The
HUNGER
of
EMPIRES

BOOKS BY R.S. MOULE

THE ERLAND SAGA

The Fury of Kings

The HUNGER of EMPIRES

R.S. MOULE

SECOND SKY

Published by Second Sky in 2023

An imprint of Storyfire Ltd.
Carmelite House
50 Victoria Embankment
London EC4Y 0DZ

www.secondskybooks.com

ISBN: 978-1-83790-461-7
eBook ISBN: 978-1-83790-459-4

For my parents. It's fine if you don't read it though.

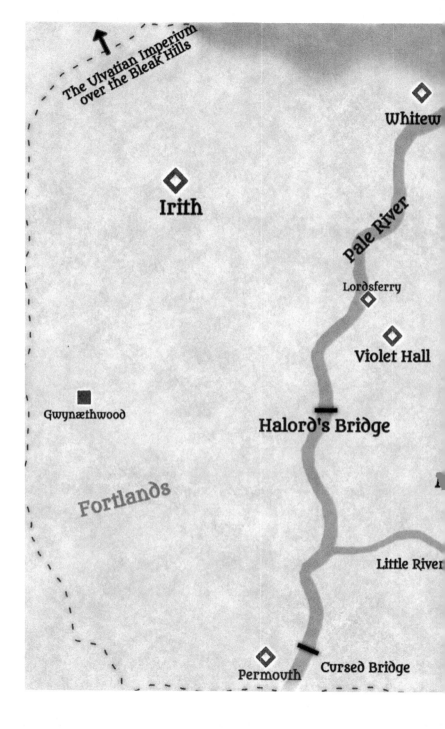

Shrouded Sea

Cliffark

ns

Marshes

Eryispek

ale

Moors

ERLAND

THE RULING FAMILIES OF ERLAND AND THEIR ALLIES AT THE END OF THE FURY OF KINGS

EAST ERLAND

King **Hessian Sangreal**, residing in Piperskeep, grieving his half-brother

His wife, Queen **Ciera Istlewick**, pregnant with a child of uncertain parentage

His son, Prince **Jarhick Sangreal**†, slain in war against the Thrumb

His first daughter, Princess **Tarvana Sangreal**, wife to Lord **Ulric Balyard**

His second daughter, Princess **Helana Sangreal**, missing, last seen fleeing the forces of West Erland

His half-brother and *balhymeri*, Lord **Andrick Barrelbreaker** [†], slain by Strovac Sigac in an ambush before the Battle of Whitewater

Andrick's widow, Lady **Viratia Brithwell**, gathering her late husband's *Hymeriker* force for war with West Erland

Andrick's first son, **Errian Andrickson**, recently freed from West Erland captivity

Andrick's second son, **Orsian Andrickson**, missing, last seen on a beach near Whitewater

Andrick's daughter, **Pherri Andrickdohtor**, apprentice to the magus Theodric

Theodric, magus and advisor to Hessian, seeking to investigate the mountain of Eryispek

Naeem, Andrick's second-in-command

WEST ERLAND

Lord **Rymond Prindian**, heir to the crown of Erland, in rebellion against Hessian Sangreal

His mother, **Breta Prindian**

His older brother, Lord **Ranulf Prindian** [†] , expired in the dungeons of Piperskeep seventeen years ago

His master-at-arms and companion, **Adfric**

Strovac Sigac, traitor to East Erland and killer of Andrick Barrelbreaker

THE ULVATIAN IMPERIUM

Kvarm Murino, merchant, returning to Ulvatia with a desire to invade Erland

His enslaved magus, **Hrogo**

His brother, Kzar **Bovarch Murino**, ruler of the Ulvatian Imperium

ORPHANS OF CLIFFARK

Tansa, a thief, last seen outside Merivale burning her brother's body

Her brother, **Tam** [†] , lover of Ciera Istlewick, executed at Hessian's command

Their friend, **Cag**

PROLOGUE

The wind swirled around the Mountain, pulling snow dust from the ground and scattering it to the cold morning air. The western horizon was cloudless, but the sky above Eryispek never was. Overhead, great grey storm clouds revolved ominously, obscuring the upper reaches and threatening more snow. What lurked there was a mystery; no man scaled the Mountain's endless peak and lived to tell the tale.

Below a high cliff of sheer, slick ice, Maghira stared up at the cave, shielding her eyes against the wind with one hand while holding her hood over her head with the other. From here it looked like a dark wound, as though the Mountain's flesh had been pierced by a sword.

This was the fifth successive day Maghira had come, hoping that the wind might have calmed enough for her to attempt the cliff. It was impassable through the cold months, but by late spring the weather had usually calmed enough to allow those who had wintered in the cave to descend. Their food would be running low by now.

Maghira had never been up to the cave. Women were

forbidden from climbing the cliff, and her father, the village's alderman, had made clear to her the grave consequences of doing so. Had it been up to him, Maghira would have stayed in their hut all year round, only emerging to be paraded before some visitor from another village in need of a wife. He was insistent that Maghira should bring fresh blood into their line. The western slope was a harsh place, where many children were born sickly. Only one of Maghira's nine siblings had survived to adulthood – her older brother, Garimo, trapped and starving up in the cave.

At her side, her younger cousin Santara looked up at her from beneath her white fur hood. 'Do you think you can get up there?'

'I believe so.' Maghira was the best climber in the village, who had once scaled the tallest pine tree in the forest and earnt a severe telling-off from her parents. She pointed to the sack of food slung over her back. 'I'll drop a rope down, then you can tie it around this and I'll pull it up.'

'My grandfather is up there as well. Papa Antares.'

Antares was Maghira's great-uncle, the hardiest old goat on the western face. Rumour was he had once killed five Lutums with his bare hands. It would take more than a storm and an empty belly to kill that old bastard.

'Do you think they're dead?' asked Santara. Even in the wind, she whispered it so quietly Maghira had to read her lips, as if speaking it too loudly might make it real.

'They'd have tried to climb down before they starved, wouldn't they? There would be six corpses at the bottom.'

Santara's face was etched with worry. 'But your father—'

'Would probably kill me.' Women were not even supposed to speak of the cave. 'But this has to be better than

waiting for them to die. What if they just never come down?'
Then she would never know what had happened to Garimo.

They trudged to the base of the cliff. The rock face
seemed to rise endlessly, all the way to the clouds and
beyond.

'Are you really sure about this?' asked Santara.

Maghira took Santara's hand and squeezed. 'Don't you
want to know what's up there? Why six men go there every
winter? I do.' As a girl, Maghira had pestered her father every
year to tell her about the cave, until finally he had clouted her
across the ear and said she was old enough now to know
better. It was the only time he had ever struck her. 'And
something strange is happening this year. The storms have
never gone on so long. And I heard that further up the slope
entire villages have vanished.'

Santara bit her lip. 'What do I do if you fall?'

'Bury me with my brothers and sisters.' Maghira would
not fall. Climbing Eryispek was in her blood. She pressed her
cold lips to Santara's cheek, secured her smaller bag to her
belt, and began her ascent.

Maghira found the handholds of past climbers easily at
first, following a sure path and clinging by her fingers, driving
spikes into the cliff to ease her passage when needed. After
an hour, she came to a slim overhang with a small hollow that
gave some shelter from the wind. She pressed herself into it,
removed her gloves to rub her numb hands together, then lay
on her stomach and peered over the edge. The ground was
no longer visible, covered by the thickening mist.

She ate some crumbs of food from her pocket, and when
she felt sufficiently rested reached up in search of more
handholds. There were none. She frowned, feeling around
for any sort of purchase. Nothing. She cursed. Unless she

could pick up the trail again she would be hammering spikes in all the way up. She drove a spike in, and began to climb.

It was colder now, the mist leaving water droplets on her face to freeze. As Maghira released a hand to pull her scarf up over her mouth, a great gust of wind rushed across the cliff, bringing with it sharp flecks of ice. She screeched as they blew into her eyes, almost letting go of the rock face. Blindly, she grabbed at her spike, clinging desperately with both hands as tiny spots of cold peppered her face. She closed her eyes, praying that the wind would drop.

Eventually it did. Maghira let out a breath. Her skin was drenched with sweat, cold enough to set her shivering. She looked upward for some sight of the cave and saw nothing, just the endless ice-white mountainside and the slate-grey clouds above.

She pressed on. Her muscles protested with every stretch of her arm, and the drive of every spike into the rock sent violent tremors up her shoulder. Maghira thought of her grandfather, gathered with her family around their fire. He had told them of a winter so cold that when the thaw came many homes held nothing but corpses, frozen to death when their fire failed. He had told her also of his own grandfather, who when the village was starving had gone down to Eryis-pool with his great rod, and returned carrying a fish the size of a stag. Maghira was of the Adrari, who since time began had dared the barren western face of Eryispek, where the men of the flatlands feared to tread. She would not die. Not before she knew the fates of the men in the cave, and learnt the secret her father was so desperate to hide from her.

Just when she thought she could climb no further, Maghira swung her arm up in search of a handhold, and her palm landed flat against horizontal ground. With a last burst of strength, she heaved herself up over the edge and rolled onto her back, gasping for breath and staring at the sky. It had begun to snow. She opened her mouth and let the flakes float down onto her tongue.

It took several minutes for her to muster the energy to stand. The cave was right behind her, a great tear in the rock at least ten feet high. Within its deep darkness, nothing stirred.

Maghira pulled a rope from her bag, tied it around a lump of rock, and threw the end over the edge, hoping Santara was still there. The rope tensed three times, and then a minute later thrice more, the signal that the bundle had been attached. Maghira hauled it up after her, strapped it to her back, and turned to face the cave.

Still nothing moved. No footprints save Maghira's own marred the blanket of snow that covered the bluff. The cave seemed even more foreboding up close. As she stared, her vision seemed to stretch in and out of focus, the cavemouth growing and contracting, pulsing in time with her quickening heartbeat.

Maghira stepped forward, and passed under the threshold of early evening moonlight that marked the entrance. The wind fell silent, and from somewhere within came the slow, steady beat of dripping water, echoing along the cavern.

Maghira contemplated the way ahead, and through the gloom saw a passage against the back wall, barely the height of a man and half-blocked by a mound of rocks as high as her waist. There must have been a cave-in; what if the others were trapped? Maghira pulled a skin of strong liquor from her pack and took a long swig, burning her throat. She replaced her gloves, approached the path, and on her hands and knees began crawling across the cold rocks into the darkness.

The rubble only covered the entrance, but once she was over and could stand again the path narrowed to a dark crack hardly a foot across, where the faraway moonlight did nothing to penetrate the way ahead. Barely able to see her own hands, Maghira gritted her teeth, turned sideways, and slipped into the darkness.

The path led downwards, deeper, so narrow that Maghira could feel her own breath against her face. Could this truly be the way the men had come? For a moment, she imagined finding her way blocked by Garimo's corpse, and fought the urge to turn and flee in terror.

Eventually, a soft, silvery glow appeared ahead of her, and the path widened to a vast cavern, its walls slick with blue ice, eerie stalagmites poking from the rock floor like splinted fingers. The air hummed with warmth, the cold of the cliff barely a memory, as though she had not just gone deeper into the Mountain but arrived somewhere else entirely. Maghira looked up at the ceiling, and the night's sky unfurled like a purple tapestry, the moon and a million stars staring down at her and casting their light across the cavern.

She could only gape in wonder. By what magic could the sky penetrate this deep chamber of Eryispek?

'By my will.'

The woman's voice reverberated around the cave, shaking Maghira's skull. The ether around her seemed to fizzle, as if the weight of Eryispek above could barely contain the power beneath the words. Maghira whirled about the chamber, searching for the source, but it was as empty as a newly dug grave. She swallowed the lump that rose at the back of her throat.

'Who are you?' she asked. 'I am searching for my brother. There are six—'

'They await you below, praying for my forgiveness. For generations, your tribe has denied me, and instead lent their prayers to the Betrayer. They have conspired against me, and left me to rot. Every man of your tribe who learnt the truth and still sought to thwart me should fear my vengeance. You alone can earn my mercy.'

The sky thundered, spitting great forks of silver-white lightning that split the sky in two, and Maghira saw the silhouette of a man atop a great peak, his arms spread wide as if in prayer, while above the sky began to blaze. Fire-tailed comets lit up the heavens, and the stars spun as if spoked to an enormous wheel. Maghira blinked against the brightness, and the man was gone. As swiftly as it had appeared, the scene faded to grey, and began to crack, leaving only the purple twilight.

'The Betrayer has grown powerful on the prayers of men and prepares to move against me. He has assembled his soul-less servants, and will soon take physical form, if he has not already. There is a girl. You must stop her going to him, and bring her to me.'

CHAPTER 1

The fog parted, and the northern coast of Erland rose on the horizon. Orsian leant over the bow railing, watching the granite cliffs grow larger as the *Jackdaw* chopped through the waves like a skimmed stone. From the shore, it might have looked majestic, but to those on the ship it was a pit of grim stenches, unwashed men and whale blubber. When they reached Cliffark, Orsian planned to dunk himself in the hottest, deepest bath he could find.

It was strange though, how little he had missed dry land.

'Sight for sore eyes, ain't it?' said Abner, the first mate, sidling up by Orsian and placing a powerful, tattooed hand on the rail. 'Enjoy the city while you can. Captain's got a mind to sail up towards Ulvatia in a few weeks. Says there's trade to be had up there.'

Orsian smiled. That was the captain's way. When he was not sailing, he was already planning their next journey. It was surprising how much he had come to appreciate his kidnappers.

'He wants to speak with you,' continued Abner when

Orsian did not reply, gesturing towards the captain's room at the rear of the deck. 'We've an offer for you.'

The captain's cabin was as large as the room below deck shared by the crew; Captain Desmont D'graw might have been one of the wiliest, most rapacious scoundrels ever to hoist a canvas, but he was also a man who appreciated the comforts of home. A full quarter of the room was occupied by an enormous wardrobe. Most men were content to set sail with two sets of clothes, but the captain feathered himself with a different raiment for each day of the month, draping himself in the finest Imperial silks and delicate lace.

'Ranulf, my boy!' he exclaimed, rising from his desk and spreading his arms wide in greeting. Today he wore a black waistcoat, dashed with a red silk scarf about his neck, and his dark hair shone like raven wing.

Of all the aliases Orsian could have chosen, in hindsight he wished it had not been the name of the long-dead brother to the pretender Rymond Prindian. None of the crew ever questioned him on it at least. Sailors recognised the value of discretion. Not knowing a man's secrets gave him one less reason to kill you.

D'graw embraced Orsian in a bear-hug, and signalled for him to take a seat, reaching to his shelf for a dusty bottle. Abner took a chair to Orsian's left.

'I always have a glass of this at the end of the voyage. Cashan. It's distilled by a sect of monks who worship the Ulvatian goddess of death.' D'graw poured them each a thimble-sized measure. 'Too much will make you temporarily blind, though it's still safer than smoking the plant they brew it from. The monks use it for a glimpse of what's beyond.'

Orsian sniffed at it warily. It smelt of rust and mouldy herbs.

D'graw raised his glass. 'To friends and shipmates. Old and new.'

Abner and the captain knocked theirs back in one, and Orsian followed suit. He gasped as the bitter nectar passed down his throat, stifling a cough.

The captain was already pouring another round. 'How've you liked your first voyage, lad?'

Orsian suspected the answer was obvious. He had taken to the sea easily; by the end of his first week Abner said he coiled ropes and climbed rigging like a veteran mariner. On a ship, a man worked for what he earnt; Captain D'graw did not accept passengers or layabouts. 'I reckon it suits me. Never would have expected that when you found me back in Whitewater.'

Abner's beard twitched in a grin. 'I know a seafaring man when I see one. You're a born sailor.'

'A born scrapper,' added D'graw, distributing the extra drinks. 'Where d'you learn to fight? Ranulf Bloodshirt, I hear the crew call you.'

Orsian felt a frisson of danger run up his spine. *Tread carefully here.* Few men learnt swordcraft at the knee of Andrick the Barrelbreaker. D'graw was probing for leverage.

Little of the *Jackdaw*'s earnings truly came from trade and whaling. D'graw was a pirate first and foremost, and no sailor could match Orsian with a blade. Right from the outset he had always been first over the rail. Initially, he had fought in a rage-driven daze, imagining the face of Strovac Sigac in every opponent, and would return to the *Jackdaw* soaked in other men's blood. That had diminished with time though; he could barely even recall Strovac's face these days. When he fought now, it was for his brother crewmen, friends like Abner and One-eyed Jahn and Tunny Burntbacon who always gave him an extra ladleful at meals ever since Orsian had saved him from being skewered by a Cjarthian privateer.

It felt more honest, fighting for your friends and your captain instead of a king who never seemed sure whether he wanted to hug you or hang you. The men of the *Jackdaw* fought for their living; they did not expect it served to them on a golden platter, bought with other men's blood.

Orsian realised D'graw was still waiting for a response, and covered himself by knocking back a second shot of cashan. It burnt like the sun. He coughed, his eyes watering. 'I had an older brother. Used to beat me, so I swore I'd get good enough with a sword that he'd never touch me again.'

It was a half-truth. Errian had beaten him, but Orsian could see in D'graw's narrowed gaze that the captain was not wholly convinced.

'I won't embarrass you by calling you a liar.' There was something reptilian about D'graw's smile. 'A man's allowed his secrets. Anyway, I'm interested in your future, not your past. When we ship out again, I want you with us.'

Orsian had known this was coming, and yet for some reason found himself hesitating. There was nothing for him in Erland. His father was dead; he had failed at being a *hymerika*; Errian was their father's heir and he would never give Orsian so much as two copper coins to rub together. It was time for him to make his own way.

So why was he not saying anything?

'Come on, Ranulf!' Abner slapped him on the shoulder hard enough to rattle Orsian's jaw. 'I like you; the captain likes you. What's the issue?'

The cashan was dulling his wits. Orsian could feel it

coursing through his bloodstream, making him sluggish. A vision of his cousin Helana swam to his mind. 'I'm a land-lubber at heart,' he heard himself say. 'Grew up in Merivale. My dad runs an inn there, and my brothers are all dead or drunk, so it's mine to take over when he passes. Left my girl there too. I mean to marry her, if she's not met someone else.'

'Oh come now, Ranulf,' said the captain, laughing and thrusting another glass towards him. 'You're still a young man! Your dad can't be that old, and as for the girl... the ladies love a sailor. Stick with us and you'll have one in every port.'

Orsian shook his head. 'My da's not well.' If only that were true. His dad was dead. Killed by Orsian's failure. 'And the girl's special to me. Won't meet another one like her.'

'What's her name?' said Abner.

'Helana,' said Orsian, speaking the first thing that came to mind. He tried not to wince. If D'graw had a passable knowledge of the Sangreal family, it would not take a genius to draw a line from the name Helana to Orsian's stolen identity.

'Ranulf and Helana, the innkeepers,' said D'graw drily. 'Fanciest pair of innkeepers I ever heard.' His black eyes bored into Orsian. 'You must think I'm a fucking fool if that's the yarn you're spinning. Do I look like a fucking fool to you, *Ranulf?*' He paused to knock back another glass of cashan. 'It's a good thing I like you and you're a decent sailor, other-wise I'd have a mind to throw you overboard with weights around your ankles. Sign on for the next voyage, and I won't say no more about it. You'll be second mate, one below Abner.'

Orsian's eyes darted around the room for anything he might be able to use as a weapon. Nothing. Even if it had not been two on one, he had seen Abner in action. The older man was strong as a bull, with thick muscles rippling under his patchwork of tattoos. In a fist fight, Orsian was under no illusions about who the winner would be.

Second mate though. He doubted there was another fifteen-year-old second mate on the whole of the Shrouded Sea.

Abner saved him from having to respond. 'Give him the fortnight in Cliffark to think about it, Captain. I told you I know a seafaring man when I see one; the lad will come around.'

'It's just a lot to take in, Captain,' Orsian protested.

D'graw was nodding slowly. 'All right, all right, lad. It's a young man's prerogative to be a little indecisive. I won't hold it against you.' He reached inside his desk. 'More money as second mate as well.' He dropped a heavy purse in front of Orsian. 'That's your share for this voyage. There's a bit extra in there as well; have one of the girls in the Siren's Storm on me. Just make sure you're sober when you come back aboard. I know you'll make the right choice.'

———

Back at the rail, watching the skyline of Cliffark grow larger in the distance, Orsian tried to unpick what had stopped him accepting the captain's offer immediately.

It's just nerves, he told himself. *After two weeks in Cliffark you'll be desperate to get back out on the water.*

But Pherri and his mother would be wondering where he was. Orsian felt a moment of guilt. He could send them a letter. Once he had sent word to his family that he was alive, he was free to pursue what he wanted. And he wanted to stay on the *Jackdaw*.

They might be dead, came a small voice in his head. Who knew what had happened after the Battle of Whitewater? Rymond Prindian might reign in Merivale. He said a silent prayer to both Eryi and the Norhai that his mother and sister lived. But he could not face them. Not as Orsian the Cowardly, the boy who ran. Better to be Ranulf, second mate on the *Jackdaw*.

That was what he would do. Find out what had happened since Whitewater and get a message to Pherri and his mother that he was alive. Then he was free to stick with the *Jackdaw*.

When the ship dropped anchor within sight of the city, Orsian was first in line to board a rowboat, with a satisfying weight of coins buried in his pockets.

'We're heading to the Old Captain Keigh first,' said Tunny Burntbacon once they were aboard, his great belly rippling with each lap of the waves. 'You coming, Ranulf? I owe you an ale.'

'I'll be along in a bit. What's the best tavern for getting news from inland?'

'That'd be the Horseman's Rest,' said Holy Gyl, a veteran navigator named for his former life as an itinerant priest. 'Other side of the city. I can give you directions.'

The harbour officials gave them only the briefest of inspections, and armed with Gyl's directions, Orsian headed down Market Road. It was his first time in Cliffark. On his previous visit the year before, he had not been able to leave Cliffark Tower, serving his father while he negotiated Hessian's marriage. The city was not so large as Merivale, but it was certainly richer. The cobbles shone, and every building was forged from stone, with glass panes in the windows. The people too. While he assumed the city must have its share of poor folk, it felt like everyone he saw was dressed in artfully arranged velvets. It made his salt-stained sea clothes feel even shabbier by comparison.

Fortunately, the Horseman's Rest was not somewhere he was likely to feel underdressed. It was a travellers' inn, with a few empty tables outside and an external staircase leading to the bedrooms. Orsian brushed down his clothes and stepped inside.

It was late afternoon, and the inn was neither busy nor empty. A dozen patrons sat at the bar or by the unlit fire. None of them looked at Orsian as he approached the bar.

'Don't get many of your sort here,' said the barwoman, appraising Orsian. 'You lost, sailor? This is a respectable establishment, not a bawdy house.'

'I'm from Merivale,' explained Orsian. 'Came here hoping for word from inland.'

'I came from that way,' said a man at the other end of the bar with a smokestick hanging from his mouth. He had the look of someone who made his living from the road, with dirty, loose-fitting clothes and a wide-brimmed hat. 'For a drink, my news is yours.' He raised an empty tankard.

Orsian handed over enough silver for two mugs of ale and retreated with the man to a corner table.

'What is it you're wanting news of?' asked the man.

'The war. Does Hessian still reign in Merivale?'

The man took a long pull on his drink and exhaled heavily. 'Aye, he reigns. Hasn't been seen in months though. Took his brother's death hard, they say.'

Orsian felt a great weight lift from his shoulders. Hessian

lived, and so his mother and sister likely did as well. 'And the war?'

'There was some battle in West Erland not long ago. I heard the Queen of Swords barely escaped with her life.'

Orsian's brow creased. 'The Queen of Swords?' What was Ciera doing in the field, and how had she earnt that nickname?

The man laughed. 'Eryi's balls, how long have you been away for? The Queen of Swords! The Barrelbreaker's widow.'

Orsian was stunned. His *mother* was at war?

'You don't know about Permouth then,' added the man with a grin. 'The West Erlanders got caught with their trousers down there!' He leant forward conspiratorially. His smokestick had gone out, but he did not appear to have noticed. 'When the Barrelbreaker died – you know about that, I assume – his wife took over the *Hymeriker*. A month later, she put Permouth to the sword. They stole all the plunder they could carry and fired the town.'

Permouth was a forge town, Orsian recalled, with the largest iron ore mine in West Erland. If it had fallen that was a great blow to the Prindian war effort. 'They make swords in Permouth.'

The man grinned. 'Hence Queen of Swords. They came away with thousands of them, all the stock Permouth had. The market's flooded with them. Got some for sale actually.'

'But Permouth is well south of Halord's Bridge. How could they get down there and torch it without any resistance?'

The man looked around furtively, as if scared he would be overheard. He was leaning so far forward Orsian was starting to worry the man's smokestick was going to drop in his beer. 'They crossed the Cursed Bridge under cover of darkness. The town never saw them coming.'

The Cursed Bridge had been raised across the Pale River a century ago, by the then Lord of Permouth. They had built in the strange black stone of the Sorrowlands, and paid the price for it. The lord and his two sons had died on the bridge, tossed into the rush of the Pale River when a sinister wind from the Sorrows spooked their horses, and thereafter nobody would set foot on it. Few gave the tales of those who claimed to have survived a crossing much credit, but how else would the *Hymeriker* have reached Permouth? And led by his mother no less. Things had truly changed in Erland since his father's death.

'And what's happened since? You said the Queen of Swords barely escaped with her life.'

The man relit his smokestick. 'There was a battle. That's all I know. News was starting to come through right when I left Merivale. Might be more news just days away.'

Orsian slid some coins across the table. 'Thank you. Get us a few more drinks. Did you say you had swords to sell?' The blades on the *Jackdaw* were the cheapest of cheap steal; he was sure D'graw would welcome better weapons.

The man's eyes lit up at the sight of silver. 'If you're buying, I'm drinking. I can show you my wares. Name's Barre.'

The man's cart was round the back of the inn, and with their drinks, Orsian and Barre headed through the rear door. Dusk was falling, and Orsian let Barre go first. He had become less trusting of people in his time at sea, and he felt naked without a sword.

'I've a half-dozen of them,' said Barre as they rounded the

cart. 'Just don't ask where I got them, and if the city guard should enquire—'

Before Barre could finish speaking, a hulking shadow emerged from behind the wagon, and brought a meaty fist down on his head. Barre barely had time to let out a grunt of surprise before he tumbled to the ground like a sack of bricks.

Orsian reflexively reached for his sword, only to remember he was unarmed. Cursing, he retreated quickly towards where the glow of the inn fell. The shadow advanced, tall and terrible, a long blade ready in its grip.

CHAPTER 2

The streambed ran west to east through Algareth's Valley, with patches of forest covering the steep northern bank and sloping grassland to the south. In spring and autumn, the creek might have flowed into the Pale River, but there had been little rain the last month, and now only a gravel path marked where it had once run.

Atop the southern ridge, Viratia raised her head over the summit, risking another look down into the valley.

'You needn't worry, Lady,' said Naeem from his horse, scratching the disfigured remains of his nose. 'Drayen has a keen eye.' He indicated the lone *hymerika* on the high hill to the east, almost a pinprick at this distance, charged with raising a banner when the time came for them to descend.

Viratia turned her horse back down the slope. 'I just don't want to miss our chance.' If they prevailed today, it would be their greatest success since Permouth. They needed it; there had been precious little for them to crow about since.

'It won't be timing that undoes us today,' said Naeem.

'That bastard Strovac was a step ahead of us at Bluefair; what makes you think he isn't again?'

Viratia did not need reminding of Bluefair, when Strovac Sigac's Wild Brigade had caught the East Erlanders beneath the town's walls. It had nearly cost Viratia her life when one of Strovac's men had broken through her guard. The scar down her cheek was only a flesh wound, but two men had died protecting her, Naeem's son Ohrik among them. The rest of them had barely escaped.

Through his grief, Naeem had counselled her afterwards that it was time for them to leave West Erland. 'We've done all we can without more men,' he told her. 'Less than ten thousand now, even with those we left to hold the bridge – not enough to strike for Irith, and if we head north to assault Whitewater, the Prindians could trap us against the sea. We cannot win this war, Lady.'

Painful though it was, Viratia had agreed. She had sacked Permouth, and the villages along the western bank lay burnt and broken, but it was not vengeance.

Today was one final chance for retribution, to fulfil part of the oath she had sworn to the shade of her husband, Andrick Barrelbreaker, the man who ought to have been here. Of her original force, it was only a few hundred *hymerikai* that remained in West Erland now. The rest had retreated across the Pale River. Half the *Hymeriker* held Halord's Bridge, and the other half stood here with her, seeking the revenge Viratia knew they desired just as much as she.

'Lady?' enquired Naeem, when Viratia did not reply.

'Even when victory was assured, Strovac risked everything to try and capture me.' He could have routed the East Erlanders at Bluefair, but had instead focused his assault solely upon their centre, seeking Viratia's position at the rear. 'Give him the chance and he will try again.'

To the west, through the valley, lay the small town of Claymeadow, where their scouts reported the Wild Brigade had garrisoned while they waited for the Prindian foot to catch up with them. Fifty brave *hymerikai* had made a dawn raid on the settlement to draw Strovac out. He would not resist another chance to capture Andrick Barrelbreaker's widow, and once they were sure Strovac had seen her, they were to retreat through Algareth's Valley as if making for Halord's Bridge.

But of course, Viratia was not among them. She was here, waiting.

Lady Yriella Gough had taken that role, disguised, atop Valour, Andrick's old warhorse. When Strovac spotted the horse and a flash of blonde hair from afar he would see no difference. It had taken months for Valour to take a rider other than Viratia or Naeem, but with characteristic patience Yriella had earnt the great beast's trust.

Lady Gough had made a name for herself since the ill-fated Battle of Whitewater. She wore mail over her six-foot frame and fought with a ferocity equal to any man's. What the men had found strange at first, they had in time embraced, and anyone spreading whispers of her taste for female paramours was now swiftly shouted down by their fellows. 'Nobody cares,' Viratia had heard one *hymerika* tell several others. 'She's got bigger balls than any of you.'

What would Andrick find stranger, me at the head of an army or Lady Gough riding his favourite horse? Almost certainly the former, if his soul had found his way above the clouds and watched her from Eryi's great feast. She could only hope that the departed heard the prayers of the living.

Andrick's absence burnt against her chest with every breath.

'I think I hear them,' said Naeem in a half-whisper.

Viratia listened, and beneath the soft wind and the rustling of grass caught frantic hooves over the dry gravel of the riverbed. Her heart quickened, and she reached for the skin of wine at her belt to lend herself courage.

From the distant hillcrest, Drayen raised a red flag, and began wildly waving it back and forth.

Viratia raised her left arm, the signal for the two hundred men behind her to ready themselves. Below, she imagined Yriella and her decoy force bringing themselves around as if preparing to make a last stand against the odds. She swallowed.

As the first clashes of steel floated up from the valley floor, she chopped her hand down. '*Charge!*'

A wordless war cry broke across the ridge. Hundreds of men with steel in their hands and vengeance in their hearts spurred their mounts over the crest and down towards the river, their hooves churning up clods of dry ground as they passed. Viratia wore no weapon, but urged her horse on all the same, surrounded by Naeem and the rest of her honour guard.

Below, the few hundred of the Wild Brigade had already encircled Lady Gough's force. Blades flashed, and the giant Strovac was in the middle of it, wearing no helmet so that men would see his long blond hair and great head and know fear, trying to cleave a bloody gash through the *hymerikai* towards the disguised Yriella. His longsword was tarnished with age, and even at this distance Viratia recognised the blade that had once been Andrick's. The same sword he had worn when he wed her, now wielded by the man who slew him.

Driven by fury, Viratia raised her voice to join the war cry. Across the valley, the other half of her force were pouring from the trees, their mail bright before the low sun and their swords raised high as they galloped towards the battlefield.

She watched as a horseless *hymerika* thrust a spear up towards Strovac's stallion. It reared, braying furiously, and with his shield hand Strovac grasped the spear by the hilt before turning it to bury the point through the man's neck, then howled as he cast his sword in a wild arc against the defenders pulled tight around Lady Gough.

Just hold on, Yriella. She would be itching to cross blades with Strovac.

Viratia's reinforcements were only a hundred yards away now, close enough that the potent stench of blood and fear reached them on the wind. Still the Wild Brigade pressed the attack.

For a few moments, Viratia allowed herself to believe that the Wild Brigade were so focused on reaching Yriella that they had not seen the hundreds of horsemen galloping downhill towards them at breakneck speed. Her hopes were dashed as a cry went up from the attackers, and suddenly they were pulling back. Not even Strovac Sigac liked his chances against a larger force preparing to encircle him.

'*After them!*' she cried, digging in her heels and urging her horse on as the Wild Brigade turned their steeds around to race west back along the valley.

The *Hymeriker* followed her. Every one of them had wept bitter tears at the death of Andrick Barrelbreaker, and every one of them had dreamt of the blood of Strovac Sigac

on their blade. For that chance they would have followed her
through fire, to the darkest depths of the earth. Viratia though
dreamt of Strovac brought before her in chains, begging for a
woman's mercy. He would find none.

*I will burn his balls first, and feed them to the dogs in
front of his eyes. Then I will carve out his eyes and make him
eat them.* The wickedness of her own vengeance sent a shiver
through her.

They thundered along the streambed. Some of the Wild
Brigade were too slow, and chopped down by the pursuing
hymerikai. Strovac was out front, but so close that Viratia
could see the bloodstains in his hair and the links of his mail.
A thrown spear whistled past her ear. She kept herself low,
willing the last reserves of speed from her mount and hoping
that others would follow her. Naeem was still beside her, and
through the fever of battle she realised he was shouting
at her.

'Lady! Lady! We need to fall back.'

Viratia stared at him. 'What?'

He pointed westward. Along the valley, two shadows
were massing on either slope. A procession of soldiers, thousands of them, spreading hurriedly into battle lines. Viratia
caught a bar of a marching song on the breeze. The Prindian
foot had caught up with them.

Viratia cursed. 'We should keep going! We can still catch
him.' But Strovac and his Wild Brigade were pulling away, as
if driven on by the sight of reinforcements.

Naeem shook his head. 'We're not risking it. It isn't worth
your life.'

It is to me, she thought to say, but stopped herself.
Naeem had lost two sons in this war, both of them on Strovac
Sigac's own blade, and no man had loved Andrick more

fiercely. She thought of her own children. Pherri, her magus babe, so bright and brave. Errian, her proud firstborn, the broken boy. Orsian. *Orsian.* They had seen neither hide nor hair of him in their months at war. The guilt rose, thick enough to choke her.

Her life was not hers to risk.

With a final pained look at the back of Strovac Sigac, Viratia raised her right arm and eased her horse's pace, pulling it around in an arc back towards the east, the *Hymeriker* following.

They rode over the high arches of Halord's Bridge at a canter, through the line of *hymerikai* who had been charged with holding their route of retreat. On the eastern side, men were already packing away their makeshift camp, and carts were brought forth to carry their injured eastward. The last Sangreal force in West Erland was going home.

'Can we be sure they won't follow us?' Viratia asked Naeem.

Naeem shook his head. 'Those men have been marching up and down the Pale River after us for weeks. They'll just be glad to see the back of us.'

Viratia turned towards the mass of mounted *hymerikai* following them, their hooves clacking against the bridge's cobbles. Yriella was with them, making a beeline for Viratia with a large bundle on the rump of her horse. She dismounted clumsily, her hair plastered to her head with sweat, and Naeem rushed to help her.

'Did we get him?' she asked breathlessly.

Viratia shook her head. 'Nearly.'

'Shame,' said Yriella. She grinned, displaying a set of bloodstained teeth. 'You might be pleased with what I caught though. Bastard almost took my head off – took four of us to bring him down.' With a hard grunt, she hefted the bundle off her horse, and threw down a man. His grey-brown hair was matted with blood, and a wound on his forehead flowed freely, soaking into a closely cropped beard. His hands were bound, but he looked up at his captors with defiance in his eyes.

Viratia gazed down at him. He had a common soldier's face, broad and sunburnt, but there was something familiar about him. He was not one of the Wild Brigade. 'Your name?'

The man spat a bloody glob of saliva onto her boot. 'I am Adfric.' His voice was hoarse. 'Master-at-arms and protector to King Rymond Prindian.'

CHAPTER 3

Drast Fulkiro sat in his top-floor study, fingers steepled and head bent over the letter on his desk.

The old boar held on far longer than I expected.

He looked up and faced the boy who had brought him the message, a slave belonging to the Temple of Urmé, pasty and pathetic in a pair of filthy shorts pulled up to above his navel. 'Did you read this?'

The slave looked surprised. 'No, Senator, I am not lettered.'

Drast studied the boy. He did not want this news reaching the ears of his rivals too soon; the election would begin in a week – every hour would count. *Better to be sure.* He reached into his desk and produced a cloth bracelet in the Fulkiro colours – red, yellow, and black – and threw it to the slave. 'You belong to me now. I'll send money to the chief acolyte. Go to the kitchens and get yourself some food. Speak to no one.'

Once the slave had departed, Drast pressed a magicked button under his desk, a relic of when the magi had ruled the

Imperium. Within seconds, Forren, his chief counsellor, joined him. Like the magi, Forren seemed a relic of a bygone age; one of Drast's father's generation, but with the vigour of a much younger man. None of Drast's guard had bladework that came close to Forren's.

'Forren, read this letter, fast.'

Forren leant over the desk to read the letter upside down. His thick grey eyebrows rose slightly as he read it. 'The kzar is dead, then. It is past time; that poison should have eaten through him in days. I was beginning to think he was holding on for his brother's return through sheer stubbornness.'

'We should keep quiet,' said Drast. 'I wouldn't put it past Senator Brunal to have the rats in the walls spying on me. Is there any word on Kvarm's return? It has been weeks since his last missive.'

'None, Senator. Sailors report black storms and waves the size of mountains. It may be that he has perished.'

'I doubt it. The Murinos are hard to kill.' It would have been welcome news, but part of Drast wanted to see Kvarm's face when he learnt that his supposed tame senator had been using Kvarm's payments to forge his own base of power. 'If he were delayed until after the election though...'

'You still mean to pursue the kzarship then?'

It was a measure of Drast's respect for Forren that he did not mind his counsellor's disapproving tone. Their bond had been shaped in the cauldron of the Imperium's war with Cylirien; they were long past the authority and deference of master and servant. 'Who else? The reformist cause requires a pillar, a lightning rod. I am our best hope of defeating Brunal.'

'You don't have the numbers. There are still too many clucking hens from your father's generation. Those like your cousin Servis, who agrees with whoever spoke to him last. And that's in a straight race between you and Brunal; Kvarm could return any day, and who knows what other candidates will lift their head above the parapet?'

Drast leant back in his chair, steepling his fingers. Forren was right. He had primed his position as best he could, and still it would likely not be enough. If Kvarm Murino returned and began campaigning, Drast's supporters would dwindle further.

'And that's before you announce your proposal to end our occupation of Cylirien. I've told you already the Senate will not support you; even among the reformers—'

'I will persuade them. Urmé's wounds, Forren, we've spent twenty years trying to hold Cylirien, and we are no closer now than a decade ago when you and I finally got out of there.' Drast did not like to dwell on his memories of the conflict; sweltering summers and frozen winters on the front line of the steppes, never sure where the next attack might come from or whether he would live to see Ulvatia again, watching men he counted as friends die one by one, year by year. 'The Cyliriens are thriving; they even have enough warriors to send mercenaries overseas to earn funds for their resistance. It is too expensive, in both gold and men. That is another reason I must stop Kvarm; his letters indicate that he wants to invade Erland, for yet another pointless, unwinnable war.'

Forren merely raised an eyebrow. They had discussed the Cylirien issue many times, and though Drast knew his counsellor agreed with him, to many Ulvatians the idea of giving up any Imperial possession would be abhorrent.

'But I cannot win without help. Forren... What of that other matter we discussed?'

'Are you sure you wish to know?'

'By Parmé, yes. If Kvarm does return, that freak of his gives him an advantage.' *He thinks himself clever; any fool can see his pet is a magus.* Drast tried to recall the maimed slave's name. Ugo? Rago? *Hrogo!* He was reasonably sure it was Hrogo.

Drast saw a strange reluctance cross Forren's face. *Is that fear?* After a few heartbeats, he lost patience. 'Come on Forren! What are you thinking?'

Forren remained silent a few moments. He walked to the window, staring down at the city as if looking for something. 'There has been a development.' Drast sensed his hesitation. 'Senator, how far are you prepared to go to become kzar?'

'As far as I must.'

'If we pursue this... Meet me in the yard, as soon as the second moon dips below Mizstel's Folly. Wear a black cloak, and do not let anyone see you leave. I'll bring your horse around.'

As Forren departed, Drast took his place at the window over Ulvatia. By daylight, the city shone, but under the glow of the twin moons the white marbled stone threaded with gold merely sparkled, the wealth of a hundred conquered cities and petty kingdoms embedded into the city's mortar, and all for the glory of the Imperium.

Drast's earliest memory was from when he was three years old: his grandfather had brought him up here, swearing that it was the best place to see the city. This had been the home of Senator Hacinder in those days, the scion of a senatorial line over five hundred years old, the head of the Senate's reformist wing, and Drast's grandfather just a first-generation senator, the son of a builder.

How they must have laughed at him. Hacinder was in the

ground now, along with his son and so many others. The three Fulkiros had buried them, bastards all.

Tonight though, he would be meddling with powers far beyond those of the deceased Hacinders. If Drast was to become kzar, it would mean wagering the very existence of the Fulkiro line. A new family chasing an old tale. The historic families publicly decried magic, while secretly embracing it within their gilded manors. The magical signalling button on his desk was trivial next to the treasures kept by families like the Murinos.

It was not only about ending the war. It was about proving to the bastards that the Fulkiros were just as good as them. Better even. Drast's loyalty to the Imperium and strength of purpose had been forged in the Eternal Legion. He was not some coddled patrician; the Fulkiros had earnt every brick of Hacinder Manor, and when his father had insisted he join the Legion to advance the family's cause, Drast had done so. It was time now to make the old man proud, to turn the Fulkiro line into a dynasty.

But if I am to beat the old families, I must follow their hypocrisy.

In time, the pale second moon approached the steeple of Mizstel's Folly, a slim tower looming over two thousand feet tall, built by the last magus kzar. The Senate of the time had killed the man, but kept the Folly. When the pale disc of Parmé began to disappear, Drast descended to the yard, where Forren had already saddled two horses. They mounted, and together rode out of the yard and down the hill towards the city.

Below, the twinkling lights of Ulvatia stretched into the distance, up into the hills and beyond, where soft plumes of smoke still rose over the horizon from the city's silver mines.

A spiderweb of marbled streets spread out before them, from Mizstel's Folly all the way to the harbour and every region in between, from the shimmering Jewellery Quarter to the haphazardly built Free District, a confused mixture of architectural styles where the towering white marble as old as the city itself rubbed up against the ugly modernity of red stone. To the east, Senate Tower rose like a gleaming blade, its great beacon glowing brighter than both moons.

The dark gave them cover, but even at a walk, Drast was conscious of the clack of their hooves on the white marble road. It echoed off the high walls of the grand houses to either side, cutting the night's tender silence.

'Do you mean to give us away with these nags?' Drast hissed.

Silently, Forren spurred his horse to a canter, and all Drast could do was curse him and follow.

As the hill gave way to a gentle slope, and the sheen of the marble road faded as they joined the more well-used streets, Forren slowed them to a trot. He did not speak until they were approaching a crossroads. 'When it happens, jump off.'

'When what—'

In a cacophony of hooves, two horsemen bolted across them from their left. Drast's mount reared, and for a moment he thought he would be tossed from the saddle. Two more thundered after them, their hooves cutting up sparks from the street, and before Drast could react, Forren grabbed him. He dragged him off the horse, slapped their mounts on the rump to set them running after the others, and pulled Drast into an alley.

'Forren, you—'

'We've got five streets to cross, and if anyone is watching

it won't take them long to realise we're not on one of those horses. Come on.'

Forren did not just take them across five streets. He dragged Drast around every block they came to and then doubled back, determined that they would not be followed. He was laughing silently by the time they stopped in the filthiest alley Drast had ever seen, with not a single scratch of gold visible on the discoloured white paving, somewhere between the Free District and the old Alchemists' District.

Drast had to resist the urge to throttle him. 'Was that necessary?'

'Better to be sure.'

Drast looked around the alley. There were many doors, but not a chink of light broached their edges. Forren looked at each of them in turn, before choosing the one nearest them, a rickety, rotten thing probably decades old. Forren turned the handle and pressed his shoulder to it, keeping his left hand on the hilt of his dagger.

It creaked open, and as the two of them stepped inside, Drast was hit by a wall of stench.

'Parmé's blade, what is that smell?'

Before them, a set of stairs plummeted into the darkness. Drast peered down, and the smell became worse than ever, a thick ball of yellow vapour that he could not prevent invading his nostrils. He had smelt death before, but this was surely the rotting corpses of a whole legion. He opened his mouth to speak, and almost retched, bending over to steady himself on the wall. Eyes watering, he saw Forren begin to descend. All he could do was follow.

For fifty steps, Drast could see nothing, feeling the brick-work with one hand and Forren's shoulder with the other. At least the precarious steps distracted him from the smell, which seemed to recede as they descended. Then, finally, he felt Forren stop, and when he stepped forward a stone floor rose to meet him. He stumbled in surprise.

Light crept in from somewhere, and Drast felt Forren grasp his arm.

'The smell passes,' said Forren. 'I suspect it's an illusion.'

'An illusion?' Many secret relics of the magi lurked in Ulvatia, but this was the first Drast had heard of a magical smell. But when he sniffed up the steps he found no trace of it, just the usual damp musk of the underground. 'But that's not possible, it...' He could not even recall the smell to describe it; it was as if it had walked through his mind and out, without leaving a trace.

'This way.' Forren indicated a decaying door, and Drast followed through behind him.

Expecting another passage, Drast was surprised to emerge into a large high-ceilinged room, with the same damp brick walls as outside, but decked for comfort. The floor was covered with thick bearskins, sticks of incense smoked on every surface, and against the wall a bookcase rose high as the ceiling, groaning with leather-bound volumes.

The plushness of the room and the smoke of the incense almost distracted Drast from the man sitting at the table in the middle, staring past him into nothingness, his features blurred by the haze of incense vapour.

Forren chuckled. 'You see him then. You've better eyes than me. I rounded the room six times before my eyes caught him, but I knew something must be lighting the incense.'

'What do you mean? He's right there!' Drast sensed he was still affected by their descent through the smell, and bent over on his knees, taking deep calming breaths through his nose, giving himself time to think. *That smell was nothing natural, and Forren could not see him.* 'Urmé's wounds. Is that a magus?'

Forren looked at Drast with pride. 'By Parmé, you're fast. There's no doubting who your grandfather was.'

Drast turned on Forren, shoving his dagger under the older man's jaw. He knew Forren could have stopped him if he wanted to, but in that moment did not care. 'You risk everything just by bringing me here. A magus! What were you thinking?'

Forren looked down his nose at Drast. 'You told me to find magical artefacts you might use in your campaign, and when I asked how far you would go, you told me, "As far as I must."' He spoke evenly, seemingly unconcerned by the blade at his neck. 'You would not be the first. Kzar Faaden used a magus to seize the throne.'

Drast relaxed his grip. 'And died screaming. I know the tale. Faaden's madness led to the Fourth Purge.' He looked again towards the desk. The man had still not moved. 'What would you have me do with him?'

'That's for you to decide. I expect you know a great deal more about the magi than I do.'

It was true. Drast had a fine collection of banned books from before the Fourth Purge, a hundred and twenty years ago. The senators lived under an unspoken truce not to look too closely into each other's secret libraries and collections. If they knew, the citizens would murder every single one of them. A little corruption was tolerated, but the magi and all who associated with them were hated.

Warily, Drast walked towards the desk. As he approached, the man's features sharpened. He was old, perhaps decades older than Forren, with long white hair and a beard both bound in a knot, and wearing a simple brown robe. The deep wrinkles in his face had a stillness to them, as if they had been carved rather than wizened by time. With his right hand, he tossed a coin with metronomic regularity, every time catching it in that same hand and flicking it again. Drast watched it land: *tails*.

Drast stood before him, keeping his hands behind his back, one resting on a hidden dagger. 'Greetings, friend.'

The old man stared past him, and flicked his coin up again and caught it. Drast watched it land: *tails*, again.

'I am Senator Drast Fulkiro.'

Nothing, again, just the same metronomic flip of the coin.

'Tails,' said Drast.

Tails. The coin landed in the man's hand, and a glaze of fog lifted from his eyes. He looked up, his gaze coming to fix on Drast. 'And who are you... to disturb my rest?' He spoke deliberately, as if struggling to recall how.

'Drast Fulkiro, of the Imperial Senate.'

The old man snorted. 'Another puffed-up popinjay in white robes. Spare me your troubles and let me rest.'

'What are you doing down in this room? How long have you been here?'

'I was sleeping, you halfwit. I've been here five minutes. Did Krutan send you? Krutan told me to rest.'

'You were down here a week ago,' said Forren, 'and you've not moved in all that time.' His eyes flicked to the coin. 'Whose likeness is on your coin?'

The old man glanced at it and shrugged. 'The dead one. His brother is Kzar now.'

'Kzar Faaden?' asked Drast.

'Yes, Faaden. Don't ask me to remember the names of all you lost lambs. Dust in the wind.'

'Faaden's been dead for over a century. You mean to tell me you've been sat here all that time?'

The old man scowled. 'My brother would not have left me for so long. Krutan swore he'd be back.'

For a moment, Drast was unsure what to do, but recovered into his most charming smile. 'Excuse me a moment. I must confer with my associate.' The magus shrugged and waved them away, staring back at his coin. Drast and Forren retreated to a safe distance.

'Parmé's blade, Forren. He says he's been down here since Faaden the Fraudulent ruled. Do you think he's telling the truth?'

Forren stroked his whiskers. 'I'm sure he thinks so. He's half-mad, clearly. It's impossible.'

'Impossible, but interesting.' A plan formed in Drast's mind. *We upstarts must take risks the Hacinders never even dreamt of.*

He returned to the table. 'Sir, I have a proposition for you.'

'Did you find my brother?' asked the man. 'Krutan wouldn't leave me.'

Drast felt a twinge of pity for this ancient stranger, then crushed it. 'It's your brother I wish to discuss. But first, please tell me, you are a magus, are you not?'

The old man looked up at Drast, eyes like slits, and pulled himself to his feet. His presence seemed to change, magnifying, turning his surroundings indistinct and distant. When he spoke, his voice rumbled in his diaphragm, and Drast felt the floor shake under his feet with each word.

'I am Krupal. Tales of my mastery are told from here to the Sea of Frost, where the world ends. Taste my power.'

The man clicked his finger, and the table between them

burst into flames. Drast stepped back, and the fire pursued
him, red and hot and terrible as blood, rushing at his face. He
cried out and stumbled backwards, shielding himself as he
threw himself to the floor.

The old man clicked his fingers again, and the desk stood
there, intact and unburnt, just as it had been seconds before.

Krupal cackled. 'You're pale as milk. Have you never
seen *shadika* before? The ungifted always scare so easily.'

Drast let the wave of anger roll over him, biting down the
humiliation. He came to his feet, dusting himself off in what
he hoped was a dignified manner. 'I salute your talents, sir. I
have read books about the magi's abilities, but I've never had
the chance to observe them before. I have also read of magi
who can read and influence a man's mind; is that another
talent of yours?'

'A trifle,' said the man with a dismissive wave. 'A rare
skill, to combine *inflika* with subtle *spectika*, but I can tread
through a man's thoughts and alter them without him having
the slightest knowledge.' He looked at Forren, with a wicked
glint in his eye. 'I could make your servant kill you. Wouldn't
that be amusing?'

Forren took a hurried step back, and Drast forced himself
to remain calm. It was written that some magi could do such
things, but also that it was not reliable, working only upon
the weak-willed and simple. He would need to choose the
most biddable of senators if his plan was to work. 'Amusing
for you, I am sure, but pointless in the scheme of things. If I
were dead, I could not help you find your brother.'

Krupal looked at him sharply. 'You know where
Krutan is?'

'Not yet, but I have much power and influence. I am sure
I can locate him, given time.'

'It should not be so hard,' said Krupal, suddenly morose. 'He was here only five minutes ago. He cannot have gone far.'

The preoccupation with his brother was most peculiar. The man either did not believe that over a century had passed, or had already forgotten. Why was an old magus obsessed with finding his brother?

'I will help you,' said Drast. 'But in return, you must do something for me.'

CHAPTER 4

Orsian took another step back from the shadow's advance. It followed, and the leaking light of the inn revealed a youth, boyish in the face but built like a boulder. He overtopped Orsian by over half a foot, and even more by width. That would have been threatening enough, but he was also carrying an ugly, blunted sword. He gripped it like a child holding a butter knife, but that would matter little if he started swinging.

'Who are you?' asked the boy. 'Tansa,' he called back towards the cart, 'what do I do with this one?'

'Don't use my name,' came a hiss from the back of the cart. 'I've told you enough times.' Orsian was surprised to see a young woman emerge. She was slim, with closely cropped hair and a smattering of pretty freckles across her cheeks. 'Just knock him out and we'll throw him in the back with Barre.'

Before the girl finished speaking, Orsian was already moving. He leapt for the cart, rolling past the boy's clumsy swing, and as he climbed into the back was relieved to see an open trunk full of cheap, substandard swords. He snatched one up and jumped down.

The girl was fast, but she had no more business holding a sword than her companion. Orsian allowed her wild swing inside his guard, leaning back to let her throw herself off balance, then grabbed her hand and bent her wrist back. She cried in pain as the blade fell from her fingers. He slammed his shoulder into her, and she sprawled to the ground.

The boy rushed forward with a yell, and Orsian did not even bother to block his lunge, just pirouetted around his great bulk and kicked him hard across the knees. The youth tumbled sideways, the sword flying from his hand.

As the boy tried to rise, Orsian placed the edge of his blade against his neck. He had not even needed it. Blunt as it was, he still fancied he could slice the boy's head from his shoulders.

The girl had recovered her sword, but instead of attacking was staring wide-eyed at Orsian. 'Don't hurt him, please.'

'Don't hurt him like you didn't hurt Barre?' replied Orsian, seething. 'What in Eryi's name were you doing out here? If you wanted to rob him then bloody rob him, you didn't need to hit him over the head.'

'He ripped us off,' said the boy.

Orsian pressed the sword against his neck. 'Not another word from you, or I'll call for the guards.'

'He did though,' insisted the girl. 'Charged us four times what he should've to cart us here from Merivale. Was always planning to rob him when he next came back.'

Orsian could barely think how to respond to that. 'Just check on him.' He gestured irritably towards Barre, still flat on his back and dead to the world.

The girl walked over and placed a finger against Barre's neck. She frowned, and checked the other side, then hurriedly held the back of her hand against his mouth and nose. 'Eryi's bones, Cag.' She looked at her friend. 'Did you mean to hit him that hard? The thieving bastard's dead.'

Before Cag could respond, the inn's back door banged open, followed by the heavy tread of armed men. Orsian turned to see half-a-dozen city guards striding towards them, followed by the barwoman. 'I knew that sailor was up to no good!' she cried.

There was a sudden scurry of feet, and Orsian's head whipped round to see the girl already shimmying over the inn's back wall. He gave a cry and raced after her. Orsian the lord's son might have spoken with their pursuers and settled the matter, but Ranulf the sailor had heard from his crewmates of the temperament of Cliffark's guards. He spared a backwards glance for Cag. The boy tried to give chase, but was driven to his knees under a barrage of truncheons.

Orsian leapt and clambered over the wall. The girl was already a good twenty yards away, running towards the city. He heard the scramble of pursuing guards and raced after her, shoving the sword awkwardly into his belt.

He kept the girl in view for a time, but was unable to keep pace as she weaved through back alleys and around surprised citizens. Orsian clipped a woman with his shoulder as he turned a corner, then stumbled and threw a desperate hand against the wall to stop himself falling. When he looked up the girl was gone.

At the next intersection, Orsian flew right, but skidded to a halt in front of a high-walled dead end. There were empty windows he might have squeezed through, but they were all too high to reach. He spun to double back, just as three blue-liveried guards rounded the corner. Orsian drew his sword.

'Put it down, lad,' said one of them. All three drew their blades, and began advancing towards him. 'Will go easier if you don't fight.'

Orsian backed away. 'You should walk back the way you came and forget you saw me.' He spun the blade twice through each hand, hoping a show of swordsmanship might dissuade them.

The guard and his fellows sniggered. 'Not a chance. You can't fight three of us.' They fanned out as far as the alley would allow, blocking his escape. Orsian took up a defensive stance.

The middle guard came at him quickly, while the other two moved more cautiously, trying to flank him. Orsian retreated, batting aside the first guard's early probing, putting the wall at his back to keep all three of them in front of him and looking for a way he might escape without bloodshed.

When Orsian ran out of room, he realised he was out of options. He sprang forward, taking the lead guard by surprise. He feinted a thrust to the right, and as the guard moved awkwardly to block, brought the flat side of his sword down hard on his knuckles. The man cried out as his blade slipped from his fingers, and Orsian drove an uppercut backed by his sword hilt into his jaw. He was out before he hit the ground, and Orsian nimbly rolled forward past the wild lunges of the two others. He leapt up and spun to face them. The odds were now only two on one, and he had the freedom to turn and run if he chose.

He retreated towards the alley's entrance, keeping his sword moving. 'You can still walk away.'

'Do you know how many will be looking for you by now?'
said one of them. 'Filthy fucking sea rat; you'll hang for this.'

Behind them, Orsian saw a pair of legs emerging from
one of the high windows, and had to cover his surprise as the
girl from the inn dropped soundlessly to the cobbles. She
made a shushing motion, and picked up the unconscious
guard's sword.

'I didn't kill him,' said Orsian, saying anything to keep
their focus on him as the girl padded forward.

The two men raised their blades again, and as Orsian
readied his defences, the girl clumsily brought the sword's
flat edge thudding down on the nearest guard's head. As the
other turned, Orsian slid forward and punched him hilt-first
across the mouth. Both guards collapsed to the cobbles.

Orsian hurried around checking them for a pulse, while
the girl collected their swords. To his relief, all three were
alive.

'Cag didn't mean it,' said the girl, rounding on Orsian
and pointing her sword towards his neck. 'He doesn't know
his own strength. He'd never hurt a fly if I didn't tell him to.'

'Seemed to hurt Barre well enough.'

'Barre was a prick,' spat the girl. 'Never wanted him to
die though,' she added miserably. 'You have to help me free
Cag. They'll hang him.'

'Are you mad? You'd have robbed me as well, given the
chance! Why should I help you with anything?'

'They'll hang you too if you don't help me. You think
they'll let you get away after this? You're not from Cliffark;
you won't last the night here without me.'

'Reckon I can take care of myself,' said Orsian, tapping
his sword against the sole of his shoe. 'Those guards were
barely better with a blade than you are.'

The girl let out a dismissive laugh. 'You going to fight the entire city guard by yourself?'

In the distance, Orsian heard the rhythm of running steps. There were still guards out, and one of the three on the ground was beginning to stir. He had no wish to kill them, and the girl was right; he could not fight them all.

'Fine,' he said, reluctantly shoving the sword back into his belt. 'Show me where I can hide, and I'll help free your friend.' The footsteps were getting closer.

'Clasp on it.' The girl thrust her arm forward, and Orsian quickly grabbed her wrist.

At the rear corner of the alley, she lifted a sewer gate that Orsian had not noticed before, and he dropped down after her. The fall was higher than expected, and he landed awkwardly in rank, shin-deep water, hopping up quickly to stop his ankle buckling underneath him. He strained his eyes against the gloom. They were in an arched, brick tunnel, with stained walls and stinking of urine.

'We're near Pauper's Hole,' said the girl, seizing Orsian's hand and leading him swiftly along the tunnel further into the catacombs, taking left and right turns seemingly at random. 'The guards don't come down here. Quickly.'

They were alone, but Orsian was sure he felt eyes on him from somewhere. He kept a grip on his sword.

They emerged into a broad courtyard, surrounded by high walls but open to the sky. Along each side were rows of stairs leading deeper. The girl picked one and led Orsian down to a filthy door, discoloured by age and marred with some dark stain that might have been blood. She knocked three times, and almost instantly a brass panel low on the door snapped open to reveal a pair of eyes.

'Maud, it's me, Tansa. We need a room.'

The eyes blinked and disappeared, and the door creaked open. The girl dragged Orsian inside, closing the door behind them.

They were in a small room, with a desk, and low corridors leading away in three different directions. The dim glow of a brazier revealed the door's guard: an old woman, shrunken with age, her face webbed with broken veins.

The woman squinted at them. 'Not seen you in six months, girl. Didn't you used to run around with your brother and that big lad?' She peered at Orsian. 'Don't recognise this one,' she croaked, reaching up to pinch his cheek. 'Got a fancy look to him.'

'My brother's dead,' said Tansa coldly. 'And Cag's got himself in trouble.' She dropped a few silvers on the desk. 'Do you have a room?'

The woman swept up the coins and plucked a heavy key from somewhere. 'Take room three,' she said, then gave them each an unnerving leer and cackled. 'Just don't be keeping me up all night.'

CHAPTER 5

A Prindian messenger brought the request for parley within an hour of Adfric's capture. The two sides met that afternoon, in the middle of Halord's Bridge. On the western bank, atop a low hill, a great pyre belched sinister black smoke and the unsettling reek of toasting flesh. The blackmasters had long given up trying to retrieve corpses, and both sides burnt their dead when they could. Word might reach their families if the deceased was fortunate enough that someone knew them, but that was all.

As she walked to the bridge's midpoint, Viratia could not tear her eyes away. Had that been Orsian's fate? No. Surely someone would have recognised him. He had been his father in miniature, ever since he was a boy.

In some ways, Orsian's loss hurt worse than Andrick's. People spoke to her of Andrick every day, and probably would for the rest of her life, but no one ever spoke to her of Orsian. Perhaps they did not know what to say; her husband's fate was certain, whereas few would be bold enough to tell her they thought her son was dead. It made her want to dig into the earth, to erect a stone declaring to the world that her son still lived.

Of her children, only Pherri remained untouched by the war. Viratia felt a stab of guilt for neglecting her daughter. When they returned to Piperskeep, she swore to spend more time with Pherri.

Behind her walked Naeem, Yriella, and a dozen others. They had left Adfric in their camp, tied between two poles with a noose about his neck. It had taken all her patience not to take his head. But he was worth more alive.

Across the hastily erected table sat Breta Prindian, beautiful as the dawn, her copper hair flowing like molten starlight. She was dressed as if for court, in a dress of green silks and black lace. Rymond Prindian was next to her, the so-called King of West Erland. He was as striking as Viratia had heard, pale and delicate as a maid, with cheekbones you could cut yourself on, even if his beauty was marred by a patchy beard. But he was so young. Too young and vain to stand against Andrick. No wonder Rymond had plotted to kill him.

Behind them lurked Strovac Sigac, a head taller than the other Prindian attendants. Viratia tried not to look at him. The monster who had taken everything from her.

The table had been laden with meat and bread and a great wheel of cheese, and there were three chairs set out opposite the Prindians. Viratia lowered herself into one, as Naeem and Yriella took those to either side.

Up close, the radiance of Breta Prindian made Viratia feel uncharacteristically self-conscious. A few months ago, she had been a lord's wife, the owner of many fine dresses, with jewellery enough to burden a mule and maids who brushed her hair until it shone. Now she was garbed in sturdy leather, and the only metal she wore was mail. Her hair was pulled back in a tail to stop it whipping into her eyes when she rode. By what right did Breta Prindian look as though she had just been washed and dressed to receive visitors?

Lord Rymond's beauty was more brittle. Up close, he was more pasty than pale, with grey circles hanging under his eyes, and the hollow cheeks of an invalid. Andrick had often said that war had been the making of him, that it had carved away the boy he had once been. Rymond had been carved by it too, and found wanting. The foolish boy was wearing a crown, a golden circlet with small points topped with dazzling emeralds. Viratia resisted the urge to laugh at his presumption.

In the background, Viratia could see Strovac smirking. Let the coward smirk when she gave him to Hessian's dungeons. Many a man had lost their mettle when brought before the rack.

'You look well, Lady,' she said, greeting Breta Prindian.

'And you, my dear,' replied Breta, as if she had not noticed the iciness of Viratia's welcome and they were two friends, rather than combatants. 'The last time we spoke, you were just a girl. Your father had invited every nobleman of Erland to his home to meet his beautiful, clever daughter.'

Viratia remembered. It had been only months before she had met Andrick. Close to thirty years ago.

'My husband could not be kept away of course. He never met a horse or a maid he didn't want to ride.'

Next to Viratia, Yriella snorted. Breta looked at her approvingly.

'You must be Lady Gough,' she said, eyeing Yriella's armour and the sword at her waist. 'We have heard a great deal about you. Could you marry my son and beat some sense into him?'

'It would go poorly for him. I have buried two husbands already.'

'I suspect they are much improved for it. Few of us are so fortunate as to love the men we marry.'

'Nor so unfortunate as to have them taken from us,' bit back Viratia. She imagined taking Yriella's sword and covering the table with Rymond and Breta's blood. 'I will speak plainly, as I do not mean to spend any more time in your company than is required. You can have Adfric back when I have the head of the man who killed my husband. Give me Strovac Sigac.'

'I had a different exchange in mind,' said Breta. 'We will give you one hundred prisoners, and your husband's ashes.'

Andrick's ashes. Viratia gripped her hands in her lap. She had heard of the indignities done to Andrick's body after his murder. 'He was burnt?'

It was Rymond who replied. 'Yes. I made sure of it. And his remains will not be part of any agreement. The ashes are yours.' He glared at his mother, and gestured behind himself to a servant holding a vast urn, who placed it on the table in front of Viratia.

She wanted to clutch it to her chest, to lift the lid and search for any faint trace of Andrick's scent – leather, iron, and sweat – but forced herself to keep her face blank. 'Thank you, Lord. But my favour will not be bought so cheaply. You will not repay the death of my husband with his ashes, nor end this war by wearing that foolish crown. You are king of nothing.'

Rymond blinked. 'I rule in West Erland, from the Dry River to the Pale River and from the Sorrowlands to the

Bleak Hills. I have been crowned by my people, by right of the Old Line.'

'Any boy can start a war.'

Rymond's blue eyes met hers. 'And any boy can end one. I propose my mother's terms: Adfric for one hundred of your captured men, with priority to be given to those who have families that rely on them. Then both sides will withdraw, so that they may plant crops and hope for a harvest before winter. There is no point to this war if both sides starve.

'In return, you will not challenge my right to rule West Erland. Those are more generous terms than many others would offer. You are withdrawing anyway, because you lack the men to continue. We also know that Hessian has demanded that you return his stolen army.'

Viratia cursed inwardly. It was a natural part of war, but if she found the spies who had informed the Prindians of Hessian's various messengers she would have them flogged.

When she did not reply immediately, Rymond continued. 'Once your men are back on the familiar soil of East Erland, what hope do you have of getting them to fight again? My men are weary too, and I have no wish to invade. Let us have peace, for now.'

He was no warrior, but Viratia had to admit to the young Prindian's intelligence. He offered a deal that would make the common soldiers on both sides think well of him for freeing one hundred of their fellows, and made himself appear wise for allowing them a brief respite from the war to prepare a harvest.

'And if I refuse?'

Rymond shrugged. 'You will keep Adfric, and those hundred men may starve. You will return to East Erland, and if you attempt any further assaults upon my lands, we will be ready.' Breta was smiling, but Rymond's face gave away nothing.

'And why should I trust the word of a man who killed my husband at a parley? Why should any true man of Erland trust you?'

Rymond at least had the decency to look slightly uncomfortable. 'Men die in battle,' he said. 'Many months before that, before there was even a whisper of war, Hessian stole my betrothed and sought to have me kidnapped. Where do you suppose that would have ended, except with my death? If I have acted dishonourably, so has Hessian.'

Viratia snorted. 'I think you know that one does not excuse the other. You will know justice for my husband, in time, all of you.' She paused, hoping that if Andrick watched her, he agreed with what she had to do. 'But we accept your terms.'

The two sides did not seal the agreement with the clasping of forearms, but rings of Sangreal red and Prindian green were exchanged to at least mark the event.

Viratia turned to leave, but as she walked away Strovac Sigac called after her.

'They didn't burn his skull. I still have that. When your men depart to feast above the clouds, you may tell them that the headless one is Andrick Barrelbreaker.'

Viratia held her head high, and walked on. She clutched the urn to her chest, trying to imagine she had not heard Strovac's words.

As she stepped off the bridge into East Erland, Viratia felt wearier than she ever had. Her legs and back both ached with so many hours and days in the saddle, and when she finally slept, she was sure she would not wake again for many meals. Perhaps she truly was ready to go home, to see Errian and Pherri again.

Adfric was waiting for them, still bound between the two poles, his cuffed wrists clasped in front of him like a penitent. He looked up hopefully as Viratia approached. 'Am I to be freed?'

She glared at him. 'It appears so. The Prindians seem to value your life.'

The old warrior bowed his head. 'I am grateful, Lady.' He stretched out his hands. 'Would someone be so kind as to remove these?'

'Not yet. First I have questions.' She gave a nodded signal to Naeem, who stepped behind Adfric and pushed him to his knees. Viratia drew her knife, and pressed it to Adfric's cheek just below his eye.

'My husband thought you a man of honour, but you've aligned yourself with his murderers, so don't expect to be treated as such. I told them they could have you alive, but I never said you'd be in the same state I found you in. So, if you value your eyes, you'll answer my questions.' She savoured the sudden fear in his face. 'Understand?'

He nodded carefully, trying to keep as much distance as possible between his eye and the blade.

'Did you fight my son Orsian?'

'I did. You already know that from Naeem.'

'I want to hear it from you.'

'He fought well, as I would expect of a son of Lord Andrick Barrelbreaker.'

Adfric gasped as Viratia pushed the knifepoint into the flesh just below his eye socket, drawing a tiny bead of crimson blood. 'You don't speak his name, you worm. Tell me what happened to Orsian.'

'He almost killed me. Managed to trap me beneath my own steed. The next I saw of him was Naeem shoving him onto a horse.'

'You never saw him after that?' Viratia tried to keep the grief from her voice.

'Never, Lady. I was injured from the fall.'

Viratia toyed with pressing the blade higher. She wavered, but decided he was telling the truth. 'And you never heard word of him after that? What happened to the East Erlanders your men chased down?'

Adfric hesitated, eyeing the knife warily. 'They were killed. Strovac gives no quarter.'

'No doubt you'd have shown them mercy,' Viratia scoffed. 'Would someone have recognised him?'

'Men do not stop to identify their foe when their blood is up.' Adfric raised his chin defiantly. 'But killing me will not bring him back. Some of your men sought refuge on the beach at Whitewater. Perhaps your son escaped by boat.'

'Do not mock me.' Viratia's eyes flashed, and the knife tremored in her hand. With a speed that made Adfric gasp, she flicked the blade against his wrist bonds, and he slumped forward in relief. 'Go. Go to your masters.'

Adfric stumbled to his feet. The ropes binding him to the poles were cut, and before anyone could refuse him he walked swiftly towards Halord's Bridge, with all the dignity he could muster.

Viratia stared after him. *I would have taken his eyes, and gladly.* But with that thought, the bright light of vengeance that burnt in her chest seemed to dim, replaced by the overwhelming sense that it was time to go home.

CHAPTER 6

Over purple heather and yellow-headed daisies their caravan trundled, a many-limbed beast snaking across the country, as certain of its destination as a running river. Eryispek dominated the horizon, enveloped in mist, rising from the rolling plains like a blade to cut the sky in two.

They came from all over. Proud Merivalers, so sure of their superiority over their country cousins. Garrulous southerners, treated with suspicion for their peculiar accent and their proximity to the Sorrowlands. A few brave West Erlanders, who had weighed the hostile welcome they would receive this side of the Pale River and come in any case. Many tribes, one people, united in their devotion to Eryi.

White-robed Brides of Eryi led them, the latest scions of the old order who had first ascended the Mountain to bring their prayers closer to Eryi. There were six of them, all ahorse, with savage-looking clubs resting on their saddles. The country had grown more dangerous since the war had begun. There were too few men left in East Erland to keep the peace, and masterless men roamed the forests and hedgerows, robbing anybody foolish or unlucky enough to come across them. Some, it was said, had even been part of the Sangreal force defeated by the Prindians near Whitewater, and turned brigand rather than return home.

They would have found ample victims among the pilgrims who followed the brides like chicks after a mother hen. Almost all were unarmed. Many were infirm, hoping that on the Mountain, Eryi would hear their unanswered prayers for a cure. Some were even barefoot, believing that Eryi would reward their humble penitence.

The pace was slow. Somewhere in the middle of the procession, an ageing bald man walked alongside a young, skinny girl with dirty blonde hair. No one spoke to or even glanced at them, as if would-be observers' eyes simply slipped past them.

Pherri had noticed the lack of attention they received, and put it down to Theodric's mastery of magic. He had insisted they would travel as part of a larger group to avoid unwanted eyes; just another pair of fanatics eager to set foot on Eryispek, perhaps a grandfather and granddaughter. So far, with a little help from Theodric's *inflika*, it had worked. From dawn till dusk, not a soul troubled them.

It had not improved Theodric's dark mood, which had travelled with them most of the journey. He had warned Pherri that they would have to sustain themselves on very little food on the journey and would not be able to practise magic as often as they had in Piperskeep. Magi required vast quantities of food, due to the energy expended by even simple acts of magic. So far, Pherri had borne the burden more graciously than Theodric, who was taciturn during the day and grumbled over the small bowl of stew given to each of them at night.

Though they were not practising magic in open sight, Theodric insisted it was necessary that he maintain the illusion around them, and travel at the slow pace of the caravan. 'There is something strange on that Mountain,' he had said. 'Whatever it is, I don't want it to know we're coming.' Some days, they travelled less than ten miles, such were the number of old and infirm among them who took so long to rise in the morning and required so many breaks to rest through the day.

Pherri remembered well the moment they had realised that Eryispek was the source of Theodric's trouble, the malign influence that had almost a year ago caused Prince Jarhick's murder, and blocked Theodric's use of *spectika* that might have prevented it. His death had thrust Erland into civil war, and since then Theodric's difficulties had become progressively worse. Pherri's father had been killed, her brother and her cousin Helana were missing, and Theodric had been powerless to prevent any of it.

It had taken Pherri to uncover the mystery. Her one foray into *spectika*, a discipline of magic that should have been beyond her, had shown things on Eryispek beyond explanation. The pale-eyed man who haunted her dreams had concocted the events that led to Jarhick's death, and it was he who had cut off her *spectika* as he had cut off Theodric's.

But other aspects of what Pherri had deduced troubled her even more. The pale-eyed man was Eryi, the god worshipped across Erland as creator of all, who held court atop Eryispek. And he was not the only power on the Mountain. *Vulgatypha.* All they knew of her was a name. A name, and a presence, even stronger than Eryi. Her message had been clear: *stay away.*

Theodric was less sure of Pherri's deductions. 'We don't

know who or what is doing this,' he had insisted several
times. It was easy for him to say that; he had not been the one
doing *spectika*, and it had not stopped him spending months
reading and researching in preparation for their journey and
waiting for the cold spring to turn to summer. 'Especially if
there are two of them. All we know is that at least one is
working against us, and working against Erland. We'll seek
answers with the Adrari in Fisherton. We've a better chance
of dealing with what whatever's up there with their help.'

Fisherton was the lowest Adrari settlement, at the south-
western base of the Mountain, where hundreds of years ago
the Adrari had knelt to King Piper, a few miles from the great
lake Eryispool. Faster ways to Eryispek existed, but Theodric
asserted that this was the best approach. There were Adrari
in Fisherton they could question, and it was the only place
they could hire guides to lead them to the swiftest trails if
they needed to seek answers further up the Mountain.

On their slow march, Pherri often passed the time by
studying their fellow pilgrims. She had rarely been so close to
the common people of Erland, and found herself fascinated
by them, by their accents, the way they formed close-knit
groups depending on which region of Erland they came from
and the state of the clothes they wore, how the parents
granted most of what little food they received to their children. Sometimes, the children played games, chasing each
other and crawling between one another's legs or throwing
sticks at a target on the ground. Several times, she had asked
Theodric if it would really be so bad for her to join in with
them just for a while. His answer on each occasion had been
a firm refusal.

When their solitude became particularly tiresome, she
instead daydreamed of leaving the pilgrims behind and

taking off at their own pace. The fates of the four apprentice priests who had grown impatient and walked off ahead of the brides had put an end to that. The caravan had found them yesterday, three hung from the bough of a great oak tree and one dead on the ground with innards spilling from his butchered belly. They were all naked; the robbers had taken everything they owned, right down to their underclothes. After that, Pherri was content to listen to Theodric on the subject.

Nevertheless, Pherri could hardly believe how long the caravan was taking to travel from Merivale to Eryispek. Wherever you were, the Mountain dominated the horizon, and on a map, there looked to be barely any distance at all between the two. Her father could have had an army there in a matter of days.

Her dead father, for whom Pherri had not shed a single tear, even when her weeping mother had held her tight and said she was leaving to fight the Prindians. It had been for the best. She would never have allowed Pherri to go with Theodric, and Pherri knew that Eryispek was where she needed to be, ever since the day she had stood with Theodric on the ramparts of Piperskeep and drawn on its power. The answer to the malady that had plagued Theodric for nearly a year was up there, somewhere. And if something up there had ill intentions towards Erland, it was up to them to thwart it.

Though it was not yet noon, some pilgrims were already beginning to tire, the stragglers stretching out the tail of the caravan for hundreds of yards. There was a cart in which some of the older and frailer travelled, but there was not room enough for all those that needed it. Up ahead, one of the brides looked back, then said something to another, who pulled a brass horn from her saddlebag and blew it to signal that they would stop.

'By Eryi's giant hairy bollocks,' spat Theodric. 'It will be next winter before we reach Fisherton.'

The magus's mood seemed to dip with every mile they stepped further from the comfort of Piperskeep. The two of them moved to rest in the shade of a tree, where Theodric produced from his bag two bruised apples.

'The way this is going,' he said between bites, 'we won't have enough food to last us to Eryispek.'

'We'll still have stew,' said Pherri. The Brides of Eryi seemed to have an endless supply of thin, watery stew.

'That won't be enough. I'll be exhausted when we get there. I'm wasting away.' He plucked the sleeve of his tunic away from his arm to display voluminous excess material.

He did look thinner, Pherri had to admit, but she had thought that was the clothes. His usual midnight-blue robes were too distinctive, and would have drawn panic had anybody recognised him. He had replaced them with the coarse tunic and trousers of the Erland peasantry. He looked like a veteran farmhand.

When he was finished eating, Theodric rose to his feet with a groan. 'I'm going to relieve myself. Stay here.'

He walked off into the trees, and Pherri turned to watch a game of tag that had broken out nearby. The children were around her age, and even skinnier, with straggly hair and bare legs, dressed in an assortment of rags and roughspun. They hooted gleefully as they chased one another, and Pherri found herself longing to join them. She cast a furtive look over her shoulder towards where Theodric had gone.

She was still looking that way when a high-pitched scream

rose from the game, whipping Pherri's head around. One of the boys was on the ground, wailing and clutching his ankle. The other children rushed over to him, some adding their horrified screams to the boy's while others stared down, fascinated.

'That's broken!' declared a girl. 'Our pig broke its leg last autumn and my da had to kill it.'

This only made the boy wail louder. His screams were beginning to draw the attention of adults now. A short woman who might have been the boy's mother was trudging towards them. 'Ryley! What have I told you about—' She looked down at his leg. 'Oh, Eryi's balls!'

'There's no call for blaspheming,' said an approaching man. A crowd was beginning to gather now. 'Let's—' He looked down at the boy's leg, gasped, and turned away looking slightly green.

Reasoning that nobody would notice her in the confusion, Pherri decided to look for herself before Theodric returned. She hurried over, and ducked around several people to reach the centre of the throng. Ryley's ankle was bent at an angle, and a grisly piece of bone had pierced his skin. He had stopped screaming, but all the colour had drained from his face, and his wide white eyes were fixed on the wound.

'Someone fetch the brides!' cried his mother.

'There's no fixing that,' said an older man. 'I saw wounds like that fighting in Cliffark, never ended well.'

Pherri had never seen a bone before, but she had heard that if properly set and fixed in place they could fuse back together, though she knew nothing of how that was done, and it was clear no one else did either. But was guiding the mending of a wound all that different to guiding a coin to fall the right way? Surely, there would be some realities where the boy's ankle healed?

She sank to her knees, ignoring the gasps around her, and placed a finger against the injury.

Phisika was the one discipline of magic that had come to her as easily as breathing, but she had never attempted anything as complicated as this. She closed her eyes, feeling for the rare paths in which the wound mended itself, drawing them into her own reality, willing that this should come to pass. Sweat beaded on her forehead, and she felt her flesh beginning to slough from her bones as she poured her energy into her magic, and in that moment it came so naturally that she could hardly have imagined doing anything else. Slowly, she sensed the bone retreating and knitting, the skin—

'Pherri!'

Theodric rushed to her, just in time to lift Pherri away from the boy as she felt herself on the verge of collapsing into the dirt. Through bleary eyes, she saw puckered pale flesh over the boy's now straight ankle. The crowd were staring at her.

'A miracle!' cried one man. 'She is blessed by Eryi!' The boy's mother was cradling his head, sobbing.

Pherri had a vague sensation of being carried away as the mob hurried after them, and of Theodric once again crafting a veil of secrecy to hide them from sight.

CHAPTER 7

As soon as they were out of sight of Lady Viratia and the East Erlanders, Rymond Prindian tore the new crown from his head. 'Get this damn thing away from me.' He threw it to a nearby servant like a soiled rag.

'You did well,' said his mother. 'The crown unsettled her.'

Crowning him King of West Erland had been her idea of course, barely a week after the Battle of Whitewater. Victory had seemed within their grasp then, with Andrick dead, but it had been only the beginning of their troubles.

Returning to Irith had been their first mistake. That had handed the Sangreals the initiative, when they ought to have harried them back to Merivale and won the whole kingdom. Within a month of Rymond's coronation, Permouth had been sacked, the second largest settlement in West Erland. Then there had been the desertions and the dissent. Some minor lords had been up in arms about Andrick's murder, and two had even gone so far as to try and march their men home. Hanging the pair had swiftly put an end to that, but it had not stopped Chieftain Ba'an abandoning the war and taking his Thrumb back to their homeland under cover of darkness. Meanwhile Strovac smirked and glowered, Adfric grumbled, and mercenary captains pestered him for payment. And none of them could agree on anything.

Even when Rymond's forces were finally able to engage the East Erlanders, Lady Viratia had led them a merry dance up and down the Pale River, attacking only where the ground favoured East Erland, and never for long enough that the Prindian forces could bring their greater numbers to bear, until Strovac had almost caught them beneath the walls of Bluefair. It had merely wasted supplies and frayed already fraught tempers. Rymond was relieved that Viratia had accepted his terms. He wanted to go back to Irith, if only so he could escape Strovac, Adfric, and his mother for at least a few hours every day.

That was all Rymond associated the damnable crown with. Not a kingdom, not even half a kingdom, just endless strife and sleeping outside. He was beginning to forget what a feather bed felt like.

He left his mother, dismissed his various attendants, and made a beeline for his tent, responding to the greetings of his lords with apologetic hurry, as if there was nothing he would have liked more than to speak with them but sadly his kingly duties made such a thing impossible.

In the months of war, tents had been lost to bad weather, poorly controlled campfires, and endless other mishaps, and so the Prindian camp was littered with all manner of shelters, some little more than four sticks holding up a sheet. Fortunately, there was no mistaking Rymond's own tent, a large square structure supported by ten-foot poles, covered with rich green and gold canvas. Stepping inside, Rymond lit the candles, illuminating the opulent Prindian wall hangings that he always tried to ignore. A chess game he had been playing against himself covered a map of Erland that was unrolled across a high table at the room's centre, and a well-fed ginger cat was licking clean a pile of chicken bones in the corner.

Rymond's attention though was drawn to his bed, where a slim, well-muscled woman lay propped upon an elbow, naked but for a single fur, her deep black hair fanned across his pillow like storm clouds across the sky. Captain-General Gruenla was not shy about chasing him for payment, nor sharing his bed on occasion.

'You're early,' he said. 'I usually don't see you till past midnight.'

She stretched, letting him glimpse her toned body beneath the fur. 'Battle gets my blood up.'

The cat had left the chicken bones and was rubbing itself against Rymond's ankle. He kept throwing the furry little parasite out, and still it kept finding a way back in and eating his food. Gruenla had named it Arka, after the hirsute Ffrisean chieftain who routinely ate enough for three men.

'And why did you give my chicken to Arka?'

'He's a growing boy. Now come to bed.'

Rymond began tugging his boots off, almost tripping over the cat in his eagerness. It looked at him with disdain and strutted out, no doubt in search of more food.

Cats were preferable to lords and warriors in many ways; their wants were easily understood, they could not talk back, and if you were sick of them you could just throw them outside. *Perhaps kingship would be easier if all my lords were cats.*

By Eryi, he was tired. Given the choice between the straw mattress with Gruenla and his own bed in Irith without, he would have gladly taken the latter. He would have flown back to Irith if he could.

Rymond had got as far as unbuttoning his shirt when he heard the tent flap open. He turned, and his heart sank to see that it was Adfric, with a face like thunder. At least it was not Strovac or his mother, but as ever Adfric had managed to arrive at the time of maximum irritation.

'What is it, Adfric? I did not give up a hundred prisoners just so you could waltz into my tent uninvited.'

Adfric was looking disapprovingly at Gruenla, who had made no attempt to cover herself. 'Forgive me, Majesty, but it cannot wait. I need to speak with you privately.'

Rymond rubbed his face in frustration. Was a moment's peace too much to ask? Gruenla was already dressing and gathering her things. 'Will I see you later?' he asked as she departed.

She winked at him as she passed. 'Come and find me. Be quick about it though, before I find some other bedwarmer.'

Gruenla left, and Rymond rebuttoned his shirt and took a seat at the head of the table. 'This had better be important.'

Adfric cleared his throat. 'You know that she is using you, don't you? She hopes you will look favourably on her and her mercenaries and allow them to stay in Erland once the war is won. Cylirien will be part of the Imperium within a decade.'

The whole damn army is using me. 'I said this had better be important. Who I bed with is not important.'

'It's about Strovac Sigac.'

Rymond would have been quite happy to never hear that name again. He was sure most of his problems could be traced back to Sigac, certainly the infighting that had plagued their war effort was a consequence of his murder of Lord Andrick, and the failure to apprehend Helana Sangreal had not helped. 'Tall, bad-humoured fellow. He's untrustworthy and almost as vexing to me as you are. What else do I need to know?'

'He tried to get me killed.'

Adfric had been riding with the Wild Brigade as they pursued the East Erlanders, he explained. When the ambush had become clear, Strovac and the rest of them had fled.

'There were four of them,' Adfric went on. 'As we were fleeing, two blocked my path and two others came up behind. I veered just as their swords whistled past my ear. My horse tossed me, and I fell straight into the path of that freakish Gough woman.'

Rymond pondered. A man bested by Yriella Gough inventing a story to absolve himself was not beyond possibility. But Adfric had come straight to him, and this was not a tale he could tell around camp to avoid being ridiculed. 'Are you sure?'

'I know when a man is trying to kill me,' said Adfric, slightly indignant. 'And his Wild Brigade didn't look friendly either. Strovac must have ordered them to do it.'

Rymond hunched forward, resting his chin on his fist. Adfric still held a grudge over Andrick Barrelbreaker's death, and did not go out of his way to hide it. He and Strovac had been at odds even before that. Rymond would not have put anything past Strovac Sigac. The strength of his arm and the fear he instilled were good enough reasons to be glad of him as an ally, but only barely.

'He means to remove your other advisors,' continued Adfric. 'To make himself indispensable in the hope that you will come to rely on him.'

Rymond sighed. 'Probably. What would you have me do though? He's our best warrior, and his Wild Brigade our finest force.'

'Is that worth him killing me?'

Rymond was tempted to say he was not actually sure. He rubbed a hand through his prickly beard. The truth of it was that Adfric was loyal to a fault, and more so to Rymond than his mother these days, but Strovac was the embodiment of erratic. If he was trying to kill Adfric, he had gone beyond being burdensome to downright damaging. 'No. Eryi's balls, he has to go. We'll deal with him once we're back in Irith. Make a plan, but tell nobody.'

By the time Rymond had managed to extricate Adfric from his tent, dark was setting in. He had been looking forward to finally having some peace, until his steward stuck his head through the flap to remind him that the servants would need to begin packing his things for the march tomorrow.

With an exaggerated sigh, Rymond poured himself a cup of wine. 'They can have one hour, but when I return they had better be finished. Just give me five minutes of peace first.'

While the steward waited without, Rymond furtively checked the pouch hidden under his pillow. Empty, as he had already known it was.

Sometimes a man needs more than wine and smokesticks. He would have to go out. Quickly, he removed his expensive garments, and replaced them with the most nondescript pair of breeches, shirt, and jerkin he owned, then wrapped himself in a vast black travelling cloak with a hood large enough to shadow his face. He was not ashamed of the habit he had acquired while at war, but he had taken pains to ensure nobody discovered it.

With a nod to the steward, Rymond left the tent. 'They can go in now. Have food ready for my return.'

Pulling the hood forward over his brow, Rymond walked around to the back of his pavilion, and wove his way between the haphazard rows of tents and campfires. The sounds and smells of a war camp in evening floated to him on the soft breeze: crackling fires, the sizzling of stringy rodents on spits, and the raucous laughter of men eager to go home, yet determined to make the most of their last night by drinking their fill of the camp's beer.

At the very edge of the encampment, by the latrine trenches, Rymond found a place covered by dense bushes and vegetation, and ducked under cover. He lowered his hood, rubbed his hands in the black earth, then ran them through his hair, muddying his golden locks to a dirty blond. For good measure, he smeared some on his cloak, and then rubbed some through his beard as well.

He pulled a small looking glass from inside his cloak, and when he looked within a stranger stared back at him. The dirt was the least of it; he had never worn a beard before the war, his once milk-white skin had been darkened by the sun, deep bags hung below his eyes, and there were lines on his forehead he could not recall seeing before.

'War truly does age a man,' he mumbled. Rymond pocketed the looking glass, raised his hood, and headed back to camp.

He found what he was looking for at the south-eastern edge; a tent almost as large as his own, but of heavy burlap and supported by poles of varying length, giving it the appearance of a lumpy, misshapen sack. Within, a warm light glowed, and he heard the murmuring of men followed by the occasional gale of laughter. Smiling, Rymond ducked inside.

Inside, around a large table formed of empty ale barrels, was the oddest collection of warriors one was likely to encounter. Two of Strovac's Wild Brigade sat next to each other, bearded and burly; three hollow-cheeked Cylirien mercenaries, including two women; a hirsute Ffrisean with an oiled black beard that drooped to his bare navel; and half-a-dozen West Erlanders sworn to a variety of lords.

They all turned to look at him. 'Do we know you?' asked one of the Wild Brigade, scowling. By his diminished stack of coins, Rymond suspected it was not the presence of a newcomer that had caused the man's poor temper.

Rymond cast off his hood. 'I'm Gunnar,' he replied, dropping his voice below its usual range and disguising his accent. 'I played before. Week ago.'

One of the Cylirien women laughed. 'I remember this one! Welcome, generous friend. Surprised you've more coin to lose.'

The table echoed her mirth, which Rymond took for a welcome. He served himself a mug of ale from the barrel in the corner and dropped into a spare chair. 'We'll see. I fancy my luck tonight.'

Had he been playing for real, Rymond would have rated his chances against any of them. Dom and Will had practically been raised in taverns; if there was a card game they did not know it was not worth playing, and Rymond had learnt from them. The table was playing triumph, a five-suit, sixty-card game that was played across Erland from palaces to pigpens.

But Rymond was not playing to win. The sums were so

small as to be below his notice, and nothing would have turned his new companions more swiftly against him than winning. He had a different prize in mind.

Rymond played for close to an hour, winning a few hands, but losing more. In some ways, losing in a manner that did not arouse suspicion was harder than winning.

Down to his last few coins, Rymond pushed all of them into the table. 'Three swords,' he declared, flipping over a hand that would usually have been good enough to win, had he not known that the Ffrisean had him beat.

The Ffrisean grinned broadly. 'Three sticks,' he replied, turning over his own cards.

'Spears, you mean,' grunted the Wild Brigader whose own stack was slowly bleeding chips.

'Either way, mine.' With hands the size of shovels the Ffrisean reached forward and pulled the coins towards him.

The Cylirien man sitting at Rymond's left let out a doleful sigh. 'Bad beat, friend.'

Rymond shrugged and pushed his chair back. 'Not my night.' As he rose, a muscle in his thigh twitched, and almost stumbling he had to grasp his chair for balance. 'Anyone got anything I can smoke to sell me?'

'Got some tabac you can have,' said the Cylirien, reaching into his leather-studded jerkin.

'I was hoping for something stronger.'

An uneasy silence fell over the table. Rymond felt a bead of sweat break from his forehead, and he had to actively tighten the muscle in his leg to stop it spasming again. The withdrawals always came the hardest when you were close to getting some. He had gone days without, and now it was almost within his grasp the longing was like a parched field seeking rain.

'You should stay away from that shit,' said the second Wild Brigader. He flashed a dark look at the Cylirien male. 'You lot should never have brought it over with you.'

'If you don't like it, don't have it,' said a Cylirien woman with the hard-bitten gaze of someone whose youth had been spent under the shadow of war. She looked at Rymond. 'Meet me around the back of the tent in a quarter-hour.'

The tremors threatened to come worse than ever after her words, but Rymond forced himself to nod, as if he did not care whether she would meet him or not. 'Fine. I'm not waiting around if you're late though.'

The woman cackled. 'Reckon you will.'

By the time she came to meet him, Rymond felt as if he was sweating arrowheads. His lungs he swore had shrunk to the size of wizened apples, dwindling with each laboured breath, and the cool night air itself seemed to have taken on a peculiar metallic taste. He strained to give an impression of nonchalance, as if he did not care whether she had the casheef or not, but the woman saw straight through him.

'You need to be careful,' she said, even as Rymond deposited the coins into her palm with a shaking hand and she slipped him a drawstring bag of the powdery, noxious substance. 'Cyliriens can take this stuff like it's ale, but you Erlanders seem to go mad for it. Ease yourself off it this time. Make it last.'

'I know what I'm doing,' replied Rymond, though his voice trembled as he said it. His tongue felt like it was made of cotton.

The woman shrugged. 'Your choice. Won't stop me selling to you.'

Their transaction complete, Rymond stumbled back towards his tent, cursing the unnamed woman, and also cursing Dom who had introduced him to casheef in the first place. Rymond had been eager to try it, for it was mentioned regularly in historic texts of Erland, apparently widely used until the plant it came from died out, but reading about it had not prepared him, not by any stretch of the imagination.

The need for it waxed and waned, but when it came it was overwhelming. He had gone five days without earlier that month, and been sure that was the end of it, but the urge always returned stronger than ever.

Rymond half-fell through his tent flap, hoping that his guards only thought him drunk. His belongings were stowed, and a plate of pork with seasoned vegetables had been left for him at the table, but Rymond only had eyes for the casheef. With trembling hands, he retrieved his pipe from under the mattress, tapped a few ounces of black powder into it, then packed it down.

Perhaps I should sleep and see if I still need it in the morning, came a small voice in his mind. Foolish imaginings. He would not sleep, not with his heart beating as if it meant to burst out of his chest. *One last hit and then I am done with it, once I am back in Irith.* The toils of war had driven him to this; in the warmth of his own bed he would have no need for casheef.

With shaking fingers, he fumbled for his flint-and-steel, and after a few attempts, the powder flashed orange with heat. Rymond inhaled, like a desperate newborn at the teat.

His heart slowed. His vision sharpened. Conversations around cooking fires became so clear it was like he was there. Over the horizon, a summer storm flashed and thundered, and in the east, the hooves of the East Erlanders' horses thundered across the plains.

To take casheef was to feel everything in the world at

once, and to find joy in it. With the deepest of sighs, Rymond collapsed onto his mattress. Gruenla, his food, the war, kingship, Lord Andrick's death, and every misery in between forgotten, as if they were no more than the whispers of the rushing wind.

CHAPTER 8

Senate Tower was perhaps the grandest building in Ulvatia. It sat atop a small hill, a shining beacon of white marble served by a single vast staircase, into which was carved the name of every single senator to have ever served. You could follow them upward, tracing every generation, all the way back to Ulvus the magus, the city's founder. For over a thousand years the Senate had stood, and seemed not to have weathered a single day. Every name stood out as if etched that morning; every towering column identical and unmarked; the stone lions so perfectly formed they seemed on the cusp of life.

Drast knew by heart where the names of his father and grandfather were. As a child he had scoured the stairs, searching for any other Fulkiros who had served in the Senate. There were none. He was no Murino nor Brunal, able to call back hundreds of years to long-dead ancestors who had trod these steps.

It took us three generations, but we are ready to challenge them.

He had not yet sought Krupal's assistance, instead preferring to try and talk wavering senators round without resorting to the magus's influence. The hustings for reformist candidates had occurred three days earlier, and Drast had been pleased to learn that of those already within the Senate, he was the frontrunner. The challenge would come from outside: from Kvarm Murino, who had returned finally from Erland the day before the hustings and who Drast had done his best to avoid, and more surprisingly the deceased kzar's daughter, Saffia Murino. Them both running could only assist his cause; there was little desire to turn being kzar into a hereditary title.

However, Drast's speech extolling the case for a full withdrawal of the Eternal Legion from Cylirien had not been well-received. Many had turned their backs, and others had left the hall entirely. He would see how today's first round of votes went first, but he suspected he would soon be seeking Krupal's assistance. He had stowed the magus in a room of his manor, and left orders that he was to be given anything he desired except allowance to leave the grounds. He could not have a rogue magus wandering the streets of Ulvatia. So far Krupal's primary concern had been gorging himself; that tale of the magi at least had turned out to be true.

Drast had risen with the sun, and been among the first to arrive, wearing a sash of bold Fulkiro red-black-yellow across the shoulder of his white senatorial robes. As the other senators milled about the stairs, there were many flashes of colour amidst the white, far more than there would have been twenty or even ten years ago. The white robes were meant to represent that, in the Senate, a man's loyalties were to the Imperium rather than his family name, but more and more preferred to garnish them with the colours of their own line.

While the reformists were divided in their support, the conservatives were almost wholly united behind Senator Naro Brunal, Kzar Bovarch's lickspittle lieutenant, as pinched and gaunt as the old boar had been fat, and with all the charm of his corpse. He had arrived in a palanquin borne by eight slaves, and was now standing near the top of the stairs, surrounded by his cadre of old sycophants.

Drast had brought with him only Forren, standing at his shoulder with a blade at his hip, and two of Drast's personal guard, dressed in silver armour and helmets topped with plumes in the Fulkiro colours. It was not unknown for elections to descend into citywide civil war between gangs of cutthroats. The ascension of Bovarch Murino, decades ago, had passed without incident, but Kzar Petro before him had bought his position at the sharp end of a blade, in a conflict that had lasted weeks and killed hundreds. Drast had no desire for such a spectacle. It would only prove them correct: that the Fulkiros were not of the right stock to be kzars, savages better suited to laying bricks and hoisting beams. Even so, Drast had stationed half-a-hundred paid blades within half a mile of the Senate. He would not start the war, but if it came, he would be ready.

Kvarm Murino had also arrived, in a carriage drawn by four coursers, each as white as Senate robes. Kvarm, not being a senator, was festooned in rich robes of purple and orange. The fine thread may have shown his wealth, but it also demonstrated a singular lack of taste and sense. Such a display would only remind senators that he was not of their ilk; merely a merchant, the younger brother to a greater man.

Saffia Murino had shown more sense. She wore a white

single-strapped dress, leaving one arm bare and the other covered by fine white lace, and her hair was bound in a head-dress with purple-orange feathers on one side and the red-green of the Brunals on the other. It was deftly done, Drast had to admit. Her dress was equal parts modern and traditional, and was similar to the senators' garb without being presumptu-ous. The headdress would delight reformers, and the Brunal colours would remind conservatives that she was not only a Murino but a Brunal on her maternal grandmother's side.

Saffia was still at the foot of the stairs, joking and laughing with senators from both factions. As Drast looked down at her, their eyes met. He raised an eyebrow in greet-ing, and she gave him an imperceptible wink.

'Senator Fulkiro,' came a sharp voice at his elbow.

Drast had been so caught up in his reverie he had not heard the newcomer's approach. For perhaps the fiftieth time that day he prepared his most charming smile, until he realised it was Kvarm Murino, standing out like a rooster among hens in his ridiculous robes. To give the man his due, he looked well for his age; he walked without the aid of a stick, and his grip on Drast's hand was firm.

'Murino.' Drast kept his voice cool. 'How does it suit you being back in Ulvatia? One hears awful things coming out of Erland these days. I hope you weren't caught up in it.'

Kvarm chuckled mirthlessly. 'Where there is war there is opportunity. I was quite moved by your speech at the hustings. Perhaps the time has indeed come to withdraw from Cylirien. I have a richer prize in mind, as you know: there will never be a better time to take Erland. I've spoken to many senators who share my sentiments.'

Many senators who have never been to war. It was an

interesting move by Kvarm though, to try and drum up support from senators looking to recapture the Imperium's glory days. 'War is unpredictable. I would have thought a merchant such as yourself would recognise the value of peace and civility over barbarity.'

'It is a barbaric place. Peace and civility are exactly the reasons we should invade. I am surprised such a storied hero of Cylirien is not keener on the idea of expanding our borders. You were quite the warrior by all accounts, one of the youngest legates in the last century. There are too few heroes these days.'

Drast could not help the bubble of anger that rose in his throat. *I have left that life behind.* His military past was a useful political tool, but he would not hear it used by a pampered merchant like Kvarm Murino as a reason to send thousands of young men to their deaths in yet another unwinnable war.

Before he could reply, Kvarm placed a hand on Drast's shoulder and leant to his ear. 'A bold move, Drast, to betray me, but you can't win. We will speak of this again.'

As Kvarm walked away, Drast felt his anger cool. Kvarm could not win; there was no reason to be unsettled by him. He knew already what Kvarm would be offering in return for his support: gold. Kvarm might be the richest man in the world, and yet here he was, scraping to the lowliest senators for just a sniff of power. Gold was gold, but power was everything.

Or, if not gold, it would be some trick with his magus. Well, Drast had his own magus now. *And won't that be a shock for him?*

Senate Tower's bells had begun to peal, indicating that

the first vote was about to begin. The senators began making their way inside.

The ballot was not taken secretly; each of the senators simply sat in their seat and raised their arm when their chosen candidate's name was called. Drast searched the marble benches for his supporters, and took a seat among them.

Proceedings were chaired by the ancient speaker Urjus Crickeli, peering over his half-moon eyeglasses from behind a desk twice his size. Even when Drast had been a first-term senator, Urjus had looked on the cusp of death, and like Bovarch every year he defied expectations. It could not be long though. When Drast was kzar he would seek to replace him with someone unerringly loyal to him.

'Come to order!' croaked the speaker, his voice magnified by the hall's acoustics and many suspected by a little magic instilled by the Senate's founders. 'Kzar Bovarch has passed from this world, and it falls to this Senate, as representatives of the popular will, to choose his successor. You are not limited in your choice to the two hundred and fifty within this room. Any free citizen of the Imperium is eligible, provided at least one senator has this morning nominated them. I have here a list of names. Should there be any further nominations required, please make those known to me now.'

'I hope someone remembered,' whispered a senator sitting behind Drast. 'If we choose a Murino from outside the Senate we make ourselves a laughing stock.'

When nobody spoke, Urjus continued. There were four nominees known to all: Drast, Naro Brunal, and the two Murinos. There were a handful of others also, some of them likely nominated as a joke, judging by the barely concealed laughter from parts of the hall when their names were called.

'Drast Fulkiro,' said Urjus. 'All those for Drast Fulkiro raise your hands.'

Drast tensed, and raised his arm in a way he hoped was not too eager. He looked around, quickly counting the hands, searching for those who had promised him their vote. It was well short of what was required, and even fewer than Drast had expected.

Damn the Murinos. His stance on Cylirien might not have helped, but that alone could not account for such a paltry showing.

The count confirmed it. Seventy-one for Drast, one hundred and three for Naro Brunal, forty-six for Saffia Murino, twenty-six for Kvarm Murino, and a smattering of votes cast for others, who having failed to secure the support of one in ten senators would be removed from the ballot.

'Order! Order!' shouted Speaker Urjus, banging his palm on his desk in response to the hubbub of conversation that had broken out as the totals were announced. 'Naro Brunal, Drast Fulkiro, Kvarm Murino, and Saffia Murino all proceed to the full ballot. Voting shall commence three days hence and then take place every second day until a candidate has one hundred and twenty-six votes.'

When Urjus gave them leave to rise, Drast was bombarded with handshakes from eager supporters. He smiled optimistically at them, agreeing that having the most votes out of the three reformist candidates was a good start, and that now the Murino supporters would have to unite around him and push him over the line, all the while silently seething.

It was never meant to be easy, he reminded himself. *Tomorrow I will put Krupal to work.*

CHAPTER 9

Tansa woke with the dawn as it crested the high window of their cell. She felt a moment of panic, until she remembered where she was. It could have just as easily been a prison; Maud's guesthouse had never been known for its décor. The walls were the same red brick as the rest of Pauper's Hole, and the only furniture was what she was lying on, a double straw mattress supported by a wooden pallet.

Cag. Shit. He would be in an actual cell somewhere. How had she slept knowing that? *I have to get him out.* She rubbed her eyes and rolled over, expecting to see her sailor companion lying beside her.

He was gone.

'Eryi's balls!' Tansa sat bolt upright. *Of-fucking-course he's run off, you idiot.* He had probably made a dash for it as soon as she was asleep. *That Norhai-cursed water rat.* The only surprise was he had not tried to rape her first.

'What's all the noise?' asked a groggy voice from below the other side of the mattress. Tansa stuck her head over the side, and there he was, curled up on the stone floor.

She blinked at him. 'You fall out of bed?'

He stretched his arms out, yawned, and rolled towards the wall. 'You claimed the bed as soon as we got here. Thought I'd let you have it.'

'Thought you sailors slept thirty to a room? You shy?'

'We don't share a hammock.'

'Is it because you stink of whale blubber? I don't mind; I've smelt worse.' Tansa was only slightly offended. From what she knew of Cliffark sailors most of them would not have taken a moment to leap into a bed with a woman, whether she agreed or not.

He waved an arm in her direction. 'Wouldn't be proper. Could you let me sleep, please?'

'Proper?' Tansa let out a manic laugh. 'What sort of sailor worries about what's proper? I thought sailors were meant to be rough as a cat's tongue; why do you speak like you've just shat yourself?'

That seemed to get his attention. He rolled over to look up at her. 'What do you mean?'

'*What do you mean?*' replied Tansa, in an approximation of his cadence, pouting her lips and turning down the corners of her mouth. She cackled. 'If you're a sailor I'm the lord administrator of the bloody Imperial Enclave.'

'I grew up in Merivale,' he said defensively. 'People speak differently there.'

'No one I met in Merivale spoke like you. Your family rich?'

'None of your business.'

'Fine. Keep your secrets, fancy boy. What's your name anyway?'

'Ranulf.'

Tansa snorted. 'Fancy name that. Sailor, my bum.'

He was awake now at least. She cast an eye over him. Ranulf's shoulders looked like a pair of prize hams, and he had arms like sturdy boughs of oak. Sailors were meant to be lithe and wiry, and grizzled by drink and saltwater, not thick-jawed and handsome. There was definitely something peculiar about her new ally.

It doesn't matter who he is. The sooner they freed Cag, the sooner she and Ranulf could be on their separate ways.

'You still going to help?'

'Swore I would, didn't I?'

'Wasn't sure a sailor would keep his word. Best get up then, though only the Norhai know what use you'll be.'

Once they were up and had greeted Maud, who fed them breakfast with a few questionable bits of bacon, Tansa dipped into her small stash of silver to pay a runner to go and see if Cag was in Cliffark's south prison. They were still in the kitchen when the boy reported back, with the unwelcome news Tansa had forced herself not to imagine: Cag had already been moved to the larger jail in the square, where they did the hangings.

'The guards were laughing about the size of him,' squeaked the barefooted boy. 'Said they'd need extra tall gallows just for him.'

It was summer, and Cliffark was suffocating in the wet heat. The clouds overhead threatened that the fine weather could give way to a storm at any moment. It broke almost as soon as they were outside Pauper's Hole, showering them with heavy raindrops.

'Put your hood up,' Tansa told Ranulf, doing the same as

they emerged onto the street. 'Guards will still be on the lookout.' He did, just as two blue-cloaked sentries turned the corner, and they shuffled towards the square.

Tansa's stomach was tight as a sailor's knot. She had already lost Tam. She would not lose Cag as well.

'We'll never get him out of there,' she said desperately. 'It's right next to the guards' barracks. You'd need an army to get in there.'

Ranulf grimaced. 'What can we do?'

Tansa thought quickly. *Eryi, Norhai, all the fucking gods – I couldn't save Tam, please just let me save Cag.* 'Sixthday is hanging day. That's three days from now. We've three days to get him out.'

Her memory of Tam thrashing at the end of a rope had faded around the edges, like a bad dream, but she remembered digging the cold earth with her bare hands to make a pit for his burning as if it were yesterday. Cag had been there for her, holding her tightly as she sobbed into his chest. Cag had always been there for her. They had all been there for each other, until that day they had lost Tam.

She and Cag had stayed in Merivale afterwards, for a while, thinking how they might avenge themselves upon Hessian. It had been futile from the beginning; he was the king and they were nobodies. The oath of vengeance Tansa had sworn did not change that.

She looked sideways at Ranulf. If they were left with no choice but to try and break Cag out by force, she would be glad to have him on their side. He had defeated three of the city guard as easily as he had defeated her and Cag. She had persuaded him to leave the sword in their room; openly carried blades were not permitted in Cliffark, unless you were a guard or a rich merchant's man.

'Where did you learn to use a sword?'

'My father taught me,' he said, as if that settled the matter.

'Is he a soldier?'

'Was. He's dead.'

'I'm sorry,' she said, placing a hand on his shoulder. 'My brother was hanged. Just a few months ago. If it happens to Cag as well I don't know what I'll do.'

Ranulf pushed her hand away and kept walking. 'Maybe you shouldn't go round robbing people then. My father died in battle; don't compare him to some common criminal.'

'My brother wasn't a criminal!' Tansa punched him hard in the arm, but it was like hitting a brick wall. 'If you think that then why the fuck are you helping me?'

Her outburst drew concerned looks from a few passers-by. Two conspirative merchants with a canopy held over them by four servants paused their conversation, and a woman frowned at Tansa before taking her daughter's hand and hastening past. Tansa looked around, and saw two guards twenty yards back studying them. 'Shit. Come on.' She hurried them on.

'Sorry,' said Ranulf eventually, once they had left the guards behind. 'Just feels odd to talk about.' His voice wavered. 'I think that's the first time I've said it out loud – my father is dead. May Eryi take him, if you believe in that. I'm sorry about your brother. I've seen innocent men die; no reason he wasn't one of them.'

Tansa nodded, satisfied with his apology. 'We don't have to talk about it. But why *are* you helping me? When I woke up I thought you'd run off.'

He looked at her strangely. 'Because I swore I would. I

have two weeks until we sail again; might as well use it to save a man's life. Better than sitting around a tavern.'

Tansa smirked. 'You don't want to go to a tavern? You could at least try to pretend you're a sailor.'

'Piss off.'

She laughed. 'Do all sailors take themselves so seriously?' She had not seen Ranulf smile yet. It was a shame; he had a nice face, with full lips. Smiling would have suited him.

It was not a market day, but Market Square was busy even so. The shower that had started when they stepped onto the street had ended just as quickly. A few hawkers were laying their wares out on spare shirts and sheets, and young men and women were congregating around the fountain at the centre, laughing as they dipped their toes into the pool and kicked water at one another. They looked around the same age as Tansa.

Will Cag and I ever be that carefree? Perhaps they might have been, if the three of them had stayed in Cliffark with their stolen gold. Tam would have been the first one in the fountain.

The jail was an austere grey building, set opposite the great white marble Temple to the Elements across the square. The Elements were not as popular as they had been before the country had adopted Eryi as its god, but she could see Ranulf's gaze was drawn to it, his eyes following the white spire up to the golden minaret.

She poked him in the ribs. 'You believe in the Elements? Thought you were from Merivale?'

'I'm not sure I believe in any of the gods. But you cannot deny its beauty.'

'I'd wager you're the first sailor to ever call something

other than a ship or a woman beautiful.' She pointed to the jail. 'Cag's in there.'

They took a seat on a bench and watched the jail from a distance, Tansa still keeping an eye out for guards. They would not take kindly to three of their fellows being left unconscious in an alleyway. There were four outside the jail, and two more on the entrance to the barracks alongside it. After a while, Ranulf wandered off and returned with a warm fish pie for each of them.

Tansa had hoped to see some weakness in the rotation of the guards, but there was none. Every two hours, two were replaced by a pair returning from a patrol of the city, and at no point were there ever less than four. She shook her head. They could not go in the front without waking half the barracks.

Ranulf seemed to have reached the same conclusion. 'Can we get on the roof?'

Tansa had run across half the rooves in Cliffark as a girl, dipping into windows and stealing anything she could grab, but nobody would ever have been foolish enough to steal from the guards. Except Tam of course. 'I think so, but there's no way inside from up there. Not that I've seen anyway.' She rose from the bench. 'We can look though. I know the way.'

She led Ranulf through a narrow street around the back of the square, finding her way as much by feeling as by knowledge. A set of crooked half-broken stairs around the side of an old brewery were concealed behind a stack of crates. She scampered up them eagerly, as she had the first time Tam had shown her, when he was eight and she was nine. The roof was slippery from the rain, but flat, and she clambered up over the edge easily, with Ranulf following behind.

Tansa had seen it half-a-thousand times, but stopped and stared nevertheless. Cliffark's mismatched rooves and towers spread out before her like a peacock's tail feathers. She doubted anyone alive knew the city as she did: above and below, every hidey-hole and cut-through, every nook and safe haven. It did not truly feel like home any more though. Not without Tam. Nowhere would.

Ranulf coughed behind her. 'Tansa.' He pointed to a corner of the roof behind them. There was a small tent-like structure; a flap of canvas set over a rickety wooden frame with a blanket inside.

Tansa frowned. She and Tam had not been the only ones to make the rooves of Cliffark their home. More than once as children they had been forced out of somewhere to make way for someone bigger and stronger. When Cag had joined them, they had taken a prime spot behind the city's great clocktower.

'People *live* up here?' asked Ranulf.

'Poor people live up here. Better than bedding down with thirty stinking sailors.'

'Fair point.' For a moment Ranulf looked on the edge of a smile. 'Did you live here?'

'Here and there. We should go, before they come back. They won't take kindly to us snooping.'

As the crow flew, the rooves overlooking the square were near, but the route required winding up and down several buildings to find somewhere to leap across to the next row. Tansa kept looking behind her to make sure Ranulf was still following, but he kept pace easily, and only once almost lost his balance when a tile skidded under his foot and threatened to take him over the edge. He grabbed for the brickwork and managed to hold on.

'Still easier than climbing the rigging,' he said, once he was sure he was secure.

'Just go slowly,' said Tansa. 'And stay low – if the guards spot you sneaking about, falling will be the least of your worries.'

One building away from the jail, they stopped and leant their backs against a chimney, shielding themselves from the view of anyone in the square. The jail's roof was flat but, as Tansa had known, there did not look to be a way inside.

'Stay here.' She crept towards the jail and leapt onto the roof before Ranulf could object.

Crouching low, Tansa explored it. As she had thought from her previous vantage points, there were no stairs leading down. She risked a look over the back of the building. There was a small yard, full of rusted iron tools, rotten wood, and other debris. A small dog was savaging a bone in the corner. It must have smelt her, because it looked up at her and started barking. Tansa quickly retreated the way she had come. There was no hope of getting in via the roof.

Safely back behind the chimney, she was shocked to find that Ranulf had company. He was holding a young boy by the scruff of the neck, pressed up against the brickwork.

'Ranulf!' cried Tansa. 'Let him go!' The scrawny boy scratched at Ranulf's grip like a feral cat.

'This little shit tried to rob me! Caught his hand in my pocket.'

'No I never,' spat the boy. 'Let me go!'

A blur of colour suddenly flew at Ranulf's back. 'Let my brother go, you bully!' A small girl clung to his shoulders, trying to wrap her tiny arms around Ranulf's neck. He paid her no mind, instead spinning the boy upside down and holding him by the ankle.

'Ranulf!' said Tansa again. 'Put him down, before the whole square sees you.'

This seemed to bring Ranulf to his senses. He lowered the boy to the ground and kept a warning hand on him while he retrieved his sister from his back, with considerably more gentleness than he had shown her brother.

'What in Eryi's name are you playing at?' he growled. 'Scared me half to death.'

'You were looking at our home,' said the boy, meeting his eye with an accusing stare. 'We were there first; you can't have it.'

'What are you talking about? I don't want your bloody home, you little shit.'

The girl started to cry.

'Eryi's blood, Ranulf,' said Tansa, pushing his hand away and gathering the girl into her arms. 'Stop it. You're scaring her. Look at the state of them; they're starving.'

'No excuse for stealing.' Ranulf released the boy and let him up to catch his breath. 'I'd have given him money if he'd asked.'

'You planning on giving money to half the bleeding world?' Tansa asked, glaring at him. 'Not everyone grew up in a house, with rich parents, and food on the table.' The girl was weeping almost hysterically. Tansa held her close, letting the tears soak her shoulder.

Ranulf opened his mouth as if to offer a retort, but whatever he had meant to say died on his breath. Tansa abruptly realised from his abashed expression how young he was for all his brawn, no older than her.

'Here,' said Ranulf, grudgingly reaching into his pocket for the remains of his fish pie and handing it to the boy.

'Share this with your sister. I'll buy you one each, if you promise not to steal from me.'

The boy snatched the morsel from Ranulf's hand before he could blink and shoved half of it into his mouth. 'Thanks,' he said, through a gulletful of pastry. 'Have you got any with pork? We prefer pork.'

'We like pork,' said the girl, rubbing a glob of snot on the back of her hand and wiping it off on Tansa's shirt.

'We'll get you some pork,' Tansa promised, lowering the girl back to the roof. 'What's the best way down from here without the guards spotting us?'

'We know the way,' said the boy eagerly. He handed the other half of his pastry to his sister and took a running leap back the way Tansa and Ranulf had come, beckoning them to follow. The girl darted away from Tansa's embrace and raced after him.

'How did you let him sneak up on you?' asked Tansa as she and Ranulf followed them. 'What if it had been a man with a knife?'

'I was on a roof, was I meant to be on the lookout for bloody assassins?'

'This is Cliffark; you should always be on the lookout.'

The two children led them back to their makeshift shelter. For Tansa it was like looking into a mirror of the past. They were just as she and Tam had been, living hand-to-mouth and surviving on their wits.

'Will you get us some more food?' the boy asked Ranulf. He dived into the ramshackle tent and emerged with a smattering of copper coins. 'Here's some money.'

'Keep it.' Ranulf dropped to a knee. 'Perhaps some cheese and wine as well, Lord?'

'Wine makes people slow,' said the boy. 'Easy to rob. Cheese would be nice though.'

Ranulf shook his head and gave Tansa a bemused look. He went to get food all the same, and returned with four more pies and a lump of cheese. They sat down on the roof facing each other, and the children tore eagerly into the cheese with their dirty fingers before tucking into their pies.

'I'm Pitt,' said the boy. 'This is Esma. What were you doing on our roof?'

'We're looking for a way to get into the jail to rescue our friend,' said Tansa. Ranulf gave her a sharp glance, as if these vagabond children might betray them. She rolled her eyes at him. 'You don't know a way in, do you?'

'Our dad's in there,' said Esma. 'Pitt says he's never coming out, but he might.'

'He's dead, Esma,' said Pitt. 'Dead. Worm food. Like Mum.'

'Ain't,' said Esma stubbornly, shoving more pie into her mouth.

'There's no way into the jail,' said Pitt, 'but I can get into the barracks. There's a window they leave open.' He looked them up and down. 'You're both too big though. You'd get stuck.'

'Can you get into the jail from there?' asked Tansa. If he could, they might get a message to Cag.

'Never tried. I don't want to get stuck in jail. Who'd look after my sister?'

'I can look after myself,' said Esma, pouting.

'Could you try?' said Tansa. 'We'd pay you.'

'Tansa,' said Ranulf sharply. 'You can't ask him to do that. He's only a boy.'

'Ain't,' said Pitt. 'How much?'

'You don't need to,' said Ranulf. 'Listen, if you've been into the barracks, do you know where they keep the guards' uniforms?'

Pitt nodded.

'Think you could steal us some? They wear those blue tabards over their armour. We'd only need two, and maybe a pair of helmets if you could carry them.'

Pitt's eyes narrowed suspiciously. 'Will you pay me? She said I'd get paid.'

'I'll buy you another pie.'

That was obviously good enough for Pitt. He ran to the edge of the roof and leapt off, heading in the direction in the jail, shouting back that he wanted the pie ready when he got back.

Esma was already eyeing the remains of Ranulf's, her eyes like saucers. 'Here,' he said with a grin, throwing the crust to her. She wolfed it down ravenously.

'What are we going to do with a pair of guards' uniforms?' asked Tansa. 'Please don't tell me you want to use them to sneak inside; the disguise wouldn't last five minutes.' It was exactly the sort of hare-brained scheme Tam would have thought of.

'I'm not stupid. That would never work. We can't get in, so we're going to rescue him in three days when they bring him out for hanging. The uniforms will help us get close to the gallows. Better than tricking Pitt into getting himself stuck in jail.'

'Yes, much better to pay him a pie to sneak into the barracks. So good of you to be looking out for him. And how is a disguise going to help *me*? There are no women guards.'

Ranulf's eyes darted to her closely cropped hair. 'You've got hair like a man.'

'I do not!' said Tansa, throwing her pie crust at him. 'I keep it short to stop it getting in my way. Better than smelling. They'd know you're not a guard because you stink of sea water and whale blubber.'

Ranulf laughed. 'I meant to get a bath as soon as I was ashore, but unfortunately you got in the way by trying to kill me. Do you know where I can get one?'

'Go to a brothel if you want a bath. The girls will be queuing up.'

'Are you two married?' interrupted Esma. 'You argue like you're married.'

Tansa spluttered a denial. There was more to Ranulf than he was letting on, but she liked his company, even when he was disagreeing with her. He had even stopped being so serious now he was around Pitt and Esma. And he seemed confident in his plan; more so than she was of Pitt successfully sneaking into the jail.

Ranulf leapt to his feet. 'I'd best be getting Pitt his pie. I'll have no money left to feed myself at this rate.'

CHAPTER 10

Most of Viratia's force had departed by the time she reached Merivale. The few minor lords brave enough to join her had led their boys home, and the peasants who toiled the land had returned to their villages. What remained was the *Hymeriker*, the Merivalers who had answered the call-to-arms, and those who followed Yriella Gough. No herald, nor clamouring citizenry, nor chorus of horns welcomed them home. The city gates were closed, and though Viratia could see guards crawling the ramparts like beetles they gave no sign they had seen their approach.

Viratia turned to look back at her column of followers. These men had earnt their rest. After their defeat at White-water, they had taken up arms again and marched under a dead lord's banner for a woman they barely knew. No mere words could express the depth of her gratitude, and if she marched again, she knew the *Hymeriker* would follow her.

But most of the rest would not. They would return to their homes, kiss their wives and children, and plant crops in the hope they would have something to bring in at harvest-time. If she ever raised her banners again, she would be lucky if one in two answered her call. She would never again march into West Erland with such strength behind her. It had been little enough to begin with.

She had led men across the Cursed Bridge and lived, torched, and plundered Permouth, and given the Prindians a bloody nose, but the men who had killed her husband walked free, and West Erland was still in open rebellion. Perhaps someday Strovac Sigac and the Prindians would face justice, but it would not be this summer, and it would not be won by her on the battlefield. In that moment though, Viratia did not care. War had wearied her; she wanted to rest her aches, to grieve for Andrick, to kiss her children.

They surveyed the city from a distance, and Yriella took in a deep breath through her nose. 'Stinks worse than my first husband.'

Naeem chuckled. 'You spend enough time here you don't notice it, but by Eryi, it doesn't half smell.' He turned to Viratia. 'I expect you are looking forward to returning to Violet Hall, Lady.'

'Even Merivale is a sight for sore eyes. I never felt so downcast as the day we made peace, but nor have I ever been so relieved to return.' Viratia pictured Pherri, with her nose buried in a book so huge she could barely carry it, her haystack hair tangled in every direction, and Errian, dripping in sweat and mud after a day of sparring in the yard. She looked to Yriella. 'Do you still mean to join us?'

The handsome warrior woman nodded. 'I've lived twenty-four years in Piperskeep's shadow. Past time I met the man I pay my taxes to.'

The three of them set their horses in a trot towards the western Ram's Gate, a long tail of men following behind.

The sun hung high, and an easterly wind filled Viratia's nostrils with the ripe stench of sweat and offal and ale. She had not spent summer in the city since she was a girl, the year she had met Andrick.

'Will you return to Tarrowton soon?' said Viratia to Yriella.

'Yes. I brought too many men to war with me. I will need to supervise the planting of crops or half my people will starve this winter.'

'Why did you bring so many?'

'Vanity, I suppose.' Yriella gave a rueful smile. 'I hoped to make a name for myself.'

'You fought well,' said Naeem. 'At Permouth and Bluefair and all the rest. If I were a bard, I would sing of the Warrior Lady, who tamed the horse of a dead man and disguised herself as his widow to come within a sword's breadth of slaying the monstrous Strovac Sigac.' He reached forward to pat Valour on the neck.

Yriella flushed with pride. 'Th-thank you.'

Naeem grinned, stretching his mutilated nostrils. 'You are still young, Lady. Plenty of time to write your tale in the blood of our enemies. By the time you reach my age you'll be sick of war.'

They were nearing the gates now, and the guards finally seemed to have noticed them. Viratia could hear their hurried cries as they debated whether to allow her entry. As they reached the drawbridge over the brown, putrid moat, Naeem looked up expectantly. The man on the battlements looked back at him, then gave a signal to someone. A moment later the gate began to creak open.

Naeem raised a hand in thanks. 'Good to see they still

know me. Though if there's any other ugly fuckers in these parts missing their nose I've not met them.'

Viratia laughed. When Andrick had been alive, she had never had much to say to Naeem and the other *hymerikai*. It was good to share more with them than bittersweet memories of Andrick.

Viratia was still smiling as they crossed the drawbridge, but her features settled as they entered the dark gatehouse tunnel. Two dozen guards waited for them at the other end, carrying spears twice their height, and shields coloured the blood-red of the Sangreals. By the crimson mark on their mail, Viratia judged them to be newly sworn *hymerikai*.

'We're to escort you to Piperskeep, Lady,' one of them announced. Viratia could not clearly see his face under his helmet, but his voice betrayed his youth. The others looked no older.

'That's fortunate, said Viratia. 'I was going there in any case. You may join my escort.' She gestured to the hundreds of warriors still making their way towards the gate.

'They're to wait outside,' said the young soldier, looking uncomfortably at the gate guards. The portcullis began to lower behind them, drawing a clamour of confused shouting from the following *hymerikai*. 'But Naeem and... the other lady may accompany you.'

'Accompany me where?'

The boy-soldier swallowed. 'To the king.'

'Is that you, Bowan?' interrupted Naeem. He laughed. 'Little Bowan the bowlegged, waving a spear in the face of Lady Viratia Brithwell? What fool made you a *hymerika*? I ought to shove that spear straight up your—'

'I will see the king,' said Viratia. 'Once I have seen my daughter and my son.'

'Those weren't my orders,' said Bowan. 'I spoke directly with the king. He said—'

'We can have this conversation at Piperskeep,' said Viratia. She did not mean to spend her day standing at the Ram's Gate arguing with a child. 'But you can send a runner and let my family know I have returned.'

Bowan looked like he might refuse, but he eventually turned to another boy and gave him orders in an undertone. The boy mounted a horse and rode away.

They steered their own horses after him at walking pace, while the others formed up around them. Their strange procession drew stares as they made their way east through the tight streets of Merivale. Half-clothed children watched from darkened doorways, the hands of their hollow-eyed mothers resting upon their shoulders, and from the alleyways the baleful glares of men young and old followed them, their clothes hanging off them like scarecrows' cast-offs.

'I've never seen it so dead,' muttered Naeem. 'When we returned from defeating Ranulf Prindian, the Castle Road was so crowded with revellers it took us almost two hours to reach Piperskeep.'

However, by the time they joined the Castle Road, running south-to-north up towards Piperskeep, a crowd had indeed attached themselves to their procession. They did not though clamour in celebration of any perceived triumph for East Erland, but with the yearning cries of the desperate and starving.

'Give us bread, Lady, anything!' cried a ragged woman so lean that her collarbones threatened to break through her skin. An emaciated child clutched her hand, and another wailed at her breast. 'My milk's dried up, and I've no—'

The woman's words were swallowed by a roar as the

crowd surged forward, forcing Bowan and the young *hymerikai* to drive them back with their spears.

'To the keep!' cried Bowan, waving his spear in panic as an aged beggar shook a clay cup in front of him. 'Before they surround us!' He dug his heels into his horse's flanks, and though the crowd did not seem particularly threatening, when Naeem and the rest followed him Viratia was forced to do the same. As they galloped away, she cast a look back towards the throng, their open mouths like black maws, their despairing shouts following her in rebuke.

'Nothing we can do for them, Lady,' said Naeem, keeping his eyes fixed ahead.

No, that ought to be Hessian. But Viratia could not so easily shake her sense of responsibility; her war had pulled men away from the fields and contributed to the shortage of food.

Matters were less desperate further up the Castle Road, where passing guildsmen waved jovially and folk raised toasts to them from tavern balconies. As they approached Piperskeep, and the city's grand inner ring where Merivale's wealthy made their homes behind gates of wrought iron, the merchants and some minor nobles were already waiting to greet them, waving their handkerchiefs. Viratia ignored them. It took more than wealth to make a lord; what did these idle city folk know of being responsible for one's own land and people? Nothing, to judge by the state of the rest of Merivale. When the war had started these people had been as much use as gems on a sword hilt.

Finally, they reached Piperskeep, and as the gates opened and then closed behind them the buzz of the city was replaced by high black walls on every side and the eerie silence of the gargoyles atop them, with their lolling tongues and stalking eyes.

'Tarrowton taxes clearly don't pay for stonemasons,' said Yriella. 'Some of these gargoyles look like they're about to fall on our heads.'

'That's just their manner,' said Naeem. 'Norhai-cursed creepy bastards.'

The yard was close to deserted, occupied mainly by more baby-faced *hymerikai*. Pherri and Errian were not there to greet their party, which was not unexpected; Viratia had not trusted Bowan's runner to properly deliver the message. She would find them later.

She had half-forgotten how imposing Piperskeep was up close, rising from the city like a giant ugly claw, an eternal reminder of the power of the Sangreals. But nevertheless, that power had waned; now only half a kingdom was ruled from the high tower where Hessian schemed.

To Viratia's surprise, their escort led them towards the keep's rarely used audience hall, where the Sangreal kings of old had once received petitioners and emissaries. It had fallen out of use in the years following the death of Queen Elyana; Hessian would more commonly refer guests to Theodric or some other underling, only receiving them himself if they were particularly important.

The chamber was long and high-ceilinged, with a three-sided balcony supported by six pillars. The far wall was covered by tapestries depicting battles once fought and won: the conquest of Erland; the Battle of Halord's Bridge, centuries ago, where East Erland had turned back the Imperium; Andrick skewering the so-called King of the Waves Portes Stormcaller to the ship's rail with his sword, while the boats behind him burnt, and blue lightning forked from the sky.

On the dais below, Hessian sat upon a simple wooden bench, garbed in rich red velvet. Sangreal kings did not sit upon thrones; a memory of the days when the Meridivals had been nomads roaming the southlands beyond the Sorrows. He looked as old as ever; grey-pale with deathly deep crow's feet, and tired hair that hung limply about his shoulders. There was something else to him though; a glint in his eye that reminded her of his younger days, when those seeking his favour had called him Hessian Honeytongue.

Viratia recognised also the man standing at his right; Lord Gurathet, a few sad strands of remaining hair looping from his crown, and his nose purple with drink. He was two decades older than her, but she could remember thirty years before a charming and broad-shouldered man with flowing blond hair. Had time been as cruel to her as to him? She had a sudden urge to look in a mirror.

The chamber was lousy with petitioners. She recognised a few faces, among them the pompous Lord Balyard of Prosbury, husband to her niece, Princess Tarvana. There was no sign though of Tarvana herself, nor Helana. Hessian clearly had no mind to find her, wherever she was, and Helana clearly had no mind to return.

The scene unsettled Viratia. What had inspired Hessian, after so many years ruling as a recluse, to hold court the day of her return? She had been prepared to confront him within the confines of his solar with the support of Naeem and Yriella. Too many of the lords present were strangers to her.

As if reading her mind, Hessian turned his attention from the two men currently addressing him, and fixed his gaze upon Viratia. He cast a withered hand to the men for silence.

'Lady Viratia,' he said. His eyes were hard as old bones. 'You honour us with your presence. Tales of your daring are told from here to Cliffark.' He raised a glass to his cupbearer for wine, and then lifted it towards Viratia in a toast. 'The Queen of Swords!'

His lips were twisted in mockery, but the court followed his toast all the same. 'The Queen of Swords!'

A servant appeared at her side, and Viratia took a cup of wine from him. She curtsied low to Hessian.

'You honour me with such a welcome, Majesty. I apologise for disturbing you. Please return to the business of the day.'

Hessian smiled chillingly. 'I was accepting oaths of fealty from my subjects. A son was born to me this morning.' He leant forward, regarding her carefully. 'I trust you will offer the same?'

That explained the presence of so many lords and ladies; Hessian had summoned them to Merivale for the birth. He had not even mentioned Ciera. It was not beneath him to kill her now she had served her purpose. Viratia had done her best for the girl, and had then gone to war and abandoned her to Hessian. She prayed the girl still lived.

The rest of Hessian's meaning was clear. He would forgive Viratia's transgressions, but if she ever again disobeyed him, by stealing the *Hymeriker* or otherwise, she would be forsworn, a traitor and an oathbreaker. Viratia had never sworn the oath herself; it had always been her father or Andrick on her behalf.

'Many congratulations, my King,' said Yriella. 'You have

our oaths.' She dropped to a knee, giving a look to Viratia that she must do the same.

'King Hessian,' began Yriella, as Viratia knelt and hurried to add her own voice, 'I pledge fealty to you; that I will pay to you a tenthweight of our yields twice annually; that I will endeavour to enforce your laws; and that I will ride to defend your realms at your request. All I ask in return is the defence of my people from all foes, both native and foreign.'

Hessian nodded, satisfied. 'I will. Though I shall not require you to defend my realms. A woman's battle is the birthing and raising of children.' He looked to Naeem. 'What of you, Naeem?'

Naeem dropped to a knee. 'I hold no lands,' he said gruffly, 'and no men save those placed in my charge by royal command. But you have my loyalty, as a *hymerika* and a simple son of Erland.'

'Good. Then I relieve you. My brother may have favoured you, but your disobedience cannot be tolerated. Lord Gurathet, my *balhymeri*, assures me you have sons more than capable of taking your place. I am told the *Hymeriker* has returned. From today, you are just Naeem, a simple son of Erland, as you say.' He waved a hand. 'You are dismissed.'

Viratia gaped, and Naeem blinked in confusion. 'Majesty. I—'

'You what, Naeem? Your king gave you a command.'

Naeem looked around, as though searching for any who would speak for him. He found no friendly faces among the lords of East Erland. Viratia could say nothing, not after having just sworn her loyalty to Hessian. His revenge for her disobedience was to punish Naeem, and thereby foil Viratia's influence over the *Hymeriker*.

Naeem blinked again. 'By your leave, my King.' He wiped his eyes, and strode from the hall, his shoulders sagging.

'Who is next to swear?' asked Hessian, Naeem already forgotten.

'I came to speak of oaths,' said a loud voice from the back of the hall. 'But not to swear one.' Every eye in the hall turned as a woman in pristine white robes strode forward through the crowd, her chin raised proudly towards Hessian. Viratia did not know her, but she recognised the robes of the Brides of Eryi. 'Do you recall the oath you swore me last autumn, Majesty?'

It was Hessian's turn to look surprised. His lips stretched in a cold smile. 'Sister Velna. Eryi has blessed me with a son. In celebration, I pledge three thousand—'

'You swore that if a son was born, you would go on pilgrimage to Eryispek.' Her voice cut across him like a blade.

Hessian's smile faltered. 'Sister Velna, I can hardly be expected to go on a pilgrimage while my kingdom is at war with itself.'

There were murmurs of agreement from the crowd.

The sister folded her arms. 'Lady Viratia returns, and you show more interest in humiliating her and her followers than in how the war is going.'

There were gasps of outrage from the crowd.

'I do not play courtly games!' Sister Velna raised her voice. 'I have no patience for hiding the truth behind honeyed words. The king swore to me an oath. A holy oath, here beneath the shadow of Eryispek. I challenge him to honour it.'

Hessian seemed to have lost patience. He rose from his seat, sending servants jumping back in alarm. 'Out! Everyone out! The elder bride and I have matters of theology to discuss.'

Viratia remained where she was while the court was shepherded out by Hessian's young *hymerikai*, corralling them towards the exit with the lengths of their spears. She waited for Hessian to tell her to leave, but he was preoccupied with Sister Velna.

From behind, Viratia heard a voice calling her name. 'Lady Viratia!' She turned to see an agitated old man with a squashed face wearing threadbare robes hurrying towards her.

She looked at him quizzically. 'Yes?'

'I'm Georald, Theodric's assistant – I'm so glad you're back. They've gone! I thought they must have left to join you, but I don't see them with you.'

She blinked at him. 'Who?'

'Theodric and Pherri. They've vanished.'

CHAPTER 11

Between shivering hours of almost-wakefulness and feverish deep sleep, Pherri dreamt, as she had not dreamt in months. A winged girl, wandering lost in a cave. Six men, laying their necks upon a block of ice for an axe made of shadow. And looming over it all, the pale-eyed man, his huge eyes like two moons.

'Find me,' whispered the winged girl. 'Find me on the Mountain.' Fierce snow swirled around her, too thick and fast for Pherri to make out her face.

All the while, at the edge of her consciousness, Pherri felt the presence of Eryispek, looming larger with each roll of the cart's squeaking wheels. Every day the cold winds grew stronger, tangling Pherri's hair and rattling the tree branches.

Some days after healing the boy's ankle, she woke fully, opening her eyes to find Theodric spooning cool stew into her mouth, looking down at her from dark, cavernous eye sockets.

'You are awake then,' he said, unsmiling, his voice hoarse. 'Can you walk?'

Pherri was unsure, but, eager for his forgiveness, she nodded.

For days, they walked in silence, each conserving their energy. Pherri felt scrawnier than ever, and Theodric looked little better. By their surroundings, they had barely come any further since Pherri had saved the boy, and still the caravan trundled at a snail's pace. In her state, that suited Pherri.

After a time, she finally plucked up the courage to speak again. 'I'm sorry.'

A wan smile touched Theodric's lips. 'Are you? Perhaps then you can tell me why you did it.'

Pherri tried not to feel ashamed. 'I wanted to see if it would work.'

'Liar. You knew it would work. You did it because you could not help yourself; I left for barely five minutes before you decided to disobey me!'

The accusation of dishonesty stung, but Pherri had to admit he was right. 'Yes, I knew I could do it. But shouldn't we be helping people with our magic?'

'It could have killed you. Would fixing a broken ankle have been worth your life? Your curiosity is not a fault – it's what led you to me in the first place – but this is no time to indulge it. We have no idea what danger we might be heading towards, and the truth is I need you. What use is saving one boy's ankle compared to what we face?'

As they walked on Pherri could not help thinking of how thin the pilgrims had been up close. Had they been Merivalers, starved by the shortages of the last winter, while she and Theodric feasted on mountains of food to power their magic? How did that serve the people of Erland? Perhaps even better than using their magic to heal would have been not using magic at all. Knowing what Theodric would think of that idea, she let the matter lie.

Each night when they lay down their bedrolls to sleep, Pherri dreamt of the winged girl again. The dream was clearer than those that had plagued her back in Violet Hall and Piperskeep, and the words the girl spoke did not change: 'Find me on the Mountain.' It did not feel like *prophika*, but as though at a distance she was actually trying to communicate with her. After several nights the same, Pherri could not help thinking that instead of seeking answers in Fisherton they should bypass the settlement and seek the winged girl on Eryispek.

Some days later, when they stopped for food where the road cut through a forest, Pherri finally gathered the courage to raise her dream with Theodric. He had always heeded her visions before, and by now he might have fully forgiven her for using magic on the boy. 'I keep dreaming of a girl. She has wings, and she said to come and find her. I think we should ignore Fisherton and head straight for Eryispek.'

Theodric answered her with a sharp look. 'Was the pale-eyed man in your dream as well?'

'Sort of. He was looming over it all, in the sky. His eyes—'

'And it never occurred to you that this might all be some design of his? That he might want us to not go to Fisherton?'

'No! It felt different, she was—'

'We have no idea what she was! Going to Fisherton is the safest course. Need I remind you how much danger we might be in? Do you think I continue to redirect attention from us for the good of my health? We will go to Fisherton – do not speak another word to me of it.'

Pherri chewed on her bottom lip, trying not to cry. It had seemed a great adventure, travelling so far from home with

Theodric, but he was nothing now like he had been in Merivale, surrounded by his books and warm fires and with servants to bring him food. And he was right: sometimes on adventures people got hurt, or died. Jarhick and her father had left Merivale on adventures, and they had died. She wished Orsian was here, but he might be dead too. Or her mother. She had won a great victory, they said, but she had heard little news of her since.

'Could we reach out for Orsian again? Or my mother. I've not heard—'

'No, Pherri, we can't. I know you're scared, but please just be quiet and let me think.'

Pherri felt the tears brimming in her eyes. Without waiting for them to fall she leapt to her feet and ran towards the forest, ignoring Theodric's panicked cries for her to wait.

Pherri crashed through the undergrowth, barely keeping her footing as knotted roots rose from the dirt to grasp at her. Yellow-green vines whipped her arms as the forest thickened around her, and soon the sky was reduced to slats of blue between the dense branches above.

She stopped, panting, leaning against a tree to catch her breath and find her bearings. She pressed her back against it, waiting for Theodric to catch her.

But there was no sign of Theodric. She scoured the trees for the path she had taken or some sight of the road. Nothing. Just the thick green and brown of the forest, eerily silent, broken only by the chirps of birdsong.

'Theodric?' she called tentatively. She shivered. The forest felt unseasonably cold.

Every direction looked the same, but she picked a course she hoped was roughly the way she had come. The trees seemed to close in on her as she walked, ageless sentinels leaning down to examine the intruder in their midst. Oaks, ashes, and horse chestnuts. She could not help looking up and marvelling at them, majestic giants humming with life, and some of the fear she had felt dissipated under their presence.

Pherri was so busy admiring the trees that she failed to watch her step. A root caught her foot and sent her sprawling. She threw her hands out but fell hard against the forest floor, leaving her palms sore and grazing her knees.

'What was that?' A gravelly voice spoke, and Pherri's blood ran cold. She looked up, and three men sitting around a fire turned towards her.

Bandits. They were smeared with grime, and bore thick, unkempt beards. One wore a helmet Pherri was sure had once belonged to a *hymerika.*

'Hello – what have we got here?' The helmeted man came to his feet. He tilted his head and sneered, pulling his lips back to reveal a set of filthy yellow teeth. 'You're lost, girl. Reckon you should walk back the way you came and forget you saw us.'

Pherri swallowed. These men were not the sort she had grown up with; these were men with nothing to lose, turned wild by the wood. The helmeted man might be their leader, but the other two looked even scarier than he did. She hurried to her feet and began to back away.

'Hold on, Si,' said one of the others, stepping forward. 'Weren't we only sayin' yesterday that it's been a while since we had a woman? Looks like Eryi answered our prayers.' This man was younger, perhaps only a few years older than Orsian, with an angry stye over one eye.

The first man snorted. 'That's a child, but if you're that desperate that's your business.'

'She could cook for us,' said the third man hopefully. He was fatter than the others, with a slack, simple face. 'Mum used to cook for me.'

Pherri took another few steps back, thinking about making a run for it. She would not cook for them, or do whatever else they had in mind.

'Don't go running off,' said the young man, pulling a rusty knife from his belt. He flashed a dark grin. 'Just want to talk is all. Why don't we go into the bushes?'

'Leave me alone,' said Pherri. 'My father will be along any moment.' Her voice came out squeaky with fear. Where was Theodric?

All three men laughed. 'There's no father here, girl,' said the helmeted man. 'You're all alone. You want to be careful, wandering around and pushing your nose into other people's business. You can go off with Hal here, and then you can cook us a nice juicy rabbit for dinner.'

Pherri backed away hurriedly. Nobody was coming to save her. She thought frantically, wracking her brain for any magic that might ward these men off her.

A deep growl came from behind Pherri, freezing her and the three men in place.

The colour drained from stye-man's face. 'Eryi's balls, run!'

The three of them turned tail and tore into the trees, leaving all their belongings behind around the fire.

The thing growled again.

Slowly, Pherri turned, her heart pounding fit to burst.

Through the trees, a monstrous black bear regarded her silently, its beady eyes like two yellow marbles, its fur rippling with thick muscle. Pherri trembled under its feral gaze.

And then, to her relief, she realised there was something odd about the bear. There had not been bears in Erland for centuries. The wind that breathed between the trees did not disturb its coarse fur. A memory stirred, of two puppies in Theodric's study, that were real and yet were no more than shadow.

'Theodric?' she whispered.

A branch cracked behind her, and Pherri turned, the shadowbear momentarily forgotten. A figure stood across the clearing. They were small, barely taller than Pherri herself, draped in an oversized coarse black cloak that covered their face in shadow. The only part of them Pherri could see was their hands, old and arthritic, clasped together over a knotted cane.

As if from nowhere, Theodric came bustling through the undergrowth like a bull in season, appearing directly between Pherri and the figure, panting hard, his bald head slick with sweat.

'Pherri,' he gasped between breaths. 'Don't run off like that... These woods... Bandits...' With a start, he suddenly noticed the bear. 'Is that your shadowbear?'

'It's mine.' Across the clearing, the figure threw back their hood to reveal the face of Pherri's one-time tutor, Delara, wrinkled and weather-beaten by a long life spent upon Eryispek's eastern side. 'And a good thing I was here too, wizard.' She scowled at Theodric. 'Those men would have killed her.'

CHAPTER 12

A fuzzy shadow of blond hair upon his crown. Unblemished skin, soft as dove wings. Fingernails like teardrops. Swaddling from the finest weavers in the city, dyed the blood-red of the Sangreals.

Ciera stared down at her son, unable to turn her eyes away. She saw none of herself in him, but his face was her father in miniature, right down to his squashed nose and the serious set of his sleeping mouth, like her father poring over accounts.

Her son had entered the world on the hottest day of the year, in this room, with the air stifling and thick with the scent of sweat, and Ciera shuddering and screaming to bring forth a squalling pink bundle of flesh.

'A healthy set of lungs,' a midwife had said as she passed the babe to Ciera. The prince bawled loud enough to shake the window frames and set the castle's dogs to howling. 'He looks just like Princess Helana did, before her hair darkened. And look at the size of him!'

Some would see his size and name him a Sangreal for

certain, as Hessian had, but there was something of Tam in the squatness of his jaw, and perhaps when his teeth came through there would be a gap between the front two, as Tam had had. Or would he have the famed Sangreal height, setting aside all doubt?

Ciera would never know for sure whether he was Hessian's. What mattered was that the king had accepted the boy as his. The Summer Prince, she heard the people of Merivale were naming him, and when the birth was announced the city bells had pealed from dawn until dusk. Rumours of his parentage might still abound, but anyone spreading those tales would be well-advised to do it far away from Piperskeep. She did not know what had become of the serving girl who had discovered Tam in her bed that fateful morning, nor of the three guards who had burst in. Nor did she wish to.

This was to be the child's nursery, and while Ciera sat rocking his cradle with her foot, servants flustered around her to make the room fit for a prince. Already her son had more possessions than most children would accumulate in their whole lives, among them a mobile of colourful woodland creatures that hung over his crib, a fishbone flute sent by the Adrari, and a miniature sword that had once belonged to Prince Jarhick.

'You need not stay, Majesty,' said one of the senior servants, Mortha, a hatchet-faced woman with a sharp beak of a nose, appearing at Ciera's shoulder. 'The little prince is quite safe.'

Mortha was to be the prince's governess, as twenty years before she had been Prince Jarhick's, charged with organising his nursery and the work of the lesser servants until he was old enough to require a steward. She was smiling, but Ciera heard the judgement under her tone. Queens were not meant to coddle their children, particularly sons. A little indulgence when they were born might be permitted, but by the time the prince was able to grip a sword and sit a horse she would be expected to see him only at formal meals, while she attended to the matter of adding to the king's brood.

Ciera could have snapped at Mortha to mind her place, but instead assumed a mask of courtesy. 'I assure you I am quite well. I will need a bed in this room. By tonight. As I've told you already.'

The woman hesitated, but after a moment gave a brief nod. 'It will be done, Majesty.'

As Mortha retreated, Ciera caught the glance and raised brows she shared with the two wet nurses standing to one side. She knew what the gossip would be among the castle servants tonight: that the queen would not be parted from her babe, like some ragged peasant woman giving birth in a field, nursing her child as she took part in the harvest and going to sleep in one room. Let them talk. After what she had endured, Ciera was immune to gossip.

This was as it would be: forever battling with others to attend her son. Princes and kings were not supposed to have mothers. Today it was overbearing serving women she could turn aside, but soon enough it would be men; counsellors, swordmasters, and lords jostling to take a place within the prince's inner circle, determined that he not spend too much time around his mother lest she make him soft.

They may try. Ciera stroked her sleeping son's face, resisting the urge to take him in her arms and wake him. She would be to her son everything her own mother had not been to her. And nobody would separate them.

A shadow fell across her, and Ciera turned to see

Hessian in the doorway. Even after almost a year married to him, just his presence was enough to send a ripple of fear through her. Gaunt as bones and dressed in crimson, like some devilish scarecrow. But he smiled at the babe in the crib, and though none would ever call her husband handsome, it lifted the years from his face. For the first time in months, no servant bearing wine followed him. Since Andrick's death he had scarcely been seen without a cup in his hand.

He looked about the room, across the army of servants and the vast collection of gifts and trinkets, and suddenly he was a king worthy of fear again. 'Leave us.' His voice was as hard and cold as a blade, and with curtsies and downcast eyes they all left through the servant door.

'Majesty.' Ciera inclined her head. 'Do you still mean to go on pilgrimage?' Hessian's journey to Eryispek was the talk of the castle.

A shadow of irritation crossed Hessian's face. 'Our preparations are to be completed soon, as much as it pains me.' He flexed his spindly fingers. 'A madwoman speaks, and a king is expected to obey like a beaten dog. I have always given the fanatics too much leeway. I mislike the look of the weather; through all that fog we have barely seen Eryispek's slope in a year. Viratia is coming also, searching for her daughter.' He stepped towards the bed, and as he came closer Ciera saw his anger melt away like candlewax before a flame. He looked down at their sleeping child and beamed. 'And yet I find myself glad of it, since it is because I have a son that I must go. He looks just like Jarhick did.'

Ciera found herself smiling also. She would never love Hessian, as he would never love her. Her first months at Piperskeep had been a torment. He had raped her in pursuit of an heir, more times than she could count, and the pain of that betrayal would never heal. And it had been rape, though she knew no man would ever name it so; she was his wife. Hessian was not truly a monster. He was just a man, and his son was proof to him that the end justified the means.

In the months following Tam's discovery, Ciera had hardened her heart to it. She had lied, and Hessian had believed, or at least wanted to believe, that the child was his. If he could forget her infidelity, then perhaps she could forget his crimes also. Few lords would have suffered her and the babe to live after being cuckolded.

No monster, and a better man than some. But she would never let him touch her again. He had his son. His rights be damned.

The babe gurgled in its sleep. 'Have you thought of a name yet?' asked Hessian.

Ciera fiddled nervously with her fingers. 'I thought we might name him for your brother. Andrick.' She held her breath, waiting for the rebuke. Would it be wrong to name a prince for a royal bastard?

'Andrick. I would journey to Eryispek half-a-hundred times if I believed it would honour my brother.' He halted, and Ciera thought she saw the shadow of a tear glisten in Hessian's eye. 'A fitting name. If he grows to be half so brave as Andrick, he will be the greatest king Erland has ever known.'

'Andrick, then.' It was a good name, and to Ciera's relief she had been correct in her judgement of Hessian. He could not resist the chance to honour his brother.

Hessian leant his long frame over the cradle, admiring his son. 'While I am away, you and Andrick will have four *hymerikai* guarding you at all times.'

Ciera had no love for spending every waking and sleeping hour stalked by guards, but she was under no illusion that her son was safe. Breta Prindian had kidnapped her, right from this very keep, and Prindian treachery had claimed the life of Andrick the elder. And then there was Lord Balyard; who knew what he would do with Hessian away? Little could have ruined the joy she took in her child, but Princess Tarvana's husband had come closer than anyone.

'And who will rule while you are gone?' she asked. There were few clear candidates. His nephew Errian, once tipped to be the next *balhymeri*, was drunk more often than not, dulling his wits with the determination of a man whose only desire was oblivion. Since the prince's birth, Piperskeep had been bustling with lords not seen in decades, eager to pay homage and swear their oaths, but Hessian dismissed most of them as halfwits and sycophants.

Hessian replied without hesitation. 'Lord Balyard asks to be my regent. He's the closest I have to a living male relative, other than Errian and Andrick here.'

Ciera's breath caught in her throat. *Anyone but him.*

———

Ciera remembered the day of Andrick's birth. For an ordinary labour, a mother might expect privacy even from her family, but the birth of a child of the Blood was almost a public occasion, and barely as soon as the afterbirth had been removed, the king's daughter Princess Tarvana had bustled into the room.

Less than a year before, Tarvana had sat with Ciera at her wedding, talking endlessly and making grand plans that their children would be the best of friends. Tarvana was pleasant enough, but Ciera found her utterly insipid; she spoke only of lords and ladies, with seemingly no interest in the war nor the whereabouts of her sister Helana. They looked similar – Tarvana was shorter, with a weaker chin, and a high forehead – but Ciera would never have believed she was related to the headstrong Helana.

Though exhausted, Ciera was glad to see her, for Tarvana's delight was evident. Ciera could not help feeling guilty for how she viewed her; Tarvana had always done her best to be welcoming. She rushed over to kiss Ciera on the cheek and fuss over the sleeping babe.

'Isn't he a darling,' she said, cooing over Ciera's bundle. 'An heir for my father, it's just wonderful, well done! And now you are free to pray for a girl next time. I always wanted a girl.'

Ciera did not want to think about that. She smiled thinly. 'Thank you.'

'He looks just like Tarrik did. And he's so close in age to Caleste, I'm sure they'll be close as twins.'

There was a rush of steps outside, and the door burst open again, revealing Tarvana's husband, Lord Ulric Balyard, and Ciera's delight turned to dread. Of the coterie of minor lords who had gathered around Hessian since Andrick's death, Lord Balyard was the meanest, and the proudest, believing that having married into the Sangreals made him practically royal himself.

He was in his mid-life, and paunchy in a way that suggested even in his youth he had never been a warrior, with a sharp widow's peak, a dry complexion with an angry tinge to it, and prominent nose. He stood in the doorway, and the whole room seemed to draw back from him. Ciera looked around for the midwives, but they had withdrawn to the room's edges.

'Tarvana,' Balyard demanded, striding towards her. 'What in blazes—'

'Ciera has had a boy,' simpered Tarvana, walking to Balyard and taking his hand, seemingly oblivious to her husband's high mood. 'He looks just like Tarrik.'

Balyard gave Ciera a cursory sneer. 'I dare say it looks like any number of people. You shouldn't be here—'

'You shouldn't be here either, Lord,' said the older midwife, finding her courage, stepping forward with a fresh cloth for Ciera. 'Birth is women's business. Let the girl rest.'

It was just the wrong thing to say to him. Balyard pulled himself away from Tarvana and advanced on the midwife, his hand twitching as if he meant to strike her.

'*Servants* do not tell *lords* their business,' he barked. The baby began to cry. 'You *dare*, you *dare* to speak to me that way, you bloody *crone*. I've a mind to—'

'Leave her be!' Ciera cried out. 'You're upsetting him.' She cradled her crying child to her breast, to which he latched on easily and began nursing, quietening him.

Balyard rounded on her, his nostrils flaring, the veins on his nose so bright they were almost purple, but the smile he flashed almost chilled Ciera's blood to ice. 'Get out,' he said, turning back to the midwives. 'You too, Tarvana. I wish to speak with our queen alone.'

Tarvana had clearly never stood up to her husband in her life. She kissed Ciera once again on the cheek, with a forced smile scratched upon her face, and hitched up her skirts and almost ran for the door.

The midwives though were made of sterner stuff. 'Begging your pardon, Lord,' said the older of them, 'but the queen—'

'The queen wants you to leave as well,' he cut across her, flashing another smile that never reached his eyes. 'There are matters only she and I should know of. Isn't that right, *Majesty?*'

The look he gave Ciera left her in no doubt. *He knows,* she realised. Had she not already been drenched in perspiration, she was sure a cold sweat would have swelled from every pore. She nodded. 'Please. Lord Balyard and I have something to discuss.' Her voice was heavy with exhaustion, barely more than a sigh.

Reluctantly, the midwives departed, leaving the two of them alone.

'So, this is the prince then.' Balyard scrutinised the child, making Ciera feel immensely self-conscious of her exposed breast. He sneered. 'Could be Hessian's, I suppose. We'll know in a few years, won't we? Blood will tell in the end.'

Ciera blinked back at him, trying to resist the urge to curl up in terror or to flee for the door. 'Lord—'

'If you were my wife, I would have thrown you from the battlements, baby or not,' he hissed, leaning over so close that Ciera could smell the wine on his breath. 'And I forbid you to have anything to do with Tarvana, or I'll dash your bastard's lowborn brains against the wall.'

'Are you well, Ciera?' Hessian asked, shaking her from her memory.

Ciera repressed a shudder, blinking away the tears. *If he is regent, he could kill me.* 'My King, Hessian—'

'I know what you're thinking. Balyard is a fool, but what choice do I have? He is my son by marriage.'

Ciera toyed with telling him his words the day of Andrick's birth. It would do no good though. It would reopen the wound of her infidelity, and Hessian would retain Lord Balyard as regent out of sheer stubbornness.

'In my absence,' continued Hessian, standing with a deep sigh, 'the kingdom is to be ruled by a council of three. Balyard, Lord Gurathet as my *balhymeri*, and you.'

Ciera stared at him. 'Me?' Her voice was so small the room almost swallowed it. That was the very last thing she had expected.

Hessian smiled, and placed a bony hand upon her shoulder. 'I am told our gate revenues are increased over two-tenths since you got me to lower the entry charge, and the market is thriving for the first time in years, only adding to our incomes. You were right, Ciera, and now you have given me a son. I would be mad not to name you on my regency council given the difficulties we face. Only within the last fortnight we have received a petition from the guilds regarding food shortages and another from the Merivale Watch demanding new recruits to help quell rising lawlessness. We are still counting the cost of a hard winter, and I don't trust Balyard to deal with it alone.'

Ciera could barely believe it. *This is what I set out to do,* she reminded herself. Cliffark had prospered under her father's rule, and now Merivale could prosper under hers. The lowering of the gate tax was only the beginning, and with a truce agreed with the Prindians, there were endless reforms she could make to alleviate the city's difficulties. The tax on using the mill had to go, and she was sure the city's reeve and his underlings were taking money for their own pockets.

'I'll do it,' she said, grasping her husband's hand in gratitude. His skin was a wrinkled map of blue veins and liver spots, and Ciera was suddenly struck by how very old he was. He had barely left Piperskeep since the death of his first wife; was he sure to survive the journey to Eryispek? No, Hessian was too stubborn to die. There was a time when she might have welcomed it, but when Andrick succeeded the throne, the lords would fight over him like dogs over a bone.

If I am on the council, I can stop them. All she had to do was outsmart Lord Balyard and outfight the rest. If she could win Gurathet and the *Hymeriker* to her side, the kingdom was hers. Balyard would rue the day he threatened her son.

As if on cue, Andrick opened his eyes, and began bawling.

'With lungs like that, he will be as fine a commander as his namesake.' Hessian seized Andrick from the cradle and passed him to Ciera. 'I'm afraid I must continue my preparations. Shall I send for a wet nurse?'

Ciera shook her head, already pulling down her dress and drawing Andrick to her breast. 'No, we shall be quite fine on our own.'

They came anyway, after Hessian had gone, and Ciera shooed them away, including Mortha, whose willing smile could not hide her disapproval.

Ciera looked down at Andrick, now contentedly suckling, his eyes closed in concentration. 'It's just you and me, little one,' she whispered. 'You and me, against everyone else.'

CHAPTER 13

'It matters not, Drast,' said the senator, reclining on a chair that could barely accommodate his vast girth. 'I must back the reformist candidate with the best chance of beating Brunal. You may have more votes at present, but that candidate is Saffia.'

Drast stretched his lips into his most charming smile. Saffia Murino was swiftly becoming a sharp thorn in his side. 'Come now, Elistar, Saffia is the continuity choice, in both senses of the word. There is nothing to suggest she will be any more reformist than her father.'

Elistar Harbon waved a dismissive hand. 'She's a pragmatist. Saffia may get votes from both sides of the Senate, but she knows which way the wind is blowing.' He leant forward. 'You should go to her. Pledge your support in return for a more reformist agenda, and a role in her administration. She might even be agreeable to withdrawing from Cylirien.'

Drast tried to hide his grimace. He would rather have become one of the slaves who cleaned Ulvatia's sewers than be another lickspittle to the Murino family.

They were in Drast's study with a bottle of his second-finest wine sitting on the table. Elistar was the seventh wavering senator he had seen today, and each of the previous six had given their assurances they would switch their vote to Drast. There were many ways to persuade a man.

Elistar drained his glass and sighed. 'You do keep a fine cellar, Drast. Men have certainly been convinced by less.'

Drast smiled obligingly. 'Another bottle, Elistar?'

'Don't mind if I do. You won't change my mind though!'

Drast rose. 'I'll send a servant. Excuse me a moment.' He already had half-a-dozen bottles in the room adjoining his study. But it was not wine that he intended to use to influence Elistar.

Next door, Krupal sat at a table, supervised by Forren, with a feast of bread and fruit before him and his eyes closed in concentration. There was something incongruous about the magus, still clad in his roughspun robe, surrounded by Drast's fine food and finer wine.

'Well?' Drast demanded.

The old magus's eyes snapped open. 'I am not a beast to be whipped to your command. You and I made a bargain, and while I sit here wading through the turgid thoughts of fools, you do nothing to find my brother. I want to see some initiative on your part first.'

Drast sighed. It was true he had done nothing to find the old man's brother. But his brother was dead, either killed in the Fourth Purge or fled and died in some godforsaken hellhole at the end of the earth. But a bargain was a bargain, he supposed. 'Forren, leave us. Do what is necessary to find Krupal's brother. Krutan, did you say his name was?'

Krupal nodded. 'Krutan von Belkarez.'

Drast did not need to state the obvious to Forren. The

best place to look would be in some pre-Purge census or
other public record. It might at least tell them where Krutan
von Belkarez had lived, provided he was not an invention of
Krupal's imagination.

'Forren will find him,' Drast assured Krupal as Forren
departed. 'You have my word. Now what do you have
for me?'

'The man next door is as vain and simple as all the
others. He lusts for gold, with no motivation other than
riches for their own sake. He once dreamt of power, but now
his ambitions are the purest, basest lusts of men.'

'Which are?'

'Wine, women, and food.'

'You might say the same of half the men in the Imperium.
How about something useful?'

The old man's eyes flashed. 'He has a daughter.'

'He has *three* daughters.'

'A *secret* daughter,' countered Krupal. 'Born to a slave.
He freed her, and now gives her a pension to raise the girl at
a secluded manse in the Free District. His family have no
idea.'

Drast blinked. 'Half the Senate keep mistresses.' Drast
had no children to his knowledge, and he preferred women
he paid; their silence could be bought. 'That he keeps his in
luxury is hardly leverage. I do not think the threat of a
telling-off from his wife is going to be enough to win his vote.'

'But he *loves* them. They are guarded at all times by six
eunuch slaves, disguised as mercenaries. If you were to
threaten their safety...' Krupal raised an eyebrow.

'I see.' It was regrettable he should have to stoop to this,
but the prize on offer made it necessary. Elistar should count

himself fortunate that it was Drast who knew, and not someone worse. 'Thank you, Krupal.'

When Drast returned, Elistar had levered himself out of his seat, and was at the window looking out across Ulvatia.

Drast joined him. 'Admiring the view?'

'Best in the city, I have to admit. How your family stole it from the Hacinders I will never know.'

Bought and paid for, like everything else I own. 'Tell me, Elistar, can you see your mistress's house from here? It's in the Free District, is it not?'

To his credit, Elistar's only reaction was a slight intake of breath. He did not gasp, or whirl on Drast in anger, as some men might have. 'How did you know? We were so careful.'

'I have eyes and ears everywhere, even in the Free District.' *Even inside your head.*

'And I suppose if I do not vote for you, you will promise some vile retribution against her.'

'Not her. Your daughter.'

That got the reaction Drast sought. Elistar spun, almost stumbled under his own weight, and grabbed Drast by the front of his robe. His eyes were ablaze, but Drast felt the fear beneath his fury.

'You dare... You dare threaten my daughter? She is not yet four; I have never known a sweeter child. Please, Drast, leave her be.'

Drast said nothing, just stared down his nose at the man before him with no secrets left. *I will use the tools I must. Some battles are won with blades, others with secrets.*

After a moment, Elistar's shoulders sagged, and his enormous belly drooped, like a half-empty wineskin. 'If I vote for you, do you swear to not reveal what you know to anybody?'

'I swear it on my life.' He meant it as well. He had no wish to harm Elistar or his daughter.

'Then I'll vote for you.' Elistar removed his hands from Drast's collar. 'And then I will retire my seat, and take them both far, far away. My other children are grown; they do not need me. My wife may be upset for a time, but I will leave her everything else.' He sighed, as though a great weight was lifted from him.

'I'm glad we could reach an accommodation. Will you stay for another bottle?'

'No. You have my vote, but I no longer desire your company.' Elistar was already casting a cloak about himself. 'You know, Drast, I always knew you were a rogue, like your father. But he'd never have stooped to something as low as this. I thought better of you. Urmé save Ulvatia if you become kzar.'

He did not give Drast a chance to respond, sweeping out the door and down the stairs with all the grace he could muster.

Drast watched the door swing closed behind him, repressing the urge to call after Elistar and apologise. He would make amends once he was kzar.

Forren returned. 'I passed Elistar on the stairs. Can I assume our friend next door found the necessary leverage to talk him round?'

'One more vote for me, and one less for Saffia Murino.' Drast gripped the back of his chair. 'But still nowhere near enough, not with both her and that whoreson Kvarm stealing votes from me.'

'She's taken votes from Brunal as well. We just need to make sure you have more than them; nobody has close to half the Senate currently. And Saffia Murino may help your campaign. The two Murinos fighting like dogs over Bovarch's bones reflects poorly on them. Nobody wants kzar to become a hereditary title.'

The door banged, and Krupal strode into Drast's study, scowling. 'I thought you were searching for my brother.' He stared at Forren.

'I've sent some of our finest men to track him down,' replied Forren, seemingly unconcerned by the anger of a man who had set a desk on fire as easily as he might have sneezed.

Krupal studied him, cocking his grizzled head slightly to one side.

'Stop that,' said Drast sharply. 'You've already tried it on both of us. It won't work, but if you do that again there is no hope of us helping you find your brother.'

So far, Krupal's powers had only worked on the most pitiable of senators; for every one whose thoughts he had been able to read, another had proved impervious, and so instead Drast had sought to talk them round, and where necessary offered them substantial bribes. So far, Krupal's faltering efforts had proved far below the mythical powers of the magi.

Krupal glared at him. 'Krutan could turn your brain to pulp with a thought. You would be more helpless than the weakest baby.'

'Have we found him yet?'

'No.'

'Then I won't worry. But I'd suggest that threatening the people looking for him is not conducive to a thorough search.'

Krupal scowled. A burst of blue fire flickered in his palm, making Forren take a nervous step back. Then it was gone, and Krupal's shoulders seemed to sag slightly.

'I'm hungry,' he said, like a mewling child.

'Then go next door and eat,' said Drast. 'More food will follow, provided you behave yourself.'

'I felt him grasping for my thoughts,' said Forren, once Krupal had left. A worried crease had appeared in the middle of his forehead. 'Do you think he could get stronger over time, now he's out of that chamber?'

'We'll ration his food,' said Drast. 'I appreciate the risk, Forren, but naught was ever gained without risk. If you meant to worry like a nursemaid, why did you take me to him?'

'What happens when we can't find his brother?'

'Once I am kzar, we'll tell him his brother went to Erland. He can follow, and we'll let the savages deal with him.'

The patter of hurried steps on the stairs outside interrupted whatever Forren had been about to say in reply, and a red-faced guard appeared at the door. 'Senator...' he said between breaths, 'Kvarm Murino is awaiting you below.'

Drast scowled. It was the second time in as many days Kvarm had appeared at the gate demanding an audience with him. 'Tell him what you told him yesterday: I am busy.' He might not realise it yet, but with his mere twenty-six votes, Kvarm Murino's campaign was dead in the water. 'If he wants to rage at my gates, let him.'

The guard swallowed. 'He's inside, Senator. In the entrance hall.'

'What? Who let him inside?'

The guard stared at him puzzledly for a moment, then looked away scratching his head. 'I'm not sure, Senator. I did, maybe? I can't remember.'

'Urmé's wounds, how—'

'The magus, Drast,' said Forren in a whisper. 'Hrogo.'

Of course. Kvarm must have gained admittance through trickery. Drast thought, quickly. 'Tell him I'll be down shortly. Forren, fetch Krupal. Go, now.'

The guard and Forren hurried off, and Drast tried to quell his rising heartbeat, as if he were once again preparing to do battle with the Cylirien horde. Kvarm's magus was a pitiable creature, but could Krupal match him? His efforts to get inside the senators' minds had been somewhat erratic.

The door to the study blew open in a thunderous explosion of metal and wood, and Drast dived for cover behind the desk, narrowly avoiding a storm of flying splinters. He landed painfully against the marbled stone and reached for his sword, before realising he was not wearing one, and instead seized a knife from his ankle sheath and leapt up.

Kvarm Murino strode through the ruins of the door, a slight, hawkish smile on his face. 'You can put the blade away. It will do you no good.' He gestured behind himself. 'Hrogo. Come.'

The ragged slave shambled through the doorway, the heavy chains that bound him scraping uglily against the marble, his legs and back twisting grotesquely under their weight. He was such a pathetic sight that Drast almost forgot to feel afraid, until the slave's eyes found his and he felt tendrils of power begin to scrape against his mind, searching for a way inside his head. Instinctively, Drast threw himself back behind the desk.

He caught a glimpse of Forren rushing through the ruined doorway with his sword raised, and Drast felt the phantom probing of his mind briefly relent as his servant thudded against the wall, thrown by some invisible force. The pressure against Drast's head resumed, and he felt an instant of discomfort, followed by a strange sensation of peacefulness.

'*Come out.*' A commanding voice echoed against the inside of his skull, and, though Drast knew it was a quite foolish response, he found himself obeying. He rose from behind the desk as the magus slowly advanced on him.

'Make him endorse me in the election,' said Kvarm. His voice sounded strange to Drast, as if it were passing through water. 'Make him tell all his supporters to vote for me.'

Hrogo's eyes were like saucers. 'I can't... We should leave. There's something... something...'

'Leave?' demanded Kvarm. 'Why would we leave? You know what to do, so do it.'

'No, please, he's coming, Kvarm—'

Hrogo let out a high-pitched wail as Krupal suddenly appeared in the doorway with fire in his eyes. His fists were clenched, crackling with ancient mastery. 'Foul abomination! You think to flee from me?'

The pressure upon Drast's skull suddenly ended. He watched as Hrogo raised his arms towards Krupal, and then the chained magus screamed as both his shoulders popped from their sockets.

'Vile weakling!' Krupal's voice sizzled with unquenchable rage. 'Disgrace! Your very existence shames me!'

Hrogo tried to lift his hands in defence as the magus advanced on him spitting fury, and screamed again as his useless arms wrenched against their joints.

Krupal flicked a finger. Hrogo's chains writhed like snakes, coursing over his skin, tightening, crushing against his bones. Drast swore he heard something inside him splinter, and then snap, and the slave collapsed to the ground, keening in agony.

'By Parmé, leave him!' Kvarm leapt over Hrogo towards Krupal and was thrown backwards against the wall. He slid down to the floor, winded, gasping for air.

'Killing you would be a mercy.' The magus stalked towards them. 'If you are found, and have any memory of this, tell them that Krupal the Great sent you.'

Krupal raised a hand. Drast felt the air change, as though it was being drawn into a great fire. The desk began to shake, and Drast had to grip it to stop himself being dragged forward. The very ether around Kvarm and Hrogo seemed to bubble like boiling water, and then disintegrated before Drast's eyes as the world folded in on itself.

Together, the merchant and the magus disappeared, and a cold horror ran up Drast's spine as beyond the void Kvarm unleashed a wordless scream of pain and madness.

CHAPTER 14

The elk strode into the clearing, as proud and patient as an ancient king. The bull was at least eighteen hands high, with antlers like the wingspan of a magnificent bird of prey that shook the leaves from the trees as it passed beneath. Its fur was the reddish-brown of summer, but here and there shot with patches of grey hoarfrost.

From between two tree branches, Helana watched, drinking in its beauty. It might be older than her seventeen years, and a father and grandfather many times over. In the dark, dense forests of Erland, the boar and the wolf reigned, but the woods of Thrumb were lighter and airier, with endless acres for these great beasts to wander.

Unlike Erlanders, the Thrumb did not hunt for sport, so Helana tried to quell her eagerness at the prospect of such a quarry. The Thrumb claimed to take from the land only what they could not go without, and not before its time. The elk's time was nigh; she knew it by its slightly lame rear leg, the way its rump shuddered, its low labouring breaths.

Slowly, Helana reached for her quiver and withdrew an

arrow, then silently laid it against her bow. It was shorter than an Erlish bow, better suited to firing from a tree. She breathed steadily, tracking the slow-pacing bull, waiting for the best view of its broadside.

Aim for the heart, below the lungs, she thought, remembering Ti'en's advice. *Too low and you'll miss, too high and you'll hit the shoulder blades. The lungs are a larger target, and still lethal, though less clean.*

Helana did not wish to settle for the lungs. She had never settled for anything. When her father had shunned her, she had scorned him rather than seek his approval, and when he had sought to see her wed, she had escaped. She was a princess, a huntress, the almost-wife of the pretender Rymond Prindian. And the elk had earnt a clean death.

She aimed, exhaled, and released.

The arrow whistled, the elk's ears twitched once, and a fletch of grey goose feathers appeared in its chest. It gave a low, bugle-like groan, wavering on its four legs, and for a moment Helana thought she had missed the heart and nicked a lung, until it sagged to the ground, sending up a cloud of dust and shaking nesting birds into the sky. It lay there like a great barrow, tongue rolling from its mouth.

'Yes!' Na'mu leapt out of a tree across the clearing and threw himself into a series of handsprings and cartwheels. 'What a shot!'

Helana's rising grin was brought back to earth by Ti'en, who quickly shimmied down from her own tree and cuffed her brother around the ear. 'If you must celebrate, do it later.' The older girl ran to kneel before the dead elk, and began praying against its head, entreating its forgiveness.

Helana climbed down after them, smiling. The exchange was her two Thrumb friends in a nutshell. They were what

Erlanders called vulgar twins – born within a month of one another to the same father but different mothers – the fifth daughter and seventh son of Chieftain Ba'an.

Still grinning, Na'mu bounded towards Helana, his red-brown plaits bouncing, and with his lanky frame enveloped her in an embrace. In Erland, such familiarity was frowned upon, but the Thrumb were a more tactile people.

'I told you we could let Hel'na have the shot, I told you!' he called back to his sister. Helana had given up getting them to call her Helana; they insisted she follow the Thrumb custom of keeping part of her name to herself, lest a vengeful spirit be listening.

'And I never disagreed.' Ti'en already had her knife out, preparing the elk for carriage to Thrumbalto. 'Now find me a sturdy branch and some twine so we can carry him.'

Na'mu strolled off, still grinning, and Helana joined Ti'en. One of the elk's golden eyes stared up at her accusingly, and Helana took a moment to lower the lid.

'You should not feel guilt,' Ti'en told her as she sawed away at the antlers. 'This will feed many.'

'I've never felt guilty for hunting anything. There's nothing tastier than the meat of your own kill. Doesn't mean I want my food watching me.'

'You should not speak so flippantly of the dead. This one gave its life so that you might eat.'

Helana could not help but smile. They might share a father, and the same freckled complexion, but Ti'en and Na'mu were otherwise complete opposites. Where Na'mu was tall and lean-limbed, with sheer cheekbones and a neat moustache, Ti'en was short and sturdy, with plump cheeks and full lips, and though carefree Na'mu showed no sign of growing up to match his eighteen years, Ti'en was as solemn and sober as a Bride of Eryi. A fierce friend though; when some among the Thrumb had questioned the wisdom of Helana being allowed to hunt in the Ancestors' Forest, it had been Ti'en who shouted them down. She was good company too, when the mood was right and with a few cups of black-currant cider in her.

Together, they strung the carcass up between two long branches, and with Ju'in – a younger boy of Chieftain Ba'an's vast brood who had been allowed to tag along provided he carried their weapons – they began the trek back to Thrumbalto.

Through a shady canopy of twisting boughs and leaves of green, yellow, and purple, Ti'en eyed the dropping sun. 'We should hurry to be back before dark.' She quickened her step, forcing the others to do the same.

'Blame your own stout legs, not mine, Sister,' replied Na'mu, momentarily pausing his tuneless whistling. 'I wager that by the time we are back, the sun will have not yet touched the horizon.'

'Does it take a wager to make you walk fast? If only it were so easy to stop you talking or whistling or existing.'

'Hel'na likes my whistling,' he replied in a tone of mock wounding. 'Don't you, Hel'na?' He turned to her and winked.

She smiled back at him. 'Better than listening to you talk, I suppose.'

In response, Na'mu mimed being struck by an arrow, collapsing in a passable impression of the dying elk that made Helana and the rest of them laugh, though they all nearly fell to the ground with him under the sudden additional weight.

It felt good to have friends again, despite the strange circumstances. Almost like what she had once had with

Jarhick; endless hunting and laughing and gambling in the barracks, before he had died and Helana's life had been upended.

Because of the Thrumb, she reminded herself. It had not been Ba'an though, she had been told, and given the chieftain's fair treatment of her she was willing to believe it. The Thrumb who had made repeated raids of Erland and fought Jarhick's invasion had been rebels under the command of Ba'an's eldest son, Ba'il; part of some power struggle with his father that even the Thrumb seemed not to understand. Ba'il was dead too now, slain by Jarhick. Helana had never asked who had killed Jarhick; it was better not to know.

When she had first been captured and brought here, Helana had expected to meet the same fate, but for reasons unexplained Chieftain Ba'an had granted her the freedom of the forest and the company of his children, in exchange for an agreement not to attempt escape. She assumed he had some plan for her, but she knew of no ransom note being sent to Merivale. It was not as though Hessian would have paid anything for her anyway.

Na'mu's prediction proved correct, for the sun was still just visible by the time they reached Thrumbalto. A great cheer went up from the trees as people saw the size of their elk, and dozens of Thrumb clad in the greens and purples of the forest shimmied down rope ladders to load their quarry into a thick-corded net, which was hauled up towards the butcher's home.

Helana stood back with her hands on her hips, admiring the forest settlement's intricate web of walkways, pulleys, and ladders, and the clever homes balanced carefully in the densely packed trees. The Thrumb lived in the branches, descending only to farm, hunt, or defend their lands. Thrumbalto covered hundreds of acres, and at the centre of it stood the Irmintree, a great blackwood hundreds of feet high, that even with Chieftain Ba'an's apartments carved into its ancient trunk still blossomed purple flowers every summer and green in winter. After growing up in a drab castle of brick and mortar, the ingenuity of the Thrumb and the verdant colour of their home were an endless source of wonder to Helana.

She had been granted a room in the Irmintree, a well-appointed double chamber blessed with large windows and a cooling breeze, and the three of them headed in that direction once they had divested themselves of the elk.

'I need a shower,' said Helana, conscious of the sweat and forest dirt that covered her. The Thrumb did not bathe, but instead caught rainwater in waxed wooden tanks with nozzles that released a fine cleansing spray.

'Be quick,' said Na'mu, 'or I'll eat all the elk without you and leave you the cock and balls.'

'I'd sooner eat the elk's than yours,' retorted Helana, creasing the three of them into giggles as they approached the pulley that led up the Irmintree's trunk. It was too high to climb by rope ladder, so Ba'an's family relied on a system of weighted pulleys.

'You first,' said Ti'en, offering Helana the rope.

Helana accepted it, but as she grasped it, the line was yanked fast out of her hand.

'Eryi's piss,' swore Helana, grimacing and cradling her badly grazed right hand. 'Which—'

The other end of the rope whistled towards her so fast that Helana had to leap out of the way. Her toe caught a tree root, and she sprawled in the dirt, letting forth a string of curses.

A gale of mocking laughter followed, and Helana rounded angrily upon her assailant as he descended to the ground. She already knew who it was: Hu'ra, Ba'an's damnable second son.

He was a handsome, well-made man of twenty-five or so, with cold eyes and a mocking, lopsided smile, wearing similar forest garb to his siblings. Still holding the rope, he sketched a mocking bow in her direction. 'I apologise, Princess. You have been with us so long. I forget how unfamiliar our ways must be to you.'

Helana advanced on him angrily, her palm still stinging, but Ti'en had already got there.

'What are you doing?' she demanded, jabbing a finger into Hu'ra's chest. 'You could have killed her!'

Hu'ra shrugged. 'When I am chieftain, we will kill invaders, not honour them with weapons and rooms in the Irmintree.' He looked Helana up and down, taking in her Thrumb-like garb and the short bow on her back. 'You should change back into your own clothes. You look ridiculous.' He added something in the Thrumb language too fast for Helana to catch, and stalked away, leaving Ti'en to unleash a string of Thrumb expletives, of which Helana caught about one in five.

'What did he say?' asked Helana, brushing the dirt from her clothes. She had picked up bits and pieces of the Thrumb dialect. Most spoke Erlish with outsiders, and were jealously protective of their own language and customs.

'"A cuckoo may lay its eggs in the warbler's nest, but it is still a cuckoo,"' translated Na'mu. 'A clever saying, if you're Hu'ra.'

'If he were not my brother I would chop his bollocks off,' added Ti'en. 'He might have killed you.'

Helana was more concerned for her dignity than her life. She had faced closer brushes with death than that. Hu'ra's hostility towards her was no secret, but this was the first time he had sought to do her physical harm. The next time, she would make sure he regretted it. 'Not sure why he's blaming me. I didn't choose to come here. If he wants me gone, he should petition his father to free me.'

'A prisoner, are you?' came a voice behind them. Together, they turned in surprise, and She'ab stepped into view from behind a tree. The shaman's face was lined and weathered, his plaits long turned to grey, but he was straight-backed and lean for a man of his years, with a shrewd intelligence in his penetrating gaze. Unlike the other Thrumb, he went about shirtless and shoeless, with only a pair of breeches cut above the knee to hide his nakedness. 'In Merivale, did prisoners hunt in the king's wood and eat at his table?'

'You know the answer to that,' said Helana. 'I am grateful for your gentle treatment, but I am a prisoner. You really think Ba'an would let me walk back to Erland?' She enjoyed Ti'en and Na'mu's company, but Erland was home, was freedom. Her father would never find her; she could go anywhere she wanted, without the threat of Hu'ra stabbing her in her sleep.

'You should be berating Hu'ra, not Hel'na,' said Ti'en. 'If she's a guest, he should treat her like one.'

She'ab smiled charitably. 'I am not berating, Ti'en, merely observing. Every morning, I uncage my chickadees, and every evening, they return. Helana, come.' Without waiting for a response, the shaman turned on his heel and leapt several feet onto a dropped rope ladder, which he began scaling with impressive speed.

'Mad old bat,' muttered Na'mu. 'Best see what he wants, I suppose; we'll save you some elk.'

Helana climbed eagerly after She'ab, not wishing to be outdone by the old man's speed. The shaman lived in his own tree, set slightly away from the Irmintree. Curiosity spurred Helana on; she had never been to She'ab's home, but oddly coloured smoke could be seen pouring from his chimney at many a strange hour.

She was panting by the time she reached the walkway, some thirty yards above the ground, though She'ab looked fresh enough to scale the same height again.

'Harder than shooting a defenceless animal, wouldn't you say?' he asked, his eyes twinkling.

'You do this every day,' Helana gasped, kneeling briefly to catch her breath. 'Why not just have a counter-weight like everyone else?'

'For the same reason I do not just lie down and die.' He sank into a cross-legged pose to look her in the eye.

'Are we not going into your hut?'

'Patience. Do you know why Hu'ra hates you?'

'That's easy enough – my brother murdered his brother, Ba'il. Neither Ti'en nor Na'mu seem to hold that against me though.'

'Neither Ti'en nor Na'mu is Ba'an's heir. For his entire life, Hu'ra has been a second son, and now he has inherited all the woes and responsibility of a first. It is a burden he struggles with, especially while so many of our people regard Ba'il as a liberator who died before his time.'

'He was not the only one who lost a brother.' She could sometimes go hours or days without thinking of Jarhick now, but the sense of something being missing was hard to shake.

'So much blood, over land that feeds so few.' She'ab

smiled sadly. 'Come.' He leapt to his feet and with a spring in his step made towards his hut.

Muttering curses at the shaman's sprightliness, Helana followed.

The wave of heat that met her as she stepped through the wooden door stopped her in her tracks. 'Eryi's blood,' she gasped. 'Is this why you don't wear clothes?' The warmth was almost a physical barrier. The fire in the chimney alcove burnt a deep crimson, so hot Helana was mystified that the whole tree did not go up in flames. The room was small and sparsely furnished, with a low table in the middle and two soft cushions to either side. She'ab took one and gestured for Helana to take the other.

'I find that heat focuses the mind.' He began to pour tea into cracked clay cups from a bubbling pot near the fireplace.

'I usually find it's a good way to burn things down. I can see why nobody else wants to live in your tree.'

She'ab chuckled. 'Tell me, Helana, what are you looking for here?'

The oddness of the question took her by surprise. 'Looking for? I'm not looking for anything. Ba'an captured me, and for reasons I don't understand brought me here rather than turning me over to Rymond.' She had barely seen Ba'an in the months since. The rebellion that ought to have died with Ba'il had resumed while the chieftain made war in Erland, centred in the Thrumb's second settlement of Barthrumb, and Ba'an was ever-occupied, either in the field himself or locked away with his council.

'Yet you make no attempt to escape, almost as if you have no desires beyond hunting and drinking. If you were not here, where would you go? Why do you stay?'

In the heat, Helana could feel rivers of sweat beginning

to run down her back. She could see She'ab's point. She had fled Merivale because she was sure of her purpose, and then that purpose had ended with the death of her uncle Andrick. And if she was truly imprisoned here, what was she imprisoned from? She had no wish to return to her father or to Rymond Prindian.

'I don't know,' she admitted. 'I suppose I don't know where I'm going. It never bothered me until Jarhick died. Now I can't go back, but I can't move forward either. It's like his death knocked a wheel off its spokes. Hunting with Na'mu and Ti'en reminds me of simpler times, before the world went to shit.' The honesty of her own response startled her. 'But I *do* want to return to Erland, whatever that means now.'

She'ab was nodding. 'Much as I thought.' There was an honest sympathy in his gaze. He placed something on the table before them, a small black leaf, curling up at the edges, shot through with strange, orange veins. 'I cannot offer you answers, Helana. It is for you to choose your path. I can only offer you truth.'

Helana stared down at the leaf, a deep sense of foreboding in her gut that set her belly churning. 'What is it?'

'Casheef. I have finally persuaded Ba'an that we have no choice but to grant it to you.'

Helana picked the leaf up by the stem and rotated it between her thumb and forefinger. 'I've heard of it.' She had drunk cashan, the powerfully strong liquor form of it, once and spent the next day violently vomiting black bile. 'I've heard it can turn you blind.'

She'ab snorted. 'If like a madman you insist on making liquor from it. And smoking it is horribly addictive, but I assure you that your body is in no danger from eating its leaf.'

'And my mind?'

'That depends on what you see.'

Helana was still turning the leaf. It was barely larger than her knuckle. 'Hardly a ringing endorsement.'

'I did not take a daughter of the Sangreals for a coward.'

'Nor should you take me for a fool.'

She'ab cocked his head, regarding her. 'If you truly want to return to Erland, then take the casheef. If you still wish to leave afterwards, I will escort you east to the Dry River myself.'

Helana looked at the leaf, and then back at She'ab. Why was this so important to him? Some part of her wanted to crush the casheef to dust between her fingers, but another more curious part wanted to take it in her mouth and then ask for seconds. It would give her back her freedom. 'Do I eat it?'

'Just place it on your tongue.'

The heat was suddenly overwhelming. Salty sweat was pouring from her forehead, dripping into her eyes, into her mouth. 'Eryi's teeth, fine.' Helana placed the leaf upon her tongue.

It tasted both sweet and bitter at once, like cinnamon and cloves. She felt it dissolve with a dry sizzle, her tongue briefly bursting with heat. She shrugged. 'I don't feel anything.'

She'ab opened his mouth to reply, but all that came out was a long, low moan, and his lips twisted grotesquely, like two worms mating. Helana blinked in surprise, and the shaman's face began to melt, first slow and then fast and then slow again, his craggy features softening until nothing recognisable as She'ab remained. He blinked twice, and two pitiless black orbs stared back at her, until they burst like overripe grapes.

Helana screamed, and covered her face with her hands.

Nothing happened. Feeling foolish, she lowered her hands, and recoiled.

The heavy, moist heat of She'ab's tent had been replaced with the crackling warmth of a huge fire. Helana looked down, and discovered that in place of her Thrumb garb she wore a flowing black dress, of the sort she had worn in Merivale after Jarhick's death.

But these surprises were nothing compared to the shock of where Helana found herself. Piperskeep's walls towered over her, and on all sides, similarly black-clothed mourners stood watching the fire. She recognised her sister, Tarvana, weeping silently and clutching the hands of her two children. Theodric stood apart from the rest with his hands thrust deep into the folds of his robes. Her uncle Andrick was there too, clad in mail, stern and stoic behind his fierce black beard, with Orsian next to him, like his famous father in miniature, which was odd, as neither of them had been there in truth.

This is the day of Jarhick's burning, Helana realised. The great blaze was his funeral pyre. Of all the days the casheef could have brought her to, did it have to be this one? To live through it once had been bad enough. There had been a feast afterwards, and Helana had drunk herself into a lonely stupor, refusing all offers of company.

A tall presence strode up from behind and stood next to her. 'Leave me alone,' she said.

'I didn't know you cared so much,' said a familiar voice.

Scarcely believing her ears, Helana turned, and there he was.

Tall and slender, with hair as golden as the sun. He wore it long, which was strange; he had always kept it short to his scalp to stop it flying in his face when he rode, but it was unmistakably him. She would have recognised that straight nose and thick jaw anywhere, with those pink lips that always seemed on the edge of mirth.

Her brother, Jarhick Sangreal, Prince of Erland.

Helana wavered on the spot, overcome by a strange vertigo, and Jarhick thrust out a swift hand to steady her. 'Are you all right? You've gone pale as chalk.'

'Fine,' she gasped. If she had been wondering whether this was truly happening, the sensation of his grip upon her arm seemed real enough. 'You just startled me.'

He frowned. 'I'm sorry, I had no idea you'd be so upset. You didn't even shed a tear when he died.'

When who died? If Jarhick was here, who was on the bier? Helana squinted into the glowing flames, and then she saw. She would have known that hollow-cheeked profile anywhere.

The corpse they were burning was her father.

She stared as the yellow flames licked over him, creeping up his long hair and spreading over his deep red gambeson. They had garbed him as a warrior, as he had never dressed in life, with a silver crown balanced on his brow and a longsword clutched over his breast.

Perhaps I should be sad. So why did she feel only relief? This was wrong, but it felt so *right* that Jarhick should live and her father should be dead. She reached out with her hand, grasping for her brother like a drowning man for drift-wood, if only to remind herself that he was *real* and *alive*, and this was *true*. Realer and truer than She'ab in that strange heat-sodden shack, and the constant sensation that nothing was as it ought to be.

Jarhick squeezed her hand between his long fingers. 'The

sooner this is done the better.' His gaze scanned the crowd of mourners. 'After Mother died, they could not escape him fast enough, and now they crowd the court like flies around a dog turd.'

Helana squeezed back, and they stood in silence for a time, watching as their father was consumed by the flames, until all that was left was ashen bones and smoking wood.

'Glad that's over with,' Jarhick muttered. Together, they walked forward and bowed their heads before the smouldering bier. 'May Eryi take him from the Earth to Eryispek above the clouds,' he whispered, and Helana could see the damp shadows of tears that stained his cheeks. She echoed him, and then Jarhick spoke the words again, loud enough for the whole yard to hear, and the congregation repeated the words back to him.

Jarhick cleared his throat. 'There is a banquet in the hall,' he called. 'My father would like nothing more than to have so many firm friends drink to his memory. Honour him with your smiles and your laughter. I can think of no better tribute.'

A hundred murmuring guests began treading their way towards the hall, clearly eager to be fed and watered. 'Complete bollocks,' whispered Jarhick. 'Father would not have pissed on half these sycophants if they were on fire. I've already got that bloody Balyard in my ear offering to advise me – I've met blind beggars who would be better suited – and that ghoul Storaut is demanding I make Andrick return some land to him. They would not even have the honour of a seat at my table if it was up to me. Balyard even thinks to discuss plans for my coronation! As if he would have anything to do with it. I would get more sense out of my chamber pot.' He rasped a bitter laugh. 'I'm glad you're here, Sister, especially since Errian has abandoned me to his Thrumb girl. Ti'en was her name, I think? You're the only one left who understands.'

Ti'en? With Errian? That made even less sense than the rest. Though Helana had no idea what she would say, she opened her mouth to reply, until the hot weight of her swimming head seemed to press the desire to speak right out of her. Her vision wavered, and Jarhick's face rippled like a reflection in a lake. She stumbled, and her foot slipped through the ground as if it were made of butter. She reached for Jarhick, and he disappeared like morning mist before the sun.

With a great gasp, Helana surfaced in She'ab's hut. Sweat was pouring off her in sheets, and her hair and clothes were plastered to her skin. The fire still burnt bright, but by the movement of light across the floor many hours had passed. She'ab still sat across from her, regarding her steadily with his sharp eyes.

Helana lunged across the low table towards him, but cat-quick the shaman caught her wrist and elbow. Helana hissed as with unexpected strength She'ab twisted her arm and forced her back towards her cushion.

Helana realised she was trembling. 'Take some tea,' said She'ab. 'It will help.'

'What was that?' Helana demanded, only her shaking limbs dissuading her from lunging at him again. 'Why would you show me that?' There were cool tears on her cheeks, mixing with her sweat like some strange elixir.

'I cannot control what the casheef shows,' said She'ab. 'Tell me what you saw.'

Painful though they were, Helana forced the words out.

'My brother was alive.' She told She'ab everything, the shaman nodding all the while.

'I have to go back,' she concluded. 'Jarhick was alive!' How could she have never seen how wrong it was, that Jarhick had died before her ever-sickly father? It was as though a shroud had been lifted from her eyes.

But She'ab was shaking his head. 'When you have walked a hundred leagues or slept a hundred nights, only then may you take casheef again. To see the world as it is not is more addictive than the most potent liquor. Some have starved themselves to death with it, for the food and drink you consume in the other place will not sustain you.'

'But it was better! It was—'

'It was as it should be,' She'ab finished for her. His eyes were soft with empathy. 'Drink your tea.'

Helana took a sip, and the hot, minty liquid spread through her limbs like a comforting blanket. Its fragrant steam seemed to clear her mind, and the world sharpened around her. As much as it pained her, it was this one that was real.

CHAPTER 15

Th-wip thunk.

The arrow flew, and found the centre of Orsian's makeshift target with a satisfying thud. He grinned. It was not difficult to hit a stationary mark at the end of a corridor, but it had been months since he had held a bow, so it pleased him all the same.

Pitt ran to the target and retrieved the arrow. Buying Pitt two pies had raised Orsian – or rather, Ranulf – practically to godhood in Pitt's eyes, and he had barely been able to get the boy to leave him alone in the days since. Pitt and Esma had returned with them to their bolthole in Pauper's.

Almost the entirety of Maud's establishment had been given over for them to prepare for Cag's rescue. Maud's curiosity when they had returned with two stray children – 'Playing house, are we?' she had cackled – had been too much for Tansa to tolerate, and she had eventually relented and told the old landlady of their plan to save Cag from the hangman.

Maud had delighted in the idea. 'My second husband,

Eryi take him, was killed by those blue buggering guards. He was a damn fool getting himself involved with Portes Storm-caller, as if he had any business throwing in with the rebels. But if you're going to rescue the big boy I'm going to help. There's a lad who knows how to make himself useful, always happy to help getting things down from the top shelf.'

Maud had no plans to leave Pauper's Hole herself, but had offered them the use of her two grandsons, Hiall and Glyn. They could barely manage an original thought between them, but they could follow orders well enough. Orsian's plan was for them to don the guards' uniforms, while he watched with the bow from a roof.

Th-wip thunk.

His next arrow found the same point as his first, and Pitt ran to retrieve it.

'I hope this isn't as useless as it looks,' said Tansa from behind him. Orsian could practically hear her eyes rolling. 'At least you've got a servant to wipe your arse now, fancy boy.'

In reply, Orsian quickly fired off three arrows in succession, grouping them as tightly as he could about the target's centre. It was fine shooting; he was sure Tansa could not help but be impressed.

'The guards won't be standing still less than thirty yards away tomorrow,' she said. 'I hope you've not wasted money on that thing. I still think we'd be better off having you on the ground with your sword.'

'You'll see tomorrow,' replied Orsian, caressing his bow. 'I could pluck a bird's feathers at sixty paces with this.'

The journey to purchase it at the docks had not been without incident. Some of the *Jackdaw*'s crew sitting outside an inn had seen him, and Orsian had waved away Tunny and

Jahn's encouragements to join them. It would take some explaining when they asked what he had been doing their first few days of shore leave. Orsian was not sure he understood it himself; all the talk on the *Jackdaw* had been of the japes they would have together. So why was he not itching to rejoin them?

'Talk me through the plan again,' said Tansa, taking a seat at the table behind Orsian. 'Pitt, go and help Maud with dinner.' Food was the quickest way of making Pitt do anything, and he ran off towards the kitchen.

Orsian sat down opposite, their knees bumping together awkwardly under the small table. Using four arrows, he marked out the shape of the square, then placed a mug to illustrate the position of the gallows. 'Once they bring the prisoners out,' he said, marking the jail with a second mug, 'you get as close to Cag as possible. Make sure he sees you, so he's ready. Glyn and Hiall will be here.' He pointed to the gallows. 'With the guards' uniforms it should be easy, provided they don't draw attention to themselves.

'Once they start bringing him up, you start the distraction. Make it as chaotic as you can. Then I'll start shooting. Not to kill, just to give them something to think about. While the guards are distracted, the boys can free Cag, then you join up with them to escape. I'll have Pitt with me to help me find a safe way down without the guards catching us.'

It had been decided that Pitt was too useful to leave behind. He knew the rooves best, and if Orsian saw anything go wrong he could send him down with a message. Esma though would stay with Maud, much to her chagrin.

'You make it sound so simple,' said Tansa, chewing her lip. 'How do you seem so sure about this? Were you a soldier or something?'

'It's simple so we can change it,' said Orsian. 'If you want to make the Norhai laugh, make a plan.'

A call from Maud followed from the kitchen. 'Dinner! Before Pitt eats everything!'

'Listen,' said Orsian, grabbing Tansa's shoulder as they stood. 'If something goes wrong, don't come back for me. I'll make my own way.' He would not let her risk her life for Ranulf. If the worst happened, revealing his identity could win his freedom.

She flung his hand away angrily. 'Don't talk like that,' she said, grabbing him by the collar, a flush rising on her cheeks. 'If you're taken, I'm coming back for you, or for Pitt, or Maud's grandsons, and don't you dare suggest otherwise. We're basically family now, and families stick together, so you can shove all that heroic shit up your bollocks.' She let go of him. 'And you better come back for me as well, or I'll make you pay.' She spun on her heel and strode off.

Family? Was that what they were? They barely knew each other. Orsian already had a family, and he had abandoned them. He rubbed his head, feeling slightly dazed, trying to shake off his worries about the *Jackdaw* and what Tansa had said about family. His focus had to be on tomorrow.

When Tansa's temper rose it was like being hit by a storm on the Shrouded Sea. To think he had once thought Helana fierce. Orsian watched admiringly as she walked away, then grinned and followed.

———

Tansa cursed herself for losing her temper with Ranulf, and for being so stupid. *Why do you care? He'll be leaving anyway.* She had blackmailed him into helping by threatening to let the guards take him; he probably could not wait to see the back of her. When Cag was free Ranulf would be gone, back to his mystery life. He was no ordinary sailor, and she hated herself for wanting to know more.

A sailor could not have shot a bow like that. He had been in control of every element; the muscles in his back and shoulders bunching just tightly enough to hold that pose, the arrow held as delicately as a needle. And then the smooth release and the thud of cedarwood against the target, right where Ranulf intended. And whatever he claimed, no seafarer could have known what he knew. A deserter from the war might have some skill and knowledge of combat, but she doubted they would have been so sure of themself, nor troubled to help her in the first place.

She struggled to meet his eye over their meal, but fortunately Pitt and Esma provided a distraction from her silence, pestering Maud for stories and bombarding Ranulf with questions, all while stuffing themselves with food. Ranulf rebuffed their interrogation with answers that were either cryptic or blatant lies, though he smiled throughout. He had a nice smile, broad and easy, with childlike dimples. Tansa wanted to believe it was the smile of a man who had found a sense of belonging in the unlikeliest of places.

Maud had produced a dusty bottle of wine from somewhere, and bid them both to drink their fill, pressing top-ups upon them if ever their cups looked close to empty. Even the children were given a watered-down measure each. Tansa felt the wine working, loosening her nerves, though she was still content to be silent, and watch as Ranulf's cheeks grew flushed and his laughter more uproarious, even deliberately falling off his chair during a mock knife fight with Esma, making the children roll about laughing.

'We should go to bed as well,' said Ranulf once Pitt and Esma had fallen asleep at the table and he had carried them to their room. 'We'll want an early start tomorrow.'

Tansa nodded. In her silent enjoyment she had almost forgotten that tomorrow was the day they would free Cag.

'You've been very quiet,' said Ranulf as they walked the short route to their rooms. Ranulf had found a bed of his own after Maud had opened the guesthouse to them. 'You've barely said a word through dinner since you told me I better come back for you.'

'Sorry about that. I shouldn't get upset over it. You're only here because I made you.'

'I'm here to keep my word,' said Ranulf solemnly. 'The right path isn't always the easy path. Quite the opposite, really.' He took her hand. His palm was warm and glazed with thin sweat. 'And I swear that if you or Pitt or anyone is captured, I'll come back for you. I just don't want you coming back for me.'

'I can't promise that.' *If not now, when?* Tomorrow he might be gone forever. She took a slow, deep breath, and launched herself at him. Her mouth found his, and when he lifted her from the ground she wrapped her legs around his waist. They fell through the door, and did not stop falling until they reached the mattress.

———

Tansa woke with the dawn, her head resting on Ranulf's torso, his coarse chest hair tickling her nostril. She resisted the urge to giggle.

Maybe he'll stay now, she thought, then immediately hated herself for even considering it. *Eryi's balls, pull yourself together. It was this sort of nonsense that got Tam killed.* There was a knot of guilt in her stomach. She and Cag were friends, and she sometimes thought that he wanted more, but Tansa could not imagine it. Not with Tam's murder echoing through every word that passed between them.

Next to her, Ranulf sighed and mumbled sleepily.

She slapped him twice gently on the cheek. 'Come on fancy boy, you said we had to be up early.' She reached for her trousers and pulled them on, followed by her boots. When Ranulf barely stirred, she grabbed a mug and threw the dregs in his face. 'Up! Up!'

Ranulf groaned. 'Is this how you treat all your lovers? This is my room we're in.'

Ranulf was her first, but she was not going to tell him that. At least if she died today she would do it knowing what all the fuss was about.

'Don't think that because I let you dip your wick means you're off the hook.' She prodded him with her toe.

Ranulf spluttered a laugh. 'Dipping my wick?' he said. 'Is that what you call it?'

'Never mind what I call it.' She threw a shirt at him. 'Get dressed.'

Maud was already waiting for them in the common area. She laughed at the sheepish looks they each gave her. 'I knew that wine would sort you both out,' she said triumphantly, slapping them both on the backside as they walked past. 'Young pretty folk should be at it as often as possible; it's nature's medicine.' She winked at them. 'You've got time if you fancy another go before you leave.'

'No,' they both said, tripping over each other in their rush to be the first to say it.

Maud shrugged. 'Suit yourselves.' She looked to Ranulf. 'Check on the pot, would you? It's rabbit stew this morning. You can serve up if it's ready.'

Ranulf almost ran to the kitchen, a high blush on his cheeks.

Maud watched him go. 'I hope him and the big lad don't hurt each other too badly.'

Tansa spluttered. 'What do you mean? Cag's my friend and Ranulf is going to help us rescue him. And it's nothing to do with you.'

'I'm not judging. I've seen how the tall one looks at you. Always nice to have a pair of bucks fighting over you. But if you're planning on keeping this one, let the other one down gently. It will be blood on the cobbles either way, but hope-fully they won't kill each other.'

Tansa did not bother to reply. *Damn interfering old shrew.* She stalked away to help Ranulf in the kitchen.

They left while the sun was still low. Pitt led the way at an eager run, followed by Tansa and Ranulf calling after him to slow down, with Maud's grandsons bringing up the rear of their strange party. The streets were not busy, but within a few hours they would be bustling with folk heading to the square. Tansa and Ranulf wanted to be in position before most of them arrived.

The square was almost deserted, save for a gang of labourers erecting the gallows. Tansa froze. It was the same lacquered dark wood as the one in Merivale, every beam thick and flawless and soaked in death. She bit down the bile that rose in her throat and bent over, retching.

Ranulf placed a worried hand on her back. 'Are you all right?'

She nodded. Her breath came as tightly as it had that day, when the crowd had pressed her from every side and the air had turned to sludge. She closed her eyes to the pain and saw Tam, his face turning blue, his bound legs kicking for a foothold that would never come.

'I'm fine.' Tansa stood, willing the air back into her lungs. Today would not be like Merivale. They had a plan, and they had Ranulf.

When she could breathe normally again, they walked to the fountain in the middle, and sat down to watch.

'I'll be up there,' said Ranulf, pointing to the roof behind the gallows. He had stashed a second bow and a sword there a night earlier. 'I want to get up there soon, so I can see everything. Hiall and Glyn, find somewhere quiet to get changed into your uniforms. Then when it gets busier grab a spot near the gallows and try to look like you belong there.'

The twins nodded and wandered off. Unlike their grandmother they were people of few words.

'Pitt, go and make sure the stairs are clear,' said Ranulf. 'I'll be there shortly.' When Pitt was gone, he took a seat next to Tansa. 'Are you sure you want to be here?'

Tansa looked at him warningly. 'Don't even think about it,' she said. 'A spot of sickness doesn't make me one of them blushing maidens you probably grew up with. You do your job and I'll do mine.'

Ranulf nodded. 'Just be careful.' He took her hand and squeezed it.

Tansa squeezed back. 'You too.'

From his perch, Orsian watched the square fill up, listening to the seagulls squawking overhead and keeping his head down. Pitt fidgeted next to him, clearly not used to staying still for any length of time.

Hiall and Glyn stood near the gallows. With their relaxed posture they stood out a mile from the true guards, but hopefully that was less obvious from the ground. Tansa was near the jail, milling around the crowds, never staying in one place for too long.

Orsian smiled to himself, remembering the night before. As first times went, he thought he had done pretty well. It had gone better than others had warned him it would. Reluctantly though, he forced himself back to the present. His attention needed to be on the here and now; that sort of distraction could get you killed in battle. He would speak with Tansa once Cag was free. But he was not planning to stay in Erland, so what more was there to say? She might be gone the next time the *Jackdaw* made port.

By the jail, a drum began to beat, a single note on the cusp of a tune. The door opened, and out came a procession of chained men, each one flanked by a guard. Orsian had no trouble seeing Cag, a stooping figure a head taller than the rest.

Tansa matched the stumbling pace of the chained prisoners through the crowd, looking for a chance to make herself known to Cag. His head hung low, and there were fresh bruises on his face. Few guards would resist the chance to put in a few blows on a defenceless man twice their size.

Tansa wished Ranulf had not been so adamant they would not kill any of them.

Halfway to the gallows, the crowd thinned slightly. Tansa pressed her way to the front. *It will not be like in Merivale.* She whistled sharply in Cag's direction to catch his eye, and he showed the briefest flicker of recognition before he was dragged on, below the ominous shadow of the scaffold.

The crowd was thickest here. Tansa looked around for a distraction. In Merivale she had accused a man of touching her to start a fight between him and his wife that had spiralled into a riot.

The first prisoner was being led to the noose. As he climbed the steps, a herald read his name from a scroll, in a high screech that cut across the murmur of the crowd.

'Kilian Tanner. Guilty of rape.'

The announcement drew an angry hiss from the crowd.

'She's a nasty, lying little trollop!' a woman cried.

The herald ignored her. 'Does any person here have the fee? Set at twenty-five gold.'

'Aye,' came a reluctant male voice. 'I have the fee.'

Tansa stood on her toes to catch a glimpse of the speaker, an older man standing next to the prisoner's wife who had cried out.

'Oh, shitting hell,' cried the prisoner. 'Can't I even get hanged without you interfering?'

The herald seemed unconcerned. 'Get him back to the jail.' He looked to the man who Tansa assumed was the prisoner's father-in-law. 'Pay the fee to the clerk there and take him away.'

There were more angry hisses from the crowd.

'Now just hold on here!' cried one man. 'We know he did

it, and not for the first time. Bugger the fee, he needs hanging!'

'Thirty gold if you'll hang him,' called a woman, drawing murmurs of agreement from those around her.

The man's wife turned around angrily, looking for where the voice had come from. 'You leave him alone! He never.'

The herald shrugged. 'It's not an auction. If you have complaints, take them up with Lord Istlewick.'

Tansa looked around. Hangings in Cliffark were not the same draw they were in Merivale, and the atmosphere until now had been restrained, far from the feverishness of the day it had been Tam on the gallows. But she had been so distracted trying to see Cag she had missed the crowd's undercurrent of impatience, now replaced by a visible discontent. Clearly many them had come only to see this man hanged. Given the smallest tinder they would ignite like dry grass.

'It could have been your daughter, herald!' Tansa cried out. 'What will you say to the next woman?'

Her outburst was echoed by the angry voices of those around her, and they shook their fists at the guards trying to lead the prisoner through the throng back towards the jail.

Tansa continued, feeling emboldened by their reaction. Maud's grandsons were near the line of prisoners, edging towards Cag. 'Hanging's too good for the likes of him! Hook his entrails and let the bastard bleed out like the pig he is.'

'Kill him!' cried a man. He drew a knife, and brandishing it wildly charged towards the prisoner.

If the guards were even slightly unmanned, they did not show it. In a blink, one drew his short sword, and raised it against the onrusher. A wiser head would have stopped, but the man ran straight onto the tip of the guard's blade. He grunted, and when the guard pulled his blade out collapsed to his knees, his blunt knife falling from his lifeless fingers.

And then with a great roar the crowd surged, and all was mayhem.

———

'No, no!' Orsian shouted helplessly from the rooftop. He had meant for this to happen when Cag was being led to the gallows, not while he was still chained with the other prisoners. Cag was surrounded by the baying crowd, and there were so many guards milling around trying to restore order it was impossible to tell which were Maud's grandsons. He had lost sight of Tansa. The crowd was so tightly packed he could not even fire an arrow to distract the guards without risking hitting somebody.

'Eryi's balls, Tansa, what were you thinking?'

He thought quickly, trying to see a way out for Cag. He was bound at ankle and wrist with three other condemned men. One clumsy blow with a blade and Cag would not be able to defend himself.

'What's happening?' asked Pitt. 'Why aren't you shooting?'

'I can't do a damn thing from up here.' Orsian threw down his bow and set off towards the square, seizing his sword as he went.

———

Tansa stumbled, almost tripping over her own feet. She had somehow fought her way to Cag, and was clinging desperately to his chain for balance against the swirling crowd.

Starting a riot had been straightforward enough – she seemed to have a talent for it – but now it had started she had no idea what to do. Hiall and Glyn were nowhere to be seen; probably they had run away as soon as the crowd surged.

'What are we doing?' Cag shouted over the din. 'Can you get these chains off?' He twisted his bulk to protect Tansa as a pair of bodies cannoned towards them, and they bounced off him to be swallowed again by the maelstrom.

Tansa shook her head. Another man reeled towards them, and this time Cag was not quick enough to stop him. His shoulder caught Tansa in the ribs as he fell and she almost fell with him, kept upright only by the chain and the strength of Cag and his fellows.

'Oi!' shouted one of the other chained men. 'You almost took us all down! Go on, leave us alone!'

Cag rounded on the man, who quailed slightly under his gaze. 'Shut up. We need to get out of here.'

'And go where?' demanded the man. 'Think we'll escape while we're chained up like cattle?'

Then Ranulf was there. He burst through the crowd towards them, his sword in one arm and a guard locked under the other by the neck. There was blood on his blade and a nasty gash down his cheek.

'Eryi's piss,' he swore. 'You were meant to cause a distraction, not start a riot.' He dragged the guard to them and held the sword to his abdomen. 'Unlock the big one, or I'll slice you open. You'll die slowly, I've seen it.'

The guard opened his mouth like he might protest, but Ranulf struck him pommel-first in the ribs. Reluctantly, the man reached into a pocket and drew out a short stubby key. Two clicks and the manacles fell from Cag's wrists, and then he bent to unlock his feet.

Ranulf shoved the guard aside to be swallowed by the mob. The guards had regrouped, and with truncheons and spears were beginning to restore order. The ground was littered with bodies, with bleeding wounds and limbs knocked askew.

'Pitt!' cried Ranulf.

Tansa had not noticed the boy before, but he was suddenly at Ranulf's elbow. 'Yeah?'

'Find us the quickest way back to Pauper's. Hurry.'

The boy blinked, turned on his heel, and started running, weaving through the crowd while the three of them struggled to keep up. Cag seemed to be limping slightly, but went first, using his bulk to cleave a way through behind Pitt. By chance, they collided with Glyn and Hiall, and Tansa had to quickly place a hand on Cag's arm to stop him shoving them aside. One of them was gushing blood from his temple, and the other's left arm was hanging lifelessly at his side. 'Where the fuck have you been?' she demanded.

'You were meant to wait,' protested one of them weakly, holding his useless arm with the good one. 'We got dragged away and beaten half to death.'

The crowd was thinner here, made up of those who had escaped the heart of the melee and those who had been content to stand back and enjoy the show with an ale. Cag's size and ugly bruises drew curious looks, but if the guards had started looking for their missing prisoner the call did not reach them. Ranulf brought up the rear, his sword hidden awkwardly inside his shirt and his eyes alert to danger.

'Isn't he the one from the inn?' asked Cag, glancing back suspiciously at Ranulf.

Tansa nodded. 'He's with us now.'

Cag said nothing.

Tansa was expecting the pounding tread of a company of guards at any moment, but they left the square without incident. Pitt took them through the back alleys, some so narrow and disused that even Tansa did not recognise them. She kept looking back, waiting for the moment when they would have to run. It never came, and if anybody was watching, Tansa did not sense them. The only witnesses were a mother cat and her kittens, eyeing them warily from their makeshift nest. Only her furious hissing stopped Pitt going to claim one. Ranulf produced some food from a pocket as they passed, scattering it to the grateful strays.

The labyrinthine backstreets came to an end, and Tansa was relieved to see the wide pavement of Market Road, the bustling anonymity of the passing crowd beckoning to her. She was so eager to reach Pauper's it took a sharp warning from Ranulf to make her wait while Maud's grandsons changed out of the guards' uniforms.

They took the stairs down to Pauper's two people at a time. Pauper's Hole was enough of a curiosity to Cliffark's law-abiding citizenry that somebody was bound to notice six of them going at once, one a small child and one a giant. Cag and Pitt went first, then Hiall and Glyn.

Tansa and Ranulf went last. She savoured the thick musty stench that rose in her nostrils as they descended into the dark. They were safe, unseen and beyond the clutches of the city guards.

'Thank you,' she said to Ranulf, taking his hand and squeezing it. 'For everything.'

Tansa never got to hear his reply. From the darkness behind them there was a draught of movement. Someone grabbed her, pinning her arms to her sides. She struggled, aiming a reverse kick towards her attacker, but was lifted helplessly off the ground and dragged backwards.

A dagger appeared at her throat, held by a meaty hand blue with tattoo ink.

'Don't struggle, girl.' The stranger's breath was hot and sour against her ear. 'Your boyfriend wouldn't want you getting hurt.'

In the gloom, she saw Ranulf, surrounded by sailors. He had somehow drawn his sword, but faced with so many he could do little more than use it to keep their knives at a safe distance. One of them leapt bravely towards Ranulf's exposed side, and lost his fingers for it, his knife and two digits spinning away where Ranulf's blade had caught him.

There was the pounding of feet from the stairs below, and Cag emerged, his eyes blazing and hands curled into fists, with Glyn and Hiall in pursuit behind him.

'That's enough, Orsian.'

Another man emerged from the shadows, dashingly attired in a bright violet waistcoat and a brimmed hat to match, an absurd contrast to the gloom of Pauper's. Ranulf was staring at him, his eyes wide, almost fearful.

It took Tansa a moment to realise that the man had called him Orsian, not Ranulf.

'That's right!' said the well-dressed stranger triumphantly. 'Bet you're wondering how I figured that one out, aren't you?' He looked at Tansa and smiled. 'I'd say by the look on your girl's face she didn't know either. Took me days to figure it out. I kept rolling it around in my head. You told me your love's name was Helana. *Helana.* It sounded so bloody familiar.

'It was Abner who worked it out in the end,' he said grudgingly, nodding to the sailor holding a knife to Tansa's throat. 'You can put the knife away, Abner. Orsian'll come quietly, won't you lad?'

'I don't know what you're talking about, Captain,' replied Ranulf, brandishing his sword warningly towards the men around him. 'I've been thinking about your offer, just like you told me, and I'm in as second mate. Just—'

The captain laughed. 'Ranulf was your distant cousin, dead seventeen years. After you ran from us at the inn and Abner realised Helana was the king's get, it all fell into place. You're Orsian Andrickson, missing and believed dead. Tell me false again and I'll cut off your girl's nose.'

Cat-quick, Abner laid his knife against Tansa's nose. She bit down on her tongue, refusing to cry out.

Across the landing Cag took an alarmed step forward.

'Careful, big fella,' said the captain, raising his hand in warning. 'Don't be doing anything silly.' He whistled, and from the shadows another half-dozen men emerged, looking mean as a pack of starving dogs.

Cag was dumb and angry enough to fight, and they would kill him. Tansa opened her mouth to shout out to him, but Abner pressed the knife to her throat and yanked her head back by the hair.

'Stay there, Cag,' said Ranulf. He looked at Tansa, and then the captain. 'I'll come with you. Now let her go.'

'Drop your sword,' said Abner.

'Take that knife off her throat first.'

The captain looked to Abner and nodded. Abner sheathed his blade and loosened his grip on Tansa's hair.

Ranulf looked at her and shrugged. 'Don't come after me.' He dropped his sword.

In the time since the captain's accusation, Tansa had drawn the dots. *He's Hessian's nephew.* By Eryi, she had shared a bed with *Hessian's nephew*? If not for everything else going on, she might have retched. She looked at Ranulf with undisguised loathing. 'Bastard. I won't. I knew you were lying.'

Ranulf opened his mouth to reply, but a sailor cracked him hard on the jaw with his knife-hand. A second man followed in with his own blow, and then a third. Ranulf slumped against the wall, and another man heaved him onto his shoulders.

Abner shoved Tansa away, and she stumbled into Cag's arms.

'He lied to all of us, girl,' said the captain, as the band of sailors retreated up the stairs. 'Best if you leave him to us though. The sea is no place for a woman.'

CHAPTER 16

Approaching the rarely used chamber of the king's council, Ciera could already hear raised voices, even over the footsteps of her entourage. In addition to a wet nurse carrying Andrick, and Lanetha, her new maid, she was also trailed by three *Hymeriker* guardsmen.

There were six guards in total, and one of Ciera's first acts since Hessian's departure had been to insist she only required three not four at any time, so that they could all rest for twelve hours each day rather than just eight. Laphor, the nominal head of them, had reluctantly agreed. He was with her today, together with Arrik and Burik, two of the former *hymerika* Naeem's many sons.

'Sounds like they're already going at it,' said Laphor from over her right shoulder. He was in his sixth decade, a grizzled, grey-whiskered veteran with scarring down one side of his face. Lord Gurathet had chosen her guard, and Ciera could not help feeling she had been given the warriors he did not want, whether by reasons of advanced age or loyalty to

Naeem, the man she knew many *hymerikai* thought ought to be their *balhymeri*.

Ciera smirked at Laphor's words. She was nearly an hour late, but had arranged for wine to be left in the council chamber. She had seen Balyard in his cups, and Gurathet's reputation was of a man who liked a drink.

She swept through the double doors in a swish of skirts and perfume, and Balyard and Gurathet leapt to their feet. She was pleased to note that they both had goblets of wine, and by the quantity left in the flagon it was not their first glass.

Lord Gurathet was near Hessian's age, but as fleshy as the king was gaunt, with a belly like an ale barrel. He was bald save for a few sweaty strands around his ears, with a bulbous nose and wild white eyebrows that were ever askew. He looked a once powerful man gone to seed through too many late meals and long drinking sessions, and unlike Balyard, who dressed in the softest velvet, wore the armour and red mark of a *hymerika*. In his youth it was said he had been of the order's finest warriors, until his father's untimely death had forced him to return home and rule his own lands.

'Queen Ciera,' Gurathet blustered, mopping his glowing brow with a handkerchief. 'We were not expecting you.'

The two men had each taken a long side of the table to themselves, so Ciera took a place at the head, facing the door. She smiled at him. 'Were you not? The king placed me on this regency council, same as you. I'm so sorry to be late.'

Balyard did not look amused. 'I believe the king saw yours as a ceremonial position.' He glanced unpleasantly towards the wet nurse, who was placing a sleeping Andrick in the cradle that had been carried down by Lanetha. 'Is the babe's presence necessary?'

'What safer place for him than surrounded by his loyal councillors, and so many fine warriors?' Ciera's gaze swept over the four *hymerikai* already in place along the two walls, the silent servants in the corners, then over their heads to the high, bright windows filled with stained glass displaying ancient Sangreal deeds. Concerningly, she noted that the four *hymerikai* already present were all Balyard's men, added to the brotherhood to increase their numbers. The *Hymeriker* was not the force it used to be. She sat down in a high-backed chair cushioned with red velvet, and Balyard and Gurathet followed suit. 'What were we discussing?'

Balyard's pursed expression made no attempt to hide his displeasure, but Gurathet seemed ready to make the best of Ciera's presence, chuckling to himself and waving away a servant to serve her wine himself, which Ciera took but had no intention of drinking. 'We were discussing the number of soldiers left in Piperskeep. Balyard proposes to leave us defenceless.'

Balyard glared across the table. 'It is an expense the treasury could do without,' he said in clipped tones. 'Feeding them, clothing them, housing them... We already have the *Hymeriker*. Now the war is over we have no need of so many swords.'

'You will if the West Erlanders come riding.'

'If the West Erlanders come, we will have to raise levies again anyway. Then they will return.'

'Return?' said Gurathet. 'You ever tried getting men back to war once they've been in the fields a few months? We'll be lucky to raise half so many again.'

'I agree with Lord Gurathet,' said Ciera. Soldiers had to be paid, but they spent their coin in the city, refilling Piperskeep's coffers. 'They should not be idle though; while

the truce holds, we can use them to support the city's beleaguered watchmen. The poorer quarters of the city grow more
violent by the day.' The Merivale Watch ought to be pleased
with that. She looked to Lord Balyard. 'But I also agree that
we ought to keep their numbers under review. We can revisit
this next month, once we know more of the Prindian intentions to honour the peace.'

Gurathet gave a satisfied grunt, but Balyard's mouth
moved as if he were chewing a wasp. He took a long draught
of wine. 'As you both wish.'

Ciera looked to the steward to make sure he was taking
notes, then smiled sweetly from Gurathet to Balyard. 'And
what else have you discussed in my absence?'

The look Balyard gave her could have cut steel. 'Those
matters are already decided.'

Gurathet's last cup of wine had emptied the flagon. He
signalled for a fresh one, then addressed Ciera as if he had
not even heard Balyard. 'The city's entry levy seems low.
We're going to increase it. More coin to pay for the soldiers
Lord Balyard doesn't want.' He chortled, his double chin
wobbling like treacle.

'It will put those puffed-up guildsmen in their place,'
added Balyard. 'If they want to moan about a lack of food, we
can show them how much worse it could be by increasing
taxes. Maybe it will make them think twice before they start
making damned petitions.'

Ciera took a deep breath to calm herself. The reduction
in the entry levy had been her proposal, and, as Hessian had
told her, the treasury was better for it. She could not tell
them the idea had been hers though; that would not convince
either of them. She looked to the steward again, a quill-thin
man with a neat grey beard. 'Frim, I believe we only recently

reduced the levy. How does its revenue compare to a year ago?' She knew the answer, but wanted the two lords to hear it from the page.

Frim blinked, as if surprised to have been asked a question. He flicked the ledger in his hand over a few pages. 'Revenue is up significantly, my Queen. Individual entries have more than doubled, and the reeve reports that takings from the market are up as well.'

'All the more reason to tax them more!' declared Balyard, slamming his cup down. 'Merchants are getting fat trading in the city. We need to make sure we're getting our cut.'

'You've heard the figures,' said Ciera, trying to keep her voice level, even as Balyard's outburst reminded her of the day he had ambushed her in the birthing room. The wine would make him slower, but it would also rouse his temper. 'Did you even ask Frim before you made the decision? Perhaps it is not so simple as you think.'

'Even the strongest horse may balk and buck at too much of the whip,' declared Gurathet. 'Revenues will improve with the truce anyway. I agree with the queen.'

Balyard's face had turned from puce to purple. 'Very well!' He shot an angry look at Frim, as if the truth of the figures must be his fault.

'We should discuss the milling levy as well,' said Ciera, sensing an opportunity. Abolishing the disliked milling levy had long been an ambition of hers. 'If we remove it, farmers will be more likely to mill and sell their grain here, rather than in Lordsferry or Tallowton.' *That ought to appease the guilds.*

'It was a hard winter,' added Frim glumly. 'There has been unrest; more folk come to the gate every day pleading for bread, and—'

That was too much for Lord Balyard. He stormed to his feet, and slammed his open palm down on the table. Gurathet had to swiftly grasp his wine to prevent it from toppling. 'You go too far, girl! I am Hessian's regent, not these guildsmen you seem so desperate to impress. Hessian may have tolerated your gall, but I—'

'*Girl?*' Laphor took a menacing step towards Balyard. 'Did you just call the Queen of Erland, "*girl*"?'

In an instant the whole room was in motion. Two of Balyard's guards advanced with their hands on their sword hilts, and with a yelp Frim threw himself behind Lord Gurathet. In the corner, Prince Andrick began to bawl, and Ciera's chair legs shrieked on the stone floor as she pushed it back to stand, shooting a look at the wet nurse to remove Andrick from the room. Blood pounded in Ciera's ears.

It took Lord Gurathet to restore order. 'Enough!' he bellowed, as Andrick's wet nurse fled from the room. He cut an imposing figure standing up, even with his wine-stained lips and sweat seeping from his forehead, and for a moment Ciera saw the warrior he had once been. 'Balyard, sit down and calm yourself, for Eryi's sake. I agree with you.'

Lord Balyard blinked, seemingly suddenly conscious of how foolish he had made himself look. 'Ah, well then.' He sank back into his chair, rubbing his temple with one finger. 'Queen Ciera, I apologise. I mis-spoke.'

'Sure you did,' muttered Laphor, stepping away, as Balyard's guards did the same.

Ciera forced herself to smile, even as her heartbeat echoed in her skull, and sat back down. She had known of Balyard's temper, but she had not been prepared for how swiftly it had risen. Even so, it would get her what she wanted. 'All is forgiven, Lord Balyard, we both only want what is best for Erland and Merivale.' She prepared to push her advantage, looking to Lord Gurathet who had also retaken his seat. 'Without the milling levy being removed, I fear we may need to get more men back in the fields, so the harvest is not diminished. Perhaps we ought to reconsider keeping on so many soldiers.'

It was not subtle, but she suspected Gurathet appreciated that. He chuckled amiably. 'Fine. Let's say no milling levy for the next two months. Then we'll have the steward check the numbers.'

Ciera sensed that the only thing keeping Balyard's temper in check was his embarrassment at being outmanoeuvred by a seventeen-year-old girl. He did not look at her or Gurathet when he next spoke, keeping his gaze levelly somewhere behind Ciera. 'We should ask the king first.' He pushed his wine away and reached for a jug of water. 'If we're making such a change we should at least seek his approval.'

It was Ciera's turn to be surprised. 'And how exactly do you suppose we do that?'

'You.' Balyard pointed over her head. 'You deal with all that, don't you?'

Ciera turned, and to her surprise saw Georald, Theodric's assistant, slightly stooped with long grey hair hanging in limp vines. She had not even noticed him as she entered. He looked no less surprised to have been called upon. 'Me, Lord?'

'Yes, you run the messenger service in the wizard's absence, don't you? Just send a man on a fast horse to Fisherton, the Adrari settlement. We'll have a response from Hessian within weeks.'

'My husband did not appoint a regency council so that

we could disturb him on his pilgrimage over trivial matters,' said Ciera, slightly more forcefully than she intended. 'Should we also ask him what colour carpet he would like in the prince's bedroom?'

Balyard seemed to have recovered his composure. His smile to her was more of a sneer. 'What's the harm? I'm just concerned about the kingdom. I'm not sure he intended for us to make such major decisions without consulting him.'

It did not stop you attempting to increase the entry levy when he had barely left Merivale. Ciera was prepared to say as much, but the magus Georald spoke first.

'We may not need a horse,' he said. His clasped hands shook nervously. 'I might be able to speak with Lord Theodric directly. He's ahead of the king, but—'

He was interrupted by Lord Gurathet chuckling again, which seemed to sap the bravery from Georald. 'Come on Balyard, let's not turn to magic just because you've lost. We can remove the milling levy for a brief time.'

Ciera was well satisfied with that. She had not expected to win everything she sought, and she was sure Hessian would not have been in favour of allowing the peasantry to use his mill for free.

'No,' said Balyard, becoming slightly shrill. 'I think—'

'I think that's quite enough governing for today,' said Gurathet. He rose with a great groan, considered the wine in his glass, and downed it. 'I'm too hungry to think any further. We can revisit this another time.'

Ciera stood as well, forcing Balyard to push his chair back and join them. Scowling, he bowed once to Ciera, and swept from the room, dragging his guards along in his wake.

Gurathet was chortling to himself, seemingly his natural reaction to almost anything. 'Strange fellow sometimes.

Balyard, I mean. Shrewd though.' The servants were already beginning to shuffle from the chamber, but Ciera hung back, suspecting that Gurathet had something he wanted to say to her. 'Majesty, I was hoping there was something we might discuss. Your lands, those your father gave you as your bride portion, would you be interested in selling them?' He named what sounded to Ciera a reasonable sum.

Ciera looked at him. In truth, she had forgotten she owned those lands. They were Hessian's strictly, but to be returned to her upon his death, to provide for her once she was a widow. She had never visited, but understood the lands to be west of her father's domains, close to the coast, a mix of farmland and marshland. 'Why would you want them?'

'Six sons.' He grinned proudly. 'Perhaps Hessian could learn a thing or two from me. Good lads, all of them, two of them are *hymerikai*, but when I die they'll be at each other's throats unless I can pass on enough land for them to share.'

'I'll think on it,' said Ciera, hastening out of the room with her guards around her. She felt an ingrained reluctance to sell the only property that she might hold in her own name. She was already the queen; what could she do with the sum of gold Gurathet had named?

'Balyard looked mighty pissed off,' growled Laphor as her three *hymerikai* escorted Ciera back towards Andrick's chamber. 'Sure you want him on your council?'

'It's not my council,' she reminded him.

'Aye, but if I had a rat scratching in my walls and stealing my food, I'd cut its head off.'

Ciera looked at him sharply. She liked Laphor's forthrightness, but there were limits. 'Lord Balyard is not a rat, Laphor.'

'No, he's worse.'

And that Ciera could only laugh at, despite herself, momentarily giddy with the morning's accomplishment. She had faced down Balyard, could safely consider Gurathet an ally, and had secured a course she could never have achieved with Hessian present. In her arms, Andrick cooed, and Ciera returned to her child's rooms as content as she had ever felt inside Piperskeep.

CHAPTER 17

Rymond ran a hand through his whiskers. He had never grown a beard before. It had come through darker than his hair, with wiry strands of black amidst the blonde. Would it disguise him in Irith, from those who had known him before the war? Perhaps, but many soldiers would know his bearded face, and the city would be full of them, celebrating having returned alive and a truce that as good as confirmed West Erland's right to rule itself.

A year ago, he would have thought nothing of going out without a disguise. His face and name were often enough to get for free what other men paid for, just so innkeepers could say that Lord Prindian frequented their establishment.

Those days are gone, he mused. It was a warm night, and he had opened the door to his balcony, giving him a view over all the twinkling lights of Irith. He could almost hear the town and the taverns below; the crashing of tankards and the rattling of dice, and the eager invitations of girls leaning from the windows of the bawdy houses.

The last time he had gone out undisguised, he had been

kidnapped and almost sold to Hessian. What a fool he had been then.

It would not do though to smear himself with dirt as he had in camp. Instead, Rymond picked up his looking glass, rushed a final hand through his beard, then sheared his face with a straight razor. Once clean-shaven, he tied his hair back in a tail, and buried it under a woollen cap.

Rymond nodded at his reflection, satisfied. It would not fool anybody who knew him well, but he should be able to go about the city undisturbed. He looked like a merchant's clerk given the evening off by his master.

He had made vague plans to meet Dom at the Smoking Sow, though their friendship was not what it had once been, not since Errian Andrickson had slain Will, their ever-cheerful companion who had tied their band together. Perhaps a return to the Sow would revitalise their friendship. The inn's popularity had only grown since the night Rymond had been kidnapped there. The innkeep had even started running tours, starting in the inn's common room, going outside to the alley where the cut-throat had caught Rymond mid-piss, and following the route his kidnapper had taken to the eastern gate. Rymond could not vouch for its accuracy; he had been tied to a horse and covered with a blanket.

He had earnt an evening to himself, duty be damned. Every other man back from the war would be drinking himself into a stupor; why not him? A mug of beer and good company was what he needed. He just had to escape the castle without his mother or Adfric noticing. His mother would assign guards to follow him, and Adfric would insist on coming himself.

The other concern that he was trying to forget about was the half pouch of casheef stashed deep within his trunk. *I should get rid of it, remove the temptation.* It was said sustained use of the herb could send a man spiralling into madness. Touching it had been a mistake from the beginning.

If he stayed in, it was inevitable that he would smoke some, and tomorrow he would be wracked with tremors and sudden chills worse than any hangover. If he could return to the old ways, he might forget all about the noxious black powder. It had been a welcome relief in camp after long days ahorse, but there was no excuse now he was back in Irith.

Fortunately, he was well-practised at hiding his comings and goings. He had always been on friendly terms with the castle's servants, not least those in the kitchen, who in his youth he had often paid to assist him in sneaking out and back in. It had been many years, but men did not forget the taste of gold.

Satisfied with his plan, Rymond set out in search of the servants' stairs, a spring in his step and his purse jangling pleasingly.

He had no sooner stepped into the corridor when he collided with somebody coming the other way. With a cry of alarm, Rymond stumbled backwards, and had to grasp the door handle to stop himself falling.

It was Adfric.

'Eryi's balls, you almost scared me out of my skin.' Rymond righted himself. 'Why are you sneaking around the castle at night?'

'I might ask you the same thing, Majesty.' Adfric's eyes flicked down over Rymond's clothes, and across his freshly shaved face. 'Were you going somewhere?'

Rymond cursed. *All I wanted was one night.* 'I was going into the town. Just to get a sense of the mood.'

'To get a sense of the mood,' repeated Adfric wryly. 'I am

sorry to disturb you, but there is a pressing matter we must discuss.' He dropped his voice. 'We should speak in your chambers, or better yet on the balcony.'

With a sigh, Rymond opened his door. *I could not even get two steps without one of them getting in my way.*

Rymond poured them each a whisky, before joining Adfric at the balustrade overlooking the city. Even if he could not go down to Irith, he could still get good and drunk. The city lights looked all the more enticing for being denied to him.

'So what is it?' asked Rymond. The whisky was strong and sweet, but did little to improve his mood.

'I've made a plan, Lord.'

Rymond looked at him, mystified. 'A plan for what?'

'For Strovac!'

Rymond bit back a curse. Between casheef and his joy at being back in Irith he had managed to forget all about that. 'What about him?'

Adfric glanced cautiously left and right, then spoke in an undertone. 'I've got a man in the Wild Brigade. Yoran, his name is, and he's near as unpleasant as Strovac. He reckons if Strovac died—'

'Died?'

'When you said I should deal with him, what exactly did you think we were talking about?'

In truth, Rymond had not been thinking. Part of him had been occupied with thoughts of Gruenla, and the other part with obtaining some casheef. He scratched his head under Adfric's glare. 'I do not know. I thought you might just... get rid of him somehow. Get him drunk and put him on a ship to Ulvatia or something.'

'This man Yoran says he can get rid of him, and that if he does, the Wild Brigade will choose him as their next leader.'

'And how much does he want paying?'

Looking slightly sheepish, Adfric named an extravagant sum. 'Plus a lordship, and a good marriage.'

It was quite probable, Rymond reflected, that this man Yoran would be just as much of a fly in his ale as Strovac. The Wild Brigade had not been chosen for their charm; they were hardened killers, and little more than that. Their orchestrated murder of Andrick Barrelbreaker might have dishonoured Rymond's name for the next century. 'Are you sure they meant to kill you? Mistakes are made in battle; how often do you think one of ours cuts down his fellow by mistake? You have no evidence Strovac is acting against us.'

'As it happens, I do,' said Adfric, pulling two sheets of crumpled parchment from his pocket and unrolling them across the parapet.

The first was a plan of troop movements Rymond had sketched out to his war council. The second was the letter he had received from their spy in Merivale, revealing that Queen Ciera had gone into labour. 'We found them both on a rider trying to sneak out of camp past our guards,' explained Adfric. 'Somebody in your council is a spy.'

Rymond stared at the letter, aghast. 'I thought I had lost this,' he murmured. That had been days ago though. 'Why did you take so long to tell me?'

'There are too many ears in camp. If there is a spy in your council, can anybody be trusted? I had to wait till I knew we were safe.' Adfric cast a suspicious glance over his shoulder, as though the spy might be lurking in a corner of Rymond's chamber. 'Who else but Strovac would have sent this?'

Rymond mused over the members of his war council.

Himself, Adfric, his mother, Strovac, Gruenla, the Ffrisean chieftain Arka, half-a-dozen lords, and Dom. He could discount many of those. Arka could not read or write in the Erlish tongue. Dom had been his friend since boyhood. He had no reason to doubt the loyalty of his lords. Unless they had been moved to treachery by the ignoble death of Lord Andrick? No, those who had been prompted to action by Andrick's death had already been removed from his service by the hangman's noose, and those who remained would not risk all for so little gain.

Gruenla... The Cyliriens were known for their fierce pride, not their subterfuge. But nevertheless, it gnawed at Rymond. Why had she come so willingly to his bed? There would have been no better opportunity to steal from him than while he slept with his clothes strewn about his tent.

'Do you have any proof it was Strovac?'

'Who else could it be?' Adfric violently drained his whisky. 'Will you be asking for proof when you find his blade pressed against your neck? The man is *poison*. He ingratiates himself deeper into your service, and at the same time hedges his bets by moving against you. He acts for himself. He always has. He bought the Fortlands off you at the head of a Thrumb army.'

'There's one other possibility.' Rymond hesitated. 'Gruenla.'

Adfric frowned. 'The Cyliriens are only interested in raising coin for their war against the Imperium. It's certainly possible.'

Rymond cursed. It pained him to admit it. 'I will keep my distance, and we should have someone keep an eye on her.'

'It will be done, Majesty. And what of Strovac?'

It had never been in doubt that Strovac acted only for

himself. Whether today or tomorrow, if he saw a profit in turning against Rymond's cause, he would do it. Rymond gave Adfric the briefest of nods. 'Do it.' They would see whether this Yoran could do what so many had failed to do and kill Strovac Sigac. 'Tell me no more of it. Was there anything else?'

'We've had a letter from the east. Hessian's had a son.'

A year before, the news would have been balm to Rymond's ears. With an heir, Hessian might have simply forgotten about him. Even a few months ago, it might have led to peace. There was little prospect of that now though. Not since Strovac had slain Andrick Barrelbreaker and spiked his head atop a pole.

The news guaranteed that Rymond's right to rule West Erland would ever be subject to challenge. He sighed, and took a sip of whisky. 'I do not intend to think about the war for at least the next week. Ideally longer if the truce holds.' He was ready to dismiss Adfric, but the older man looked to have something else on his mind. 'Is there anything else?'

Adfric nodded. 'The Imperium, Majesty. There's rumours they might have a new kzar. If their eye should turn upon Erland—'

Rymond held up his hand. He was not going to trouble himself with a power hundreds of miles away, divided from Erland by the Shrouded Sea and the Bleak Hills. 'We have enough to fear from our enemies today without borrowing fear from tomorrow.'

———

It took a promise to consider carefully his concerns about the Imperium, but Adfric grudgingly allowed Rymond to leave without an escort. Though, as he rode towards the New Quarter, Rymond still swore there were two men trailing him. As long as they did not interfere with his evening he supposed he could live with it.

He found himself thinking more on Strovac Sigac. The warrior's low cunning might see through the intent of this man Yoran in an instant. With his size and ferocity, how could Strovac be assassinated? It would have to be a dagger in the dark, preferably while he was drunk and asleep.

It was safer not to think on it. Should the plan fail, it would at least be plausible Rymond had not known anything if he forced himself to forget about it.

The town was busier than Rymond could ever recall. People filled the streets, and the revelry was still good-natured enough that the guards had not intervened. Barrels of ale had been rolled outside, and soldiers still covered in sweat and dust from the march were drinking their fill. The dancing had already started, and between songs the air was alive with cries of 'King Rymond!' and 'West Erland!'

The Smoking Sow was abuzz with light and noise, spilling cavorting shadows into the street and filling the night air with laughter. Rymond threw a gold piece to a wide-eyed stableboy and handed him the reins as he dismounted.

The inside was thick with people, and Rymond had some difficulty locating Dom. A boy elbowed past him, forcing Rymond to one side and narrowly missing a table. It took him a moment to realise that a purse had disappeared from his pocket, and by then the boy was already out of sight, lost in the throng. He cursed. There were some downsides to being in disguise. At least he kept a second, heavier purse tucked carefully inside his shirt.

A high whistle caught his ear. He turned around looking for its source, and saw Dom, waving to him from a table.

'That boy just filched from my pocket,' Rymond complained, taking a chair.

Dom grinned. 'I asked him to. It's your round.'

Sure enough, the boy was at their table a moment later, carrying two foaming mugs of ale. He dropped Rymond's purse into his palm, which he shoved quickly back into his pocket as Dom laughed.

'You seem happy,' observed Rymond, shouting to make himself heard over the din. Before, it would have been Will japing with him; Dom was the more serious of the two, usually thinking about women rather than fooling about with his friends.

'Why wouldn't I be?' Don grinned. 'Back in Irith, with all my limbs. No disrespect, Ry, but I hope you don't mind if I stay here when you next march. The soldiering life is fine for some, but I need a deck beneath my feet.'

'With any luck, we won't be going to war ever again,' said Rymond, though even as he spoke he knew it was a lie. East and West Erland would not endure as separate realms for long. 'To friendship!' he cried, lifting his tankard towards Dom.

'To kingship.' Dom raised his own and the two of them crashed their drinks together, sending beer foaming over the rims.

They spoke of small things for a time, reminiscing on youthful hijinks, with fresh ales being regularly delivered to their table, and Dom even managed to make a joke about his night in the dungeon after Rymond's kidnapping, a subject he had not found the least bit amusing the year before. They never spoke of Will though; there seemed to exist an unspoken accord between them not to dwell on their dead friend, at least until Rymond was eight drinks deep.

'I'm sorry about Will,' he said, putting an arm around Dom's shoulder. 'If I'd—'

'We don't need to talk about it,' said Dom. 'Wasn't your fault.' He looked up at someone's approach, and his face broke out in a grin. 'Anyway, there's someone I'd like you to meet.'

Rymond looked up too, and found himself gazing into the face of a woman, tall and slender, with delicate elfin features and long, dark lashes framing blue eyes large enough to drown in. She wore a long cloak, clasped with a silver brooch, and a red hat with short blonde hair poking from underneath it. A smokestick dangled from her elegant fingers.

'Hello,' said Rymond. *Eryi's blood, she's beautiful.* 'Nice hat. Could I—'

With a smile, the woman held out a second smokestick, which Rymond took gladly.

She lowered herself into a spare chair, and Dom draped an arm casually over her shoulders as she turned to kiss him on the cheek. 'Ry, this is Alcantra. We met in Whitewater.'

Rymond felt his heart sink slightly. He and Dom had shared women before – not at the same time of course; there were limits – but by the way he and Alcantra were looking at one another Rymond doubted this would be one of those occasions.

'My love, you did not tell me your friends were so handsome,' purred Alcantra, her eyes twinkling. There was a slight accent to her speech. 'I'm almost sorry I met you first.'

Dom laughed. 'King Rymond must aim his sights a little higher than the likes of you and me. No doubt we'll see him

married to some lord's daughter before the year is out. We
should enjoy his company while we can.'

Rymond inhaled on his smokestick, and as soon as the
fumes hit his lungs the world seemed to return to focus.
Alcantra's features sharpened, making her somehow even
more beautiful, and the sights and sounds of the Smoking
Sow rose brighter and louder than before, with each conversation distinctly audible.

Rymond let the smoke out, and the effect lessened, but
he did suddenly find himself feeling a little more sober. A
bemused grin broke out across his face. 'There's casheef in
this!'

Alcantra beamed, showing two rows of perfectly straight
white teeth. Rymond was struck with the sudden urge to kiss
her. 'I heard you like it, Majesty.' She reached inside her
cloak and produced a small pouch. 'This is the good stuff, not
the sawdust you Erlanders insist on sucking into your lungs. I
say we retire to my room and enjoy it. It's not often I get the
chance to smoke with royalty.'

Rymond's heart beat a little faster at the sight of it. *So
much for quitting.* That small measure of casheef had taken
the edge off, but he needed more.

'You in, Ry?' asked Dom.

Rymond's hesitation lasted barely a moment. *By Eryi, it's
not every day one returns from a war.* 'I'm in.' He looked
quickly around for the men he suspected Adfric had sent to
follow him, but saw no sign of them. The three of them rose,
eased their way through the crowd, and sneaked out into the
back alley.

'The last time I was here I had a knife to my throat,' he
told Alcantra, as she linked her arm in his, with Dom on the
other side. The night felt alive; every star as bright as silver,

and every garbled conversation floating from the inns as clear as if someone were speaking it in his ear. Three returning soldiers argued good-naturedly over a dice game, while a pair of lovers in a nearby alley whispered sweet nothings to one another. Rymond was giddy on the sensation. 'The company is considerably more attractive this time.'

'Don't think I won't hit you for flirting with my woman,' said Dom. 'Wars have been fought over less.'

'My dear friend, I was talking about you.'

Dom laughed, and Alcantra giggled. Rymond had not noticed before the high boots she wore. Their sharp heels clicked against Irith's cobbles, almost throwing up sparks.

Alcantra led the way, weaving between the knots of revellers, towards the other side of the city. Rymond had expected her to turn towards the walls and the cheaper flophouses, but instead she steered them into the Old Quarter, to a well-made, brown-beamed inn, with garlands hanging over the door and a third storey. Alcantra opened the front door to a hall bright with candlelight, and a servant appeared to take their cloaks.

Rymond looked around. Even by his own standards, it was an opulent establishment, with rich carpets, a pleasant cinnamon smell in the air, and smooth, spotless banisters leading up a wide staircase.

He looked into the common room, and found it empty. 'Are you the only guest?'

'I rented the whole inn. I like my privacy.'

Rymond was not sure why anyone would need to rent an entire inn, but he did not want to seem nosy by prying into the matter. 'Rich as well as beautiful. How on earth did Dom trick you into bed?'

Alcantra covered her mouth in mock horror as Dom slid

his arms around her waist from behind. 'My virtue remains unblemished. Dom, defend my honour from this cad.'

'I wouldn't dare, not against the mighty warrior king of West Erland. Let's get him completely fucked on casheef first, that way I might stand a chance.'

'If you insist, my fearless defender.' Alcantra passed Rymond and Dom another smokestick each. One hit, and Rymond felt the peculiar sense of relaxed alertness return. He could hear the splatter of urine against an outside wall, and the argument of a couple two houses over, but he no longer cared why Alcantra had troubled to rent a whole inn.

He followed them upstairs. Alcantra's room took up the whole top floor, perhaps a third as large again as Rymond's own spacious chambers, with a huge four-poster bed, a fireplace at either end, and a carpet so soft he was struck by the urge to run his toes through it. Then, he asked himself if he wanted to do it, why did he not just do it? Grinning, he pulled his boots and socks off, collapsed into a soft chair, and began balling his toes through the lush wool.

From somewhere, Dom handed Rymond a tumbler of whisky, and Alcantra produced a pipe not unlike Rymond's own.

'The tabac muddies the high,' she told him, passing it to him. 'Try this.'

Vaguely, Rymond recalled that one of the reasons he had gone to Irith tonight had been to avoid taking casheef. But when a beautiful woman seemed intent on plying you with the stuff, what was a man to do? He lowered his lips to the pipe and inhaled.

The effect was instant. Waves of awareness crashed against Rymond's consciousness, until his whole body seemed to be vibrating, the impossible sensation of the whole world happening at once, too fast for him to hear or see. Existence narrowed to a black pinprick, and then, as Rymond exhaled, exploded in a riot of sound and colour. Somewhere, Alcantra and Dom were laughing, and though Rymond was not sure why he found himself laughing along with them. Rymond's mouth was moving, speaking simultaneously a low, creeping whisper and a jumbled, excited babble, both too slow and too wild for him to understand. The crescent moon crept towards the horizon at the speed of a galloping horse, and in the blink of an eye the summer night faded to purple and to blue, and a yellow sun rose in the east.

Rymond blinked, and sunlight streamed in through the open window, burning his eyes. With a moan, he fell to the floor, his head on the verge of splitting into four parts. He strained to hold them together.

'Eryi's balls,' he moaned. He grasped for a cup left on a table, gagged on a mouthful of oily whisky, and spat it across the carpet. He curled into a ball, groaning at the ache engulfing his whole body.

Truly there is no way to make a hangover worse than to add casheef. Even just that thought was enough to send a sharp spike through his brain. What Alcantra had given him was so potent it would have brought down a boar.

Rymond levered himself slowly to his feet, leaning on the chair for support.

Dom was sitting by the window, shirtless, a smokestick between his fingers and Alcantra curled up beside him, still dozing. He grinned. 'Enjoy last night?'

Rymond's head pulsed. 'I think so. What happened?' He had the sense that he had embarrassed himself horribly.

'You got back here, rambled nonsense for five minutes,

then fell straight asleep.' Dom laughed, while Alcantra smiled sleepily. 'All the excitement went to your head.'

'Right.' Rymond ran a hand through his greasy hair, relieved. 'Well, I'll be off then. Sorry if I was any trouble.'

With a swift farewell, Rymond pulled his boots on, made for the door, and walked gingerly back down the staircase. Hoping it might silence his headache, he reached for a smokestick. He took a drag, then instantly regretted it; the whole staircase spun, and he was forced to grasp the banister for support as he tried not to vomit.

It had been a very strange homecoming.

CHAPTER 18

It was the first day of summer in Ulvatia, and the city was sweltering. Children and youths were throwing themselves into the harbour by the dozen to cool down. Those who still had places to be made their way about the city in sheltered palanquins, accompanied by entourages of slaves, carrying water and waving huge fans. Most had made the wise decision to stay in their homes, not least those who the night before had enjoyed the masked celebration marking the anniversary of the Second Purge, when Ulvatia's ungifted had risen and toppled their magi overlords. The water in the city's fountains had been replaced by wine for the night, and many were nursing sore heads.

Drast Fulkiro's malaise, however, was a very different sort. His headache was not from overindulgence, but from another sleepless night worrying about the man he wished he had never met – the magus, Krupal – and the man whose name was on the lips of every senator in Ulvatia – the missing Kvarm Murino. Drast laid his head against the cool marble of his study window, trying desperately to think of a solution.

Voting had continued, and the kzarship was now a three-way contest between Drast, Naro Brunal, and Saffia Murino. Drast had swept up most of Kvarm's votes, and he now had over a hundred, narrowly behind Brunal. A few more rounds and support for Saffia would fade away. The contest was his to lose. And yet, investigations into the disappearance of Kvarm continued, and though nobody had yet drawn a connection to Drast – Kvarm had evidently kept his visit to Hacinder Manor a secret – he was sure it was only a matter of time.

If anyone discovers I freed Krupal, it will mean my execution. What the magus had done to Kvarm and Hrogo should not have been possible. Drast had only wanted to persuade a few senators to vote for him, not remove them from existence. The magus' power, unchecked, could bring about not only Drast's demise but the demise of the whole city.

And he was growing stronger. Krupal's attempts to invade Drast's mind had become persistent, like a constant knocking. He and Forren had shared their concerns in clandestine whispers, both too afraid to speak openly.

To Krupal's face, Drast had been nothing but grateful; he could not dispute that the magus had saved him. He had rewarded Krupal by giving over to him his finest guest bedroom, in the opposite corner of his estate.

I will become kzar. Then Forren can tell Krupal that his brother is in Erland, and we can be rid of him. Then he would be safe; with no body, Krupal was the only thing linking him to Kvarm's disappearance.

Drast jumped to his feet as the door to his study crashed

open, revealing Forren, his clothes askew, and breathing as though he had taken the stairs three at a time.

'They found him, the brother,' he gasped. In one hand he clutched a book, and in the other a square package wrapped in distressed leather. 'In a house, in the old Alchemists' District.' He placed the package before Drast. 'Most of it was destroyed, but the leather kept this intact.'

Drast pulled back the leather. Krupal's face stared up at him from a painting. Not scowling as Krupal did, but eerily calm, with one eyebrow slightly raised and the beginnings of a smile at the edge of his lips, as though sharing a private joke with himself.

'This is the census for that district from the year before the Fourth Purge,' continued Forren, pulling a scroll from under his arm and unrolling it. 'This is how we found the house.' He pointed to the entry for the address, which listed one resident: *Krutan, son of Karved, magus and senator.*

'Were they twins then?' asked Drast. That would explain why Krupal was so desperate to find his brother.

Forren shook his head. 'We looked everywhere. Karved had only one son: Krutan. There's no record of a Krupal anywhere. We thought the records might just be lost, but then we found this.' He placed the book on the table so Drast could see the cover and title: *The Creation and Care of Shadowtwins, by Krutan von Belkarez.*

Drast looked from the book to the painting, and back to the book, his mouth widening in horror. 'Urmé's wounds... Did Krutan pull a version of himself from another world? Is that even possible?'

Forren nodded grimly, and opened the book. 'It's all in here; the state we found him in was a form of hibernation, intended to replicate sleep. *"If left in that state for more than a month, the mind of the subject may degrade. If left for longer than a year, all my observations suggest that the subject will become wilful and uncooperative, and potentially descend into madness. My advice in such cases would be to destroy the subject, rather than wake it."* My best guess is that during the Fourth Purge, Krutan put Krupal into hibernation for safety, and was killed before he could return.'

'Gods...' Then Krupal was even more unpredictable than they had thought. Drast stumbled into a chair as though he had been winded. What had he and Forren unleashed upon the world? It had been bad enough when they had thought Krupal only a magus. 'I had hoped to remove him once I became kzar. I was going to tell him Krutan was in Erland. But we have to kill him, don't we?' *Not just for my own sake, but for the sake of Ulvatia.*

'Yes. He's too dangerous. We can't have a magus's pet twin running around. We're putting ourselves and the whole Imperium at risk. What if he decides to do to us what he did to Kvarm?' Forren dropped his voice to a whisper, as though Krupal could be listening. 'We'll wait till dark, then we'll go to his room. I've told a dozen of our best swords to be ready.'

'Make it two dozen.' What Krupal had done to Kvarm and Hrogo was etched on Drast's memory. 'Could we go for him while he sleeps?'

'If he sleeps. Who knows what he's doing in that room?'

Drast suppressed a shiver. 'What if we don't send him any food, so he's weak and can't use his powers? No, then he'll know something is wrong. Could we dose his food with a sedative?'

'It might slow him, perhaps. I wouldn't rely on it.'

'Parmé damn him!' Drast ran both hands through his

hair, soaking it with a sheen of sweat from his forehead. He rose and began stalking the room, calculating.

'Incendiaries,' he said finally. 'We have some huyar somewhere, surely?' He had seen in Cylirien what huyar explosives could do to armoured men; not even Krupal would stand against that.

Forren hesitated. 'I believe we have some in safe storage. Huyar is temperamental though; if we use too much—'

'Use all of it. Set it under his room. I don't care if the whole wing goes up. We'll tell everyone it was arson, a Murino plot.'

'I don't like it. What if the whole house comes down around us, and at the end he's standing in the middle of the rubble and we're all dead? Let me go in with soldiers. He can't kill us all.'

'He might.' Drast glanced at the chest where he kept his rarely used sword; it was not seen as proper for senators to carry them. 'Set the huyar, and set this near it.' He scrabbled in his desk for one of his magical artefacts, an ensorcelled bead that could be heated by its twin, and handed it to Forren. 'If we need to, that should get hot enough when I press it to set the huyar off. And I'm coming with you.' It was Drast's fault that Krupal was free; he would not hide while other men sought to clear up his mess.

———

Drast spent the day's remaining hours writing missives to allies and would-be supporters, massaging their fragile egos and assuring them that he would meet with them tomorrow. When the light faded, he claimed the sword from his chest, polished it till he could have shaved in it, and took a few experimental thrusts, skewering invisible foes like a child at play. When he had left Cylirien and taken up his father's senatorial seat he had hoped never to have to wield a blade again.

As night fell, he stowed the sword in his belt, and descended to the courtyard, where Forren waited with twenty-four armoured guards. One of them carried a flaming torch, its pale orange glow lending an eeriness to their meeting. They were not slaves, but salaried free men. His elite guards. They ate better than Drast's finest horses, and it showed in their smooth skin, and the taut muscles that bulged beneath their leather armour.

Forren greeted him. 'Senator. Your men await you.'

'Did you set the huyar?'

'Yes.'

'And what have you told them?' he asked, low enough that the guards would not hear.

'I've told them the man you invited into your home as a guest and advisor is in fact in league with Senator Brunal.'

Drast indicated his approval. A small and necessary lie. If they learnt he had knowingly entered into a deal with a magus they were just as likely to attack him as Krupal. Better to let them discover that on their own.

Forren signalled for the guards to follow, and Drast stepped in behind them, fingering his sword every few steps to remind himself it was still there. As they drew close to the wing containing Krupal's room, Forren doused their torch to give them the cover of darkness.

Forren went first, opening the door with a soft scrape. They crept up the stairs, ears alert to every sound above them. Nothing stirred. The wing was silent as a crypt.

Drast left them briefly to allow himself a peek into the

room below Krupal's. The clay vases storing the huyar gleamed sinisterly in the half-light of the moons through the window, like misshapen gravestones. The earthy, sulphurous smell of the alchemical powder sent a shiver along his shoulders. The odour reminded him of war.

He caught up with them on the floor above. Forren stood at Krupal's door, surrounded by soldiers. Drast swallowed. They had been as quiet as two dozen armed men could be. For the first time in his adult life, he said a silent prayer to Urmé. He nodded to Forren.

Forren flung the door open.

A blaze of light flooded the hallway. Drast shielded his eyes and followed behind his soldiers.

Krupal stood with his back to them, gazing out of the window. Every lamp and candle in the room radiated light. Forren and the rest drew their blades.

'Senator.' His voice was sharp as swords, controlled in a way Drast had never heard before. Krupal turned, keeping his hands buried in his robes.

We shouldn't let him speak, thought Drast. *We should rush him, and make an end of this.* But he found himself replying. His sword weighed heavy in his hand. 'We found Krutan's house. He's dead.'

Krupal blinked. 'I expected so. Too long has passed.' A sadness passed over his eyes. 'Are you here to kill me?'

'Yes,' said Drast.

'Then try.'

Forren moved so suddenly that Drast barely saw him. His sword whistled towards Krupal, too fast to evade, a cut that would slice his torso in two.

But Krupal was not there.

He was standing by a bookshelf, on the adjacent wall, hands still buried in his robes.

He smiled. 'In some existences, I was here when you arrived. In some I was by the window. In some I was not here at all. In none of them did you strike me.' Drast felt something shift, like time folding over on itself. 'Lay down your weapons.'

The magus's voice rumbled with authority. Drast stared as his guards struggled against his command, their swords shaking as they fought to hold onto them.

Krupal frowned, then brightened with realisation. 'Ah. Too much against their nature. They are well-trained pets.' He thought a moment. 'Kill each other.'

With a shout, two guards turned to one another and plunged their blades into the other's stomach. Another shoved Forren out of the way to swing viciously at the other's head. The air sang with sparks as steel clashed against steel.

Drast stared in horror as his trained men destroyed themselves. One was pushed from the window. Another was sliced from balls to brain, spilling his guts over the floor. A severed hand landed at Drast's feet. In the chaos, Forren was shouting, but none heeded him.

Drast looked down at the steel in his hand. He had forgotten it was there. Krupal was watching, satisfaction spread across his face. Hardly daring to believe his own foolishness, Drast stepped towards him.

Krupal took no notice. Emboldened, Drast lunged. The magus's eyes flashed, and a guard's fist caught Drast in the side of the head.

Drast fell hard against the floor, the sword tumbling from his grasp. He whirled around, ready to pull his attacker down to the ground with him, but the dead-eyed guard only stood next to Krupal, daring Drast to try again. Across the room, Forren was trying to reach him, but a phalanx of four soldiers held him back. The rest lay on the ground with Drast, dead or dying.

Krupal shook his head. 'You men, who believe you can bend others to your will. You only rule because of the follies of my kind. When the sun rises and when it sets, you are all men, destined to serve the true masters: the magi.

'Krutan saw this. He was the greatest of his age; he worked in secret, rediscovering much of what was lost. I was his first; the first of a new breed who would re-establish dominion over man. Until they killed him.' His voice grew bitter. 'Until they killed all of them.

'I have learnt much from treading through your senators' minds. The Fourth Purge you call it, when the ungifted finally spilled all the magical blood left to you. And what has it got you?' He gestured to the window, towards Ulvatia. Out of the corner of his eye, Drast saw Forren still trying to break through the line of guards. 'A dying, decadent empire, of a dying, decadent people. I pity all of you.'

Drast scrabbled in his pocket for the bead, and the world exploded into fire.

CHAPTER 19

Orsian coughed himself awake, the taste of blood rich and metallic against his tongue. He retched, and spat a thick glob of it on the floor.

It was pitch dark, and his hands and feet were bound to a chair. He ran his tongue around his teeth, and was relieved to find them all still there. His jaw was throbbing.

Orsian struggled against his bindings, but the knots did not give a fraction of an inch, and his chair seemed to be bolted to the floor. He felt the rhythm of the water. The gentle lapping of waves against the hull suggested they were still at anchor.

He shook his head at his own stupidity. *Ranulf, from Merivale, to be wed to Helana.* He could not have given them a better clue to his identity if he had worn his father's banner.

A door creaked, and lamplight flooded the room. Orsian saw coils of rope, barrels stacked three-high, and moisture on the walls showing the waterline. He was in the hold, deep in the bowels of the *Jackdaw.*

The bobbing light approached him, held by a burly figure half-ensconced in shadow. 'You should have run when you had the chance.' Abner stepped into the light, holding a bowl of broth.

Orsian's dry laugh reawakened the pain in his jaw. 'I wasn't going to run! Honestly, I—'

'Nah, lad. You would have.' Abner placed the bowl on the floor and clapped him hard on the shoulder. 'Told you I can see a seafarer, but I can also see when someone's got other places they want to be, even if they can't admit it to themselves.' He pulled another chair from somewhere and sat opposite him, knee to knee. 'We're not going to harm you, Orsian. Not if your uncle plays fair.'

'The bruise on my jaw says different.' Orsian flexed his fingers, wishing he had a sword. Even a knife would do. 'So, what's the plan? Stroll into Piperskeep, present me to Hessian and expect a reward? Hessian will clap you in irons.'

'The captain's writing a letter to him as we speak. Then we're back out to sea. Bit earlier than planned, but needs must.'

'He won't pay. You don't know him.'

Abner grinned, a golden molar glinting in the lamplight. 'Aye, but I know you. Deny it all you want, but there's something tying you to Erland, and it ain't just that pretty girl, not that you'll be seeing her again any time soon by how she looked at you. Men run away to sea because they can't fucking stand their families, and it's clear you ain't one of them.' He shrugged. 'Maybe Hessian won't pay, but there's bound to be someone else rich who cares about you.'

'My brother hates me. Wouldn't give you two bits of flint.'

'That's brothers for you.' Abner thoughtfully curled a

finger through his beard. 'Truth is, there's others we reckon might buy you. There's a new kzar in the Imperium, and word is that Erland's on their shit list. Reckon they'd pay nicely for a king's nephew. Might even get a bidding war going; the captain would like that. We bear you no ill will. It's just business.'

Orsian laughed. 'Great, thanks for that.' He shook his bound wrists against the chair. 'Thank you, Abner, for kidnapping me, dragging me to sea, and now kidnapping me again so you can ransom me. I understand though, just business.' Strong as Abner was, Orsian was so furious with himself for trusting D'graw he reckoned he could have given the first mate a decent fight.

Abner's face darkened. 'Kidnapping, was it? You were just a scared lad, miles from home, in enemy territory. You wouldn't have survived a week. We gave you a home, lad. And if the Imperium buy you, you might just wish you'd stayed Ranulf of the *Jackdaw* for the rest of your days.'

Orsian bit down his temper. He could acknowledge a grain of truth in Abner's version, but no more than that. 'Fine. You did right by me, in your way. Will you let me out of these bindings once we're out at sea? Won't be as if I can run anywhere.'

'Aye, reckon that'll be fine.' Abner patted Orsian on the knee. 'We sail with the tide, around dawn. Once we're an hour offshore, the captain should let me release you. You're still popular among the men; they'd be glad to see you up and about. Once the ransom's paid, if you did decide you wanted back aboard the *Jackdaw*, you'd be welcomed back with open arms.'

Abner lifted the broth from the floor. 'This is your dinner. I'm not spoon-feeding you, so you'll just have to drink it down, I'm afraid.' He held it up and poured the lukewarm liquid slowly into Orsian's mouth.

He stood. 'I'll be back with your breakfast in the morning, and to untie you. If you need to make water in the night, I'm afraid you'll just have to piss yourself. Sorry, captain's orders.'

Orsian shook his head in disbelief as Abner departed. He had never held any illusions about the sort of people D'graw and Abner were, but he had considered them his friends. He had lied to them, but what person would have told the truth? This was where the truth had brought him. His head felt thick as mince, and his eyelids were growing heavy. His head drooped into his chest, and he fell back to sleep.

He woke groggily, with his mouth feeling like cotton, and a dull pain behind his eyes.

Drugged. Obviously. Captain D'graw did not trust him awake, even bolted to a chair in the ship's bowels. He had no idea what time it was, but no doubt he had lost precious hours in which to escape. He listened to the lapping of the waves. They were still at anchor, but he felt the stirring of life elsewhere on the ship. The crew were preparing to set sail.

He strained his arms against his bindings again. He tried rubbing the knots against themselves, but gave up quickly. It would have taken several days to fray such coarse rope. He slammed his weight one way, then the other. There was no give in the chair at all. Whoever had bolted it to the floor had known their business.

His ears pricked at the creak of a board somewhere behind him, so soft it might have been his imagination.

'Hello?'

If D'graw meant to kill him, Orsian was reasonably sure

he would have done it already. The creak must have been a natural movement of the wood.

Another creak. Closer this time. Orsian tried to crane his neck to catch a glimpse behind him. Not Abner, nor D'graw. Some pirate with a grudge?

'Hello,' came a small voice in front of his chair.

Esma was standing in front of him, looking immensely pleased with herself.

'Esma! You scared me half to death!' His voice echoed in the vast expanse of the ship's belly. He winced, and dropped his voice to a whisper. 'What are you doing here?'

'Rescuing you, silly.' She gleefully held up a serrated kitchen knife the length of her tiny forearm. 'Tansa sent me. They tried to send Pitt, but he didn't fit.'

Orsian was too surprised and grateful to question how she had got in, or the wisdom of Tansa's decision to allow it. It proved at least that Tansa was as good as her word, even if she did think him a liar. 'Can you cut through my bonds? Be careful.'

He winced at the cold steel on the inside of his wrist, but the knot split open and Orsian's hands were free. He rubbed them together and shook the feeling back into his fingers.

'Thanks. Give me the knife, I'll do my feet.' He freed himself fully and stood up. 'How do we get out of here?'

'I got in through a porthole.' Esma looked at him doubtfully. 'You won't fit though.'

'Is there a boat waiting?'

Esma nodded. 'A rowboat. Tansa's there, with Pitt and the big boy.'

'Did you come in port or starboard?'

Esma looked at him blankly, and pointed to the starboard side.

'Let's go.' He dropped to his haunches. 'Jump on my back.'

Esma looked at him like he had grown a second head. 'I can get myself out. You'll need to find your own way.' She placed her hands on her hips, daring him to contradict her. 'Tansa says get up on deck and swim to us before you're seen.' She did not bother to wait for his reply, just ran back the way she had come and slipped out the door without even waving to him.

Well, fair enough then. Orsian had seen soldiers with not one-quarter of Esma's bravery. She reminded him slightly of Pherri. If he made it out of this alive he swore he would buy her and Pitt as many pork pies as they desired.

Orsian found a water barrel and dunked his head. The drugged broth had left him groggy. He slapped his face and submerged himself a few more times for good measure. He was drenched when he finished, but he felt more prepared to take on the lower decks of the *Jackdaw* and fight his way free if he had to. First though he needed a weapon.

He walked as quickly as he dared, stopping at every corner, listening for the sound of footsteps. The cabin where the crew hung their hammocks was on the port side. He crept to the door, and placed his ear to the keyhole. At sea, there could be men sleeping here at all hours of the day, but he was hopeful that they would all be on deck getting ready to make sail. He turned the handle, and entered.

The cabin was empty. Orsian breathed a sigh of relief. He recognised his sea chest in the far corner, *Ranulf* carved into it in crude lettering. He found the key hidden under a loose plank and opened it. To his relief, his sword was still in there.

Orsian was so intent upon the sword that he only just heard the heavy rush of feet behind him.

He turned just in time. The sailor ran directly onto the point of his blade, and it pierced all the way through him.

Orsian wrenched the blade free as the man fell, ready to face a second assailant yards behind his dead friend. This one was considerably larger, and looking at Orsian with undisguised fear.

'Tunny, it's fine, I won't—'

Tunny Burntbacon took one look at the steel in Orsian's hand and ran for the door, hollering for help.

Orsian cursed, and sprinted back to the corridor, towards the ladder up to the deck. There was no sign of Tunny. His feet pounded against the wooden planks; every man aboard might have heard Tunny shouting, but if he was quick enough he could be over the rail before anyone knew where he was.

But the scene that greeted Orsian on deck as he reached the top of the steps was not two dozen sailors focused upon their work. They were on deck, ready and waiting for him, knives at the ready. Orsian looked around for some obvious weakness in their formation, but every route was blocked. He gripped his sword tighter.

The sound of slow clapping came from the quarterdeck. Orsian looked up, and there was the captain, majestic in his leather sea-coat and a tricorn hat.

'You have strange friends, Orsian,' said Captain D'graw, leaning over the upper rail. 'I'll give most men a chance, but I draw the line at bringing a five-year-old girl to sea.'

Abner stepped forward, carrying a thrashing Esma as easily as he might a coil of rope.

'I'm eight!' she yelled. 'Let me go!' Abner tried to cover

her mouth, and she bit down hard on his hand. The big sailor yelped, drawing unrestrained laughter from the crew.

'Such a spirited child. We wouldn't want anything to happen to her, would we Orsian?' D'graw smiled. 'Drop your sword down the hole.'

Orsian hesitated. He was vastly outnumbered, but he would have backed himself to at least kill a few of them, maybe even to forge a path to the rail. But the risk was not worth Esma's life. He dropped his sword back down the ladder.

The sailors moved in immediately, but this time he was ready for it. One of them threw a punch, but Orsian dodged it and moved to put the hole between himself and his assailant. *Just stay alive. Give Tansa a chance to come for you.*

'That's enough,' said D'graw, staring daggers at the man who had tried to strike him. He looked at Orsian. 'You cut Bernat's fingers off in Cliffark. You ever heard of a sailor who couldn't grasp a rope? He's itching to do the same to you.'

Orsian stared up at him. 'Reckon you should have let me go. Then Bernat might still have his fingers.'

'Never been an option. You were too good a sailor, and now you're too valuable a ransom.' He smiled wryly. 'I should have seen it from the first day: boy of your age, showing up on the beach after a battle, fancy sword and knowing how to use it... What could you have been apart from a lord's son?

'Abner persuaded me to be gentle with you, but your little escape attempt has changed my mind. You'll go in the hold again, with leftovers twice a day, and only the rats for company.

'And we can't forget your desertion. And you would have, don't even try to deny it. What was the punishment for desertion in your father's army? Not much left of it since he died, from what I hear.'

'Death,' said Orsian. 'Beheading.'

'And people say pirates are cruel.' Some of the sailors looked discomfited; a few even whispered a short prayer. 'I'm more civilised than that, fortunately for you.' D'graw stroked his chin. 'Twenty lashes. That ought to knock some of the pride out of you.'

Orsian swallowed. He had seen men take the lash when they were at sea, for minor misdemeanours like stealing from the hold or striking a fellow sailor without due cause. Abner wielded the whip, and even five lashes was enough to cut a man's back to ribbons and leave him screaming for his mother. Twenty could kill a man.

A dozen firm arms grabbed him and marched him towards the foremast. Three men grabbed him by each arm, pulling him so that his face was pressed up against the wood and bound his hands together the other side. His heart was hammering in his chest, the sweat already flowing.

I will not cry out. He gritted his teeth. A whip cracked twice behind him.

'Sorry, lad,' said Abner. 'Don't think I'll go easy on you.' He moved to where Orsian could see him, and removed his shirt. 'You can still see my scars,' he said, pointing to his back. 'Worst I ever took was twelve. It stung worse than a whore's tongue for two weeks, but I survived.'

'Did you thank the man for it afterwards?'

'I did. He was my father.' He cracked it once more to test it, splitting the air like a snapping dog. 'Taught me humility. Maybe if a few more lords took a whipping when they were young, the country wouldn't be in the state that it's in.'

He paced backwards, measuring out the distance. An

eerie quiet had descended over the crew. Even the waves seemed to have fallen silent. He tested it a few more times, cracking it within a few feet of Orsian's head.

Orsian clenched his teeth so hard they shook. *I will not scream.*

The lash came down, fast as lightning.

It burnt like hot iron against his spine. Tears welled in his eyes. But he did not cry out.

The whip cracked a second time. A grunt of pain escaped Orsian's lips. His shirt was already cut to ribbons. He felt the salty sting of sea air against his back.

A third time, and then a fourth so quickly afterwards he barely had the chance to feel it. His knees buckled. His face slid uncomfortably down the mast, but next to the pain in his back it was as gentle as a woman's kiss. Its sting was so sharp he would have sworn he was cut to the bone.

A fifth time. He felt his skin split, and finally he screamed.

Abner did not wait. Orsian's scream was cut short by the sixth lash, breaking a fresh laceration from left to right.

This will kill me. Surely this will kill me. He gritted his teeth for the seventh, willing himself not to scream for a second time. Somewhere, a thousand miles away, sailors were shouting. He heard the sharp song of steel being drawn; a memory of battle, when he had thought he knew what pain was.

The seventh lash never fell. Orsian's senses slowly returned, and he realised the sound of steel was not a feverish imagining. The sailors were not shouting at him, but at the blue-clad city guards who were streaming over the rail.

Orsian forced himself to his feet, and managed to turn and look at the chaos unfolding across the deck. The guards were clambering up from rowboats below. He watched as a sailor struck one flat in the face with an oar, and another broke a bucket over his foe's head, before being run through with a sword in retaliation. Had the sailors not been distracted by the spectacle of his whipping, they might have repelled the guards easily, but now there were over a dozen on deck, working together to protect the others as they clambered up.

D'graw was on the quarterdeck, bellowing orders and brandishing his sword wildly. Half the sailors were trying to stop the guards gaining a safe area in which to mass their troops, and the other half were streaming all over the place in search of weapons.

One man who was ready was Abner. His whip cracked, and two guardsmen fell, clutching their faces. Seeing the danger, one of their fellows aimed a crossbow. The bolt caught Abner in the shoulder just as he was pulling back for another lash. He fell back, whip flailing uselessly.

Orsian looked round in alarm as a figure appeared. To his relief, it was Tansa, with a knife that she immediately turned upon the rope tying him to the mast.

'Th-thank you,' he gasped.

'Thank me once we're out of here.' She pressed a sword into his hand. 'Can you walk?' She shoved an arm under his shoulder. She smelt of saltwater and firewood.

He felt a little unsteady, but nodded. 'Where's Esma?'

'Already got her.' She pointed to the starboard side, where Cag was clambering over the rail, Esma clinging to his shoulders.

Enough guards had now gained the deck to push the sailors back. D'graw had come down from the quarterdeck and forced his way to the front of the melee. His hat and clothes were askew, and there was a trail of blood running from a deep gash in his cheek, but he cut down two guards as quick as blinking. It seemed to give heart to the sailors, who pushed back in unison, trying to drive the soldiers back into the water.

Orsian realised something was burning, the thick smoke filling his nostrils. There were few things more feared aboard a ship than fire.

D'graw must have smelt it too, because suddenly he was pointing to the bow. 'Fire on the foredeck!' he cried. 'Water!'

Orsian looked behind him. Curling tendrils of smoke were floating from the *Jackdaw*, and growing larger.

'We need to leave,' said Tansa, pulling him towards the rail.

Orsian's legs did not want to do what he told them to. He stumbled, almost taking Tansa down with him. 'Why is there fire?' he asked weakly.

'I lit it. Wanted as many distractions as possible.' She shoved him over the rail. 'Climb down the ladder.'

Orsian did as she said, the wounds in his back protesting vehemently as he clung to the rungs. When he was three feet from the bottom, his legs gave out. He slipped and fell into Cag's arms.

Orsian was just awake enough to watch the *Jackdaw* burning as they rowed away. Blue-clad guards and mismatched sailors were leaping into the sea as fire fed its way along the deck. As he slipped from consciousness, he swore he could see two figures working tirelessly to stem the flames. One wore a fine tricorn hat, and the other was shirtless, and built like a bull.

CHAPTER 20

Despite Theodric's vehement protests, Delara joined their travelling band, at Pherri's urging.

'She saved me from those men,' Pherri had insisted, during the aftermath of Delara's shadowbear sending the bandits running, after Theodric had threatened the Lutum woman with all manner of magical injury. 'If she meant me harm, why would she have interfered?'

'She tried to poison you, Pherri!' Theodric's fierce scowl had not moved from Delara. 'Who knows what she's planning? If she means no harm, why is she skulking around in the shadows following us?'

'To stop you reacting like this, wizard.' Delara croaked a contemptuous laugh. 'If anything, you're following me; the Mountain is my home, remember? Pherri has nothing to fear from me. If she wishes to do magic, she can live with the consequences.'

'See?' said Pherri. She had enjoyed having the Lutum woman as her tutor, despite her belligerent approach. 'It did no harm in the end; you said so yourself.'

'Pherri.' Theodric spoke through gritted teeth. 'Might we speak alone a moment?'

Delara had waved them off, with a promise to remain just where she was, and Pherri retreated into the trees with Theodric.

'Are you mad?' demanded Theodric. 'Not only did she try to deaden you to magic with bogroot, but you said you saw a connection between her and one of the powers on Eryispek! She isn't trustworthy.'

Pherri remembered well what she had seen, the imperceptible thread that linked Delara to the power that named itself Vulgatypha. 'But you've said yourself we don't know what's working against us. Delara might not even know about the connection. What better way to deduce what's going on than by watching someone we know is linked to it?'

In the end, Theodric had relented. Pherri had known his curiosity would eventually outweigh his distrust, and so it came to pass that Delara joined their party.

With that settled, Pherri had expected to play peacemaker between Delara and Theodric all the way to Eryispek. Instead, however, the two of them fell into a silent routine. Theodric barely spoke while they walked, focused upon the *inflika* that kept them from others' sight, and Delara seemed content to ignore them both. In the evenings, they shared a fire, where Delara and Theodric studiously ignored one another.

Delara joining them had at least improved the food on offer. She had a short bow with her, and on their second afternoon together journeyed into the woods. She returned with a pair of rabbits, which she skinned and cooked herself.

'Lutums eat what's on offer,' she told them. 'I've shot

snakes and mice and even the odd lizard; rabbits are easy by comparison.' Even Theodric was grateful.

Some days later, the grass thinned to wet mud, and the chill winds from Eryispek began to rain powdery snowflakes down upon them, melting on Pherri's pink cheeks. Every day it began to feel a little less like summer.

'How many days to go?' Pherri asked when they made camp for the night. Their fire was pitifully small, and all Delara had been able to find was a single stringy vole for them to share.

Delara shrugged. 'A few. Are you sure about Fisherton? They're more fish than man. They sell their daughters to mermen in exchange for treasures from the depths of the lake.' The old woman spoke through chattering teeth, huddled under several layers of fur. 'Damn these old bones. Only savages would live somewhere with so little of the sun's warmth.'

'You should enjoy such talk while you can,' said Theodric to Delara. 'They won't take kindly to it in Fisherton.'

Delara snorted. 'Don't I know it, wizard. I'll keep my own counsel once we're there, have no fear.'

'Why do you do that?' asked Pherri. 'Call him *wizard*, like it's an insult.'

'Because that's what he is.'

'Then what are you?'

'The sort who's had their life ruined by folk like him. Running about convinced that magic means they have some wisdom that eludes other folk and they've the right to determine who sits upon this throne or that throne. I've met a few others with magic in my life, and the one thing they had in common was wanting a quiet life.' She prodded the fire with a stick, making the sparks dance. 'But that would never have suited Theodric the Wise, the king's closest confidante, the bogeyman who keeps Erland under his bootheel.'

Theodric's face reddened slightly. 'You don't know the first thing about me. Nobody handed me power on a silver platter. My birth was as low as any man's.'

'And you're lucky for that. As soon as my family learnt what I was, I was no longer a person, just a beast of burden to be yoked.'

'So it's my fault your family mistreated you? If I held a grudge for every kicking I took when I was making my way up in the world, I'd be the most vengeful man alive. You're an old woman. Let it go.' He got to his feet. 'Pherri, I thought we might practise some magic this evening, if you have the energy.'

Pherri leapt up; she felt no worse the wear from healing the boy's ankle now. Even if what Delara said was true, what better way for Pherri to prevent people trying to misuse her than becoming as powerful as Theodric? They departed, leaving Delara alone by the fire.

'Mad old woman,' grumbled Theodric as they walked. 'We've learnt nothing from her so far.'

'She only wants to protect me,' said Pherri. 'There's nothing to indicate she knows anything of Vulgatypha.' The unfamiliar name felt strange on her tongue, like her mouth was made of bark.

'She's lied before. If she were not such a useful hunter, I would leave her behind.'

Theodric led them far from the camp, away from the other pilgrims to a small hill, with fair visibility in every direction. Ethereal snowflakes danced under the moonlight.

'I am anxious for news of the war, and Piperskeep,' said Theodric. 'I am going to try speaking with Georald.'

'With Georald?' Theodric's nervous assistant was miles away, back inside Piperskeep. He supposedly had some small skill in magic, though Pherri had never seen it.

Theodric smiled. 'Weakened as my *spectika* is, I am sure I can find another magus, particularly one so known to me. He has a presence. Not much of one, but enough, I think.' He sat down and closed his eyes. 'This will be a good lesson for you. Tell me what you remember of Georald.'

Pherri thought. 'He's kind. But nervous. He has a squished face and grey hair.'

Theodric grunted approvingly. 'Focus on your image of him, and try to channel it to me. It will improve my own recollection of him.'

Pherri held tight to her memory of Georald. Theodric had told her of magi being able to speak to each other across vast distances, using a combination of *shadika* and *spectika* to create a proxy of the person they sought to speak with. She felt Theodric's own vision of Georald, which he twisted up with Pherri's own, and the twin images vibrated as Theodric threaded them together and poured them into the air.

Slowly, Theodric's projection began to gain features. Pherri stared open-mouthed as the body sprouted ears and a nose, and eventually long grey hair.

Theodric cut the link between him and Pherri, and a spectral Georald sat in front of them, his robes shining like icicles under the moonlight.

'Oh,' he said, worriedly. 'This is interesting.' If Pherri squinted, she could see Theodric's rooms in Piperskeep behind him.

'Never mind interesting,' said Theodric. 'I want to make

this quick. What news of the war? And what of the king? Is he well? Is the child born?'

The apparition blinked. 'A healthy boy,' said Georald, as proud as if he had sired the child himself. 'Where are you?'

'Approaching Fisherton. What other news is there?'

'Oh.' Georald smiled brightly. 'They'll be so relieved! Lady Viratia returned over a week ago, and was most distraught to find you both gone. She's coming to find you, and the king! They've already left, but I'm sure if I send a rider to tell them—'

'You'll do no such thing.' Theodric knotted his brows. 'We require the utmost secrecy.'

Pherri had to resist the urge to cry out and speak to Georald herself. What did he mean, her mother was coming?

Georald's spectral smile faltered. 'But I promised Lady Viratia! If I—'

The connection from Theodric to Georald tremored, and the ground beneath them shook violently for several seconds. Pherri stumbled and had to grab Theodric to stop herself falling.

'What was that?' asked Georald.

Behind Georald, a shadow rose. A silhouette, with pale blue eyes bright as the dawn, holding a blade spun from darkness. The shadow seized Georald by the neck, and drew the edge across his throat.

'Georald!' screamed Pherri. She made to leap towards the shadow, but Theodric grabbed her by the hair, pulling her back.

Ghostly black blood flowed from Georald's neck in a torrent, his mouth wide and terrified. He gave them a final pleading look, before his image began to spasm and distort, and across the miles that separated them Pherri felt the life leave him. Theodric's connection to him flickered, and died.

It was like a candle going out. Pherri and Theodric were suddenly alone, in the dark, the snow falling thicker than ever, so heavy they could barely see.

CHAPTER 21

A clamorous banging shocked Ciera from her slumber, so heavy and insistent that the door rattled in its frame as if it might burst open any moment. In the cot beside her, Andrick stirred and began to cry.

Ciera was on her feet in an instant, seizing Andrick and rocking him with soothing words, her heart pounding. There were three *hymerikai* outside her door; who would be bold enough to stride past them and begin hammering upon her door? Assassins did not announce their arrival, nor did they come by day, and soft morning light was already floating through the window. There was some mistake; perhaps she had somehow slept through the calls to open?

'I'm coming!' She pulled down her nightdress, and put Andrick to her breast. There would be no surer way to embarrass the would-be entrant than the risk of seeing the queen's naked nipple. She opened the door, and recoiled as Lord Balyard's fleshy face gawped down at her. He shoved his way in, forcing Ciera to take several fearful steps back. Four *hymerikai* with Lord Gurathet followed Balyard inside, and behind them Mortha with the two wet nurses, and most surprisingly of all, Princess Tarvana, whose eyes were puffy as though she had been weeping.

'What is the matter?' asked Ciera. She held Andrick to her more tightly. 'Has something happened?'

Lord Balyard looked at her, and then with a grimace averted his eyes. 'Would somebody cover her please? This is unseemly.'

'To be fair to the girl, we have just barged into her room,' chuckled Lord Gurathet. 'Let the women sort her out. Go on.' With another laugh, he urged the younger wet nurse forward, and Mortha advanced with her.

'I can cover myself,' said Ciera, trying to sound braver than she felt. She pulled her shawl tightly around herself and Andrick, and backed away from Mortha, putting the cot between them. 'Now will somebody please tell me what is going on?' She could not help the note of hysteria that crept into her voice. 'Where are my guards?'

'I sent them away,' said Gurathet. 'The man Laphor was most reluctant. He should have more respect for his *balhymeri*.'

'We're here for you,' said Lord Balyard. 'We have indulged your peasantly desire to stay with your child for too long. Now hand over the prince before I order him taken from you.'

'What?' Ciera swore her heart nearly stopped, and as she hesitated Mortha tried to snatch Andrick from her. Ciera stepped away, almost stumbling, and Andrick began to cry. 'No! I command you to stop!' Her pleas fell on deaf ears, and the two wet nurses came at her from the other side, trying to pin her in behind the crib.

'I command here,' shouted Lord Balyard, a red flush rising upon his face. 'Seize the child!'

'Eryi's blood, Balyard, calm down,' said Gurathet. 'There's no need to frighten the poor girl.'

'What is going on, Lord Gurathet?' asked Ciera. She was panicking now, edging backwards to distance herself from Mortha's grasping hands.

Gurathet scratched his neck, and when he spoke he did not meet Ciera's eye, preferring to keep his gaze fixed at a spot on the wall. 'Lord Balyard and I have reached an agreement. The prince will be taken into his custody, and you are removed from the council. It's what's best for the kingdom.'

For a moment, Ciera did not understand. Then she saw the look that passed from Balyard to Gurathet. 'You did this for land, didn't you?' She stared at Gurathet, barely believing it. 'Just how many hectares did he offer you?'

Balyard laughed, savouring Ciera's rage. 'Lord Gurathet gave me a most generous price.'

Gurathet reddened. 'Do you know how much land *six* sons require? I offered you the chance to sell me yours, and you balked.' He reached into his sleeve for a handkerchief to wipe the sweat from his forehead.

'You don't need to justify yourself to her,' said Balyard. 'She slew the wizard, need I remind you, and no doubt has committed no end of other wicked crimes.'

'I did what?' demanded Ciera. 'Who—?'

'Don't even try to deny it. You knew I could use the magus to contact the king and tell him of your treachery. You had him killed, didn't you? Georald was found dead in his room with his throat cut. No one but you had any cause.'

The idea was so absurd that Ciera barely considered it worthy of a response. She gave a laugh, and then stepped quickly away from Mortha as the Eryi-forsaken woman made a grab for Andrick, who was still crying. The wet nurses were coming at her from the other side, the three of them trying to trap her. She looked around for something to defend herself, anything, but she was completely cut off with the women closing in on her. 'Lord Gurathet, you cannot believe this!'

The lord shrugged his broad shoulders as if the matter was beyond his control. 'There'll be an investigation, but it's best you aren't on the council while it's happening. You can stay in your own rooms. You'll have every comfort. I'm sorry.'

'Liar!' spat Ciera. There were tears welling in her eyes. She had misjudged Gurathet utterly, though he at least had the grace to look ashamed. 'You don't believe that!'

'You can see why I came to you, Lord. The girl is half-mad,' said Mortha. She had closed the gap as Ciera was forced into a corner, and extended her arms towards Andrick. 'A queen sleeping in the nursery, and feeding a prince from her own breast? I've never heard the like.'

'Be quiet,' snapped Balyard. 'Just get the prince.' He looked at Ciera, now as far away as she could get from him. She was still cradling Andrick, who was bawling so loud that they were all having to shout to be heard.

'You can't do this,' said Ciera desperately. 'I command the *Hymeriker* in the name of my son, Andrick Sangreal, of the Blood, to stop this!'

'You think you're so clever, don't you?' sneered Balyard. 'So special, and all because the blood of the Meridivals supposedly runs in your son's veins. You had no business being on my regency council. Your commands are meaning-less. Gurathet is *balhymeri* and he stands with me on this. Anyway, I have my own Sangreal.' He looked to Tarvana, whose tears were flowing in rivulets down her cheeks. 'Tarvana, as we discussed.'

Ciera knew she must look awful, pale and terrified, with her hair all over the place and still wearing her nightgown, but Tarvana likely looked worse. There were heavy bags under her swollen eyes, and her lower lip was trembling. She said something to one of the *hymerikai*, too quietly for anyone to hear, barely daring to look at him.

Balyard's voice cracked like a whip. 'Speak up, wife!'

Tarvana looked to him fearfully. 'Take the prince into custody,' she said, more loudly. She looked to the four *hymerikai*. 'Take the prince.'

'Is this what it's come to?' asked Ciera. 'The last time Sangreals gave opposing orders to the *Hymeriker* it plunged East Erland into civil war.' The Grandsons' War, when three descendants of King Piper had each sought to claim the crown. 'Is that what you want?' Tarvana would not even look at her.

Lord Balyard was smiling. 'You heard her. Take the queen to her chamber and keep her there. Bring the prince to me.'

For a moment, none of them moved, until Lord Balyard gave a sharp look towards his wife. 'Do as my husband commands,' Tarvana said quietly, keeping her eyes fixed on the floor.

The four warriors advanced. Ciera shrieked, stumbling backwards, clutching Andrick to her chest. He was bawling fit to burst, his face red and scrunched, his mouth a bottomless black maw. Ciera's back collided with the wall, and she slid down to the floor, weeping uncontrollably along with Andrick. She would make them kill her before she let them separate her from her son.

The *hymerikai*, however, were obviously reluctant to lay their hands on her, or Andrick. One of them awkwardly tried to prise him away, but the babe screamed louder than ever, and the warrior flinched as if he had been burnt. 'She won't give us him, Lord,' he said foolishly, looking back towards Balyard.

'Oh, Eryi's blood, stand aside.' Mortha pushed past him, and Ciera cried out as Mortha slapped her with such force that it set her ears ringing. 'Give him to me!'

Her intervention emboldened the guards, and between the five of them they wrenched Andrick from Ciera's grip. Mortha held the squalling babe triumphantly, as Ciera folded to the floor, sobbing as if they had ripped her heart from her chest.

'Get her out of here,' said a voice a thousand miles away. A pair of strong hands lifted her, and as she was carried away, Ciera reached helplessly for her child, feeling as if her whole world was collapsing beneath her feet.

CHAPTER 22

The jetty was ancient and rotten, with wild moss growing on the poles that held it above the waterline. It was barely larger than the barge they travelled on, but when the captain flung a line around the cleat it held fast, though the Little River threatened to drag it downstream and the jetty along with them. It was past midnight, and through the darkness snowflakes glowed in the moonlight as they spiralled down from Eryispek before disappearing into the river.

Viratia stepped over the rushing water and onto the landing. The Little River ran dangerously fast. If you fell overboard, your corpse would wash up over the falls in Eryispool before anyone even thought to look for you. The upside of this was that travelling by barge they had reduced a journey that might have taken over a week on horseback to only a few days.

Not that we got here any quicker. Viratia turned to watch the rest of them come ashore. They had spent a week waiting for Hessian to ready himself for the pilgrimage he had promised Sister Velna, days Viratia had spent pacing the floor, worrying about how she would find Pherri and trying to care for Errian.

It had pained her to leave her eldest child again. When she had left for war in the spring, Errian's drinking spree had been less than two weeks old. Longer than it ought to have been, but less than many. Rymond Prindian's father might have called that breakfast. On their return, Viratia had expected to find Errian itching to return to war.

But Errian had still been in bed, in a miserable below-stairs room littered with wine bottles, with vomit in his tangled beard and his blond hair hanging in greasy strands about his face. He still had his youth, but his once chiselled body was beginning to soften, with a pot belly rolling over his waistband.

It was not something Viratia had been prepared to stand for. She had sent for a half-dozen pails of water, and thrown them over him one by one.

'Whatwa'tha' for?' he slurred, looking at least awake, if not yet sober.

'For the three months I have spent at war, while you sat here drinking yourself to an early grave. Did your father raise a man, or a coward?'

She had hoped that might sting Errian's famous pride, but instead he buried his face in his hands and wept, like the child he had once been. 'I killed him. He died because of me.' He reached for the bottle of wine on his nightstand, before Viratia swept it away from him.

He had been confined to his rooms, once they had been cleaned, while she figured out what to do with him. Any servant caught giving him wine or anything else was to be flogged, and no one was permitted to visit him.

And now Viratia had left him again, and who could say

what state he would be in when she returned? It pained her, but she had no choice. Pherri was her youngest, and, if Georald's suspicions were correct, Theodric was dragging her into something dangerous beyond any of their understanding. Viratia knew little of magic, but if there was something on Eryispek that had spurred Theodric to go in person then it was not to be trifled with. That did not though give him the right to pull her daughter into it, magus or not.

I should never have left her. Viratia carried the guilt like a yoke around her neck. She had given Pherri over to Theodric because she knew the frustration of feeling shaped by others into something you were not. She had never expected it to lead to this.

Viratia had been ready to ride for Eryispek the same day she had learnt of their departure. With a small guard and spare horses she might have made it to Fisherton already.

The mistake had been waiting for Hessian. Once it had become clear that the elder bride intended to hold him steadfastly to his oath, he had insisted they travel together. 'Don't be foolish,' he had told her. 'You will travel with me, by barge. It has been a decade since I set foot on the thing, but I am assured that it is still river-worthy.' He had then spent a week arranging his regency council and other affairs, and then cost them another half-day by insisting upon travelling to their embarkation point on the Little River separately, along some ancient Sangreal escape tunnel that ran out of Piperskeep instead of riding through the city.

Hessian followed Viratia off the barge with an escort of a dozen young *hymerikai*, and two pack mules bearing their supplies. The king had asserted he would travel only with the warriors he considered loyal, those who had sworn their vows recently and not gone to war with Viratia. The sure-footed mules had fared better than most of them on their journey, seemingly content wherever they were left provided they were fed hay three times a day.

Naeem came next on shaky legs, green and queasy. Viratia had taken him into her service as soon as she could find him after Hessian's dismissal. Men such as Naeem were not made for hanging up their swords to rust, and he had been a *hymerika* for more than half his life. He had lost his breakfast over the side of the barge several times, and his attempts to cure himself with drinking had only made matters worse. When he stepped off the jetty and felt solid ground under his feet, he fell to his knees. 'Blessed Erlish soil,' he said, kissing the wet ground. 'I shall never set foot outside you again as long as I live.'

Viratia had hoped Yriella Gough might join their expedition, but she had insisted she must return to Tarrowton. After Naeem came Velna, leading two much younger Brides of Eryi. All three bore long wooden staffs, though how much use they would be if their band encountered trouble Viratia was not sure. The youngest of them, Sister Aimya, assured Viratia she was seventeen, though she was slender as a reed and barely a finger over five feet tall. She had been better company than Sister Velna on their river voyage at least, with all the easy confidence of youth in her favour. As tiresome as Viratia found the elder bride's devotion, she was glad of their presence; Velna meant to continue up Eryispek as far as they were able in proof of her faith, so if Hessian and his guards turned back before Viratia rescued Pherri, the brides would be their only allies.

It had been two days here from Merivale, and Viratia would be content to make the return journey by horse if it meant never again having to be in such close confines with so many people. Between the smell of the pack mules and the shouts of the young *hymerikai* playing dice, Viratia had longed for the relative peace of a war camp.

Before them, a dark dirt path led onward, crowded by wild woodland on either side and with Eryispek looming ahead like a great curtain drawn across the sky. The silver-white moon was bright, illuminating the dark dense pine forests that grew up against its gentler lower reaches, before giving way to mist and spectral snow as it reached into the clouds and beyond. Just looking at it was enough to make Viratia feel dizzy.

'I mislike this,' Naeem murmured next to her, looking towards their path. 'There could be all manner of evil in these woods. I'd sell my boots for a swift horse.'

'There are eighteen of us,' said Viratia. 'Could a troop of brigands trouble us?'

'It's not brigands I'm worried about. There are parts of this country that have never felt a man's eye upon them. Who can say what beasts hide in the darkness?'

'Are you scared of the wood nymphs?' asked Aimya with laugh. Viratia noted how quickly she had detached herself from Sister Velna to join them. 'Where I grew up in the marshes, we feared the water nymphs. I expect you'll be safe; they only take the young and beautiful.'

Naeem laughed with her, but his words had already dampened the spirits of the party. Viratia saw several *hymerikai* casting nervous glances into the woods, and their hands grasping for their swords at every sound.

'Waiting for daylight won't make this any quicker,' barked Hessian. 'The sooner I lay a foot upon the Mountain the sooner I can go home and deal with the Prindians. Stop dickering and move, before I leave you all behind.'

The king's outburst settled matters. They would walk through the night, guided by the torches borne by Hessian's *hymerikai*.

Hessian rode upon one of the pack mules. He had bullied his horsemaster into forcing a mount aboard the barge with them, but the animal had gone wild, and the captain had been adamant that he would not sail with it aboard. It looked terribly awkward, Hessian's long legs hanging either side of the mule, but the beast bore him without complaint.

As they walked, Viratia found herself as disquieted by the forest as Naeem. The trees seemed to lean in on them, reducing the sky to a thin strip of moonlight, illuminating their party like a beacon amidst the shadowed greenwood. The mountain wind shook the trees, and the rustling leaves and creaking branches seemed almost as if they were talking to each other. Every so often, she swore she could hear voices of men on the breeze, but when she peered blindly into the darkness she saw nothing.

'I hear them too,' murmured Naeem, fingering his sword hilt. 'There's something out there, and nothing friendly.'

'Be quiet,' hissed Aimya. 'The only thing out there is wolves, and they won't trouble this many. Just because you're scared of the dark is no reason to scare the rest of us.' Several of Hessian's young guards had stopped, raising their torches towards the forest and casting strange shadows. 'There's nothing out there.'

An owl flew over them hooting, and Aimya almost leapt out of her skin, spinning her staff in a full circle before she came to her senses.

'Bloody owl,' she muttered, blushing.

Naeem chuckled darkly. '"There's nothing out there," she says. You'll learn, girl. There's nothing *nothing* about a forest this close to Eryispek. It has an evil feel to it. I'll be a happier man when I feel the sun's light on me again.'

They walked on in silence. A *hymerika* began to sing 'King Piper's Glory' in a halting tenor, until a dark look from Naeem quieted him. Viratia would have welcomed something to her ears other than the wind through the trees, and the boy had a pleasant voice.

'We should sing of the glory of Eryi,' said Sister Laurane, a plump, rosy-faced young woman. 'No evil in this forest would dare stand before the light and wisdom of Eryi.'

Sister Velna cuffed the girl on the back of the head. 'Foolish child. Song does not keep evil out, deeds do. That is the whole reason for this journey. Do you think we would make pilgrimage if songs alone could prove our faith?'

'No, Sister,' said the girl quietly, biting her lip.

'Good. Don't make me regret bringing you.'

Viratia shook her head. She had never loved the Brides of Eryi, nor understood the regard in which they were held by some. There was comfort to be had in the quiet dignity and good humour of priests, but none from these joyless harridans. No wonder Aimya preferred to walk with her and Naeem. Sending Viratia to the brides had been a common threat of her father when she misbehaved. Perhaps Aimya's father had done the same and followed through with it.

'How many *hymerikai* did we set out with?' asked Aimya. 'Twelve?'

'Aye, twelve,' said Naeem, still casting glances about the forest. 'Why do you ask?'

'Two of them are missing.'

All three of them looked back and forward, counting. Aimya was right: of the twelve men and six torches, only ten and five remained. Viratia's heartbeat quickened. How long had they been gone?

The wind seemed to rise around them, deafening Viratia's senses. She reached for the knife she carried against her leg. Naeem moved to place himself between Viratia and the forest, while Aimya did the same on the other side. 'Swords!' cried Naeem, drawing his blade. 'Protect your king!'

Four guards immediately drew their blades and surrounded Hessian, but the other six only stared at Naeem in wide-eyed panic.

For a moment, the wind died, and Viratia heard running feet. The dark silhouettes of men appeared against the trees, dozens of them, with axes and cudgels and spears.

Naeem's blade flashed, and warm blood splattered against Viratia's face. A ragged man collapsed before her, with a gaping wound in his throat. The tip of Naeem's sword was grisly with blood and flesh. Viratia had not even seen him approach.

The rest came running from the forest, shrieking with fearless bestial cries. Some wore armour and the tattered uniforms of lords they had once served, others were garbed in thick animal skins. Viratia kept herself low and close to Naeem, her long knife clutched in her fist. In all her months at war, she had never been so close to combat without a wall of armoured men to protect her.

Viratia looked for Hessian. He was still atop his mule, and had grabbed a spear from somewhere, wielding it with some skill to hold back the mob of bandits that had surrounded him and the young *hymerikai*. They seemed to be holding their ground, letting their attackers come to them and manfully deflecting their wild blows while finding flesh with each of their own strikes.

Some of their fellows were not so lucky. Viratia shouted a warning as a former soldier in a spiked helm crept behind a hard-pressed *hymerika* and buried an axe in his spine. Velna's staff spun, sweeping the attacker's feet from under him, before a *hymerika* stuck a dagger in his eye. Another *hymerika* collapsed shrieking as a fur-clad man wrapped around his shoulders with his teeth buried in his neck before two more rushed in to club him to death with their cudgels. Nearby, Aimya was holding off four of them by herself, leaping past their attacks and whipping her staff around weightlessly, sending them sprawling backwards with precise blows to the jaw and groin.

Viratia only just heard Naeem's warning as one of them slipped past him. She acted on instinct, and with a wild stab buried her knife in the man's chest. He fell backwards, the axe raised over his head slipping from his lifeless fingers.

Viratia stared down at the man's corpse. He was gaunt to the bone, the shape of his skull visible under his tight grey skin. His furs were soiled and threadbare. Viratia shuddered. *If he had been armoured, I would likely be dead.*

A pair of armour-clad assailants lurched towards them, and Viratia backed away behind Naeem, clutching her dagger. Naeem easily parried an axe, before slipping inside the man's guard to grasp him from behind and pull back his head to open his throat. As the other moved towards Viratia, Aimya appeared from the darkness, and with a vicious two-handed blow of her staff caved his head in from behind with a sickening crunch of bone.

'The last bastard almost got me,' she said with a grimace, wiping her hand against the side of her head and pulling it away bloody. There was a shallow cut under her ear.

'Think that's all of them,' said Naeem.

Viratia looked around. He was right. Only one attacker still lived, and not for much longer, dying noisily on the ground from the wound in his belly. One of Hessian's guards silenced him with a thrust to the heart.

It had felt like hundreds when they had come screaming out of the trees, but there were not even three dozen of them, and each of them as lean and hollow-cheeked as the next, with dark sunken eyes and ribs protruding like overground tree roots.

'They had us two-to-one.' Naeem rolled over a corpse with the toe of his boot. 'If they'd come at us together instead of running at us in twos and threes they'd have given us something to worry about.'

Their own losses were not insignificant. Three of Hessian's guards lay dead, and Sister Laurane had taken a deep axe wound to the thigh which Velna was tying a tourniquet around. There was no sign of the two *hymerikai* who had gone missing, but the seven who lived had barely taken a scratch between them, and were staring pale-faced at the corpses they had made, both proud and repulsed. They were too young to have seen true combat before. Hessian was of course fine, though he was breathing heavily and no less pale than his guards; even in his youth he had not been a warrior.

'Stop staring and make yourself useful!' Velna snapped at the soldiers. 'Get Sister Laurane up onto that mule. You as well, Aimya!' They jumped to obey.

'What happened to Ed and Sim?' asked a *hymerika*.

'I'll double back and check.' Naeem snatched an unlit torch from the ground and lit it from another. 'Let's hope the poor bastards only got lost.'

Viratia doubted it. She looked about their victims, avoiding the lifeless eyes of the one she had killed. She had once asked Andrick about the men he had slain. He said that he did not regret a single death, but that their faces haunted his dreams even so. She prayed that she would not see her own attacker's face when she slept tonight, with his gaunt cheeks and deep-sunken eyes.

'Well, I found one of them.' Naeem had returned sooner than she had expected. 'What's left of him.' He threw down a hand, bleeding and ragged where it had been torn from the arm. 'Wolves have been at him.'

'Wolves?' laughed Hessian. 'Wolves don't sneak up like thieves and take people without making a sound. Perhaps those men ate him; they looked starved enough.'

As if in answer, something howled behind them, deep and dark enough to run the blood cold. A dozen other cries answered, all around them. The night came alive with the baying of wolves, hungry for prey.

CHAPTER 23

'Show yourself!' demanded Theodric. He whirled on the spot where they had watched Georald die, a bright light emanating from his hand, melting the snowflakes.

There was no answer. The only sounds were the patter of snowfall and the whispering wind.

Pherri shivered. It had grown very cold suddenly. Her tears were freezing on her cheeks.

'We need to move,' said Theodric. He rubbed his face in frustration. 'That was a mistake. A huge mistake.' He suddenly grasped Pherri by the front of her furs. 'If that happens again, you run. You run and you don't look back for me.'

Pherri fought to hold back the tears welling behind her eyes.

'Come on.' Theodric grabbed her hand and hurried back towards the camp.

Pherri could barely see through her tears and the swirling snow, but Theodric did not slow, not until the dozens of fires around which the pilgrims gathered came into view.

'I think we're safe,' he said, without much certainty.

'Is Georald...?'

'Dead? Yes.' Theodric rubbed his pale face. 'I should not have done that. So much risk, for so little gain.' His eyes were bloodshot. 'Was that the figure from your dreams?'

Pherri shivered. 'Yes. The pale-eyed man.' She wrapped her arms tightly around herself. 'Why would he kill Georald?' An idea ignited in Pherri's head like oil to a flame. 'It killed him so he couldn't tell my mother where we are! He wants us to come to him!'

'Could be all sorts of reasons,' said Theodric, eerily calm once more. 'Might have been a warning, or it might have been to stop us communicating with Piperskeep.' He stroked his chin thoughtfully. 'Come on. I'll think while we walk.'

He did not speak again for a long while, not even once they were back at their fire. Delara had gone to sleep, and the flames had burnt low. Theodric sat, silently and slowly adding wood to it.

Pherri waited, squinting into the darkness at every disturbance. A pack of wolves howled in the distance, making her jump. A shadow passed across her, and her veins ran with fear before she realised it was only a man on his way to make water.

It felt like hours, but finally Theodric spoke. 'Either this pale-eyed man wants to scare us away, or he wants us to come to him.'

'If he wants us to stay away, why not kill us?' asked Pherri. She had never seen anyone die before. It had happened many tens of miles away, but it had felt as real as if it had happened in front of her. She imagined Georald, silent upon the old stones of Piperskeep. Would anybody realise he was gone? Or would he lie there for days, food for the castle mice, until somebody noticed the smell and grew brave enough to enter Theodric's rooms?

'I don't know.' Theodric poked at the fire with a stick. 'We are travelling blind, towards an enemy we are not even sure the name of. And my allies are a girl of twelve, and an old woman who hates me even more than she hates herself.' He shook his head. 'I should never have involved you with this. Because of your talent and intelligence sometimes I forget how young you are. The best thing I could do would be to go back the way we came, return you to your mother and beg her forgiveness.'

'But you won't,' said Pherri, with more confidence than she felt. She had started them on this journey, and she meant to be there for the end as well. He could not send her home, not so close to Eryispek. 'He said that my mother was coming. With the king.' Pherri bit her lip. If her mother caught them she would be dragged back to Violet Hall.

'They are likely many days behind us, even travelling on the king's best horses. Depending on what we learn in Fisherton, we could be halfway up Eryispek before they reach where we are now.' Somewhere in the trees an owl hooted. 'And we are leaving now. I mean to be in Fisherton by morning.'

'I thought we were still days away?'

'At this pace. But the enemy has seen us now, if he had not already. We have no hope of secrecy, so we shall have speed. Wake Delara.'

Moving silently, Theodric departed towards where the Brides of Eryi had made camp. As night drew in, the fires around them had begun to dim as pilgrims made for their beds. Pherri shook Delara, and she opened her eyes immediately, as if she had been only feigning sleep.

'We are leaving then?' Delara cackled. 'What did the wizard do?'

Theodric returned, leading three tethered horses, by which time a deep darkness had descended over the sprawling camp. He raised a finger to his lips, and led Pherri to the smallest, a white pony. Delara grumbled, and refused Theodric's offer of assistance onto her mount, pulling herself up by the saddle. Pherri held her breath as they rode through the camp, expecting someone to cry out at any moment, but whether due to the hour or by some magic of Theodric's no one stirred.

They were many miles away before one of them finally spoke. 'A thief as well,' said Delara. 'Is there no end to your talents?'

'Be thankful that I didn't leave you behind.'

Delara snorted. 'I won't be thanking you if they catch us and we have to fight off those angry shrews.'

'They won't catch us. I scattered the other three; they'll spend the whole morning rounding them up again.'

Some hours later, as they crested a forested ridge and the sky began to turn from black to violet, Fisherton appeared in a depression below them. The town was arranged in concentric circles around an imposing stone marker, next to a post with several signs pointing in all directions. By a covered paddock of mules, a dirt road led north into Eryispek's foothills, weaving towards the great lake of Eryispool. Every house was built in wood, and despite the hour smoke still rose from several chimneys. By the shadows moving in the dim light of the long building on the opposite side of the square, the town's inn was beginning to stir with the dawn.

'We'll head down,' said Theodric. 'Hopefully the inn has rooms.'

They dismounted, and with slaps to their rumps Theodric sent the horses back the direction they had come from. 'No sense in keeping them,' he said. 'They won't fare well once we reach Eryispek.'

They began their walk down the slope, Pherri in between Theodric and Delara. Pherri raised her hand to her mouth to stifle a yawn. Their midnight ride was beginning to catch up with her. She only hoped that in a soft bed she would not dream of Georald's demise.

The memory of Georald's death was still occupying Pherri when she felt herself seized from behind, and a leathery hand clamped tightly over her mouth. *Bandits!* She tried to cry out, and the hand pressed down harder, as the point of a blade appeared at her neck.

'Quiet.' Her captor's voice hissed in Pherri's ear like a rusty hinge. Pherri's eyes flicked left and right, and saw Theodric and Delara had their own assailants, pale figures clad in bearskins holding rags to their mouths and dragging them to the ground.

'Bring the girl,' said a woman Pherri could not see. 'Quickly.'

Pherri was too scared to struggle. Her wrists were swiftly bound, and she let herself be hoisted up onto a man's shoulder, leaving her face pressed against his back. His clothes reeked of stale sweat.

'And the other two?' rasped a man.

The woman seemed to hesitate. 'Leave them. They'll be out till morning.'

'There's someone in the trees,' came the anxious voice of a second man. 'They're watching us.'

'We should kill them,' said the first man. 'If—'

'There's no time,' hissed the woman. 'Come on.'

Their fellowship turned and broke into a run, away from the forest and Fisherton and towards Eryispek. Suddenly furious at the gall of these strangers, and with herself for being taken so easily, Pherri sensed for her bearer's heartbeat. If *phisika* could be used to heal, could it not also be used to harm? Men fell dead all the time. A myriad of the man's possible ends spread out across her mind: a knife in the dark, a raging fire, a brief shudder in the night, but she only had eyes for one. She willed his heart to *stop*.

The man gasped as if he had been punched in the stomach. His steps slowed, his body shuddered, and like a felled tree he toppled forward as Pherri slipped from his failing grasp.

She landed to the side and rolled away. She reached for the will to free her bonds, and the threads broke apart in a moment. Killing had been easier than saving a boy's ankle; death was an inevitability, certain in a way that a healed wound could never be.

Pherri rushed to her feet, and stepped straight across the path of the woman she had heard. She was tall, young, with strands of wild, white-blonde hair flittering from beneath her hood, and as the first faint light of dawn rose beyond Eryispek, the shadows it cast seemed to spread behind her shoulders, almost as if she had grown wings.

'I dreamt of you,' said Pherri. The words fell from her lips almost by accident, and seemed to steal the last of her strength. Her will faded like the receding night, as her knees buckled and the ground rose to meet her.

CHAPTER 24

Drast woke to the sound of bells. A low rumble of bellowing brass, pierced by the high howl of the ascension bell. That meant only one thing: the election of a new kzar.

He looked down at his body. He recognised the furnishings of his own home, but he was in an unfamiliar bed, and his arm was held in a sling. His throat was bone-dry.

'Forren!' he called. His voice grated like sandpaper. 'Forren!'

There was a sound of shuffling feet outside, and the door opened. A physician in blue medical robes appeared, old and wizened, with tufts of hair sprouting from his ears and a long nose supporting a pair of thick eyeglasses. 'It is good to see you awake, Senator.'

Drast tried to speak, but could emit only a pained croak. He rolled awkwardly out of bed and stalked to the table, ignoring the ache of his legs and the stabbing pains in his torso. He drank straight from a jug of water, and almost gagged with relief as the cold liquid flowed down his barren throat.

'Where is Forren?' he demanded. 'And why are the bells ringing?'

'Forren is sleeping. He may never walk again without a stick, and his left arm is burnt raw, but he came personally to fetch us with the fastest mounts from your stable. He has barely left your side the last four days. I had to insist he get some sleep and allow his own wounds to heal.

'You have extraordinary luck on your side. Both of you. A whole wing of your home is burnt to cinders, along with who knows how many of your people.

'As for the bells, there is no great mystery there. You hear the high bell of ascension: Saffia Murino is the kzar. She defeated Senator Brunal by one hundred and twenty-seven votes to one hundred and twenty. A few of your loyalists battled to delay the vote while you recovered, but it was not to be. I am sorry, Senator.'

Drast was silent for a few heartbeats. He gave a wry chuckle, then slammed the jug's handle on the edge of the table, breaking it. 'Where did my votes go? Saffia Murino was nowhere.'

The man looked at him quizzically. 'I'm only a physician, Senator.' He held out a scroll. 'Perhaps you can ask her yourself. She said to send for her once you were awake.'

Drast snatched it from him. It was there, in Saffia's own hand. She was sorry to hear of his misfortune, and the damage to his home, and would be grateful to be informed when he was awake and well enough to receive visitors. Signed *Kzar Saffia Murino of the Ulvatian Imperium.*

Drast threw the scroll onto his bed. He would reply later.

'Can I examine you, Senator?' asked the physician. 'You have some nasty burns on your legs, and at least one fractured rib. All will heal, with time, but you will need rest.'

Drast let the man examine him. The physician had a competent air, and seemed entirely uninterested in the origins of the fire that had claimed half Drast's mansion and killed several people. He finished by listening to Drast's heart. He grunted encouragingly, then gathered his things and made to leave.

'Sir,' asked Drast when the physician was at the door. 'Was there an old man found among the dead? Long grey hair, wearing a brown robe.'

The physician raised his eyebrows. 'I have seen none among the dead like that.'

'What about wandering the grounds?'

'I believe I would recall such a man, Senator, dead or alive.'

Drast sagged onto his bed, feeling suddenly drained. Was Krupal gone? Could his body have disintegrated in the inferno created by the huyar? Drast doubted it. He had the abrupt urge to run from Ulvatia and never return.

He found a mirror and washed himself in a basin of perfumed water. His face was red from the fire, and his eyebrows were singed. Something in his torso stretched painfully when he raised his hands to his face.

When he felt suitably cleansed, he went to the window. The east wing was a charred shell. The roof was destroyed, and support beams jutted from the masonry like the ribs of an ancient corpse. One wall looked on the verge of collapse. Repairs would cost a small fortune. Through the damage, he thought he glimpsed what had been Krupal's room. It was burnt black.

Every step I have taken since Forren showed me that underground room was a mistake. Except perhaps being willing to sacrifice himself to kill Krupal. Nobody could say he had not done his duty as a proud son of Ulvatia. Not that he would ever tell a soul.

But where was Krupal? The man was too crazed to let Drast get away with trying to incinerate him with huyar. He had the sudden urge to check under the bed.

Gods, if he's gone, he's gone. Just be thankful.

There was a knock at the door, and Drast looked up, for a moment fully expecting it to be Krupal come to finish him off. It opened, and to Drast's relief it was Forren. The doctor had told it true: his right arm clutched a stick, and his left arm was covered in horrific burns from the shoulder down. Half his hair on the left side of his charred face was gone.

'Urmé's wounds. I am so sorry, Forren.' Drast rubbed his face. 'How on earth are you still standing?'

'I sought the best physician in the city,' he croaked, his voice half-a-whisper. 'I have a salve that I must rub onto it every two hours. Completely numbs it.' He pinched a section of burnt flesh between his fingers, making Drast wince.

'Did he escape? Did any of the guards survive?' They would have to remove any witnesses.

Forren shook his head. 'All dead. I was able to drag you out from the worst of it, but I never saw Krupal. We've tripled the guard, but there's been no sign of him.'

'At least he's gone,' said Drast, as if saying it could make it true. 'Would you help me dress? Saffia Murino has requested to see me.' He hoped someone had shown the foresight to put his clothes in the room's wardrobe. '*Kzar* Saffia Murino,' he added. Drast brought his fist down hard on the windowsill, then cursed furiously at the pain in his hand.

It should have been me. Urmé curse them all; Saffia, Krupal, and the rest.

With their injuries, it was difficult even between them, but they eventually managed to dress him. Drast would not come before Saffia as a supplicant in senatorial clothes; he dressed simply, as though he was going into the city on errands. Supporting one another, he and Forren weaved their way downstairs like sailors crossing the deck in a storm. By the time they got to the yard and were able to call for horses, they were both soaked in sweat, and Drast swore his ribs were trying to pierce his torso. He suppressed a scream as he vaulted onto his horse.

They drew peculiar looks as they traversed the city towards Murino Hall, and no wonder. Drast expected the fire had been visible for miles, and if he knew Ulvatia little else would have been discussed for days. The ascension bell was still ringing. He tried to close his ears to its mockery.

'Is it true you brought a magus from across the sea and tried to hatch a dragon, Senator?' one woman called after him from a shop doorway.

Drast turned on her, drawing a painful protest from his torso. 'It was a fire, nothing more. If you spread rumours like that I'll bring you before the law.'

The woman looked away, but Drast caught the eye of a man next to her and nearly fell from his horse in shock as Krupal's wizened face stared back at him. 'Forren! Ri—'

The words caught in his throat as Drast looked again, and an ordinary man stared back at him, regarding him strangely before walking away.

Drast wiped the sweat from his forehead. *I am seeing things. Whatever they treated me with is jumbling my wits.*

At Murino Hall, a knot of senators moved past them as they dismounted. They looked at Drast curiously, but did not greet him. A few days earlier they would have been pushing past each other to speak with him.

I am yesterday's news. There were a few kzars who had been elected at a second attempt, but Saffia Murino was younger than him, and seemingly in fine health. She might be kzar for the rest of Drast's life. If he had made a deal, she might have found some position for him, but there was no chance of that now. The last thing a new kzar needed was to attract scandal, and half his manse burning down in mysterious circumstances was perhaps the biggest scandal of the decade. At least it had perhaps distracted the city from Kvarm Murino's mysterious disappearance.

In a daze, he approached the doors, flanked by a pair of burly guardsmen wielding pikes. One of them whispered something to the other behind a hand, eliciting a chuckle from his partner.

'Senator Fulkiro,' Drast said wearily, drawing the scroll from inside his vest. 'Saff— Kzar Murino is expecting me.'

One of the guardsmen rapped on the door. A slave girl opened it a moment later, and with a wide-eyed look at Drast's burnt face bid him and Forren to enter.

He remembered the vastness of Murino Hall from his last visit; a reception of the old kzar's years ago, to mark the anniversary of some imagined triumph. The foyer was grandly appointed, built in gold and white marble threaded with purple and orange. Eight huge columns supported the high ceiling, and at the far end, two staircases curved up to a long carpeted landing.

If Bovarch is looking down at this he will be pissing himself. In his ambition, Drast had killed both Bovarch Murino and his despised brother, and then Drast's hubris had seen his daughter elected instead. By the time Saffia died, the Murinos might have ruled for a century.

A bell was ringing somewhere in the house, marking their arrival. He was heartily sick of bells.

A few minutes later, Saffia appeared at the top of the stairs. She had already donned her white senatorial robes, trimmed with gold to mark her position. Drast had never thought her any more than ordinary to look at, a dark-haired young woman with a long, curved nose and a narrow, boyish shape, but he had to admit that she cut an elegant figure, and the silver circlet atop her head only added to her poise, so too the jewels that adorned her fingers and dripped lavishly from her ears.

'Senator Fulkiro.' She looked genuinely shocked to see him. 'I did not expect you to come yourself; if I had known you were awake I would have come to you. We were so sorry to hear of your injuries and the damage to your home. Is it salvageable?'

'I hope so, Your Excellency. I only woke today, so I have not yet been able to assess the damage.' He bowed, as was expected, and Forren followed awkwardly, gripping his stick.

'And you rushed straight here! You great fool, Drast. Your man looks like he's about to keel over.' She clicked her fingers at a pair of slaves, who disappeared and quickly returned carrying an absurdly ornate chair, which Forren almost fell into.

'Put him in the conservatory with refreshments,' she said, snapping her fingers again. 'Senator Fulkiro and I will speak alone.' The slaves picked up the chair, with Forren sitting on it, and disappeared before either he or Drast could protest.

'Follow me, Senator.'

Drast climbed the stairs, and Saffia led him deeper into the house, to a room she had obviously made her study. A great hardwood desk sat by the window below a towering bookshelf, but she gestured him towards a soft chair at a low table and sat down opposite in a chair so large it might have suited a buffalo. Polished golden wall sconces shone like bright suns in their own firelight, making the white marble floor blinding to look upon.

'The desk was my grandfather's,' said Saffia. 'And this chair was my father's. I like to keep the family's artefacts close. Which is one of the reasons I was so distressed when my uncle disappeared. He owned something of great value, which I had hoped to inherit if he died.'

The magus. Drast tried to keep his expression neutral. 'More furniture?'

Her eyes narrowed. 'There are whispers he visited you the day he disappeared. Is it true?'

'Yes.' There was no guilt in admitting that. 'I hoped to broker a deal for his support, but our positions were too far apart. I was as shocked as anyone when he did not turn up for the next round of votes.'

'I'm sure. And I assume your explanation for the fire at your home is just as innocent?'

'We are investigating. If you have any ideas I would be grateful for them.'

Saffia looked away, smiling and shaking her head. 'Do you know why you lost, Drast?'

Because I was unconscious and you stole all my votes. 'Why?'

'Because you are too clever to have a proper appreciation of risk. You seek the path that is fraught with danger, assuming you have the wits to correct matters when things inevitably go wrong. I knew you would overreach; I just had to make sure I could take advantage when you did. The disappearance of my uncle helped as well of course.' She plucked a bottle of wine and two glasses from a shelf and began pouring. 'And now I am the kzar, and you are a fool who burnt down his own house.

'I don't know how you killed my uncle, but I know enough to be sure you must have broken every law in the Imperium a dozen times over. He was as dangerous as any man in the world, which is why I never engaged him directly. That *creature* of his is better off dead as well in truth. You did me a great favour, and for that I will make sure that you are protected. You will not be pursued for his death, and we will devise some believable lie about your fire.

'But you are going to do something for me in return. You are thoroughly unsuited to being kzar, but your recklessness makes you well-suited to other tasks.'

'Such as?' Drast leant forward, intrigued now. Unless he was mistaken, she was offering him a position.

Saffia took a sip of wine, and lifted a scroll from the shelf. She unrolled it, revealing a map, recently copied.

'Do you recognise these borders?'

Drast examined it. 'It's the Imperium, but as it stood two hundred and fifty years ago.' He pointed to an expanse of empty plain north of Cylirien. 'That's where we built the second Athlehem.' He moved his finger south a little, to a marker indicating a settlement. 'That's where the first one was, before the Cyliriens burnt it to the ground.'

Saffia regarded him approvingly down her beaked nose. 'That's more than most could say. As long as their larders are full and their coffers overflow with gold most senators don't concern themselves with the provinces. And what do you notice about this map?'

Drast pointed to a river in the west. 'The curve of the River Trevath has changed, but otherwise the Imperium's borders are much the same as they were then.' *Proof of our folly in Cylirien.*

'Indeed.' Saffia moved her finger south. 'The Erlanders beat us, and we were so shocked that someone had the gall to fight back that we came home and didn't leave our homes again for centuries except to try and bully the Cyliriens into becoming Ulvatian.'

'You agree with me then, about the fight to hold Cylirien.'

'Yes. Although I also agree with my uncle. Erland is ripe to be conquered.'

No. It is madness. Thousands will die. 'The Bleak Hills prevent us moving south; of the forty thousand Kzar Naaro sent to Erland—'

'Ten thousand died on the way,' finished Saffia. 'More or less. I expect the numbers were exaggerated to make the defeat seem less shameful.' She shook her head. 'Many times I argued to my father that we ought to expand southward. If we could take Erland, the whole continent would open up for us. Thrumb to the west, Ffrisea to the east. Ours. Wealth and land enough to raise the whole Imperium, from the lowest slave to the highest senator.

'My father never wanted it. He was content to play politics with that gaggle of white geese and waste the riches of our empire paying girls to bounce about on his prick.

'In any event, all the Imperium hears tales of and fears Andrick the Barrelbreaker, the man who fights like a demon and inspires devotion like a god.

'But no longer.' Her eyes glittered. 'The Barrelbreaker is dead, and his country divided against itself. My contact there tells me that it is ripe for conquest. All the fury of the Imperium will cross the Bleak Hills, to wage red war upon

Erland. The Imperium will be great once more. It may be the only good idea my uncle ever had.

'Sadly, I am a woman, and for all the equality the Imperium offers, it will not suffer a woman to lead an army. I need a man. A man with experience of war, a hero who other men will follow. A man who is devious, and bold to the point of recklessness. A man who is in my debt, and whose obedience I can rely on.' She gave Drast a look of triumph. 'Can you think of a man like that, Senator?'

Drast barely heard her. His ears beat with blood, like the drums of war leading him across the mountains.

CHAPTER 25

'You'll need to carry him,' said Tansa as she and Cag hauled Orsian from the rowboat.

'If it were up to me we wouldn't have gone after him at all,' muttered Cag, hoisting Orsian up.

Tansa ignored him. Cag had complained constantly about the idea, but she had known he would come through for her. Not least because Pitt and Esma had refused to have anything to do with him unless he would help their friend Ranulf.

Not Ranulf, Orsian. She should have seen it the first time she spoke to him. No sailor would have helped her, and he spoke and carried himself like a lord. The difference had been obvious the moment he had faced down the sailors in Pauper's; even stationary, the sailors seemed to swagger with the rhythm of the waves, while Orsian was steady as an oak.

His uncle killed Tam. The four words she could not stop invading her thoughts every other hour, though she knew that Orsian did not share a single slice of blame. He had not even been in Merivale at the time. But there was another part of her, the small part where she had buried the memory of burning Tam's mutilated body in the woods, and that part wanted to cut off Orsian's head and return it to Hessian in a box.

Ranulf, her friend. More than a friend. Orsian, her enemy's nephew.

It was still early, but word must have spread of the fire in the harbour. They were moving in the opposite direction to the crowd, most of whom were fortunately too eager to see a burning ship to pay any attention to their strange band.

After a while, Esma began to flag, having to be encouraged along by Pitt to keep her little legs moving. Tansa swept the girl up in her arms. She had done brilliantly. They had wanted to leave her behind with Maud again, until Esma had threatened to scream the whole district down about their plot to turn the guards upon the *Jackdaw*'s crew. Thank Eryi she had persuaded them.

When Orsian had been captured, once she had admitted to herself that she could not just leave him, Tansa had despaired. It would have taken a small army to overwhelm the crew, and there was no question of hiring even a single small-time ruffian; they barely had two pennies to rub together. She had even considered the awful idea of going to Cliffark Tower and telling Lord Istlewick that the king's nephew had been kidnapped.

It had been Maud's proposal in the end. Everyone in Pauper's knew that Wyatt the moneylender had contacts among the city guards; he offered them low-interest loans in exchange for inside information and turning a blind eye to his many other nefarious activities. Tansa had no trouble believing that; Wyatt would do anything for profit. The last time Tansa had seen him he had traded her their stolen

Imperial coins for Erlish currency at a fifth of its usual value.

They had cornered Wyatt in his shop. The old miser had been reluctant at first, but once Cag, Glyn, and Hiall had taken care of his two sentries and threatened to extract the money he had shorted Tansa the year before, Wyatt had agreed to pass an urgent message to the guards that the man who had been rescued from the gallows crewed on the *Jackdaw*, which would be lifting anchor the next morning.

Eventually, their ragtag band made it back to Maud's guesthouse. Orsian still had not stirred. Maud tended to his back with a soothing poultice, gasping at the strips of torn flesh that ran from shoulder to rear. She let them lay him to sleep in her own bed.

The room was warm and the bed was soft, enough so that Orsian did not want to leave. So when somebody started repeatedly slapping his face he pushed them and rolled over to the other side.

Orsian's assailant did not relent, and a second stranger began pulling his hair and flicking his ear.

He had been dreaming. Dreaming about drowning, and a burning ship upon a sea of blood, and a hundred corpses on the seabed, grasping for him.

Abner and D'graw's faces had been among them. But that had not been his fate. His friends had rescued him, friends who had known him by another name, but friends all the same.

Orsian rolled over, and threw the laughing Pitt and Esma off him to the end of the bed.

'You're awake,' cried Esma, jumping up and down in her excitement, narrowly missing Orsian's feet. 'Finally. You've been asleep forever.'

Pitt was more serious. 'They've said to call you something else, but I don't like your other name. Can I keep calling you Ranulf?'

'If you like.' Orsian looked around. The room itself was as dark and tumbledown as any part of Pauper's Hole, but the furnishings were fitted for comfort. The bed was big enough for four, with pillows stacked three-high, and there were soft sofas and exquisitely carved furniture that looked like they belonged in a lord's castle. 'Where am I?'

The door opened, and Maud appeared.

'He's awake!' she cackled. 'Are you well rested, young master? It's been a long time since I had a man in my bed.'

Orsian started. '*Your* bed?'

'This is my room. I patched you up as best I could. Your back looks like a field that's been ploughed by drunk oxen. I insisted you take my bed, once you'd stopped bleeding everywhere. Will cost you a pretty penny, mind; turfing an old woman out of her bed doesn't come cheap. I'm just glad Tansa didn't jump in there with you, not that you were in any fit state for it.'

She was already dragging the sheets off, ready to be washed. Orsian took the hint and got up, quickly pulling on the spare clothes someone had left for him.

'That's what you get for messing with pirates,' said Maud, eyeing his back.

'The *Jackdaw*'s at the bottom of the harbour. That's what they get for messing with me.'

'Not how I heard it. You're lucky that girl came after you, after all those lies you told. And don't expect me to be bowing and scraping and calling you Lord. That nonsense doesn't belong down here.' Maud snapped a fresh sheet out of a trunk. 'Now get out of my way. It's nearly dinner and I want to fix the mess you've made of my bed.'

Orsian shuffled away, tottering slightly on his sleepy legs and trying not to stretch his wounds, while Pitt and Esma ran off ahead of him. He eventually made it to the kitchen, where Cag and Tansa were seated. They looked up as he entered.

'You're awake!' Tansa rose to embrace him, kissing him on the cheek. He hugged her back awkwardly, conscious of the shape of her body pressed against his. And of Cag glaring at him from the far end of the table.

'Thanks for coming after me,' said Orsian. The words felt too small for the measure of what they had done for him.

Tansa smirked. 'You told us not to, remember? Nearly didn't, but Pitt and Esma wouldn't hear of it.'

'Where did the guards come from?'

'I called in a favour with... Look, it doesn't matter. He owed us. He told the guards that it was the crew of the *Jackdaw* who interrupted the hanging. They didn't need much more convincing than that; the guards aren't big on pirates who reckon they're whalers.'

'I saw it sink.' Orsian tried not to dwell on the men who had been onboard, men who only a week ago he had called his friends.

Tansa nodded soberly. 'That captain went down with it, and the big tattooed one probably. The guard have tripled their patrols of the harbour because folk keep trying to swim down looking for gold.'

May Eryi take them. Orsian felt a twinge of pity for D'graw and Abner, then crushed it. They had kidnapped him twice after all.

Abner had been right about one thing though: as much as Orsian had tried to deny it to himself, his place was in Erland. Taking a whipping could really make a man see the truth of himself.

'What did they want with you?' asked Tansa.

'They were going to ransom me to the king,' said Orsian, taking a seat. 'Or the Imperium. Don't think they'd worked that part out yet.'

'There's one thing I've been wondering,' said Cag. 'How did a fancy lord like you end up onboard in the first place?'

'It was after the Battle of Whitewater,' said Orsian. He had no wish to say anything further on the matter.

'Were you one of them that ran away? I heard most of them turned bandit. "Pirate" sounds better, I suppose.'

'I'm no coward.' Orsian's hands clenched into fists. 'They tricked and murdered my father before the battle even started. I was knocked out and my horse ran off.'

'Sounds like running away to me.'

A hot fury rose in Orsian's veins. His back was burning and Cag was built like an outhouse, but he would not sit here and be called a coward by a sneering boy who barely knew one end of a sword from the other. He made to rise, staring daggers at Cag.

'I'll have no fighting under this roof!' Maud hobbled into the kitchen. She glared at them. 'If you want to fight you can do it in the yard so I can at least charge for the spectacle.' She looked at Orsian. 'And I know you're a young lord who probably plays at iron sticks with his friends, but my money would be on him, especially while your back is bandaged up like a poxy tart.'

Tansa pushed Orsian back into his seat. 'Don't.' She

turned to Cag. 'And you don't either. Orsian saved you, or have you forgotten?'

With a dark look at Orsian, Cag shoved his chair back from the table and stormed out, slamming the door behind him hard enough to leave the hinges rattling.

We may have saved one another, thought Orsian, *but I don't think we're going to be friends.*

Maud shook her head. 'Was going to ask the big lad to do it, but if you're well enough to start fights I reckon you're well enough to be useful. You can make the stew, put those soft lordly hands to use for once.'

While Orsian struggled with the stew, Tansa sent Pitt and Esma away and set to laying the table. For a woman running an inn out of the most lawless acre in Cliffark, Maud was fastidious about the correct way to eat a meal. Tansa would miss her when they left.

Left to where though? That was a question. Cag was a fugitive, and not one easy to hide. They could not stay in Cliffark, unless they planned to live in Pauper's and never leave.

'What will you do now?' she asked Orsian.

He was bent over the pot, stirring. 'Put the carrots in, probably.'

It was a weak jape, but Tansa could not help laughing, and Orsian looked back at her with a grin. 'You know what I mean. Guessing you won't be going back to sea?'

His face fell, suddenly serious. 'I'm going to Merivale,' he said, with iron certainty. 'There's a war to be won.'

The war. Of course. If there was one thing lords loved, it

was a war. It had been Ranulf she had hoped to rescue, but it was Orsian the lord she had come back with. 'I thought it was the war that made you go to sea.'

Orsian stirred too quickly and sent stew sloshing over the cauldron's rim. 'I should never have left. And Abner told me the Imperium means to invade. I can't leave my family to face that alone. My mother's out there fighting; how could I live with myself if she died because I wasn't there? I have to go back. Because Cag's right, even if he's wrong: I have been acting like a coward; I abandoned my family because the thought of going back to them was too difficult.'

Merivale. The idea of returning filled Tansa's heart with dread. She only had to close her eyes to see the distant figure of King Hessian, watching from the balcony as Tam danced at the end of a rope. The fork she was placing tremored in her hand. How could Orsian fight for a man like that?

He really was going to leave her. A lump caught in Tansa's throat. It had been easier when he was Ranulf. Then she could cling to the chance that he might stay. But she could not compete against the pull of duty and family. That was who he was; he had shown that by helping her save Cag.

She wanted to grab him right there and drag him to her bed. He could not leave her, not after what they had shared together. That he was so prepared to cast her aside and run back to Merivale filled her with fury, which only made her even more furious with herself. She did not need some lying lord to protect her; as long as there were fools to rob she did not need anybody.

He turned to look at her again, still stirring the stew. 'Makes me nervous when you go quiet, like the way the wind drops at sea before the storm comes. I keep worrying you're going to sink one of those knives into my back.'

Tansa put down the last of the cutlery with a clatter. 'If you want to leave, then leave. Not stopping you.' Did he have some fancy lady back in Merivale, with dresses and long hair and that shadowy stuff rich girls put on their eyes?

Orsian blinked at her. 'I stayed to free Cag, as we agreed, and I get the feeling he doesn't want me sticking around.' He scratched at his neck. 'You could come with me, I guess? Just I expected you to stay in Cliffark.'

It took every ounce of restraint for Tansa not to slap him. 'What a generous and enthusiastic offer, Lord Orsian. Just the words every girl wants to hear. *"You could come with me, I guess?"'* She barked a laugh. 'Should have expected it, I suppose; I know how you lordlings treat the commonfolk: get your jollies and then get the fuck out.'

Orsian's ears flushed bright red. 'I didn't mean it like that! I—' He stopped uselessly. 'Why are you so angry with me? I've done everything you asked! I'm sorry I lied; I had no choice. Why did you come back for me if you hate me?'

Tears began to form in Tansa's eyes. She threw down the last of the cutlery and fled.

Orsian watched Tansa rush out of the kitchen and back to her room, slamming the door shut behind her, his mouth hanging open in confusion. What had he said?

I'd be leaving anyway. What difference does it make whether it's Merivale or the sea? She doesn't have to come.

He turned back to the stew, and a moment later hissed in pain as someone clipped him hard on the ear.

He whirled around. 'Just what—?' He pulled up open-mouthed as he realised it was Maud. The old woman had somehow sneaked up behind him.

She jabbed angrily at the stew with a ladle. 'You're burning it, idiot.' She elbowed him out of her way. 'Can't deal with stew, can't deal with women. Must be a real fancy lord to have lived this long being so bloody useless.'

Orsian took a calming breath and stepped aside. What was it with the women here and attacking him? 'Sorry. Was a bit distracted.'

'I heard.' Maud lifted the cauldron off the fire with surprising strength and set it to one side. She turned on him. 'Just what is it you're playing at, boy? My home ain't a brothel, and that girl deserves better than being treated like a whore.'

'I didn't!' Orsian spluttered. 'I mean—'

'You did.' Maud jabbed him in the chest with the ladle. 'You lied to her, tupped her, and she rescued you, and then you were ready to just up and leave! Surprised you didn't leave a pile of coins on the bedstead!' She jabbed him again. 'That girl's had more hardship than some folk have in their whole lives, and I won't have you treating her like that, lord or not.'

'But that's not fair! I stayed to rescue Cag, and I did that, and it's not like I dragged her into bed, and I never asked her to rescue me!'

Maud rolled her eyes so hard they threatened to disappear into her skull. 'Oh spare me the problems of young handsome lords. *"The girl took me to bed, and saved me, and I never wanted any of it."* Just why do you think she went back for you? The girl's in love with you, you bloody idiot.'

Maud's outburst stunned Orsian into silence. He shook his head as if to dislodge the sudden fuzziness that had come over him, and covered it by taking the ladle from Maud to serve the stew into bowls.

'I sound nothing like that,' he muttered eventually, then before Maud could reply called, 'Dinner's ready!' eager for everyone else to join them so he could be free of their conversation.

The meal was quiet. Cag had not returned from wherever he had stomped off to, and both children seemed tired, so partway through Orsian had to carry Esma to bed.

It ought to have been a celebration, Tansa reflected. Their first meal with Orsian since the rescue, and perhaps a goodbye to him as well. He had not said when he would be leaving, but he did not strike her as a man to let the grass grow under his feet. How much longer would she have him for? Perhaps tomorrow. She sighed. Her stew tasted like ashes.

Maud kept their ales topped up, but did little to force a conversation, until eventually she stood and announced that she was going to bed. 'You as well, boy,' she told Pitt, who was licking the last of his stew from the bottom of his trencher.

'But I'm not tired!' he complained, his lips stained brown with stew.

'Don't care. Boy your age needs sleep.' Maud took him by the shoulder and guided him down from his seat. She looked to Orsian and Tansa. 'Leave some stew for the big lad if he comes back. And no more shouting, or the neighbours will be round complaining.' She left, dragging an openly yawning Pitt with her.

Tansa felt Orsian's gaze on her, but could not meet his eye. She had embarrassed herself earlier, and did not wholly understand why. Only Tam had ever made her lose her temper like that. 'Sorry,' she said eventually, not looking at him. 'Shouldn't have shouted at you.'

'It's fine. I was being an arse. I've not even properly thanked you for saving me. I doubt there's anyone else in the world who would have come back for me. Thank you.' He shook his head. 'Doesn't seem enough really, words. If it weren't for you, I'd be out on the Shrouded Sea wrapped in chains.'

Tansa shrugged. 'You did it for Cag. We're even now.'

She watched him spin his tankard in small circles, stirring the ale within, his face sombre. What was he thinking of when that dark look came over his face? She knew, she thought. After so many months, Tam's death no longer felt like an open wound; it was more like a scab now, only sore if she picked at it. Three months at sea had not done the same for Orsian.

'You're thinking about your father,' she said.

His mouth twisted. 'I'm still surprised every day when I wake up and he's not there ordering me to go out and practise. I'd like to speak to him again, just once.'

'What would you say?'

'I'd apologise.' He sipped at his ale. 'If it weren't for me, he'd still be alive.'

'Do you really believe that?'

'Maybe. Maybe not.' He shrugged. 'But I can't let the shame of it stop me going back.' He looked at her, his dark eyes deep as coalpits. 'I'm not free, Tansa. I can't just do as I please and damn my family. I've been away too long already.' He took a deep breath. 'But if I were free, I'd want you.

That's why I asked you to come with me. If you can stand to be with a man whose life is not his own, the offer still stands. Truthfully, I can't imagine going back without you.'

Tansa's heart fluttered in her chest. *He does want me.* Back to Merivale, where she had burnt her brother's body, without prayer or ceremony. But she could face it, with Orsian there. She would have to.

She stood, taking a long drink of ale, her mouth suddenly both too wet and too dry. She walked to him, and bent down to kiss him softly on the mouth, sending a spasm of fire through her.

'*Yes,*' she whispered. She lowered herself into his lap, holding his face in her hands. '*Yes.*'

CHAPTER 26

Ciera paced her room, watching the low evening light from the window move across the floor. Another day gone, and another day of confinement. A week had passed now, and still Lord Balyard and the guards at her door remained indifferent to her pleas. She had been given new guards, of Balyard's choosing.

Just what is it with the men in this family and locking me up?

She had thought herself so bold and clever for outmanoeuvring Balyard, but she had underestimated Gurathet's greed. Beneath the bluster was a heart every bit as avaricious as Balyard's. She doubted it had even taken much land to turn him.

Ciera had barely bothered to think about the ridiculous accusation that she had killed Georald. His door had been locked from the inside, and her guards could account for every hour Ciera spent outside her chamber. It was a pathetic pretext to confine her, but with Gurathet in his pocket it was all Balyard needed.

Instead, her thoughts lingered on her son, Andrick. She felt pathetically grateful for the meagre hour a day they allowed her with him. Desperately, she had hoped that if she was deferential to Balyard, meek and mild as her captor expected women to be, he might relent and at least return Andrick to her.

'I will leave it up to his governess,' Balyard had said without looking at her when Ciera asked if she at least might be able to see him for more than an hour a day.

Of course the Eryi-accursed Mortha had refused her. 'This is how it's done, Lord,' she had said to Balyard. 'Princes are raised to be kings; they should not be coddled.'

Mortha. Ciera had been all sweetness and charm with her as well, as if that would have made a difference. The thought of her fussing over Andrick's nursery filled her with rage.

Eryi take them all. I will show them a queen's vengeance. She could waste no more time on tears; she needed to act, to correct matters. But all her solitary plotting had borne no fruit. She was trapped here, seeing nobody save for her guards and her maid Lanetha, who brought her meals but was not allowed to speak with her.

In frustration, Ciera seized the poker from the fire and brought it down hard on her dressing table, leaving its imprint in the wood and propelling a vibration up her arm that sent the poker clattering to the floor.

Immediately the door flew open, and there stood Tarwen, one of her *hymerika* jailers, tall and rangy with a black spade-shaped beard and a grim countenance. He scowled. 'What was that?'

'Nothing. I dropped something.'

'Well, don't, or Lord Balyard will hear of it.' He slammed the door shut, and Ciera heard the bolt being replaced.

Ciera stared after him, wishing that the poker was a sword and she had the skill to wield it. The other *hymerikai* assigned to guard her were all just as cheerless as Tarwen, chosen for their loyalty to Balyard and their fierce indifference to Ciera's plight. Laphor and her old guard would have sympathised, or even been prepared to speak with her to make the hours go quicker, but Balyard would risk no allies around her.

How am I to get my son back and depose Balyard if I am stuck in this room? Laphor might help, and she was sure some of the other *hymerikai* would be on her side also, especially if they learnt that Gurathet had effectively sold their loyalty to the highest bidder. But what use was that? She had no hope of speaking to Laphor.

But as Ciera returned the poker to the hearth, she remembered something. A vision of Hessian shimmered before her eyes, emerging from her fireplace with cobwebs in his hair and a goblet of wine gripped in his fist.

There is a way out. Dozens of times the shriek of metal on stone had been the harbinger of Hessian coming to her bed. It had never occurred to her – she had always been half-asleep when he arrived, and done her best to forget afterwards.

The embers were long cold, and Ciera explored the edges of the hearth with her fingertips, searching for a seam or something that might open it, but the granite fireplace was tight against the brickwork. Ciera had small fingers, but not even a child could have found a gap to grasp.

She kept searching, forcing herself to be patient. She

even resorted to trying to lever it open with the poker, but that was no more useful than her fingers.

After several fruitless minutes, Ciera gave up. It was hopeless. Perhaps it could only be opened from the other side? She cursed herself for not looking more closely when Hessian had left the same way.

Exasperated, she slapped her hand against the masonry.

The wall gave a sharp noise. A brick shifted, and something mechanical whirred within the stone. The right-hand side of the fireplace clicked and rotated slightly, revealing a dark annex inside what until then had been solid masonry.

Open-mouthed, Ciera cautiously pulled at the hearth until the gap was wide enough to slip inside. It was dark within, so she doubled back to retrieve a candle.

There were cobwebs and dust everywhere, and it smelt of mould, but here and there were signs of someone's passage: handprints that the dust had not yet reclaimed, and a discarded wine bottle that made Ciera jump as her foot collided with it and sent it clinking down a set of spiralling wooden stairs. It smashed loudly far below, and Ciera was sure the whole castle must have heard it.

With bated breath, she waited for the sound of running feet and the click of her chamber door. All she could hear though was her own heartbeat, and the deafening, rushing silence of a stairway that above her ascended into the darkness, and below fell into the depths of the dungeon.

If they find me gone, I will never get this chance again. Ciera looked back through the gap to her chamber. Carefully, she pulled the fireplace towards her, until only a soft chink of light was visible; enough to find her way back, and hopefully too small for anyone searching her room to find.

Unsure whether to go up or down, she ascended, keeping an outstretched palm against the walls and clutching her flickering candle, wincing with every creak of the wooden stairs. At the floor above, the staircase ended, and Ciera emerged into a corridor with three passages going in different directions, each high enough for a man but no more than a yard wide.

Ciera examined each of them in turn. All were draped with stringy cobwebs, and down one of them she thought she heard a distant drip of water. None looked inviting. She lifted her candle high, and chose one at random, peering into the gloom, hoping for some indication of where it might go.

An unlit wall sconce gave her the answer. Ciera reached out and plucked the long grey hair that had caught on it, unmistakably Hessian's.

She took a moment to get her bearings, orientating herself to her room below and evaluating the direction of the corridor.

Hessian's solar. With a shiver, she realised that this was the path he must have walked when he came to visit her. For a moment, she half-expected him to come looming out of the darkness, his pale face glowing like a skull in the candlelight.

Eryi's balls, get a grip. Heart pounding, she crept down the corridor, her feet whispering against stone.

When she reached another spiralling staircase, this one even tighter than the one before, she knew she was right. Ciera set her foot to the first step and began to climb. It was noticeable how clean and well-swept this part of the tunnels was compared to the rest. She looked down, and felt a moment of dizziness at how the stairs plunged into the castle depths, lit by a soft, distant glow.

No wonder Hessian had barely emerged from his solar. *He could prowl the entire castle with none of us being any the wiser.*

She had been worried about what she would do once she reached the top, but the way out was made clear by the presence of a single wall sconce, slightly askew, with no candle in it. Ciera grasped it and turned it horizontal. It squeaked, and before her an entire section of wall creaked open into the light of Hessian's chambers.

She had been so enthralled by the passage, and so eager to find her way, Ciera had not taken even a moment to decide what she would do once she reached the solar, nor what would happen if there was somebody already there. She stepped into the light, and came face to face with a young servant girl, who until a moment before must have been dusting something. She was backed against the far wall, her eyes like cartwheels.

If she screams, I'm finished. Though her heart was threatening to leap out of her mouth, Ciera raised a placating hand. 'It's all right,' she said forcing a smile. 'It's only me.'

The girl remained silent, and Ciera was suddenly struck by a memory: a straw-haired slip of a girl, timid as a mouse, who forever ago had left her flowers in her chamber every morning, until the day she encountered Tam in Ciera's bed and her screams brought the guards running.

'I remember you.' Ciera gasped. 'You helped me dress, that morning, when— What's your name?'

The girl's face brightened. 'You remember me?'

Ciera beamed. 'Of course I do.'

Before Ciera could think to say anything else, the girl was racing towards her. She half-leapt at her, throwing her skinny arms around Ciera's shoulders as Ciera instinctively crouched down to embrace the girl.

She buried her face against Ciera's neck, suddenly overcome. 'I'm Haisie,' she managed to say through her sobs. 'I'm sorry, I thought, I thought... When I saw that boy, I was so scared. I—'

'You're alive,' whispered Ciera, holding the girl to her, letting Haisie's tears soak into her dress.

After a few moments, Haisie pulled back, sniffling, and Ciera produced a handkerchief from her sleeve to wipe the girl's stained cheeks. 'I hid. I was scared. I thought someone would come for me, but they never did.'

Painful as it was, Ciera forced herself to recollect the morning Tam had been found in her chamber. The three guards who had caught him had never been seen again, and Ciera had assumed Hessian had arranged for all the witnesses to be killed. 'I'm glad you're safe.'

Haisie sniffed again, covering the handkerchief with yellow-green snot. 'Can I come and work for you again? I have to clean the king's rooms now, but no one comes in here. I hate it. It's cold and scary.'

Ciera brushed Haisie's hair back behind her ears. 'I would like that too, but first you have to help me.' She looked over towards the solar door. 'Are there any guards outside?'

'No. Not since the king left.'

Ciera thought quickly. She was unlikely to ever get such a chance again. Haisie was trembling, and Ciera took her gently by the shoulders and looked into her eyes. 'Haisie, I need you to do something for me. I need you to find someone, and bring them here, but you can't tell anyone. Can you do that for me?'

The girl's bottom lip wobbled, but she nodded.

'Do you know Laphor? He's an older *hymerika*.' Ciera realised that to Haisie likely everyone was old. 'He's bald, with bad scarring from a burn on his cheek and neck, and a bent nose. He should be in the barracks. Can you get him for me, please?'

Tears welled in Haisie's eyes. 'I've never been to the barracks. The soldiers scare me.'

Ciera took the girl's hand in hers. It was freezing cold. 'They scare me too.' Ciera had a sudden idea. She pulled a silver bangle from her wrist, an old piece of jewellery decorated with an etching of her father's crest, a sea eagle on the wing. 'Give this to him, so he knows you've come from me. If you come back with him, you can keep it.'

'People will say I stole it.'

'I'll buy it back from you. If he won't come, just run away. I won't be angry.' Ciera hoped she had not misjudged Laphor.

The girl took the bangle in both hands, holding it up to her face and turning it over and around, admiring the way the sconce light reflected in it. 'I'll do it. I'll bring him back, I promise.'

She hugged Ciera, and ran off as fast as her scrawny legs would carry her, giving a quick wave as she closed the solar door behind her.

With a deep breath, Ciera stood. It was risking Haisie's life, but what choice did she have? She did not believe the Norhai would have placed the girl right where Ciera needed only for her to fail. Any gods regardless, the sheer unlikeliness of it gave Ciera renewed hope, even as her stomach churned like the Shrouded Sea on a stormy night.

With Haisie gone, Ciera surveyed her husband's room. She had never thought to see it herself; he only summoned here those who were useful to him, and her only use had been in the bedchamber. There was a table in the shape of Erland with an upturned flagon marking Eryispek, and several swords hung on the wall, though she doubted Hessian had gripped one in decades. A cabinet laden with wine bottles stood in the corner, and there was a double door of paned glass leading onto a balcony overlooking the city. A fire burnt in the hearth, and Haisie had lit every wall scone, so the room glowed with warm yellow light. From down in the city, it would have looked like a great lighthouse, a marker for all the world that Hessian Sangreal reigned in Piperskeep.

I should have somewhere like this. Summoning people to her chamber was nowhere near as impressive as forcing them to climb to the highest point in the city. This was why it was essential that she beat Balyard and Gurathet; without authority, when Hessian died, what was she? A former queen, doomed to be locked away and forgotten while others ruled in her son's name. The small power Hessian had granted her had slipped through her fingers as easily as water. She needed power in her own name.

When she heard the click of the latch, Ciera was sitting at Hessian's table, and had poured herself a glass of ruby-red wine, so noxious that she had been forced to water it. Haisie led the way, and Ciera had to hold herself from leaping to her feet as Laphor entered behind her.

More footsteps followed, and Ciera panicked that she had misjudged Laphor, then felt a surge of relief as she realised it was two of her other guards: Burik and Arrik, Naeem's sons.

'We've not got long,' said Laphor. 'Need to be back in the barracks before anyone notices.'

'I didn't tell you to bring others,' said Ciera.

'Need someone to watch our backs. Burik, get outside that door and listen for anyone coming up the stairs.' Laphor joined Ciera at the table and began pouring glasses of wine. He sniffed at one and made a face. 'Pigswill stuff you nobles drink, begging your pardon, Majesty.'

'Are we going to fight back against Balyard?' asked Arrik eagerly. He was around Ciera's age, with a squat body and his father's stout jaw, but with a broad, flat nose and no grey in his hair. 'We'll stand with you, we all—'

'Hush your trap,' growled Laphor, thrusting a glass of wine into Arrik's hand. 'The queen'll tell us why we're here. Until then, we know a great fuck load of nothing.' He glanced at Ciera. 'Begging your pardon, Majesty.'

Ciera smiled. *He knows why we're here, otherwise he would not have come.* She needed him, someone, any sort of ally who would stand for her. 'You were right before. When I moved against Balyard—'

'You shouldn't have held back,' agreed Laphor. He looked at Haisie, who was now exploring the section of wall where Ciera had entered. 'Is she—?'

'I trust Haisie completely.' The girl turned and beamed at her.

Laphor grunted. 'Fine.' He sank into a chair. 'Never thought I'd live to see another *balhymeri* after Lord Andrick. Was easier with him. A man knew right from wrong then, friend from foe. Now the king's gone, we've got some useless regent, and the *balhymeri* is a man even older and more foolish than I.' He took a glug of wine.

'What's been happening since Balyard imprisoned me?' asked Ciera.

'The entry levy's back up, and the milling levy, and

Balyard's placed a per-resident tax on every dwelling and sent in his thugs to get them to pay. The city's even more agitated than before, and this time it's not just the guilds kicking up a fuss. There are more folk than ever congregating at the gate calling for bread. The Merivale Watch is stretched to breaking point, and Gurathet has sent half the *Hymeriker* to watch Halord's Bridge. Balyard doesn't know what he's messing with.'

'Why's Gurathet sent men to the bridge?' asked Ciera. Surely the truce had not failed already.

'Rumours. Fighting in the west, if tales are to be believed, which I don't. Without the king's wizard, scouting is more confused than ever. It's either late or wrong or both, or sometimes they seem to report things that haven't even happened yet.'

Fighting in West Erland? Ciera hardly knew what to make of that. Good news for East Erland, but it did not alter her predicament.

'There must be dozens ready to support you,' said Arrik. 'We all—'

'I told you to shut it,' said Laphor. 'I don't like Gurathet being made *balhymeri*, and I like taking orders from Balyard even less, but are you ready to stake your life on which men in the barracks will see it that way?'

Arrik blanched. 'Well—'

'The answer's "no" if you've got the sense your mother birthed you with.' Laphor leant forward in his chair. 'Majesty, you need your son back, and you want Balyard and Gurathet gone. You understand we can't achieve that ourselves?'

'I've no other choice.' There was a lump in Ciera's throat. 'How many *hymerikai* do you think would follow me?'

'None I'd vouch for. Gurathet's unpopular, that's for sure, but men still need someone to follow, and that's not me.' Laphor glanced at Arrik, as if suddenly concerned about the younger man's opinion. 'There's only one *hymerika* who I think they might follow, if he got himself sober. The man you need is Errian Andrickson.'

CHAPTER 27

In every direction, all Drast could see was death.

They called it the Bleak Hills, this desolate hinterland of rolling knolls. The Bone Hills would have been just as apt. There might be nothing to eat, but there was a fine collection of human bones. Thousands upon thousands of slaves and soldiers had perished when an Imperial army had last braved this crossing, and their remains were everywhere, the soil so arid that they had barely decayed. There were no predators large enough to feast, and their bones had stayed where they fell, pecked clean by time and scavengers.

The Imperium then had had forty thousand, and still it had not been enough. Pedrian Sangreal, the first king of all Erland, had driven them back from the Pale River all the way back to these hills, and killed every son of Kzar Yoratho for good measure.

Drast had twenty-five thousand men, and sufficient food that most should survive the march, but only twelve thousand from the Eternal Legion, three companies comprising nine thousand infantry and three thousand riders. The rest were mostly slaves, under the command of an assortment of senators.

Some of these he was glad to have. A thousand *prifectai*, Imperium-owned slaves bred and trained for the single purpose of violence, all over six and a half feet tall and rippling with the muscle necessary to wear the crushing weight of their steel plate; fifty war zebrephants owned by Senator Plutacto, nearly thrice the height of a man and armoured in huge sheets of chain mail, each attended by a dozen slaves to feed and control them; three mangonels and their firing crews, all disassembled and dragged in rickety wooden carts.

Others, he would gladly have left in Ulvatia, had they not needed every man that could be spared. Senator Bouteli the Belly had brought a thousand eunuchs, commanded by forty disgraced former legionnaires, and insisted he would go into battle with them on an enormous palanquin that required eight men to lift. They would be the first to die if Drast had his way. Senator Lorima, an eccentric elderly widow who had taken over her husband's Senate seat, commanded a force of five hundred warrior women, all identically garbed in golden scale armour with absurdly large metal nipples. The best Drast could say of them was that they would be more use than Bouteli the Belly.

That was all Saffia Murino had given him. Twenty-five thousand soldiers and slaves, and seemingly every one of them miserable and fearful, save the *prifectai*, who felt nothing and thought less. To Drast's irritation, even the legionnaires had been heard to complain. They were not fit to polish the swords of the men he had led in Cylirien. When he had asked Forren about the source of disquiet in camp, he had not been pleased by the answer: 'You can't see Urmé this far south. It disturbs the men to see only one moon in the sky.'

Drast had not even realised. In response, he swore that the next man he heard complain about anything would be force-fed zebrephant dung. He could not say the threat improved morale, but at least he did not have to listen to any more pathetic whining.

Drast did not even know how far there was still to go. He had heard that the mountain at the centre of Erland was so high the barbarians thought it endless. If they were close, he ought to be able to see it against the distant sky, but he could see nothing beyond the windblown clouds of dirt and detritus, obscuring the horizon behind a dark mist. A few days before, the winds had risen to a howling storm, and every man had been left covered in a grey dust, and spent the next day hacking it out of his lungs.

That thrice-damned bitch has sent me here to die, Drast thought, for the dozenth time that day. *I paid my dues in Cylirien, watching good men perish.* And now he would have to do it all again. It would have been better had he never thought of becoming kzar. He angrily kicked a rogue shinbone across his camp. The whole damn place was a graveyard.

'Patience, Senator,' counselled Forren, as he struck a match to spark their tiny cookfire. Despite his injuries, including the horrific burns to his left arm, he had refused to be left behind, and was bearing the journey better than many younger, more able-bodied men. 'We should save our fury for the Erlanders.'

'The Erlanders are nothing to me.' Drast removed his boots and lay down a blanket for himself near the fire. It was Saffia he was angry with.

He had to give her credit for the scheme. Kvarm's disappearance and the fire at his manor had left Drast too vulnerable to refuse her. And if he was fighting a war, he could not make trouble in Ulvatia by reminding people that she had stolen the election while Drast was unconscious. Either he succeeded and Saffia became the first kzar in generations to expand their territory, or Drast died, and her rule was secure.

'There is an opportunity here, Senator,' said Forren. His fire had caught, and he was carefully fanning the flames with a scrap of cloth. 'General Hallas who first suppressed the Cyliriens was elected kzar within a year of his return.'

'And died from an untreated wound a month later. I know our history.' It was a long-standing argument. It was a measure of his affection for the old soldier that he did not mind being lectured by him. Without Forren's counsel he had no prospect of victory.

Drast looked into the rising fire, and recoiled as Krupal's wizened face appeared in the flames. He shrieked and leapt to his feet, reaching hurriedly for his sword.

But there was no one there. The only thing that burnt in the flames was wood.

Parmé damn it, I am seeing things. It was not the first time either; there had been the occasion in Ulvatia, and during their journey he had already imagined he saw the ancient magus on a distant hill, and disguised among a knot of slaves. Knowing that Krupal was still out there somewhere was beginning to affect his nerves. The stress of returning to war was getting to him.

If he meant you harm he would have come for you already, Drast told himself.

'Are you well, Senator?' asked Forren, looking up from the fire.

Drast glanced back to where his slaves had just finished erecting his vast tent. It was the size of his study, made of thick cloth in the Fulkiro red-black-yellow stripes that gave some protection from the worst of the cold. 'I'm fine, Forren. Call me when our dinner is ready.' It was approaching the time of his weekly appointment with Saffia's agent, and a few moments to himself might calm his jumpiness. Drast paced towards the tent.

Safely inside, he retrieved the object Saffia had bestowed on him from the bottom of his trunk. A golden looking glass, faded with age and cracked near the bottom, wrapped tightly in black cloth. He had seen purses that could hold beyond their capacity, and boxes that could transport letters thousands of miles in an instant, but never anything so fascinating as this. If only it had not been such a constant source of vexation.

He unwrapped it, and the face of a beautiful young woman stared back at him.

She was blonde, short-haired, and milk-pale, with inscrutable diamond-hard eyes. Drast was immediately filled with loathing; this girl had been almost as much a torment to him as Saffia Murino.

'You're late,' she said. She had declined to provide her name.

'An army does not march according to your schedule,' he replied, sitting down and setting his back against his trunk.

'More's the pity. If it did you would already be in Erland.'

Drast looked to the heavens. 'Which you have told me nothing of! If I was there already, I would be as blind and clueless as a newborn!'

'You will know when you need to,' she said, 'but

currently you can't even tell me how far away you are. How many miles today?'

'Because nobody has made this crossing in over a century!' Drast had searched his library, and found that none of the reports gave a straight answer. One soldier's account claimed the crossing had taken four months, but the diary of a battle magus suggested it had taken less than two. 'Surely you can tell me something? I don't want to come down from these hills and find King Hessian's host waiting for me.'

'By your unnecessary delay and all your worrying, I am starting to think that you fear the Erlanders.'

Drast grunted a laugh. *I am many things, but I am no coward.* 'Speak to me of fear when the long grass rustles in the depths of winter and you do not know whether it is the wind or a troop of Cyliriens come to kill you. Speak to me of fear when you have found your friends nailed to trees by their hands with their feet cut off and left to bleed out. It is not the Erlanders I fear, but your folly.'

She sighed, and adjusted the mirror slightly. 'There's no need for theatrics; I have information for you.'

Drast saw at her neck a silver brooch clasping a cloak. She pulled on a red hat and adjusted it to an angle, as might have been fashionable in Ulvatia thirty years ago. 'Where are you going?'

'It does not concern you.' She paused to light a smoke-stick. 'Now do you want to know or not?'

Drast did want answers, as little use as they might be. 'I would be grateful.'

'The two sides have agreed a truce,' she said. 'The rebel Rymond Prindian has returned to Irith.'

'So the west is no longer undefended.' Drast cared little for barbarian politics, but Kvarm's whole justification for this invasion had been that the Erlanders would be too busy fighting among themselves to mount a defence.

'It is not a problem. I have already begun to turn the situation to our advantage.' She dabbed perfume against her slender neck. 'Assuming you are mere days away, which you surely must be by now unless you are marching in circles, this is the last time we will speak before your arrival. When you reach Erland, you are to divide your force into three. You are to take command of the Legion's infantry and whatever slaves you need, then march directly for Irith. The rest you are to divide between following the coast and sweeping in on Irith from the north, and going further inland and coming up from the south. Whatever defence they muster will not stand against a three-pronged assault.'

Drast could feel the colour rising up his neck. Just who did this *girl*, this *nobody*, think she was? 'This is my army. I was winning battles when you were still some nasty, knock-kneed little brat, and I will deploy it *as I see fit*.'

'You asked for information, and I am giving it to you.' The girl was not even looking at him. 'My plan is the best way to ensure your victory. The kzar does not want you fucking this up like you did that business with the fire. Now if you'll excuse me.' She put the mirror down, and as she did Drast caught a final glimpse of a large comfortable chamber and a four-poster bed before it was covered by a dark cloth.

He flung the mirror onto the bed. *Let's see her dismiss me like that when I arrive with an army.* He would have to follow her plan though. All he knew was to go to Irith; he had no idea how many the Erlanders might raise in defence, how they were armed, or who commanded them.

But if I win a resounding victory, who will dare try to claim it from me? The glory would be his, and once he was in

Irith, he would deal with this nameless girl, whoever she was. There were all sorts of ways one could come to an unfortunate end during a siege, or in a war camp.

———

The next morning, the sun pierced the smog that hung over the Bleak Hills for the first time in weeks, and white clouds were visible in the distance. The mood of the whole army seemed to lift. Drast heard no more whispers of their doom, or ill omens.

That afternoon, his horse crested a hill. The wastelands ahead seemed endless, but the black mist melted away, revealing to him a distant shadow, obscured by a shroud of fog, and so faint it might have been a mirage.

Eryispek. Even from here, he knew it could be nothing else. There was presence to it, as though it had stood since before the creation of the world. For a moment, he could almost hear the whistling wind showering the land in sheets of ice, and the war cries of drunken barbarians.

Forren appeared behind him. 'That's it, then.'

Drast nodded. A long way from his study, with its soft chairs and tended fire. He looked back the way he had come, the wasteland stretching on into the void, his tired army snaking behind him like the tail of whipped cur.

Win or lose, Saffia Murino had sent him here to die. Well, he would scorn her by living. And in her arrogance, she had given him an army.

'The road back to Ulvatia is through Erland,' he muttered. If he could win here, he could win in Ulvatia. A swift victory was what was needed, to prove himself, to prove the idiocy of the Cylirien occupation. He would be a hero, the general who made the Imperium *imperial* again. Saffia Murino thought herself clever, but she did not understand men as he did. If he took Erland, the Eternal Legion would clamour for him, and when he returned a conqueror, the people would clamour for him too. And then, when he took the kzarship from her, who would object? The Senate? Drast would deal with the Senate.

Drast smiled. 'We will do good work here, Forren. When we are finished, the world shall once again tremble before the Imperium.' *And Saffia Murino will know not to underestimate Drast Fulkiro.*

CHAPTER 28

In his chamber mirror, Rymond scratched at the collar of his silk tunic, cursing how uncomfortable it was, and that he had to wear it at all. He finally gave up on the collar and cast an emerald-green cape about his shoulders.

The coming celebration had been his mother's idea. 'A new king must be generous,' she had told him. 'The families that supported you expect a little gratitude.' Rymond had hoped they would be as weary and reluctant as he was, but Irith Castle was full to bursting with the lords he had ridden to war with and their families. Rymond would have been happier with a celebration for those who had fought, noble and common alike, but his mother insisted that this was the way these things were done.

One person who would not be attending was Gruenla. Tales had reached Irith of shepherds seeing strange fires in the heights of the Bleak Hills, and Adfric had suggested that sending Gruenla to investigate with her Cyliriens would get them out of the city, just in case she was the spy. Rymond had reluctantly agreed.

Rymond dismissed the servants, resisting the urge to scour his trunk for more casheef, and made his way towards the hall.

He could already hear the hubbub from within as he approached; he could not ever recall the castle being so busy. Every time he encountered his steward the man looked ready to give up and keel over. Rymond entered through the private antechamber, next to the hideous throne he tried to avoid, and a sea of faces quietened at the sight of him as the cadre of musicians fell silent.

Rymond raised a hand to quell the few whispers still audible. 'Thank you for coming.'

The hall burst into applause, which echoed off the high ceiling and thick walls, followed by cries of 'Eryi's blessing on King Rymond!' or 'Hail King Rymond!' or even just 'King Ry!' Rymond could not help grinning, then as the applause dampened, he realised he was expected to say something. His smile faltered.

'Thank you all for coming!' he repeated awkwardly. 'And be welcome to my meat and mead. The last time I had so many staring at me, it was the East Erland army. Fortunately, the crowd before me is significantly fairer to look upon.'

They laughed politely, and Rymond tried to hold back a grimace. It was part of being king, he supposed, that everyone was required to laugh at your weak jests.

'I hope to speak to every one of you before the night is over! I, and all of Irith, welcome you. Drink your fill, be merry, and speak to me of anything other than war!'

A ripple of laughter followed, and Rymond sensed he had said enough. With some reluctance, he descended the dais into the throng of waiting subjects.

For an hour, he walked among them, and sometimes

almost began to enjoy himself. Lady Storaut, half as old and twice as engaging as her husband, insisted that one of her five unwed daughters would be a perfect match for him. Lord Darlton the Younger, not truly a lord while his father still lived, wanted to refight the Battle of Whitewater using cups of wine, but was continually thwarted by people retrieving their drinks. Adfric kept a merciful distance, and Strovac Sigac was nowhere to be seen.

'I hear you've been returning to your old haunts,' came a sharp voice from behind Rymond, during a brief moment when he had stepped away to recover himself.

With a sigh, Rymond turned around. 'Mother, I had one night at the inn on my return.' She wore a sleek silver-white dress, studded with emeralds, and her copper hair had been elaborately curled. 'Since then I have hardly left the castle.' Most evenings he spent in his chamber, smoking casheef on the balcony.

'Even so, you have left it to me to deal with your realm. Coinage, taxation, land disputes – all of it has fallen to me. Why are you avoiding your duty?'

'Because I saw enough of you at war.' That was part of it. The other part was that he feared if they spent too much time together she would uncover his casheef habit. It had been easy to hide in the chaos of a war camp, but Irith Castle was his mother's dominion. 'I'd have thought you'd be glad I was leaving those matters to you. What do you want, Mother?'

'I want you to start acting like a king. Whatever you may think, I did not crown you so I could rule myself. Thrones are not only won and lost on the battlefield; if you fail to take responsibility for your realm, there will be a line of foes ready to take from you. I hoped war would be the making of you, and yet I fear you have not changed at all.'

Rymond's reply was interrupted by an exchange of shouting from the entrance, and he looked around in alarm as Adfric came barrelling towards him to place himself between his king and the disturbance. The guests had all turned to look as well; the rising voices and general uproar indicated some disagreement.

'Stay behind me, Majesty,' said Adfric, gripping his sword hilt.

'Eryi's balls, Adfric, take a night off. Hessian is not going to murder me at my own feast.' Rymond slid past Adfric to see Gruenla and her Cyliriens standing toe-to-toe with several of Rymond's guards. One of the mercenaries had a burgeoning bruise under his eye, but mercifully no one had drawn steel yet. Rymond hurried through the throng.

Gruenla caught sight of him. 'Majesty, Imperials! Imperials—'

'I've told you it's bollocks!' said a guardsman, cutting over the top of her. 'There's been no Imperials in West Erland for over a hundred years!'

'What do you mean, Imperials?' demanded Rymond, shoving his way through the last of the guests with Adfric following behind.

'To the north-west coming down from the Bleak Hills,' said Gruenla. 'I saw them with my own eyes!'

As the sun rose, Rymond found himself astride a horse once again, staring westward into the dew-sprinkled grass at their long charcoal shadows. Adfric rode beside him. For all

Rymond's complaints, he was glad to have him at his side. The man was utterly unwavering in his duty; Rymond would not have been able to rouse an army without him. Some five thousand rode alongside them, all veterans of the campaign against East Erland. It was fortunate timing to have so many lords already in Irith attending the feast.

'Are you sure about this, Majesty?' said Adfric. 'What if Gruenla's lying and it's a trap? Even if she's just mistaken, you've put the fear of the Norhai into these men for nothing.'

'What choice do we have? If the Imperials have crossed the Bleak Hills...' It did not bear thinking about. The last time they had invaded West Erland, the country had rolled over and ended up yoked to the East. 'I know she might be lying; that's why we're leaving her and the Cyliriens behind.'

'We should keep our force here and send out scouts.'

Rymond shook his head. 'We can scout better from the field. If the Imperium is out there, I want to attack while we have surprise on our side.' It was what Andrick Barrelbreaker would have done. 'Did you find Strovac?'

'No sign of him. I found enough of the Wild Brigade but they refused to answer any command other than Strovac's and wouldn't tell me where he was hiding.'

That was a blow, Rymond had to admit. The Wild Brigade were the fiercest warriors in his army. 'Well, we can't wait for them. Raise my banner.'

Dutifully, Adfric lifted their emerald-green standard. Rymond held up a fist to the men behind him, and squeezed his calves against his horse's flanks to urge it forward. Behind him, five thousand men followed, and the calm of the morning was broken by the clip-clop of hooves, the rattle of mail, and a deafening war cry.

As they made camp that night, Rymond, like Adfric, was beginning to wonder if this was indeed some trick of the Cyliriens. All their scouts reported nothing, and Rymond could sense his men's unease. Fighting the East Erlanders, they had known who their enemy was, where they were, and how they fought. Now they were riding blind; the enemy could be four times their strength or might not exist at all. Gruenla claimed there were at least five thousand, but how much was that worth?

Rymond stared into his campfire, inattentively spooning stew into his mouth, wishing he had some casheef.

'You look like you're chewing a wasp, Lord.' Across the fire, Adfric hunched over his own bowl of stew. His master-at-arms had once seemed as vigorous as a man of Rymond's own age, but after the wound he had taken at Whitewater and his brief imprisonment at the hands of Lady Viratia he was beginning to look his years. His well-kempt beard had faded from ash to snow, and he had winced at the crack in his knees as he sat down. 'Here.' He tossed a wineskin over the fire. 'Spot of wine usually cheers you up.'

Rymond threw it back at him. 'Not tonight.' If he drank, he would want casheef even worse, and as there was none, he would drink more. He tipped back his bowl and emptied the remaining stew into his mouth, then set it aside and came to his feet. 'I'm going to bed.' The prospect did not thrill him; there had been no time to pack his usual grand tent, so he was making do with a small shelter lent to him by Lord Darlton. 'Wake me if anything happens.'

Inside, he lay down on his straw mattress and closed his eyes.

It felt like only a few moments later that he was woken by Gerant, his young servant, poking his head through the tent flap. 'Majesty, there's a scout here; he says he's seen something!'

Rymond sat bolt upright. Cursing, he pulled his discarded clothes back on and crawled through the flap.

The scout, a skinny boy little older than Gerant, was deep in conversation with a frowning Adfric. 'Majesty!' Adfric beckoned Rymond over. 'Tell the king what you just told me.'

'Barely five miles away!' the scout said breathlessly. 'I was about to turn back, but there was one more hill, so thought I'd take a look from there. There are *thousands* of them!'

Eryi's balls, Gruenla was right. So was Strovac the spy? What would he be getting up to in Irith unsupervised? Or was this Gruenla's trap, to place Rymond in harm's way? This was no time to worry about it. 'Were they settling down for the night?'

'Looked that way.'

'Are they more or less than us?'

The boy swallowed. 'Perhaps double.'

Rymond scratched at the rash on his neck. He might spend weeks amassing that sort of strength. 'Adfric, ready the men to march. We'll leave our gear here.'

'Majesty, night marches are treacherous,' said Adfric. 'We should send some scouts closer to their camp, get a better judge of their strength. We don't know—'

'Adfric, given their numbers there's no better time to attack!' Rymond laughed, his cheeks flushing with both thrill and fright at the prospect of battle. 'They might not even know we're here! We won't get a better chance than this. Ready the men. Leave everything we can behind.'

Within a half-hour, they were back in the saddle. The men grumbled at first, but once they heard their enemy was so close they were passing wineskins back and forth between them again as if they had never made camp.

At their head, Rymond had summoned Lord Storaut and the portly Rudge Darlton. 'We'll hit their camp from three points of the compass. Storaut, you'll come from the west, and Darlton, you from the east, while I come up from the south. When we're within a mile, Adfric will dip my banner and we'll divide. Once we're positioned, watch for a torch. That's the signal.'

Rudge Darlton was grinning heartily. 'Never thought I'd get the chance to cross swords with an Imperial! We'll send the bastards to their black-hearted gods, have no fear on that, Majesty.'

'And if the battle should turn against us?' said Lord Storaut.

Rymond's gut rumbled. Just like Storaut to pour cold water on his plan. 'Make for Irith. We'll hold them there.'

The two lords departed to their soldiers, and Rymond was left with Adfric and their scout. 'What's your name?'

The boy swallowed. 'Brant, Majesty.'

'Lead on, Brant.'

They rode by torchlight at a slow canter, but the summer night was cloudless, the stars shining bright overhead, and as they left camp, Rymond passed the order that all lights were to be extinguished. 'Can you find your way by starlight, Brant?'

'My father grazes sheep on these lands. I could find my way blindfolded.'

Adfric offered Rymond a wineskin, and this time he took a long measure before passing it to Brant.

At some point, the ground began to rise slightly, and Rymond could make out the ridge of a hill against the inky sky. 'We're almost there,' whispered Brant.

Adfric dipped the banner, and Rymond looked back to see their forces divide, Storaut going left and Darlton right.

They crested the rise, among the cover of wild foliage, and Rymond gasped as a vast patchwork of tents and fires came into view below. He could only imagine they had chosen the low ground to avoid their camp being spotted. Brant's assessment of their strength had been correct, but what surprised him was the grandness of some of their tents. The one at the centre of their camp could have held his own vast tent three or four times over, with six sides and striped in a garish red, black, and yellow. Beyond it, at the camp's far edge, were what looked to be great mounds of earth, but even straining his eyes through the darkness Rymond could not deduce what they were. More tents? They did not look like tents. Piles of waste? It would take weeks to produce so much.

'Majesty?' asked Adfric. Rymond glanced over, to see him holding his flint against an oil-soaked rag held by Brant. Looking down the hill to their west and east, Rymond could make out the forces of Storaut and Darlton, half-hidden in the shadow of trees.

There was no sense in delaying. Rymond drew his sword, and a racket of steel hissing against leather followed as every man behind him did the same. Sparks flew as Adfric struck his flint, and the oiled torch ignited.

With a wild yell, Rymond drove his horse forward, and

thousands of men thundered after him, churning up earth and screaming for West Erland.

Their noise lent heart to Rymond, who for a moment forgot to feel afraid. He was no warrior, but he had learnt from his time at war that in battle the key to survival was never to hesitate, never to show fear, and never to leave Adfric's side. He had his own bodyguards, six men in mail painted Prindian green, all fearsome fighters a match for any *hymerika*. They fanned out around him, ready to intercede with steel should anyone come too close to their king. If it went to plan, Rymond would not cross blades with anyone; his role was to get the men to follow him, to see that their king shared the dangers they faced in his name.

As they roared into the Imperial camp, Rymond caught his first glimpse of the enemy. Gaunt, glass-eyed men in rags stared up at them, around tents little more than twigs and sheets.

The West Erlanders rode straight over them. Rymond lashed out with his sword, but before he could see if his victim was dead their horses were already past them, as thousands of warriors thrust into the Imperial camp.

These ragged men were everywhere, fleeing in terror and crying out in a foreign tongue as Rymond's Erlanders charged straight over their flimsy tents. Rymond lashed out as a few came within sword range, but he soon realised it was pointless; they were not even armed.

'Make for the pavilion at the centre!' Rymond cried, raising his sword to point their way. If there were men worth killing, they would find them there. To both sides of the camp, he caught flashes of torchlight and the clash of steel as Storaut and Darlton joined the slaughter.

Rymond drove forward as the rest followed in his wake.

Torches were thrown and lanterns smashed, spilling flaming oil everywhere and igniting fires. All around, the Imperials were fleeing. Rymond began to wonder if his fears had been uncalled for; he could have ridden into any Erlish village and encountered more resistance.

But as they neared the centre of the camp and the tents grew larger, Rymond realised his hubris. The unarmed, ragged men they had ridden down were slaves, and the true soldiers of the Imperium were lining up ahead behind long rectangular shields, in armour that shone golden under the starlight and visored helmets with great purple plumes that added an extra foot in height.

An Imperial shield wall formed before him, a hedgehog of long spears, and Rymond brought his horse to a halt barely in time. The rest skidded and pulled up with him, but one man failed to stop and rode straight into it. His horse screamed as it galloped into a spear and its rider went flying over the Imperials.

Their foe took heart from the Erlanders' hesitation, and cried out with one voice as they stepped forward, thrusting their weapons. Rymond barely pulled back in time to stop his horse being skewered, but others were not so lucky, going down under a flurry of Imperial spears.

'Retreat!' Rymond cried, whirling his mount around. The Imperials were as disciplined as their reputation; they had formed up quicker than he would have believed possible. For a moment, he wondered if he could have made a fatal error.

Then the other two-thirds of their force crashed into the Imperial flanks.

The shield wall buckled, and broke, as two torrents of horseflesh thundered through them. Rymond thought he saw

Rudge Darlton in the midst of it, swinging a flail in every direction and smashing skulls like melons.

'Forward!' cried Adfric, and Rymond rode with him.

As with the slaves, it was more butchery than battle, but at least these men were armed, and Rymond did not feel quite so guilty as he cast about him with his sword. An arrow nicked his shoulder, and as he turned looking for his would-be killer a second Imperial thrust at him with a spear, which he sliced the head off before burying his sword in the man's neck. The air was alive with the cries of triumphant Erlanders, as the Imperials broke and ran before their three-way assault.

Heedless of the caution he knew he ought to have, Rymond urged them onward. 'Take that pavilion!' If they could capture their commander—

The horn that split the night was so loud it was wont to deafen him; a chilling, endless howl that drowned out the chaos of battle and twisted Rymond's blood. After several moments, it faded to an echo, and the whole battlefield fell silent, as if waiting for something.

There came a chorus of trumpeting near as loud as the horn itself. Rymond stared towards the far end of camp, where by the glow of a hundred tiny fires over a dozen mountainous shadows galloped straight for them. They were enormous, striped white-on-black, with strange long noses that moved of their own accord and tusks near as long as a man, covering the ground with long strides that shook the earth beneath their feet. One raised its trunk and released another great bellow, before the rest added their own cries in a hellish cacophony that seemed to echo off the sky and envelop the night.

'Zebrephants,' Rymond breathed. He had thought them

a myth. At least he knew now what those mounds of earth had been.

They had no hope against such behemoths. 'Retreat!' The great beasts were fast, faster than Rymond could have imagined. He was not sure if anyone heard his command, for they continued to gape as if they could not believe what they were seeing. More than one Erlander was pierced by an Imperium spear as they gazed on in wonder.

With his own horn, Adfric broke the spell. He placed himself directly in front of Rymond, and blew long and loud. 'Retreat! Retreat!' He blew again, a mournful wail that hung over the field like smoke.

And this time, the Erlanders listened. They scattered whichever way they could, heedless of the Imperials who were lashing out with their spears and rushing to reform their shattered shield wall. Purple-fletched arrows flew, and two men near Rymond fell screaming.

Rymond felt a hand on his reins and cried out in alarm, until he realised it was Adfric, guiding his horse. Rymond set his heels to its flanks, and together they galloped away, the thundering zebrephants now so close that the ground was shaking. 'Retreat! Retreat!' His men had done well, but they could not stand against the zebrephants. Better to retreat now before the Imperials could bring their greater numbers to bear.

They rode hard for their camp. Adfric was panting, and blood was seeping from his shoulder and down his mail. 'It's nothing, Majesty,' he told Rymond when he caught him looking. 'Just an old wound reopened.'

'What do you make of their strength?' asked Rymond as they swiftly packed their camp up, once Adfric had sealed his wound with a burning tree branch.

'Too many slaves. They'll be days trying to recover them and getting them to march again. And did you get a look at those legionnaires? Boys, the lot of them.' Adfric thrust the last of his belongings into his saddlebag. 'All these years I thought the Imperials were to be feared.' He gave a low laugh, and Rymond saw him wince at the stretch in his shoulder. 'If they had a hundred more of those zebrephants I might worry, but you can't win a war with a dozen of them. And think what it takes to feed them!'

Rymond let himself by reassured by Adfric's words. What use would those beasts be in a siege of Irith?

'And well done, Majesty. We'll make a warrior of you yet.'

It was the faintest of praise, but Rymond welcomed it.

Dawn was breaking as they began their journey back to Irith, once Rymond had been assured by Adfric that this was the right strategy. 'We know they're coming now, Majesty, and they won't know our land. We'll send word to your lords and pick them to pieces before they come within sight of our walls, zebrephants or not.'

Irith rose on the horizon with the sun at its back, as a cluster of crows twisted overhead. It looked quieter than Rymond was used to; there were no coils of smoke over Irith Castle's kitchens, and the gates were shut. He could only suppose that they had closed them against the rumoured invasion, and that the fires had not been lit without a king there to cook for.

Storaut and Darlton had joined Rymond at the head of

their march. Darlton was a plump ball of excitement, keen to relive every sword swipe and spear thrust.

'...the way you led them down that hill, Majesty.' He chortled and gratefully received the wineskin Rymond tossed back to him. Darlton had insisted this was a West Erland victory, the first of many, and they ought to celebrate it as such. 'It was like Halord the First reborn! Not even King Pedrian—'

'We should not overdo it, Darlton,' croaked Storaut, looking his years and worse for their night's march. 'An Imperial force in our lands is no cause for celebration. We should send out scouts to track their movements.'

Rymond grinned at Darlton's acclaim even so. Their best estimate was that their lightning-strike attack had slain or injured over a thousand Imperials. And he had also gone almost their whole march without thinking about casheef.

He was surprised to see the gates were closed, and they did not open even as their host approached. The battlements were deserted. Rymond stopped below and called up to them. 'Ho! Your king demands entry!'

There was a moment of stillness, the city so eerily quiet that Rymond could hear the wind rushing between the merlons. Eventually, a spot-scarred guardsman appeared. He gave a nervous salute. 'Sorry, Majesty! Gate should be up in a moment.'

'We took all the good men with us,' muttered Adfric as the gate mechanism creaked. The master-at-arms swore his wound was fine, but the strained look on his face told different.

When the double gates were half-open, Rymond urged his horse through, with Adfric, Darlton, and Storaut alongside him. Then as he passed below the walls, the gate paused. The mechanism spluttered and began to creak the other way.

'What are you doing?' Rymond cried towards the gatehouse, at the men inside he could not see. 'There's still—'

On the battlements, a shadow stepped out, and with the rising dawn shining on the figure's mail it took Rymond a moment to recognise him. The hulking shape of Strovac Sigac came into focus, sword in hand.

'Strovac! What's going on?' An urgent dread settled in Rymond's belly.

The giant smiled. 'Heard from a good friend you want me dead.'

From the opposite gatehouse, Alcantra stepped into view, leading two Imperial legionnaires, and Rymond's heart and stomach sank right into the pit of his bowels. A nervous laugh escaped his lips. 'Now hold on. Just what—'

'What's going on here, Strovac?' blustered Darlton. The gate had closed now, and soldiers' confused shouting was audible over the wall. 'I know you and I haven't always seen eye-to-eye, but—'

'It's over, *Majesty*.' Strovac spoke over Darlton, addressing Rymond, his lip curling in mockery. 'I might have been half-minded to stay faithful to you, if not for your baseless accusation.'

Rymond's smile faltered. 'Now, hold on... Your men tried to kill Adfric. There was a spy in our camp! They were passing information to Hessian! If it wasn't you, I'm sorry, but you—'

'They were passing it to me,' said Alcantra, with a pointed smile.

Before Rymond could reply, a voice came from behind him. 'It was me, Ry.' And though he knew whose voice it was, he could not allow himself to believe it. Dreading what he would see, he turned his horse.

On the deserted road stood Dom, garbed in the fine clothes of a lord with a black cape streaming behind him, and surrounded by a company of Imperial legionnaires.

'Why, Dom?' asked Rymond. His voice sounded piteous, pleading. 'Is this because of Will?'

Dom laughed, his teeth gleaming like pearls. 'No, it's because of you. I tolerated you for Will, and you got him killed. I've seen enough to know that West Erland is better off without you.' He sniffed. 'Thanks for all the wine and gold though. All you're good for.'

Rymond looked back at Alcantra, and a cold horror raced up his spine, remembering waking in her room with only casheef-hazed memories for company.

Alcantra dangled a drawstring between her fingers, and even at this distance, Rymond's mouth went dry at the sight of casheef. '"*In casheef, truth*," the monks say.' Her smile was sharp as a razor. 'You told me everything.'

'Strovac!' Adfric had finally found his voice, while beside him Storaut only stared in bewilderment. 'Enough of this. End this madness, and we'll forget your treachery.'

It's too late. Rymond looked about. Members of the Wild Brigade and gold-armoured legionnaires were streaming from the gatehouses, from inns, from tailors and tanneries.

'I think not, Adfric.' Strovac pointed his sword towards them, looking down its edge through his cold, beady eyes. 'Take them. Do them no harm, unless they fight.'

Adfric's sword was already unsheathed, and Lord Darlton reacted only a millisecond later, drawing his own. 'No!' Rymond cried. There were dozens of them, descending on the four mounted lords like a horde of rats. Rymond let himself be pulled from his horse, but as he fell, saw Adfric cut two men down in the blink of an eye, and for a moment it looked as if he might fight his way free, until someone grabbed his bridle, and the throng dragged him down in a whirlwind of blades.

Something heavy and coarse was pulled over Rymond's head, and a drawstring drawn to cinch it to his neck. His sword was wrenched from its scabbard, his knife thrown to the ground, and then his hands were bound behind him by a tight cord that bit into his wrists.

He was dragged away, his boots bouncing on the cobbles, Strovac's high laughter ringing in his ears.

CHAPTER 29

Fisherton sprang up out of the wilderness as the morning's first rays of sunlight appeared from beyond the Mountain. The trees parted, and there it was, several dozen buildings upon the rising slope, circled around a high stone marker and a simple wooden sign indicating Eryispool was five miles north.

Viratia fell to her knees, sucking in deep breaths as if she had just surfaced from a river. Never had she been so relieved to see civilisation.

The wolves had harried them for two days all the way from the Little River, snapping at their heels, forcing them to turn and fight. Each time, they would drive the wolves back, leaving a handful of their brethren as corpses against the dark ground, and for a few miles they would dare to think themselves safe, only for the tireless howling to begin again, and for snarling jaws dripping with saliva to burst from the darkness. They had been able to take a few hours' rest in an abandoned hut, and for a time the wolves had left them alone, but as soon as they departed the howling pursuit had begun again. The second time they stopped, they had been forced to take refuge in the trees. The strangest part had been that the wolves had retreated to wait again rather than go for the mules.

Viratia looked around at her companions. Sister Laurane had died, bleeding out atop the mule when there had been no time to treat her. Two more of Hessian's *hymerikai* had fallen also; when two wolves had gripped Hessian's mule's legs in their jaws and almost tossed Hessian to the ground, they had been the two to go to him. They had fought the beasts off and paid with their lives, pulled to the ground under the mass of numbers.

Viratia had not even known their names. She promised herself she would learn them, not least so Hessian could be made to honour the families of the men who had saved his life.

Naeem was beside her, bent double with his hands on his knees, red and breathless. 'I've not run that much in decades,' he gasped. 'Never known wolves to act like that.' There was a wound at his knee, an angry black bitemark dripping blood.

He was not the only one injured. Viratia's ankle throbbed where she had stumbled, and there was a gash at her shoulder where a wolf had leapt at her from behind before Naeem's sword had sliced through its back. All the surviving *hymerikai* had cuts and bruises. Only Hessian and the two remaining brides had escaped wholly unhurt. Sister Aimya had swapped her staff for a *hymerika*'s spear, which she had wielded with such skill it seemed part of her arm.

Naeem saw Viratia looking at his injury. 'Just a scratch, Lady.'

'At least they weren't rabid,' said Aimya, leaning back with her hands on her hips, taking deep breaths, savouring the dawn air and looking as though she could run the same distance again. 'Eryi alone knows what got into them.'

'I would have said they were hungry, were it not for the dozens of corpses we left for them.' Naeem pushed his sweat-drenched hair back from his face. 'And those men we killed... little more than beasts themselves. I won't set foot in that forest again, not for as long as I live.'

Viratia could not help but agree. It seemed a long time ago that Aimya had mocked Naeem for his superstition.

'Fair-sized town,' said Aimya, considering Fisherton. A well-built inn stood opposite them, across the square, with a wooden tankard over the door. A crescent of smaller huts surrounded it, and a pair of mules not unlike their own were tied up around the side. The chimney was piping smoke, and there was a scent of cooking meat on the air.

'Aye,' said Naeem. 'But where are they all?'

As if he had been summoned, a stout, short man emerged from the inn, whistling tunelessly and carrying a pair of buckets. On edge, the five remaining *hymerikai* all reached for their swords.

The man stepped back, dropping his buckets with a clatter. 'Easy, friends!' He spoke like he was chewing through gristle. He was ghostly pale, bald save for a pair of wild whiskers, but he looked healthy enough; the belly protruding from beneath his furs suggested he did not miss many meals. 'You're the second group of outlanders we've seen this week. There was trouble with them; I hope we'll be having no trouble with you.' He gave a sharp whistle. There was a bustling behind him, and people appeared in every doorway, barely dressed, but holding heavy whalebone axes or with flint-headed arrows notched against their bows.

Viratia cast a contemptuous look over the five *hymerikai*.

'Put them away.' They all obeyed, to her relief. She had not come this far only to start a skirmish with the natives.

Hessian raised an arm to the assembled Adrari. Even upon the mule, there had been times when Viratia thought he might not survive their pursuit through the forest, but something about the presence of men had stirred some life into him. 'Forgive my men. It was a hard journey, and we are weary. I am King Hessian.'

At Hessian's words, the man's eyes grew wide as the Pale River. He fell to his knees, not paying the least bit of notice to the mud at his feet. The rest followed, throwing down their weapons and dropping to the ground. 'Forgive me, Majesty,' the man pleaded. 'Our town is yours.'

Hessian beckoned them to their feet. He nodded to the stone marker beneath the signpost. 'Is that where Dacar of the Adrari knelt before King Piper?'

'It is, Majesty. We have been loyal subjects of the Sangreals ever since, all of us. I'm Haim, the alderman.'

'The bond between the Adrari and the Meridivals goes back generations; I am proud to stand where that bond was formed. If you can provide us food and lodgings we will see you fairly rewarded.'

Hessian dismounted the mule, and immediately was surrounded by fur-clad Adrari, almost falling over themselves in their eagerness to lead him to their inn.

'You'd think he was Eryi himself,' muttered Naeem.

The inn was simple, the furniture a mishmash of old wood and carefully carved whalebone and its walls draped in furs against the cold, with a fire burning in one hearth. Haim, apparently not only the alderman but also the innkeeper, wasted no time in getting a second fire going, and soon their party was spread across the inn. Viratia took a table with

Naeem, but when Aimya tried to join them, Velna ushered the girl away to the next table.

A hearty breakfast of bacon and root vegetables with mugs of mead was soon placed before them by Haim's wife, who introduced herself as Kari. They ate quietly, save for Hessian's young guardsmen, giddy with the joy of having survived both an ambush by bandits and a pursuit by wolves, and eager to relive every swing of their sword. It was too much for some of them, who could not help falling asleep at the table.

They deserved it, Viratia had to admit. Of the twelve they had set out with it was no accident that these five had survived.

'They'll know real battle one day,' said Naeem. 'It's not all so easy as slaughtering starving men and culling wolves.'

'Let them have their moment,' said Viratia. 'In a day or two they will remember the friends we left behind, without even a funeral pyre.'

'There is none so beloved by Eryi as he who falls in his service!' cried Sister Velna from the next table. The elder bride had declined the offer of food. 'When their souls find their way above the clouds, pyre or not, he will honour them as if they were his own children.' Beside her, Sister Aimya rolled her eyes.

Viratia only wished she could be so certain. Did Andrick feast with Eryi? Or were the ashes of the dead only ashes, and the bodies unburnt no more than food for worms? And what truly lurked on Eryispek? 'Pardon me,' she said to Kari as she slid more bacon onto their plates. Across the room, Haim was speaking nineteen-to-the-dozen to Hessian, while the king smiled through gritted teeth and helped himself to liberal measures of mead. 'Your husband mentioned a first group of outlanders who passed through. Who were they?'

Kari frowned. She was pale as her husband, with grey hair that looked to have been cropped with a knife. 'Strange business that. I'd sent my boy to the forest to catch something for the breakfast pot. He was pissing about in the trees as he does and saw the whole thing. Fight or something between these outlanders and a few snowheads. We found two outlanders the next day, bound and drugged, and a snowhead man dead nearby.'

'Snowhead?'

'Them from up Eryispek. We're one tribe supposedly, but we've more in common with you flatlanders than them. Didn't see them myself, but—'

Viratia leant over the table towards Kari. 'Who were the outlanders?'

'Never gave names. An old woman – didn't like the look of her, not had Lutums in these parts for generations – and this bald fellow. They set off sharpish, once they'd woken up a bit, off up the Mountain. My lad swears he saw them snowheads steal this girl who was with them.'

Pherri. Viratia's heart leapt. 'How long ago?' she demanded. 'Can I speak to your son?'

'Couple of days ago it was. I'll find him; probably still asleep knowing his lazy arse.'

Kari disappeared in search of her son, and Viratia buried her face in her hands. *A few days.* If not for Hessian delaying them at Piperskeep and then the wolves they might have beaten them here. She had been so close.

They took Pherri. The bald man was Theodric, but why was Delara with him? Viratia's one hope had been that the magus would protect her daughter, but he seemed to have gone out of his way to place Pherri in danger. It had been only his efforts that had stopped Delara poisoning her.

Kari returned, steering a skinny, shaven-headed boy of around twelve towards their table, his eyes half-closed like he had just woken up. Kari jabbed him in the shoulder. 'Tell this lady what you told me, about what you saw the other night.'

The boy rubbed his eyes again and yawned, revealing a gap where his two front teeth ought to have been. 'They tied up the man and woman, then one of them picked up the girl and tried to carry her off. She killed him though; one of the others had to carry her instead.'

Kari grabbed her son by the ear, making him yelp. 'Don't you be spreading that tale again. How would a little girl—'

'I saw it!' The boy freed his ear and leapt away. 'She did magic, I'm telling you! She did something, and he just fell over. You saw – there wasn't a mark on him!' Kari swiped for him, but the boy danced past her and ran for the door.

'You get back here, you bloody little liar!' she called after him. 'Pay his tale no mind; had I not seen the two outlanders come wandering into town the next morning I'd not believe a word of it.'

Viratia had heard enough. She slid a pair of gold coins across the table towards Kari. 'Thank you. We'll need a guide, and supplies for a dozen, as much as we can carry.'

Naeem had seemed content to listen, but now spoke up. 'Steady now, Lady. We're in no shape to go straight on after the last few days. Might be all right if we had horses we could sleep on, but we don't. We'll move quicker on the morrow.'

'There are mules; I saw them outside.' Viratia would not delay for a minute while Pherri was in danger. 'Andrick was famed for marching through the night and the next day.'

'But we marched for Andrick. Some because we loved

him, others because they feared him.' Naeem pointed across the room to Hessian's guardsmen, of whom only two were still awake. 'Think they love or fear you enough to follow you up Eryispek on no sleep? Some of them have probably never left Merivale before.' He took a long draught of mead.

The fatigue beneath Naeem's words made Viratia suddenly aware of her own tiredness. She pushed the hair out of her face and rubbed at her eyes. She could not afford to be tired. 'Just us two will go. We don't need them.'

Naeem glanced at Sister Velna and the next table and lowered his voice. 'Lady, I regret to tell you that we do. We just faced down men with the sense of beasts and beasts with the sense of men. Those wolves weren't hunting for meat; they knew us. Whatever is on that Mountain, whoever's taken your girl, you won't help her by getting yourself killed. Sounds like Theodric's already after these kidnappers anyway, and the wizard's not a man to be trifled with lightly.'

That did not stop him losing Pherri. Viratia stared at Naeem levelly. 'Six hours' sleep, then we go, while it's still light.'

Kari gave no indication she had heard anything pass between them. 'There's three rooms you can take. I'll give the king his own, and put the men in together and the women in together.'

From the next table, Velna sniffed. 'The truly devout have no need of feather beds, sustained as we are by faith in Eryi. The first women to make this pilgrimage had no such luxury, and nor do we. Lady Viratia may have her own room; we shall sleep in the stable.'

Behind her, Sister Aimya looked to the heavens. The younger bride wrapped herself in one of the furs given to

them by the Adrari and traipsed off in the direction of the
small lean-to stable they had seen outside.

Viratia watched her leave. *That girl's an enigma.* Rail-
thin, but deadly with a spear. Pretty too, with a storm of
golden hair hidden under her hood, and by the way some of
the *hymerikai* looked at her as she passed, Viratia was not the
only one to have noticed. By the slight smile Aimya gave
them she knew it too. Perhaps not all the Brides of Eryi were
so devout as Sister Velna thought.

'I'll head off as well,' said Naeem, wincing at the pain in
his knee as he stood then downing the last of his mead. 'I've
never been one to fall asleep at the table.' He made for
upstairs, taking another tankard from the bar as he left.

Alone, Viratia chewed at her nails, like she had as a girl.
Something on Eryispek was amiss. What had Theodric come
searching for? If she found him before he found her daughter, Viratia would make the magus wish he had never set eyes
on Pherri.

She looked across the room, to where Hessian now sat
alone.

He might know something. The Sangreals had ruled East
Erland for three hundred years; what dark secrets had been
passed down from father to son in that time?

She went to join him, and sat down opposite. 'We must
be on our way again in six hours. Pherri was here just days
ago.' She did not honour him with his title; such things
seemed to matter far less after their flight through the forest.
Outside Merivale, away from his power, he was an old man
much like any other.

Hessian chuckled. 'And who gave you command? We
will leave when I say we leave.'

'I'll go on without you then.' Naeem would come with

her if she pressed him, she was sure of it. 'But tell me: what do you know of Eryispek? What power acts against us?'

He looked at her blankly. 'Power?'

'The men who attacked us, and the wolves. That was not bad luck, Hessian. Something is trying to stop us reaching the Mountain.'

He stared at her for a moment, and then threw back his head and laughed, startling the sleeping boys at the next table. It was a bleak, creaking sound, not far from a death rattle. 'A few nights outdoors and Naeem's peasant tales have got to you. Banditry and beasts in the forest do not require some sorcerous conspiracy.'

'Wolves do not chase men for miles when there is fresh meat on the ground. And why had they not troubled the bandits? Why did they leave the mules?'

Hessian shrugged. 'Have you ever tasted mule? We were probably just in their territory.' He sipped his mead. 'Leave me. I have no intention of moving on today. Haim tells me we can cut days off our journey by rowing across Eryispool, once their fishermen return, so that's what we'll do. And remember: once I touch Eryispek I am going no further.'

Trying to hide her fury, Viratia rose in a rush from the table. Truly he was mad. But if he knew anything, he had hidden it well.

As Viratia walked back towards her table, Sister Velna flagged her down. 'Fear not, Lady. Sister Aimya and I will travel as far as you require. Faith will be our guide, and if your daughter holds her love for Eryi steadfast in her heart, no harm shall come to her.'

'Thank you, Sister,' replied Viratia through gritted teeth. 'That is most reassuring. The quickest route is across Eryispool; we'll go by boat. Excuse me a moment.'

She walked to the bar, where Haim was still polishing his tankards.

'What's up there, on Eryispek?' she asked. She was too tired to waltz around the point.

Haim exhaled in a low whistle. 'Depends how high you go. You've got Adrari settlements all the way up this side for miles. Above that... well, beasts and snow and such! I learnt young I was better suited down here.' He laughed. 'The cold turns some of them funny in the head. Did my wife tell you—'

'She did,' said Viratia. 'But I think you know there's something more up there than just snow. Something's been trying to stop us from reaching here ever since we stepped off the barge.'

Haim shook his head, and turned his back to her, busying himself at the rear of the bar. 'No good comes of asking that question. I came down here to avoid all that.'

'Tell me. My daughter is up there.'

'Was she the girl my son saw?'

'She's twelve.'

'I shall pray for her, and for you. But I can't tell you anything.'

Before she could enquire further, Haim fled through the back of the bar, leaving Viratia no surer of anything. What trouble had Theodric dragged Pherri into, dragged them all into? The idea that Pherri's magic might have allowed her to kill a man only made her more afraid.

INTERLUDE

Maghira emerged from the downward path into a cavern similar to the one above, the words of the voice still ringing in her ears. *'There is a girl. You must stop her going to him, and bring her to me.'* Ponderous stalactites hung from the ceiling, and a fire glowed at the centre, with a handful of people sitting around it. Relief rose in Maghira's heart, and as the figures turned to look at her, she recognised her brother Garimo, pale and gaunt, with deep bags under his eyes and his furs dirty with wear.

'Maghira!' Garimo rose and rushed towards her, and his embrace almost knocked the breath from her. She was shocked to see how thin he was. 'What are you doing here? Did Father send you?'

'Bringing you food,' said Maghira, dropping her sack in front of him. 'But I don't understand. There was something—'

'We do not need your food.' Their uncle Antares hobbled towards them with his staff. 'How did you get here? Do you have any idea what you've done?' The lean months had not diminished his presence, his eyes blazing beneath his heavy brow.

'We watched for weeks,' protested Maghira. 'It is late spring; we thought you must be trapped up here by the bad weather.'

'I have survived seventy winters. Do you think bad weather would stop me coming back if I had a mind to?'

'We had to stay, Maghira,' said Garimo. He stood half-a-head taller than Antares, but he still quailed slightly before him. 'The—'

'Not another word.' Antares's staff was whip-fast. It struck Garimo on the temple, and the younger man stumbled back clutching his head. Maghira cried out in protest. When she was younger, Antares had often sat her and her cousins on his knee and told them the stories of their people. He had been kind then, laughing readily, with a mug of mead in his fist. But this was not that man; this was the wild man who had once killed five Lutums with his bare hands. 'Bad enough that she has come here.' Antares shook his stick towards Maghira, as if he meant to hit her next. 'We'll take the food, but you need to leave. You are lucky to be alive, assuming the village does not kill you for this desecration.'

'I would hear how she reached us first,' came a calm voice. Ruhago, another of Antares's generation, was approaching from the fire. In the village, he was famed for his wisdom, but also for a long-standing feud with Antares. It was said that either would have made a fine alderman, had they been prepared to accept the authority of the other. Ruhago was as lean as Antares was brawny, with cool grey eyes like a winter's sky. 'Perhaps she can help us. What did you see in the chamber above, Maghira? How were you able to reach us?'

Antares did not even turn to look at him. 'Better she does not speak of it. The punishment is death. This is a sacred task, bestowed upon us by our fathers and their fathers before them. Do you mean to throw that away, just because some bloody fool girl has climbed the cliff?'

'Easy, Antares, Maghira meant no harm.' Either to placate Antares or perhaps because he thought to rile him further, Ruhago placed a hand on his rival's shoulder.

Antares whipped around with his staff, which Ruhago avoided with a swift backward step. The two elders squared up to one another, Antares chest-to-chest with Ruhago as each tried to speak over the other. Maghira sensed that tension had been building between them for months. Garimo tried to push them apart and was shoved aside by Antares.

The sound of splintering wood accompanied by an animalistic roar shocked the squabbling elders to silence. Three men still stood by the fire, among them Charones, the strongest man in the village, with a chest like a buck and shoulders as broad as Eryispek. Even he looked to have been diminished by their time in the cavern. He had smashed his great club to smithereens against the ground, and was staring the others down, almost daring them to try his patience by resuming their quarrel.

'We vote,' he said, tossing his broken club aside. 'I am tired of your quarrelling. We vote and that is the end. Antares wishes to send her away, and Ruhago wishes her to tell us what she saw. I vote with Ruhago.'

No man argued, not even Antares, though the scowl he gave Charones could have curdled milk. Garimo also sided with Charones. The other two were Tremares, another testy elder of Antares's generation, and Cleone, a wiry hunter who it was said knew Eryispek's pine forests better than any man alive. Tremares sided with Antares, but Cleone voted with the rest.

'Madness,' spat Antares.

'Looks like you're staying, Maghira,' said Ruhago. 'Let's get around the fire and share out that food.'

They encircled the fire, Maghira taking a spot between Garimo and Charones. The big man smiled at her and passed her an extra fur, which Maghira gratefully wrapped around herself. Opposite them, Antares scowled, but when the food was passed to him he did not refuse it.

Maghira looked into the fire, and realised with a shock there was no wood. It burnt without fuel, with twisting red flames that seemed to sprout from the earth itself. She stared, spellbound.

'It's real enough,' said Ruhago, following her gaze. 'Don't be tempted to put your hand in to check.'

'How?' Maghira tore her eyes away from it, and looked at Ruhago. His furs hung off him like rags and his old skin was stretched tight across his skull, but his eyes were bright.

'We will come to that. What happened to you above?'

'A voice spoke to me. She said you had conspired against her and were praying for her forgiveness, but that I could earn her mercy by finding a girl for her, before the "Betrayer" does. Who is that?'

A tense quiet filled the cavern, disturbed only by the crackling fire. Several moments passed before Ruhago spoke again. 'Do you know the story of how Eryi came to be worshipped all across Erland?'

Every child on Eryispek knew that. 'When the Meridivals came to Erland we agreed to support their conquest if they took our god.'

'Indeed. And do you pray to Eryi?'

Maghira nodded, confused. Was Ruhago going to take her through hundreds of years of Adrari history before he told her what was going on?

'And what do you know of the god of the Lutums?'

The Lutums lived on Eryispek's eastern side. Once they had fought the Adrari, but now mostly just fought each other. 'False gods,' she said, reciting the words she had heard half-a-hundred times. 'They worship the Mountain itself, as the pillar of gods they call the Norhai.'

An uneasy silence again spread around the fire. Her brother Garimo shifted anxiously.

'This is wrong,' said Antares. 'You go too far, Ruhago. Our ancestors—'

'Our ancestors were wrong,' said Ruhago. 'The goddess spoke to her; how much plainer do you want it, Antares? This madness has consumed our people for too long. Maghira, the Norhai were real.'

A harsh wind whistled through the chamber. Even through her furs, the hairs on Maghira's skin stood on end.

It took her several seconds to understand Ruhago's words. If that were true, then why did the Adrari worship Eryi? Eryi was the creator of all, who lived at the summit of Eryispek, beyond where mortals could tread.

'Does that mean Eryi... Is he not real?' She felt shaken. Why would Ruhago suggest something like that? 'But the Lutums are—'

'Savages,' said Antares.

'Misguided,' said Ruhago. 'The Adrari remember, but the Lutums have forgotten. The Norhai created the world, and forged the Mountain as their connection to it. Then, in their madness, they almost destroyed everything they had built.

The Norhai fought a war among themselves, which only one of them survived. She—'

The fire suddenly sizzled, flashing violent blue and purple sparks. Maghira shifted back in alarm.

'That's her,' said Ruhago.

Antares chuckled darkly. 'She's angry again.'

The fire crackled in rebuke. Maghira stared. It moved unnaturally, as if alive. She was overcome with questions. Why then did the Adrari pray to Eryi? And how had the last of the Norhai come to dwell inside Eryispek? 'But if the Norhai are real, then Eryi—'

'Also real,' said Ruhago grimly. 'Though barely a god. Eryi—'

The fire crackled again. '*Your talk serves me not. I have told Maghira what must be done. Bring me the girl with straw-coloured hair, before the Betrayer finds her.*'

Old Tremares rose suddenly. 'Antares is right. This is madness. We are here to keep the two of them in balance, not to serve her whims. I won't do it; it's treason, blasphemy. If—'

Maghira threw up her hands as a stalactite burst with fire, and a bolt of forked purple lightning flashed upon Tremares. Even with her eyes covered, she saw every bone in his silhouette flare a terrible white. His rising scream was cut off, and the chamber filled with the awful scent of burning flesh.

The voice rang out through the chamber. '*See the price of disobedience, and understand the limits of my mercy. Your prayers are no longer enough.*'

Through a haze of mist, skeletal trees crowded around them like wraiths, their bare branches creaking in the light wind that blew down Eryispek. The sun still lurked behind the great shadow of the Mountain, no more than a glow against the pale morning moon, still hours from rising high enough to burn away the mist.

Striding through the steep snow alongside Charones, Maghira looked down at the straw-haired girl, beneath a mountain of furs upon the wooden sled he pulled, her eyes flickering as she floated in and out of wakefulness. Had Maghira seen Pherri only as she was now, she would have wondered why they had gone to such trouble for her, but the fate of Cleone had made her power clear enough. The hunter had borne the hardship of their long trek down Eryispek more tirelessly than any of them, yet when he seized Pherri had fallen dead without a mark on him, as suddenly and surely as Tremares.

All the while, Maghira felt the weight of the goddess's will pressing down upon her, her command a constant refrain beating against the backs of her eyes. '*You must bring her to me.*'

CHAPTER 30

Pherri woke again, feeling more alert than she had in days, and looked around. Charones still dragged her sled, and beside them Maghira was setting a swift pace, gliding across the snow with easy long-limbed grace. Through the trees, she saw the three other Adrari men patrolling their flanks and rear, clad in heavy furs and snowshoes that left marks like bear prints where they trod.

Their path avoided Eryispek's main trails, staying hidden on the steep slopes amidst the dense pine forest. Behind them, Pherri could just see the sparkling waters of Eryispool below, where a sole boat was rowing fast for the near shore, leaving a tail of white surf in its wake. They had reached Eryispek's slope only the morning before, after several days' swift walking around the lake and through the foothills.

She supposed she ought to have been scared, but the Adrari did not treat her as a foe, instead going to every effort to ensure her comfort. Something in these pale strangers' faces told Pherri that her kidnappers were more afraid than she was. If it was fear of her, that was understandable, after the fate she had dealt Cleone. For all they knew it was only the limits of her strength that prevented her doing the same to them.

If they had only spoken with us rather than kidnapped me, he might still be alive. Pherri would have recognised Maghira as the girl from her dreams immediately. They might have been able to come to an accord, instead of fleeing into the night and leaving Theodric and Delara lying on the cold ground with their hands bound.

Her questions to them fell on deaf ears. Maghira was distant and evasive. Her brother Garimo was kind, but whenever he spoke with her beyond mere pleasantries the sour-faced Antares would hiss at him to tell her nothing. Charones seemed the friendliest, but Maghira kept him in check with sharp glances whenever he looked down to speak with her.

They stopped in a small clearing, just as the sun was finally cresting over Eryispek and the mist began to fade. Maghira gave a high-pitched whistle, and the other Adrari trudged back to join them.

'We should not stop here,' said Ruhago. 'The wizard and the Lutum woman might be only hours behind us.'

'If you were worried about that, you should have killed them,' said Antares. 'They will not catch us; a Lutum and a flatlander do not know the Mountain as we do.'

Maghira leant against a bare-branched tree, regarding them. 'We will not stay for long. If they are chasing us, they will have to rest as well. The sooner we have a fire to warm ourselves the sooner we can be on our way again.'

'It is not them we should fear,' said Antares. 'We have

taken too long finding the girl. Should the Betrayer's servants catch us—'

'They will not,' said Maghira. 'Her instructions have not changed. We are to bring her Pherri.'

'We do not serve her whims, as I have told you before; our task is to keep them in balance. With every passing hour, the chance his servants find us increases. You've heard the tales from up the slope of whole villages disappearing. They are on the move. I will not risk the girl falling into his hands. You know what must be done.' He cast an eye over Pherri's sled, fingering the hand axe at his belt.

Pherri stared back at him. Did Antares mean to kill her? Panicked, she reached for her magic, but with her rising heartbeat it slipped away like a dream. She tried to rise, before Charones pushed her down and moved to stand between her and Antares.

'Try,' he said.

Antares's hand did not move from his axe.

'Stop this,' said Maghira. 'You know he is already breaking free. Bringing Pherri to the goddess might be the only way to stop him. No one is killing anyone.'

'Tell that to Cleone,' said Antares. 'Without him, our going will be even slower.'

'I will not speak of this again. Gather some firewood. Now.'

Grumbling, Antares wandered off into the trees, as the other three men did the same. In the middle of the glade, Maghira began to mark out a circle of rocks for the fire.

Pherri rose from her sled and wrapped her furs around her. She approached Maghira, treading awkwardly across the thick snow. The Adrari had shown little concern that Pherri might flee; where would she have run to?

Maghira did not even glance up as she approached. 'I dreamt of you,' said Pherri. The older girl's eyes were half-hidden by her white fur hood. 'Wandering lost in a cave. And of a man, with eyes pale as moonlight.'

As Pherri spoke, a sudden chill wind crept over them both, shaking the boughs above and scattering pine needles. The two of them looked towards its source, and as swiftly as it had come on the wind died, back to the gentle breeze that had been with them most of the morning.

Maghira's gaze flicked over Pherri's shoulder, to where Antares was regarding them hawkishly as he stripped branches from a tree. 'We should not speak of this here.' Maghira looked about warily as if somebody else might be watching them. 'We don't know how powerful he is. If he—'

In the pines behind them, up the slope, the crack of a branch split the wintery stillness.

Maghira's head whipped round towards the noise. 'Did you hear that?'

Antares was already trampling back to the clearing, reaching for the great whalebone axe at his back. 'I told you, girl. We should have—'

From behind them came a brief shuffle of hurrying feet across the snow, and a staff was thrown over Maghira's head and jammed up against her neck. The girl's eyes bulged as she grabbed it and tried to wrench herself free, but her assailant clung on and dragged her backwards, the weapon tight against her windpipe.

'Keep your hands to yourself, snowhead.' Delara's face appeared over Maghira's shoulder as she manoeuvred the Adrari girl to place a tree trunk at her back. 'Pherri, get behind me.' Up the slope Theodric appeared from behind a pine, gaunt but otherwise unharmed. 'Think yours is the only tribe that can move quick and silent through the snow? I was sneaking through these forests before you were even a twinkle in your father's eye.'

The other Adrari had drawn their weapons, and were advancing upon Delara, murder in their eyes. 'Stay back or I'll break her neck!' she cried.

Theodric rushed forward to stand at Delara's shoulder. 'Nobody needs to get hurt here. Drop your weapons.'

'Don't reckon you're in a position to be making demands,' said Antares. He tossed his hand axe end over end and caught it again. 'You really think you can harm her before I put this axe between your Lutum whore's eyes?'

'Whore, is it?' Delara cackled. 'Better a whore than a milksop old man. Try it and see what happens.'

Charones and Ruhago looked to have been on the edge of complying with Theodric's demand, but at Antares's words seemed to steel themselves. Charones beat his huge whalebone club against the ground, and Ruhago reached for the axe slung over his back. Delara's grip tightened upon Maghira's neck, and Pherri felt Theodric reaching for his magic.

'Stop!' Pherri threw herself in front of Theodric and Delara, just as Garimo did the same before the Adrari. 'Let her go,' Pherri told Delara. 'Please. She's a friend.'

'Friend?' Theodric stared at her. 'Pherri, they kidnapped you! They could have killed us all!'

'But they didn't! Maghira is the winged girl from my dreams! Please, let's just talk with them.'

Delara shrugged. 'Have it your way then. I'm not in the habit of saving those that don't want saving.' She released one hand on her staff and kicked Maghira stumbling into her brother's arms.

Maghira turned on Delara, rubbing her neck where the

staff had bit into it. 'Try that again and I'll break your arm, witch.'

Delara raised a wizened eyebrow. 'Then give me no cause to, girl. Consider it fair payment for sneaking up on us in the dark.'

'The wise woman watches her back,' said Antares. 'Especially a Lutum wandering through Adrari lands.'

'We came here seeking answers,' said Theodric, before Delara could offer a riposte. 'Pherri's dreams are not enough reason to trust you. If you can convince us, we will come with you willingly.'

Maghira considered him, still rubbing her neck. She looked around at the other Adrari. 'We should get the fire going. If you will both sit, I will tell you all I can.'

She looked to Antares in expectation of disagreement, but the old man merely grunted. 'Tell them then, if that's what you want. Might be that we all die in this madness anyway.'

The day was beginning to brighten, but the snow was falling in earnest, and it took the Adrari some time to get their fire started. Theodric and Pherri sat down together on a fur, with Delara on one side and the Adrari arrayed opposite them.

Pherri craned her neck, looking up at Eryispek's steepening slope. The snow looked thicker by the mile, and its upper reaches were as ever hidden in cloud and fog. When they were settled, and the fire warm enough to ease the chill from their bones, Maghira spoke. 'Ruhago. Tell them all you told me.'

Across the fire, Ruhago glanced warily from Pherri to Theodric. 'This tale has not left the tribe in centuries. Would that a better man than me were the one to tell it.'

Antares grunted. 'We can agree on that. If we're going to tell it, it ought to be done properly. I'll do it.'

'You can *both* tell them,' said Maghira.

Ruhago nodded. 'I would hear from you first what you think you know.'

He was looking to Pherri as if she would be the one who would answer, but Pherri's eyes slid to Theodric. 'We believe there are two powers on Eryispek,' said Theodric slowly. 'One, or perhaps both of them, is working against Erland. We came here seeking answers.'

Ruhago spoke. 'All across the flatlands, people give thanks to Eryi, the creator of all, who hosts our dead in an endless feast above the clouds. But the gods who, with fire and earth, forged the world and those who dwell upon it were the Norhai, making their will known to mortal men through the Mountain. And, just as they built the world, they nearly destroyed it. Thousands of years ago, they fought among themselves a war that almost split the sky in two, raining meteorites and lightning as men cowered and prayed for the gods' mercy.'

'*Some* say thousands,' interjected Antares. 'Others say longer. But it was well before the Meridivals began riding horses and forging steel, well before even the Imperium. The Heavens War lasted centuries and, at the end, just one of the Norhai survived. Our people gave thanks to her, glad that they no longer needed to pray to a dozen different gods, all eager to earn the favour of their new goddess. More fool them. They might have guessed the goddess who slew all her kin would be an evil bitch.'

'We don't know she killed them,' said Ruhago. 'But gods are fickle creatures, and this goddess was no different. She was alone, and with her kin passed the last trace of what gentleness and goodness she may have had. Through the Mountain, she sought to bring the world under her bootheel, no longer content to let mortal men be free to live as they please. Her name was Vulgatypha.'

The mountainside was deathly still. Even the leaves on the trees seemed to have stopped their trembling to lean in and listen.

'Some resisted,' said Antares. 'One such man was Eryi, a magus of rare talent. For three days and nights, he battled Vulgatypha atop the Mountain, as a hundred other magi lent him their strength to cage the vengeful goddess.

'They succeeded, but it came at a cost. The strength it took to defeat her blew the magic right out of a generation of Erlanders, and when the boat people came across the sea, we had no defence. Some of us were forced up the Mountain, and others fled west, into the lands beyond the Dry River.'

Pherri's mouth was bone-dry. 'What of Vulgatypha and Eryi now?'

Ruhago took up the tale again. 'The only vessel with the strength to hold a Norha was one of their own creation: the Mountain. What had once been Vulgatypha's source of power over the mortal realm became her prison. All that keeps her locked away is Eryi, trapped himself atop this endless Mountain. He sacrificed himself, so that the rest of us might live.

'So you are correct. There are two powers, Eryi and Vulgatypha, locked in a war without end, each imprisoned by the other. She is trapped in the Mountain, and he at its endless peak. A perfect balance, we thought.'

'So we should help Eryi!' said Pherri eagerly. 'If he was free...'

But Antares was shaking his head, and Pherri recalled the pale-eyed spectre who haunted her dreams and killed Georald. 'The centuries have been no kinder to him than to her. The man our ancestors called Eryi is only a memory. All that is left is a shadow, as cruel and capricious as any of the Norhai. He shakes at his bonds not because he is our ally, but because he seeks our doom.'

'So why worship him?' said Delara. 'Why spread this lie across Erland? Always knew we Lutums had the right of it.'

The other Adrari were staring daggers at her, and Antares looked ready to issue a riposte before Ruhago spoke over him, his voice level. 'It is only the presence of Eryi that keeps Vulgatypha's power in check. Eryi was strong, but alone he could not hold back the will of a goddess, and our ancestors lent him their prayers to balance against her power.'

'But you lot forgot,' rumbled Antares, staring at Delara. 'You returned to the old ways. She drew strength from your prayers, from your devotion to the Mountain and the Norhai, and there were too few of us to hold her back.'

'When the Meridivals came from the south,' continued Ruhago, 'our ancestors saw an opportunity to protect the balance for generations: a people with the strength of a country behind them, lending their prayers to ours.

'It worked. It worked too well. Eryi spread across the flat-lands like fire, and the balance was undone. For generations, we failed to heed the warnings, and now he rattles his chains like the angry, vengeful demigod he is. For generations, we few Adrari who remember have watched Vulgatypha as well, deep within the heart of the Mountain. She feels him waking, and her fury is terrible.'

Maghira's face was like stone, but she shot a filthy look across the fire at Ruhago and Antares. Ruhago at least had the grace to look ashamed. 'So, there's your answer,' she said. 'Two gods, each as bitter and vindictive as the other, locked in balance. It is only now that balance might be upset that the Adrari men thought it might be worth telling somebody.'

Delara spat into the fire. 'Ever as it was. Men so sure they know best. And who do you serve, girl?' If she was surprised to learn that Eryi was real, she did not show it.

Maghira shifted uncomfortably. 'I serve Vulgatypha, so that neither of them may be freed. Eryi has grown strong on Erland's prayers and oaths, strong enough to influence our world, as you have seen, and his power grows by the day. If we do not act, he will free himself.' She looked to Pherri. 'It is he who has summoned you here. He seeks you, though we do not know why. I am to bring you to Vulgatypha, to keep you safe.'

'What?' Theodric lunged to his feet, and the Adrari rose with him. Pherri stood too, but Theodric moved in front of her, placing himself between her and the Adrari. 'Safe? You think we're going to come with you after what Ruhago just told us? That I'm going to sit by and watch you deliver Pherri to some thousand-year-old goddess who tried to end the world?'

'If you had seen what I have seen, you would under-stand.' Antares had drawn his axe, and was fingering it threateningly. 'For decades, I have watched the goddess rage against her bonds. All that holds her back is Eryi, and he her. An eternal struggle, with no victor.

'But she fears him now, as she never did before. In my great-grandfather's time, she was the stronger: Vulgatypha was there at the creation of the world. But she cannot hold back the oaths of all Erland. If Eryi frees himself, the world will tremble. All we can do is restrain him. We must, even if it means helping her.'

Their circle fell silent as all considered his words. Snow still fell, and the fire still crackled, but otherwise all was still. The mist seemed to be rising again, closing around them, separating them from everything save their companions.

'You wondered why you could not use your magic as you could before.' Pherri looked up at Theodric. 'This explains it: he has grown powerful enough to block us from the strength of the Mountain. What if he did it to summon us here?'

'Or what if this Vulgatypha did?' countered Theodric. 'We're being led to her blind as children.' He surveyed the five Adrari. 'Do what you must, but we won't be coming with you. We're leaving.'

Delara levered herself to her feet, and joined the Adrari surrounding Pherri and Theodric. Pherri looked sharply at her. 'Did you know about this?'

'I heard rumours that Eryi was real. A heresy, or so I thought.' There was a brightness in Delara's eyes, seemingly invigorated by Maghira's revelations. 'Adrari or not, if they're helping the last Norha, I'm on their side.'

'I should never have let you come with us,' said Theodric, backing away from her and the advancing Adrari. Pherri had seen Delara's magic now; in a battle between her and Theodric, she did not know who would triumph. 'You are treacherous to the bone.' Pherri could feel the anger rolling off him, his face strained in a tight grimace. 'So much for protecting Pherri.'

'I was trying to save her, you fool! If it had been left to me, she would have had the magic burnt out of her and you would never have pulled her into this.'

Antares and Ruhago were still edging towards Theodric with their weapons drawn, but seemed reluctant to attack. Pherri wanted to tell Theodric and Delara to stop, but her voice caught in her throat as the two magi stared at one another. She felt Theodric reaching for his magic.

'Stand down, all of you,' said Maghira. 'I have been told nothing of bringing either of you.' She indicated Theodric and Delara. 'The only one Vulgatypha spoke of is Pherri, and I will leave the decision to her. Whatever her choice you are free to leave or come with us as you please.'

'You can't leave the decision to a child,' said Antares.

'I trust Pherri will make the right decision,' said Maghira. She looked to Theodric. 'And I have no desire to fight a magus. Will you abide by Pherri's decision, wizard?'

Theodric looked at Maghira. 'I will, if you and yours will. I do not wholly believe you will cast off a goddess's whims so easily.'

'Believe me, I trust her no more than you do. But if we do not help, then Eryi will rise.' She looked to Pherri. 'What do you decide, Pherri?'

Pherri felt the eyes of everyone fall upon her. She wiped away a globule of snot that had formed under her nose, and took a sip of icy water from her flask to clear her head.

She remembered the dark, fearful presence from her dreams, the pale-eyed man, who had tormented Gelick Whitedoe, and the same shadowy figure who had slain Georald. There had been a malignancy to it, like a once sturdy tree rotted by parasites, and a fetor of remorseless vengeance that would not be slaked. God or not, this figure had ill designs upon all of them. She closed her eyes, and his ashen gaze stared back at her, causing her eyes to leap open again.

Her heartbeat quickened as fear flooded her veins. For as long as they were upon Eryispek, she was in danger. What fate waited for her if Eryi took her? She wanted to flee, to put as many miles between her and this evil as possible.

And yet, would that save her? Georald had been slain miles from here, inside the walls of Piperskeep. If Eryi's reach was so vast, perhaps nowhere was safe. And Maghira said his power was growing, that all that held him back was the waning powers of this Vulgatypha.

Pherri fingered the coin in her pocket, a memento of when she and Theodric had first discovered her powers. She felt the same sense of destiny she had felt that day, that she was taking a decision that would follow her the rest of her living days. And more than that, perhaps echo across all of Erland. A whole country, with its fate poised between the fortunes of two gods, like balancing a coin on its edge, knowing that someday that coin would topple, one way or the other.

And it falls to me to stop that. Pherri's resolve almost crumbled under the weight of that realisation. This was a war greater than any between East and West. Some twist of fate had brought her to the attention of two gods, and she would have to walk a path of finest gossamer to keep these two powers in balance.

'I don't even know what they want with me,' she whispered. She was talented with *phisika*, but her *shadika*, *inflika*, and *spectika* fell far below the powers of Theodric, and of Delara. Any powerful act of magic left her drowning in exhaustion for days.

She realised that everyone was still staring at her. She looked up at them, the campfire dancing in her pupils. Her legs trembled in the cold, and she gripped Theodric's hand to stiffen her resolve.

In her head, the balanced coin wobbled on a precipice, but did not fall. Pherri would not allow it to fall.

'I will go with you,' she said to Maghira. 'I will speak with Vulgatypha.'

CHAPTER 31

In Hessian's solar, Ciera stood at the balcony window. Far below, a thousand lights illuminated Merivale, its rain-soaked streets shining like a shimmering lake bathed in the sombre glow of the moon. The two sources of light seemed to mingle with each other, tangled by the low haze of chimney smoke that hung over the city beneath a cloudy grey sky.

It was four nights since her clandestine meeting with Laphor, four days of pacing her room and savouring the brief hours she spent with her child. Laphor had sworn he could bring Errian here, and that Andrick Barrelbreaker's son was the man to lead their nascent rebellion. Arrik and Burik had not been so convinced. Arrik had proclaimed him a washed-up drunk, and Burik had been no kinder.

For all her time in Merivale, Ciera had heard tales of Errian, as furious in battle as his father and as handsome as Prince Jarhick. Those tales had taken on a darker tone after his capture, and since his sad return people spoke only of the shambling figure in soiled clothes and a bedchamber covered in empty wine bottles and tankards, if they spoke of him at all.

Only Laphor had been enthusiastic. 'That washed-up drunk could beat you with a blade with both hands tied behind his back,' he had told Arrik. 'And I won't hear any man tell me Lord Andrick raised a drunk.'

And so Ciera had tonight returned to her husband's solar, tiptoeing in the dark from her bedchamber and emerging from the passage with broken spiderwebs in her hair and cloaked in dust. Haisie had been waiting for her, with a thick robe and a mug of spiced wine fresh from the pot. It was summer, but Hessian's solar was always cold, and her effusive gratitude had made the girl beam with pleasure.

'When you're queen again, can I serve you?' Haisie had asked. After, she bit hard on her lower lip, and cast her eyes on the floor.

By her tone, Ciera assumed the girl had spent the last four days rehearsing and readying herself for that question. 'Of course.' She had poured a measure of the hot spiced wine into a spare cup and given it to Haisie, who had looked at it as though it was the most wondrous thing she had ever seen.

From below, Ciera heard the staccato of booted feet on the stairs. She tensed, casting a nervous glance towards the wall she had entered from. Quickly, she ran to the door and bolted it. If someone other than Laphor knocked, she and Haisie could be away through the tunnel long before they broke the door down.

Someone tried the handle, and found it locked. 'Open the door, quickly,' came a muffled voice. 'Quickly, quickly.'

She recognised his gruff burr immediately and hurried back to the door. Snapping the bolt back, she opened it to reveal Laphor, who was for some reason carrying a large sack which he dropped to the floor. Following him were Arrik, Burik, and Errian Andrickson, towering over the rest of them, straight and sober with a sword at his belt in leather armour embossed with his father's three-barrels banner.

'We just passed that bastard Tarwen in the hall,' said Laphor. 'Gave us a look like he knew we were up to something. Best hope he doesn't come looking.' He bolted the door again.

Ciera was busy staring at Errian. His hair and beard had been trimmed, and his eyes were bright and clear. He looked at least two inches taller than when she had last seen him, half-drunk at breakfast in the hall while she was still pregnant, and as handsome as a portrait.

Errian felt her eyes on him. 'Yes, I'm sober,' he said, failing to keep the irritation from his voice. 'Thought I ought to be, so I'm not fool enough to join you in this madness.'

'You're a *hymerika*, Errian,' said Laphor. 'You said the words same as we did.'

'And I've stuck by them. I never swore an oath to a queen nor to commit treason.'

'It's not treason,' said Ciera. 'Balyard and Gurathet have imprisoned me under false pretences, and kidnapped my son.'

Errian shrugged. 'Even supposing that's true, men follow who it pleases them to follow, which you might have noticed. You should forget it. Balyard's been merciful so far, but he won't be if you challenge him. It won't be house arrest for you, it will be the dungeon.'

'He wouldn't dare,' said Ciera, trying to disguise the terror that blossomed in her gut.

'It's not as hopeless as it sounds, Errian,' said Laphor, positioning himself at Ciera's shoulder. 'Gurathet's taken most of the *Hymeriker* west to hold Halord's Bridge. Most of those left are Balyard's men. We can take them.'

Ciera looked at him. 'More men to Halord's Bridge?'

'Word is the Imperium's taken West Erland. If they march east, we can only hope Gurathet holds them. Can't say I have much faith.'

'But that can't be true, the Imperium's not been seen in Erland since—'

'Since the days of King Pedrian, near two hundred years ago.' Laphor's voice was grim. 'I didn't want to believe it either.'

'All the more reason this is madness,' said Errian. 'You want to stage a coup right as the Imperium invades?'

'You want to leave the defence of East Erland to a fool like Balyard?' countered Burik. 'He's already brought Merivale to the edge of revolt with his taxes. The folk shouting at Piperskeep's gate are getting more desperate by the day.'

'I don't like the look of some of them,' added Laphor. 'It ain't guildsmen delivering petitions no more. Lots have been turning up with weapons. Some are going after the gated streets as well; there's not enough watchmen to keep the peace.'

'It will only get worse,' said Burik. 'The Watch was already stretched thin; with most of the *Hymeriker* gone the city could start ripping itself apart any day now.' He shook his head, his mouth twisting in disgust. 'What happened to you, Errian? We've trained together since we were old enough to hold a sword, this isn't you. The Errian

Andrickson I knew did what was needed, consequences and odds be damned.'

Errian looked his friend square in the eye. 'And look where it got me.'

'Derik died to free you!'

'Exactly.' Errian gave a bitter laugh. 'A lot of good men died because I rushed off to try and avenge Jarhick. And Jarhick was worth fighting for; you lot aren't.'

Burik spat on the floor. 'Coward. Orsian was twice the man you are. He wouldn't stand by while Balyard and Gura-thet let the Imperium roll over us.'

Ciera gasped as Errian's sword came free of its sheath in the blink of an eye. He advanced on Burik, his face a mask of anguish, his blade rippling in the hearth light. Burik pulled his own sword free, but as Errian's fell, Ciera could see his guard was not coming up fast enough.

Her scream caught in her throat as Laphor's blade rode to meet Errian's, and they clashed together in a shower of sparks.

Errian turned on Laphor. Three times he brought his blade down, and three times the older man met his swing. Ciera saw though that he never attempted to strike Errian in return.

As Errian stepped back, Ciera thought she caught a grin on his face. 'Coward am I, Burik? This coward would have cleaved you from chin to cock if the old man hadn't been here.'

Colour rose beneath Burik's beard. 'Going for your sword like that when a man's not expecting it is coward's work. Orsian met his foes on the field, fair and square, and he never let himself get captured.'

Errian's gaze hardened, his blue eyes like deadly sapphires. 'Mention my brother again and I will kill you. He let my father die. I'm still twice the warrior he was, not to mention I'm alive.'

'Shame Strovac let you live. Killing you would have been a mercy. A year ago you'd have been raging with me; you wouldn't just have threatened to cleave me from chin to cock, you'd have done it. What's the use of you if you're too afraid to fight?'

'Maybe I just like you enough not to kill you.'

'I need your help, Errian,' said Ciera, speaking before Burik could try and continue their quarrel. She had never been so close to a swordfight, and she tried not to let her fear show. 'It's not just for me, it's for the kingdom. Balyard's—'

'An arsehole,' finished Errian for her. 'But what makes you think you'd be any better? And how do I know you didn't kill the wizard?' Suddenly, he grinned. 'I'll fight Burik for it. He beats me, I'll follow you. He doesn't, I walk away.'

Arrik laughed. 'You must be drunk if you think you can beat him after four months staring at the bottom of a tankard.'

Errian's glance at Arrik was barely even cursory. 'All three of you then. I'll kill you first.'

'You won't kill anyone,' said Laphor. He lifted the sack Ciera had been wondering about, and with a clatter poured four wooden training swords onto the table, narrowly missing the flagon of wine.

Errian snorted. 'Do you just carry those around?'

'I watched Naeem and your father train you since you were no higher than my knee. You could never resist a chance to test your strength.'

'Toys,' said Errian dismissively, though Ciera thought she saw doubt in his eyes. Whether because he found the wooden swords disagreeable or because he was surprised by Laphor's intuition, she was not sure. 'I've not fought with one of those since I was twelve.'

'Good,' said Laphor, taking up a sword and tossing another to Errian. 'Means I'll win.'

Errian caught it easily. His gaze narrowed as Burik and Arrik took up their own wooden blades. 'If I land a blow on all three of you before you land a blow on me, you'll pour me a wine and then leave me the fuck alone.'

'Little chance of that,' said Arrik, swishing his sword through a series of figure-eights. Burik swung his twice and nodded, while Laphor and Errian kept theirs at their sides.

Errian moved so fast that Ciera barely saw him. He lunged forward towards Burik, and as Burik's sword came up in defence Errian kicked out at his opponent's hilt, then hurdled Laphor's low cut that would have caught him on the knee. Burik's training blade spiralled away, and Errian's sword, that a moment ago had been moving left, swung right in a vicious arc that struck Arrik's head, sending the younger man sprawling over the table.

Behind Ciera, Haisie shrieked. She had forgotten the girl was there. Ciera turned and Haisie rushed to her.

Errian retreated, putting himself a few paces away from Laphor and Burik, who had retrieved his sword. Arrik was awake, but dazed, blood trickling from his temple. Errian laughed. 'They must have been desperate to make that boy a *hymerika*. I've fought better twelve-year-olds.' He raised his sword again as Laphor and Burik advanced, one going to Errian's left and the other to his right. Together they charged him, bringing their blades down overhand, but Errian simply ducked and turned underneath them, and Burik had to twist awkwardly and leap away to avoid Errian's blade striking him on the hip.

They came again, and Errian parried a few strokes of Laphor's, the two blades meeting in a cadence of wooden clacking, while giving ground to avoid Burik coming around him. Ciera pulled herself and Haisie out of their path as their dance headed towards the hidden door.

She could see what Burik and Laphor were doing. Laphor was making no true attempt to strike Errian, simply doing enough to keep him occupied while the swifter Burik tried to get around his defence. There was sweat on Laphor's brow and Ciera could hear his breath coming heavier, while Errian's grimly determined visage gave no indication he was tiring at all. But despite his longer reach Errian could find no way past Laphor's guard, not without letting Burik past his own.

As Errian's back touched the wall and Burik lunged forward for a killing strike, Errian dropped his guard and threw himself towards Burik. Their shoulders thumped together, and Burik stumbled backwards, while behind Errian, Laphor's strike clattered against the wall where Errian's head had been a moment before.

As Burik backpedalled, Errian thrust his sword forward like a needle, the tip striking Burik square in the throat. Nevertheless, Ciera thought she saw a look of triumph in Burik's eyes as he toppled backwards, for Laphor was already moving against Errian's exposed back, ready to bring his blade down across his shoulders.

The blow never came. Errian ducked underneath as the

wooden sword passed overhead, spun on his heel, and planted the tip square in Laphor's gut.

The older man froze in place as if it were a mortal wound, and let his own weapon fall harmlessly onto the lush red carpet their bout had led them to. 'Well fought, Lord Errian,' he said between breaths, his eyes twinkling. Behind Errian, Burik was pulled to his feet by a slightly unsteady Arrik.

Errian gave a glib laugh. 'Waste of my time. Try me again when you've learnt to tell one end of a blade from the other.' Without another word, he let the training sword slip from his fingers and strode for the door.

Ciera realised she was still holding Haisie's hand. She let it fall, then sank into a chair, utterly deflated. Laphor had let her put her hopes on Errian, and now all their prospects had been sunk on the outcome of a stupid game because men could find no better way to solve their disagreements. Had she not been so tired she might have been angry, but she was long past that now.

She looked up as Laphor approached the table, and was surprised to see he was grinning. He reached for the wine and poured himself a cup.

'Why are you smiling?' asked Ciera.

Laphor chuckled. 'That boy's been ready to fight anyone about anything his whole life. In an empty room he'd probably fight himself. We just reminded him how much he enjoys a scrap, and how much more he enjoys winning. It won't be the last you hear of him, Majesty. I guaran-fucking-tee it.'

Tired and disheartened, despite Laphor's reassurances, Ciera returned through the hidden passage to her room, silently wondering how it would feel to be as good at anything as Errian was with a blade. If Laphor had told it true, that was the first time Errian had held a weapon since his capture by the Prindians. No wonder he had been sure men would follow him.

She was well-practised now at entering and exiting the hidden doors. On the wrong side of the fireplace, she pulled the wall sconce clockwise, and with a familiar screech the hearth shifted an inch. She pushed it the rest of the way and stepped inside her chamber.

Ciera had barely let out a breath before a huge hand clasped over her mouth. She was still holding her candle, and tried to thrust it into her assailant's face, but a second hand grabbed her wrist and twisted until it slipped from her fingers. She felt a sinking dread as her attacker pushed her against the wall.

But it was not Tarwen, nor any of the other rotating cast of warriors made to guard her. It was Errian, and he was grinning as if the whole thing was just a brilliant ruse. He let go of her wrist, so Ciera reached up and slapped him.

It barely seemed to register with Errian, but he released her. 'Sorry. Had to make sure you didn't scream.'

'How on earth did you get in here?' Ciera's eyes scanned the walls, as if a second secret passage might reveal itself.

'Through the window. Was a tighter squeeze than when I was a boy. Came straight here after I left Hessian's solar.'

'This is all just a game to you, isn't it? Whatever you felt you could not tell me before, out with it. I'm tired and I want to go to sleep, not that I've got anything worth getting up for.'

'I came to say that I'll do it.'

Ciera blinked at him. 'You'll what?'

'I'll fight for you. Never liked Balyard. Never liked Laphor either, come to think of it, the old bellyacher, but at least he knows what it is to fight. And if Balyard thinks he can lock the queen away, just imagine what he might do to me if I start being a problem for him.'

It took all Ciera's sense of propriety not to throw her arms around him. 'Thank you, thank you! Will you tell Laphor and make a plan?'

'Just leave it to me.'

'Here's the little prince, my Queen,' said Mortha, handing the swaddled babe to Ciera. The governess had shown nothing but deference since she had usurped Ciera, but Ciera could sense the insolence behind her smiles. Andrick stirred slightly, but did not wake. Ciera herself did not feel particularly well-rested; after Errian's visit she had tossed and turned through the night. He had not told her what he would do, nor when, only that she should be patient.

'Try not to wake him,' chided Mortha. 'I've only just got him down.'

Ciera eyed her coldly, but rather than spitting a retort restricted herself to a quiet smile. Mortha would live to regret parting a mother from her child. If Eryi and the Norhai were just and Errian was as capable as he seemed to believe, this would be one of the last times the hag would see the little prince, or indeed the inside of Piperskeep. A hard thing, for a woman of such advanced years to find a new position.

She moved to a rocking chair at the corner of the nursery, with a good view of the door and the two *hymerikai* stationed to either side, and tried to calm herself. What if whatever Errian was planning went wrong? *I might never see Andrick again.* Ciera reflexively clutched him tighter to her, then silently scolded herself for worrying so much. Laphor was careful, even if Errian was not.

The room was on the keep's south side, and even through the stout walls Ciera swore she could hear the angry clamour of men at the outer wall. By the volume, Burik had been right; the protests against Balyard's taxes and treatment of the city were getting worse. The sooner she could get rid of Balyard the sooner she could start putting matters right, if it was not too late by then.

Trying to ignore the noise, Ciera focused her attention upon Andrick. He was bundled in red swaddling, and with each gentle breath he took the soft skin around his nose fluttered slightly. So small, so perfect. She rocked the chair, ever aware of Mortha eyeing her from the corners of her beady black eyes as she pretended to do embroidery.

Ciera half-dozed for a time, savouring the simple pleasure of her son's warmth against her. She was abruptly shaken from her reverie by three ascending chimes from the twelve bells atop Piperskeep, sounding third bell.

Mortha sat up with a start. 'Those bells,' she complained.

She was about to add something, but was interrupted by a commotion at the door. A man shouted something, followed by the sound of running feet on flagstones.

'What was that?' asked Ormo, one of the guards, an older man with small cruel eyes like a pig.

Tarwen scowled. 'I'll go and look.'

Something in this exchange seemed to stir a sense of alarm in Mortha, for as the *hymerika* opened the door she cried, 'Wait!'

Too late. As the latch lifted, Errian barrelled into the door like a thunderclap. His shoulder connected with Tarwen's face, sending him staggering backwards, and followed up with a sweeping kick to the man's legs to put him on the ground. He was followed immediately by Laphor, who as Errian rounded upon Ormo flung himself at the prone Tarwen, drawing an ugly dagger and setting it under the man's eye. 'Not a sound,' he hissed.

Ormo had his sword halfway out of his scabbard, until Errian clocked him with a right hook that sprang his head back against the wall and tumbled him to the floor. Arrik and Burik brought up the rear, clasping a guardsman each with their hands tight over their opponents' mouths.

Mortha opened her mouth to scream but Errian was on her in a second, and it died in her throat as he loomed over her. 'Scream, and you die,' he told her, his voice sharp as breaking ice.

Errian looked around, first at the two *hymerikai*, one out cold and one trapped beneath Laphor with a blade laid against his cheek. The two trapped by Arrik and Burik had given up struggling. 'Bind and gag them,' Errian told them, moving swiftly to check on the unconscious Ormo.

As Laphor released the knife to reach for bindings, Tarwen began struggling. He spat in Laphor's eye, and drove a knee between his legs, drawing a pained grunt from the older man, and for a moment it looked as if he might win free, until Errian drew his sword and pressed the point of it to the man's throat. 'Bind him, Laphor.'

'Fucking treacherous whoreson,' spat Tarwen as Laphor bound his wrists. 'Balyard will have your heads for this.'

Errian released the press on the man's neck so Laphor could gag him. 'Only if we lose.'

'Your father—' Tarwen did not get a chance to finish his sentence before Laphor shoved a ball of cloth into his mouth and tied it with a rag.

The whole affair had taken little more than a minute, barely time for Ciera to register what was going on. 'You could have told me it would be today,' she hissed, coming to her senses. 'I never thought—'

'Would have been too late otherwise,' said Laphor. 'Balyard's pulled all the watchmen from the city to hold Piperskeep, at least those that haven't deserted, the Norhai-cursed fool. The rioting's already started; you can see the fires from the battlements. Unless someone gets a handle on this mess there might not be a Merivale left by tomorrow.'

'Of the *hymerikai* left we think at least half will be with us, once they realise what's happening,' said Errian.

'You mean you've not gathered them already?' Ciera was aghast. 'How many of you are there?'

Errian answered with a smirk. 'Well, there's us four, and that servant girl of yours who drew them away from the door for us.'

Those must have been Haisie's running feet Ciera had heard. Of course. 'You mean we're committing a coup with only four swords?'

'We're getting you and the prince to safety first,' said Laphor.

The commotion had woken Andrick. He gurgled irritably, and before he could cry Ciera quickly pulled down her gown and gave him her breast, which he latched onto eagerly. She looked to where the four captives were being dragged into a corner by Burik and Arrik. 'We don't have time for this,' she told them. 'There could be more along any moment.'

Errian looked at her, but quickly averted his eye from Ciera's bared breast. 'We don't have time for you to be doing that either!'

'Well, it's either this or he screams the keep down.' Ciera stood and turned her gaze on Mortha, where the old woman sat in her chair, her shaking hands gripped around her embroidery. 'Will you gag her as well?'

Errian and the rest were just finishing the last of them. 'The old woman? What for?'

'You don't know her.' Ciera felt a burst of fury rise in her chest. Balancing Andrick on her hip, in a few short steps she crossed the room, and slapped Mortha across the face. The governess did not cry out, but her embroidery slipped to the floor, and Ciera's handprint was fiery-red upon her cheek.

'Stop that!' Errian grabbed Ciera's hand before she could strike Mortha again. 'We need to leave.'

Ciera's feelings came in a rush. Her relief to have Andrick safe in her arms; her hope of overthrowing Balyard; her hatred for the vile Mortha. Tears swelled in her eyes, and she bit down on her lip as it quivered. Errian was right; there was no time. She took a few quick breaths to steady herself. 'Are we ready to go?'

Errian nodded. 'Can you walk with him... like that?'

Laphor interjected. 'You've just seen her deliver a slap that my wife's ma would have been proud of with the babe on the tit; I'd say the queen can manage a walk.' One of their prisoners began to stir and Laphor silenced him with a jab of his boot.

'Fine,' said Errian. He moved to the door and peeked into the corridor. 'It's clear.' He ushered Ciera out, followed by the three warriors. The four of them formed a diamond around her and headed away as fast as they dared.

'Where are we going?' asked Ciera.

'Your chamber,' said Errian. 'We'll get you inside the walls, then we'll go and deal with Balyard and whoever he's got guarding him. The girl's waiting with blankets and food for you to take in there with you.'

Ciera's heart was in her mouth as they traversed the castle, fearing at every corner that they would find themselves face to face with Lord Balyard and half-a-dozen guards. A tortoiseshell cat swishing her tail watched them from atop a statue as they hurried past. Twice they encountered servants, a young girl and an old man carrying a ewer of water, but Errian pushed them aside and growled at them to keep their tongues behind their teeth if they knew what was good for them, and before Ciera could object to their treatment, they were past.

When they reached the final corridor before her chambers, Ciera let out the breath she felt she had been holding ever since Errian had burst in.

They were no more than twenty yards from the door when there was a clatter of footsteps, and far at the other end of the hallway Lord Balyard rounded the corner with four *hymerikai* in tow. He looked furious, his blotchy face even redder than usual. 'Stop them!' he cried. His guards wrenched their swords free and began racing down the corridor.

Ciera's instinct was to turn and flee, but Errian grabbed her dress at the back and half-dragged her towards the door, so fast she barely kept her feet under her. 'Get her inside!' he yelled, kicking it open as he pulled his sword free. Ciera found herself bundled through the door with her three *hymerikai*, just as Andrick began screaming. From behind her came the sharp notes of steel on steel as Errian's blade clashed with the first of Balyard's men. He had set himself in the doorway, his sword flashing so fast it was little more than a silver smear in the air. It ended when Errian shouldered his opponent aside, straight into a second man. Before the others could reach him, he stepped back and slammed the door shut, dropping the bar with a clunk and twisting the key to lock it.

'That won't hold them long,' he said. He looked exhilarated, as though he could not wait for them to break apart the door so he could cross steel with them again. 'Go!' From behind the door came Lord Balyard's voice, calling angrily for an axe.

Ciera rushed to the hearth. She was so flustered it took her several goes to find the right brick, and the fireplace groaned open, its shriek mingling with the thud of axe blows against the heavy door into a hellish cacophony that made her ears ring.

There was a crunch of splitting wood. 'Swords up!' cried Errian. Burik wrenched open the fireplace and Ciera stepped inside. Behind her, Haisie scurried out from under the bed and raced after her, carrying a sack and a large flagon of water. Once she was inside, Burik wrenched the hearth closed, plunging them into darkness.

In all the commotion, Ciera realised she had forgotten a candle. Heart in her mouth, she heard the bar being thrust aside, and men stepping over the ruins of her door.

'Where is the prince?' demanded Balyard. 'Throw down your swords, tell me where they've gone, and you can leave with your lives. Otherwise I'll have your heads, traitors.'

'The only traitor I see here is you, Lord,' came Laphor's voice muffled by the walls. 'I swore an oath to those of the

Blood, not to you. Restore the queen to the council and leave, and maybe we'll let *you* live.'

'You are four against six. Stand down.'

'Never.'

There was a shout, followed by the clash of swords, as for the first time in over two hundred years, Piperskeep ran with the blood of *hymerikai*.

CHAPTER 32

Helana threw herself to the ground, breathing hard, savouring the grass's soft smell and the prickle of heather against her skin. Her face and arms stung from sweat and sunburn, and she wrenched off the cap of her skin to take a long draught of the sweet honey liquor the Thrumb favoured. A red sun was setting over the forest, like a great ball rolling along the treetops, casting long shadows and turning the trees to dark wraiths.

Did I feel the sun's warmth in the other place? Her father's funeral pyre had burnt hot, but that could have been the heat of She'ab's own fire. Every day, her memory of the vision faded, as though her mind knew the tale was false and sought to be rid of it.

A hundred leagues, She'ab had said she must walk before she again took casheef. She was surely approaching that, after weeks spent dragging Na'mu and Ti'en through the Ancestors' Forest, across steep hills and plunging valleys. And now she was not even sure she wanted to. Those few minutes with Jarhick had provided her no answers, only questions. She could still ask She'ab to escort her to the Dry River and return to Erland, leave the whole confusion behind.

Na'mu crested the rise and slumped down next to her. 'I'm not walking a step more without a rest.'

Helana passed him her skin. 'Nonsense, we barely got above a stroll. There are men thrice your age who would not complain half so much.'

Na'mu took a long slurp, and then coughed at the liquor's acid sting. 'We Thrumb are meant for climbing trees, not ploughing the earth like horses.'

Ti'en soon followed them, slower and steadier but not near so out of breath. She dropped to her haunches and took a slow draught of water before reaching for the liquor. 'Now we know why you Erlanders are so desperate for our land; because your own cannot satisfy your mad desire to walk everywhere. Will your father be satisfied with the findings of your scout mission?'

Helana smiled. 'My father has never been satisfied with anything. How far would you say we've walked these past few weeks? More or less than a hundred leagues?' She had sought to speak with She'ab again several times now in the weeks since her casheef trip, but the shaman had always found reasons to avoid her, including one occasion where she thought she had finally cornered him only for him to leap for a stray rope and disappear into the trees.

Ti'en exhaled. 'A person's worth is not measured by the miles on their feet. How far even is a league?'

Helana grabbed the liquor from her and took another reckless swig, letting its warm stickiness run down her chin. As soon as they got back to Thrumbalto, she would demand that She'ab spoke with her. He might not owe her more casheef leaf, but he owed her answers. She did not believe he had not known what she would see.

She had not told Ti'en that in another world she had married Errian, Helana's cousin. How did a person tell someone something like that?

'You look troubled,' said Ti'en, as Helana handed the liquor to Na'mu. 'Are you ever going to tell us what happened with She'ab?'

Na'mu spluttered. 'I told you, Hel'na, the man is a few apples short of a bushel. If he's the reason you've been dragging us on these forced marches, I beg you to forget it, for the sake of my feet.'

Helana smiled away their queries. She had not told them, because she did not want them to believe she was mad. Na'mu would dismiss the whole thing as a drug-induced fever dream, and Ti'en would likely start chasing She'ab through Thrumbalto yelling at him.

'I'm sorry,' she said eventually. 'I—'

'Shush!' Ti'en suddenly threw a hand over Helana's mouth. 'Listen.'

Helana pushed Ti'en's hand away, but remained silent. Against the distant whisper of the forest, she caught the rhythm of approaching horses.

'I'm sure it's nothing,' said Na'mu. Even so, he came to his feet, with a hand ready over his belt knife.

Pursued by the beating of hooves, two men burst from the forest into the open ground at the foot of their hill, which was enough to bring Helana and Ti'en rushing to their feet as well. The men ran frantically. Their hair was short and unbraided, and by their garb Helana recognised them as Erlanders, her countrymen.

They were less than fifty yards past the tree line when

the first horseman broke from the forest, riding one of the stout ponies favoured by the Thrumb. With a cry of rage, he tore down upon the two fleeing men, waving a wickedly tipped spear. He launched it overhand, and it whistled through the air to take the first of his quarry in the back.

There were others pouring from the trees now, more Thrumb waving spears and howling. The second man turned and sank to his knees, and though it was too far to hear over the Thrumb war cries, Helana swore she saw his lips form the word 'mercy'.

The horseman rode him down. An iron-shod hoof connected with the man's temple and sent him sprawling, his head leaking like a broken wine barrel.

His killer yanked the spear from the first corpse and thrust it into the air, while his fellows surrounded him, howling and trampling over the two dead men.

'That's Hu'ra,' muttered Na'mu.

The chieftain's heir sat proudly upon his mount, though Helana was sure she could have outridden him. Still waving his bloody spear, his eyes sighted the three companions atop the hill, and gestured his fellows to silence.

'An invasion!' he called up, targeting Helana. He gestured towards the two corpses. 'Your Erland dogs are running amok through our lands, stealing and pillaging wherever the mood strikes them!'

Helana and her companions stared down at him. 'Is he going to charge us?' asked Na'mu in a half-whisper.

Helana was long tired of Hu'ra's hostility. In Thrumbalto she had been prepared to let Ti'en defend her for the sake of appearances, but out here away from the eyes of others she meant to speak as she liked. 'A most fearsome invasion, Lord!' she called down to him. 'I commend you for vanquishing them so ably. Should I write a song of your victory?'

Hu'ra's face darkened. 'There are hundreds of them! Streaming across the Dry River like flies to a banquet. I've been hunting them all day.' He jabbed his spear into the nearest corpse. 'If my father cannot see reason, I will do what he won't.' Howling, he raised his spear to the sky, and spurred his mount towards the slope. His six companions followed, crying and waving their spears as they thundered forward, churned the grass to dust beneath their hooves.

'By the Ancestors...' Na'mu's face had gone pale as ash. 'He's mad.'

Ti'en had drawn her bow and was setting an arrow to it. 'Hel'na, you should run. He wouldn't dare hurt me and Na'mu.'

Helana was not so sure. She had seen what men were like when their blood was up. 'I won't run,' she vowed, drawing her own bow and laying an arrow against it. The slope they found themselves on was steep; a small shield wall might have held a force many times their size, but the three of them – untrained, unarmoured – stood no chance.

They were halfway up the slope when Hu'ra pulled his spear arm back. Helana tensed, swearing she would put an arrow through his eye before she let him launch it.

She was so focused upon Hu'ra she did not see the horsemen riding hard from their right. A slingshot whirled, and a nut-sized stone grazed Hu'ra's temple. He turned towards its source, and an armoured fist met his chin, spinning the Thrumb heir from the saddle.

Alarmed, his outriders spurred towards him, only to pull up with their mounts skidding and neighing in protest as they saw their leader's assailant.

Chieftain Ba'an met them, dressed for war with a wolf pelt over his shoulders, and backed by six men of his own, his scarred face terrible as thunder. Spears fell from the hands of Hu'ra's men to clatter upon the earth while in the dirt Hu'ra stumbled to his feet. There was blood pouring from his nose, and he was favouring one leg from the fall, though no bones appeared to be broken.

'Father,' he managed to lisp in the Thrumb language through a mouthful of blood. 'She—'

Chieftain Ba'an slid from his horse and laid a vicious slap upon Hu'ra's cheek that sent his eldest son spinning back to the ground.

What followed was a string of Thrumb curses, delivered with such speed and fury that Helana caught not a word that spewed from Ba'an's mouth. Hu'ra tried to say something, and was rewarded with a further slap.

'I've never seen him like this,' whispered Na'mu.

'Is it not enough that I must deal with rebellion in Barthrumb? And now I must deal with your insolence as well!' roared Ba'an. He looked to Hu'ra's companions. 'Take him back to Thrumbalto, before I think better of letting you go.' Helana just about understood his Thrumb. Despite his beating, Hu'ra had clambered to his feet, and was staring at his father with unguarded hostility. 'Confine him to his chambers, under guard.' Ba'an turned to some of his own men. 'You four, see that it is done.'

He remounted his horse, and set it in a canter towards Helana and her companions. 'Princess Helana. Forgive me.' He spat in the dirt. 'I am cursed with disobedient sons.' He cast his gaze upon Ti'en and Na'mu. 'You two are not much better.'

'Not much better?' demanded Ti'en. 'How were we—'

'I told both of you there was trouble again at the border!' Ba'an switched suddenly to Thrumb, and said something too quick for Helana to follow, but it seemed to quieten her friends well enough. Na'mu looked chastened, and though her eyes blazed just like her father's, Ti'en stayed silent.

'You will take Hu'ra's horse,' said Ba'an to Helana, pointing back down the slope. He passed his eye over Ti'en and Na'mu again. 'You two can walk back on your own.'

Ba'an sent Hu'ra and his escort ahead, and then he and Helana settled into a slower pace, riding side by side at the head of a column. It was the first time Helana had been alone – or near enough – in his company since he had captured her in West Erland. She watched him at the edge of her vision. His skin had likely once been as pale as Ti'en and Na'mu's, but had been burnt to bronze by the sun, and the sickle-shaped scar that marred his face was white as bone, like the slimmest of crescent moons. His jaw was heavy and square, topped by a flat nose and blue eyes as pale as summer skies, and his red-brown plaits were shot with specks of grey.

'I did not know of the invasion on your border,' Helana said after a time. The sun was almost below the horizon now, and only the narrowest shafts of pale light illuminated their path back through the forest. 'If I had known I would not have gone out.' A lie, of course; she had nothing to fear from a few West Erland peasants.

Ba'an gave a throaty chuckle. 'Invasion is perhaps over-selling it. Refugees, one might call them. I am not without sympathy; that is after all how the Thrumb came to occupy these forests. I rode out to assist them, only to find my son had already slaughtered them.' A dark shadow passed across his face. 'Everywhere, I am hamstrung by advisors, who demanded I tell you nothing of what was occurring, and then delayed me so that Hu'ra could get there first. If I could prove they sought to thwart me, I would have them before a *djurica.*'

The Thrumb's laws were something of a mystery to Helana. The chieftain had certain powers he could exercise without supervision, but he was required to tolerate men on his council if enough Thrumb supported them, and to take their views into account.

'I did not know the Thrumb were refugees,' admitted Helana, after a long moment of silence.

Ba'an grunted. 'Long before your people came up from the south, Erland was ours. The supposed native Erlanders were once invaders themselves. They drove us as far west as they could and kept the rest for themselves. No doubt my people did the same once, but that tale is lost to time. Conflict and exodus are common to all people.' He paused, and Helana got the sense that he was contemplating something, chewing it around in his head like a tough piece of meat. 'Do you know why the Thrumb wear their hair in six plaits, Helana?'

Of all the things Helana had thought he might say, that had not been one of them. For the first time she realised that he was using her whole name, not cutting out a syllable as Ti'en and Na'mu did. She shook her head.

'So we can tell our own world from the next.'

His words came so low that Helana barely heard them over their horses' plodding hooves. When Helana realised what he meant, the breath caught in her throat. *Of course. At the funeral Jarhick wore his hair long.* 'She'ab told you?' Perhaps Ba'an was angry with him for sharing Thrumb secrets with her.

'We will speak more of this when we return,' said Ba'an.

Dark had fallen, and Helana could see his features by the glow of a following guard's burning torch, but the chieftain's hard face remained inscrutable.

When Thrumbalto came finally into view, the trees were aglow with fires. 'We'll meet in my chambers,' said Ba'an, once they had handed their horses off to servants. 'Go back to your rooms as you would usually. Someone will meet you.'

Helana did as he directed. She was though mystified by the secrecy. Were all rulers as paranoid as her father, or did Ba'an genuinely have something to fear from a few disgruntled Thrumb and one foolish heir? And what did she have to do with any of it?

At the base of the Irmintree, Helana unhooked the length of rope from the trunk, gave it a swift yank to free the counterweight, and let it lift her into the air.

It took only a few seconds to reach the high gangway, and when Helana dismounted the rope without stumbling she felt a moment of satisfaction. She had been as clumsy as a foal her first few weeks among the trees, but now she could ride the intricate system of ropes and pulleys with the practised grace of, if not quite a Thrumb of her own age, at least no longer a toddler.

The walkway was only dimly lit by distant torches, and there was no sign of anyone. With a shrug, Helana began walking towards her hut.

'Helana.'

She nearly fell from the walkway as She'ab's wrinkled face materialised from the shadow of the tree trunk.

'What are you doing?' she hissed. 'For weeks you refuse to speak to me, and then—'

The shaman clamped a hand over her mouth. Helana

fought, but she had forgotten how damnably strong he was. '*Shush*. No one must see you.'

Reluctantly, Helana stopped struggling, and after a moment She'ab released her. 'Come,' he whispered, gesturing along the gangway, towards the other side of the tree.

Helana's room was the other way to the one She'ab was suggesting, along a straight walkway suspended between two branches that supported her chamber. There was nothing this way, just a curved path that circled around the Irmintree's thick trunk. Nevertheless, she let the shaman lead her.

The reverse of the tree was deserted, as Helana had known it would be.

'Are you lost?' she asked. 'The only way to leave is back to the ground. Trust me, I've tried.'

She'ab smiled, his eyes aglow under the distant torchlight. Wordlessly, he crouched to press a knot in the wood. It clicked and disappeared into the tree, and She'ab hooked a finger through it and pulled.

An entire two-foot-by-two-foot section of bark swung open, revealing within its hollowed-out insides. Helana could only gape.

She'ab's grin was as wide as the mouth of a river. 'I hear the Sangreals of Merivale are fond of secret passages. So are we. I'll let you go first.'

Too amazed to respond, Helana crouched, and wriggled through the gap. The interior was stifling hot. Helana gazed up the hollow trunk, and hundreds of feet above, a solitary light glowed.

She'ab ducked through after her and with a click closed the entrance, plunging them into deep darkness. He sprinkled some powder onto an unseen wall-torch, and it burst into flame, revealing beside it an iron-rung ladder built into the tree itself.

'It's quite a climb,' said She'ab, still smiling, pointing up at the distant blaze.

'Terrific. Do you think you could smile a little less maniacally? It's giving me the creeps.'

This only seemed to encourage him. 'I'll let you go first,' he told her. 'Just don't fall. I do not think the chief would forgive me.'

Helana began to climb. It proved easier than the rope ladders commonly used in Thrumbalto, though a few times her feet almost slipped on the cold, curved iron of the rungs.

'Why is it metal?' she asked, after the third time it happened. 'Nothing else in Thrumbalto is.'

'To avoid rot. These steps are used maybe once or twice a century. They were originally wood, for use by an old chieftain's mistress, until her foot went through one of them and she fell. They found her body at the bottom a week later.'

'Wonderful. I'm so glad I asked.'

After what felt like a thousand rungs, the ladder came to an end. Helana pulled herself onto a wooden platform, and She'ab appeared a few seconds later.

A high door in the wood swung open, and Helana sprang to her feet. Chieftain Ba'an stood there, silhouetted against the glow of a fire.

'Were you seen?' he asked She'ab.

The shaman shook his head. 'One of Hu'ra's friends tried to follow me. I went to a privy, and when he stepped into the one next to mine he got locked in. So unfortunate how those locks keep breaking.'

Ba'an chuckled. 'If only all my foes were so easily dealt with. Come in.'

The room was generously proportioned. The fire in the hearth crackled and swam with warmth, while the wooden floor was bedecked with a huge black and white striped pelt of an animal Helana did not recognise. The chair Ba'an gestured Helana towards was just as rich, plumply cushioned in soft green velvet, set over a table draped with a heavy silk throw and surrounded by matching chairs. Helana had never been to a whorehouse, but she imagined they might look a little like this.

'Do you think me immoderate?' Ba'an asked wryly, taking a seat opposite Helana as She'ab did the same.

'You hide it well, but the trappings of the rulers of Thrumb are not so different to those of Erland.'

'Power takes its toll. Please forgive my indulgence.' He moved to pour tea, which smelt as the tea in She'ab's hut had, giving Helana a momentary flashback to the bittersweet, powdery taste of the casheef.

She pushed the cup away from her. There would be no better time than this to seek answers from She'ab. She looked at him pointedly, and he met her gaze. 'What is the casheef for?'

She'ab exchanged a look with Ba'an. Some understanding passed between them, as if Ba'an were giving his shaman permission for something, but it was the chieftain who spoke first. 'What do you know of magic?'

'Nothing. I know nothing. Why won't you answer my question?'

Ba'an raised an eyebrow. 'I was led to believe there was a magus at Piperskeep.'

'Theodric. He never told me anything of magic.'

She'ab sighed. 'This is taking us nowhere. I believe you know now, Helana, why we Thrumb wear our hair in six plaits? That tradition is older than our use of casheef. There was a time when we could explore other worlds without it. That is all magic is – the bringing and giving of things from other realms.'

The casheef was more magic than anything Helana had ever seen from Theodric. 'Can you do magic like Theodric then? Can I?' Even as she asked the question, she knew it was not so. Whatever magic was, it was not something she could touch.

Ba'an smiled sadly. 'No Thrumb has done true magic in over a thousand years. The casheef grants us no more than a peek through the keyhole.'

'But it does show us things,' said She'ab. 'Sometimes, we see things as they are here, identical events occurring in worlds apart, a hundred times over, as if we are troupers in the same play with each world its stage. And sometimes we see things that are different, yet so real they seem almost truer than what we know ourselves.'

'And sometimes, we see the same, different thing over and over again.' Ba'an stared at her over his steaming tea. 'For almost a year now, the casheef has been showing us somebody. Someone who ought to be here.'

'Something has gone wrong, Helana,' said She'ab. His usually dancing eyes showed no trace of mirth. 'Your brother was not meant to die. He should never even have come here. What you saw proves it.'

Helana's mouth was as dry. Absently, she reached for her tea, and the aroma nearly made her gag. 'But he *is* dead.' Her eyes began to fill with angry tears. 'And I've lived with that. I had *got over* that. How does it help me, help anyone, to know what *should have* happened?'

'You are not the only one to lose somebody,' said Ba'an. 'Ba'il, my son. It pains me to remember him now, to recall who he was, before his rebellion. His followers say that he spoke of a voice in his head, telling him he must throw off the yoke of Erland. This voice led to his death, and who knows how many more?'

'There is more to this than meets the eye,' said She'ab, 'and there is one person who is key to everything. In every vision I saw, she was here.'

'Well, now you've got me!' Helana threw up her arms in despair. 'What now? Is everything fixed? Does Jarhick live again?'

Ba'an shook his huge head. 'Not you, Helana. A young girl, small, with hair like straw. Her name is Pherri.'

CHAPTER 33

Orsian had thought Cag might choose to stay in Cliffark, but he would not leave Tansa, and she would not leave him either. Now, the whole way to Merivale, Cag had barely said two words to him, and every step Orsian felt his resentful eyes boring holes into the back of his head.

Each night, as the purple twilight turned to black, Tansa would come to him, and wrapped in their cloaks they would move beneath the stars, their bodies hot and eager, their clumsy lips crashing together like shield walls to mask their sighs. As they dozed afterwards, he could always tell by Cag's low breathing across the fire that he was only feigning sleep.

He cast an eye behind him. Tansa, sitting comfortably on her mount, flashed him a smile. 'You sit a horse as well as any lady now,' he told her. He meant it.

'*Better* than any lady, just like everything else I do.' She winked.

Orsian grinned. Sometimes, he wondered whether he would have found the strength to come this far if not for

Tansa. Twice, she had overcome the odds to save the people she cared for. Just as she had not abandoned him and Cag, he could not abandon Erland. And she understood that, he thought; why else would she have agreed to come with him? Through his own deception, Cag's jealousy, and a difference in birth as wide as the Shrouded Sea, they had come to rely on one another.

Yet he could not shake the sense that beneath the smiles and fierce passion there was something Tansa was not telling him. He did not grudge her having secrets – how could he? – but it left him with a sense of unease all the same.

They met the first refugees when they were still two days from Merivale. A trickle of ragged peasants heading east, and one man leading a raw-boned donkey bearing two young children.

Orsian knew by the look of them they were not Merivale folk. They were dressed in the rural style, in sturdy home-spun yellowed with sweat. There were a dozen of them, hollow-cheeked and gaunt. The grain shortage in the wake of the Prindians' first attack of the war had hit people hard.

'We should help them,' said Pitt, from where he sat with Esma in front of Orsian. Tansa and Cag had never ridden horses before, so Orsian had taken both the young orphans on his mount.

Orsian raised a hand to the man with the donkey. 'Where are you travelling?'

The peasant looked up at him. 'Anywhere. Never thought I'd see Imperials in East Erland, until that fat lord surrendered the bridge.'

Abner's rumour about the Imperium had been true then. Orsian closed his eyes. *If Halord's Bridge has fallen...* 'What fat lord?'

The man scowled. 'Lord Gura-whatsit. We told him how many they were, but he wouldn't listen; said the Imperials were no match for his *hymerikai*. Half our village is probably slaves now.'

Orsian remembered Lord Gurathet, a great blustering fool of a man. What had Hessian been thinking? 'Come with us, you'll be safest in Merivale.'

The man spat again. 'Damn Sangreals have failed to protect us twice now. West Erlanders already killed my wife last harvest and Hessian never lifted a finger. I'm taking my kids to safety.' Without waiting for a reply, he tugged on his donkey's rope and walked on, followed by his companions.

'You'll starve,' Orsian called after him. 'There's nothing that way but marshes.'

'Better starved than a slave,' the man shot back over his shoulder. 'That's all you be by winter if you go to Merivale. West Erland's gone, and we're next.'

Tansa reined her horse up next to his, and placed a hand on his arm. 'Let them go, Orsian.'

'Maybe we should turn back as well,' said Cag, struggling to bring his mount beside theirs. The horse did not bear its rider's weight gladly. 'We might ride straight into them Imperials.'

'You're welcome to leave,' said Orsian. 'I'm going to Merivale.' He urged his horse onward with rather more force than he intended, drawing a high scream from Esma as it broke into a fast canter and a cry from Tansa to slow down.

But Orsian did not slow. With every stride of his horse, Merivale came a little closer.

Within an hour, they met their second group of refugees, a portly older man, with a family of six and servants following him. He had no livestock, but by the servants and the cut of his clothes, Orsian took him for a landowner. Not a lord, but wealthy enough to pay other men to till his fields for him.

He too refused to follow them to Merivale. 'All my day labourers went to the city,' he told Orsian. 'More fool them. I saw that beast Strovac Sigac riding with the Imperials. He raped my daughter last autumn, and now no man will marry her.' He scowled at a drab, mousy-looking girl behind him.

Blood began to pound in Orsian's ears. *Strovac Sigac*. In his mind's eye, an axe flashed, and Andrick Barrelbreaker fell from his horse.

Something must have shown on his face, because the man recoiled fearfully. Mutely, Orsian led Tansa and Cag on their way, leaving the landowner and his party to walk east.

'Ain't his daughter's fault,' said Tansa, scowling back at the man. 'Thought being a lord meant you could whip men like that?'

'Strovac Sigac rides to Merivale,' replied Orsian, not hearing her. A hot sweat broke upon his forehead, like the rush of humidity before a storm.

As Tansa had known they would, they caught the smell of Merivale on the eastward wind before it came into focus. The great towers of Piperskeep rose forebodingly, silhouetted like a hand clutching for the distant grey-white shadow of Eryispek.

'That's the biggest thing I've ever seen,' said Pitt with wonder, craning his neck up at it.

'It's not as big as the sea, stupid.' Esma elbowed her

brother in the ribs, and Orsian had to place a hand on his shoulder to stop him tumbling from the horse.

'My uncle's solar.' Orsian pointed to a slim tower spiralling from the main keep.

Tansa tensed at the memory of Hessian on the balcony, watching impassively and sharing jokes. She shut her eyes, and her brother's swollen purple face flashed in her mind.

She had sworn an oath that day. An oath of vengeance against Hessian, and it weighed more heavily upon her with every mile.

It felt like a bad dream sometimes, that the person to whom she felt closest in the world should be the nephew of the man she most despised. Her hatred for the king smouldered like an ever-burning candle, and yet Hessian did not even know who she was and would not care if he did. She wanted him to see her, to know her grief, and her rage.

What will I do if Orsian introduces me to him? The thought of kneeling before Hessian made her tighten her grip on the reins, and her horse whickered unhappily. She could not do it. Not even for Orsian.

She could have left Orsian on the *Jackdaw* in Merivale and named it justice – a nephew for a brother. But that would have been the petty justice of lords, cutting off your own hand to cure a broken finger. She wanted to love the living, not the dead. So why was Tam's face still the last thing she saw every night before sleep took her, even with Orsian lying next to her?

'We should enter by the King's Gate,' said Orsian. 'Hopefully someone recognises me.'

Tansa urged her mount to a trot behind Orsian, and Cag brought his into step next to her. 'He keeps ordering us around like we're servants,' he muttered. 'Why are you standing for it? Why are we even here?'

'Maybe if you hadn't got yourself arrested we could have stayed in Cliffark.' Ever since Cag's rescue he had done nothing but complain.

Cag snorted. 'Liar.' He kept his voice low. 'It's because you love him.'

'What bloody business is that of yours?'

Six months ago, Cag might have recoiled from her anger, but too much had changed since then. 'It's my business because I won't lose you to some fucking lord who orders us around like we're nothing!'

'Lose me? You never fucking had me!' She had never seen Cag in that way, and never would. Looking at him was too much like looking at Tam.

Orsian had stopped his horse to turn back and see what the commotion was. 'You can argue once we're inside the walls, unless you want to be trapped out here when the Imperials arrive.'

Cag looked at him hotly, his cheeks flushed red. 'Anything you say, *Lord*. Should I polish your boots and brush down your horse once we arrive as well?'

Orsian scowled, but said nothing, and set his horse to a trot. Tansa followed, as reluctantly did Cag. Back in Cliffark, Orsian might have let Cag get a rise out of him, but since their departure his focus upon getting to Merivale had been arrow-sharp, doubly so since their encounters with the fleeing peasants.

The city grew larger, until its great grey walls loomed over them, and the stench of the moat was vile enough that Tansa had to cover her nose with a scrap of cloth. There was another scent on the wind as well though, the acrid smell of fire and ashes, and a faint cloud of smoke hung over Merivale like a portentous spectre. The drawbridge was down, but the gate was closed.

Orsian called up to the battlements. 'Ho! Open the gates!'

He waited a moment, but nothing stirred. There was no creak of a winch to lift the portcullis nor rattle of the bar being removed; only the light breath of the wind and the snorts of their horses. Tansa recalled the battlements over the gate being occupied by four men when she had last entered Merivale.

'Perhaps they don't want you back,' said Cag.

Orsian did not even look at him. 'Something's wrong,' he said, his eyes scanning the parapets of the southern wall. 'They only close the city at night usually, and Hessian never left the gate unmanned. That the drawbridge is still down suggests someone closed it in a hurry.' He rode up to the gate, and rapped three times on the heavy wood, to no response.

'Do you want me to try and climb the wall?' asked Esma. 'I bet I could.'

'I'd be faster,' said Pitt.

Orsian shook his head. 'Come on, we'll try the Ram's Gate.'

But the Ram's Gate too was closed, and the sight that met them as they circled the wall took Tansa's breath away. There were people, hundreds of them, a sea of flesh spread across the plains like a besieging army. But they were no army. Some might have been prosperous farmers, but others wore little more than rags, and their camp had no order to it, with people huddled in threadbare cloaks around meagre fires in threes and fours.

'More refugees,' murmured Orsian, though Tansa did not

need his words to see that. Many of them had the same haunted look as those they had seen on the road and appeared to have escaped the Imperium with no more than the clothes on their backs. A few half-naked children chased one another, shouting gleefully, but otherwise the mood was sombre.

As their party approached, the swell of peasants looked up, as if these new arrivals might prove their salvation. 'Food!' cried one woman with two children no older than Pitt and Esma as Orsian came within a few yards of her. 'Anything you can spare for us!'

'What's happening here?' asked Orsian. 'Why are the gates closed?'

'Wish we knew,' said a sturdy-looking man, coming to his feet from a nearby fire. 'We arrived yesterday and found them like that. We've all tried calling over the wall, but there's no one there.'

'I swear I saw someone up there yesterday,' called another man, 'but when we shouted they didn't even look at us.'

It was as though the whole city had disappeared into the ether, leaving behind nothing but silent stone and this collection of hungry mouths. With a grunt, Orsian turned his horse towards the gate, and Tansa followed. They came to a stop on the drawbridge.

'Should I climb the wall now?' asked Pitt.

Orsian shook his head, his jaw tight.

Tam could have climbed the walls as easy as breathing, but Tansa saw little hope for the rest of them. It was over thirty feet high, and the mortar was flush with the stone, leaving nothing to use for handholds.

'What if they all went to war?' she suggested. 'Or fled when they heard the Imperium was coming?'

'The whole city can't have fled; we'd have seen them.' Orsian cupped a hand to his mouth. 'Hello!' The only answer Merivale gave was the echo of his own cry off the walls.

Pitt tugged at Orsian's shirt. 'Ranulf, I need to pee.' He still had not got used to calling Orsian by his true name.

Orsian sighed. 'Go in the moat. Just don't fall in.'

Tansa watched him dismount and help Pitt and Esma down also. Pitt ran off to relieve himself in the moat while Esma busied herself collecting the daisies that grew among the long grass. Tansa dismounted also; it did not seem they would be travelling further any time soon.

Orsian stood at the edge of the moat, brooding over the high wooden gate that barred their way. 'This doesn't make any sense,' he said as Tansa approached. 'I don't like that burning smell in the air either.' He ran a hand through his hair. 'We need to get that gate open.'

Tansa placed a hand on his shoulder. 'It's fine. One more night sleeping outside won't kill us.' She wondered how Hessian was faring. If the city was abandoned, perhaps he was dead?

'No, you don't understand. We *need* to get that gate open. When the *Hymeriker* and the rest get back, or whatever's left of them, they'll be stuck outside, and the Imperials will crush them. If they fall, Merivale will fall too, and Erland is finished. They might be only hours away.'

'Is there another way in? Something secret?' There had been a postern gate on the edge of Cliffark, long forgotten and used by smugglers until Lord Istlewick had learnt of it and had it bricked up.

Orsian rubbed his jaw. 'Maybe.' He touched her hand. 'Stay here. I'll walk up the western wall and look, it's too narrow for horses.' There was less than a yard of earth between the moat and the walls. 'If I find anything I'll come back, or let you in here.'

Tansa kissed him, and watched him go. She reached into a saddlebag for one of their last skins of water, and sat down to wait.

'He won't come back,' said Cag from behind her.

Tansa turned round to fix Cag with a stare. 'Course he will. He came back when you were going to be hanged, though I'm starting to wish we hadn't bothered.'

'Only because it was him who got me captured in the first place. He's a lord, Tansa; we're nothing to the likes of him. His uncle killed Tam!'

'Did you think I've forgotten? Orsian didn't kill him, Hessian did.'

Tansa craned her neck, looking up to the high tower that Orsian said was the king's solar. *He could be up there right now.* She ran a finger along her sheathed dagger. She had never killed a man, but she supposed kings died just as easily as other men. There was no magic to it – a stab to the heart, and Hessian would die like anyone else.

But his death would not bring Tam back to her. She dug her fingers into the soft, moist earth. She could have Orsian, or she could have vengeance for Tam. But she could not have both.

———

It was several miles before Orsian found a gap in the wall, a jagged rift in the stonework less than a foot wide and five feet high. Looking inside, he saw a winding passage leading deeper into the walls, widening as its route deepened.

Orsian stooped and squeezed through, scraping his jerkin against the stone and brushing his head against the low ceiling. He did not have to go too far before he came face to face with a heavy portcullis, wrought from black iron heavy with rust. Through the lattice grill was the stone wall of a building, but above was open sky, and looking left and right Orsian's spirits rose to see the inside of Merivale's walls.

In hope rather than expectation, he spread his feet wide and crouched to grasp the portcullis at the bottom. Straining, he lifted it a few feet before his strength gave out and it crashed back to earth, only narrowly getting his feet out of the way.

Orsian looked upwards, searching for a mechanism that would raise it, but found nothing. In frustration, he kicked the sole of his boot against the gate. He had only replaced one locked entry with another. Merivale's bells that rang to mark the passing of each hour ought to have chimed by now. Their absence was perhaps even more troubling than the lack of gate guards.

The sound of footsteps behind him sent a frisson of danger up Orsian's spine. He whirled round, already reaching for the sword at his waist.

'Pitt.' He sighed with relief. Esma was with him, and they both wore mischievous grins like they had been caught filching desserts from the kitchens. 'What are you doing here? How did you get away from Tansa?'

'Her and Cag were arguing,' said the boy. 'We said we were going to play with some of the children we saw.'

'We thought coming with you would be more fun,' added Esma, smiling gleefully.

Pitt pointed to the base of the portcullis. 'With some big stones you could prop it open.'

'Great,' said Orsian. 'All we need is some loose stones then. Do you see any?'

'Might be some on the other side. If you lifted it again, we could crawl underneath and check for you.'

Orsian rubbed at his face. 'Are you so eager to die, Pitt? We don't know what's waiting. And what if I drop it on you?'

'We're too quick,' said Esma. 'Bet I can find a big stone before Pitt does.'

'Bet you can't,' said Pitt, jabbing his sister with a finger.

Orsian looked the portcullis up and down, as if he might break it open with the sheer force of his will. But other than waiting a few centuries for the iron to rust he had nothing. 'Fine. But be quick. I don't know how long I'll be able to hold it.'

He braced his back against the gate while Pitt and Esma crouched in the dirt either side. With a snarl, Orsian pushed from his knees, and shifted it a few feet off the ground as Pitt and Esma darted underneath fast as whippets. He held it a few more seconds to be sure they were safely through, then let it drop.

'Stay together,' Orsian told them through the iron lattice. 'And don't talk to anyone. And no stealing.'

Pitt looked up at him. 'But how do you expect us to bring something back without stealing it?' Before Orsian could reply, he and Esma raced off, holding hands and hollering gleefully.

Tansa will tan my hide if they don't come back. With nothing to do but wait, Orsian slipped down to his haunches and stared through the bars, marking time for their return.

He did not have to wait long. Pitt and Esma returned,

dragging a small anvil between them, smiling despite their obvious struggles. It must have weighed more than either of them.

'How did you get that?' asked Orsian, wondering how they had distracted a blacksmith long enough to take something so cumbersome.

'It was just left in the street with everything else,' said Pitt. 'We've not seen a single person.'

'They're all gone,' added Esma.

They were not lying, which made Orsian all the more concerned. *What by Eryi has happened here?* 'Good work, now put it next to the gate. When I lift, you need to push it underneath, quickly.'

Orsian raised the gate again, his legs and back protesting furiously, and this time when he dropped it he was rewarded with a satisfying clang. The anvil left little over a foot beneath the portcullis' iron spikes for him to crawl under.

Bad way to go if that gives way and the whole thing falls on me. Gritting his teeth, Orsian dropped to the muddy ground, and shimmied through as fast as he could.

'That was well done,' he told Pitt and Esma. He stood up, brushing the dirt from his clothes. 'Now get back to Cag and Tansa and wait. I'll get the big gates open.'

Pitt looked crestfallen. 'But aren't we coming with you? We might be able to help again!'

'No.' He did not know what dangers lay ahead, but if he voiced his worry aloud it would only encourage them to follow. 'There's no need; from here I can just walk up to the castle. Why don't you race back? Winner gets a pork pie.'

Orsian had barely finished speaking before Esma dived under the gate and ran back into the darkness of the wall, Pitt following a few steps behind.

Relieved to have got rid of them, Orsian considered his surroundings. By the odours of urine and decaying flesh in the air, he had emerged near a tannery, hidden on the city outskirts away from passing trade. So where had Pitt and Esma got an anvil from? The sight that met Orsian as he rounded the first corner at least partly answered that question, but also raised a hundred more.

The street was scattered with debris, as if some flash of wind had swept through the city and turned all the unwanted possessions out of people's homes. A shoe, caked with mud; barrels leaking ale, beset by flies next to an over-turned cart; a tunic that had been torn down the middle, half left on the ground and half hanging from a gable.

But still no people. From a few streets away came the snarl of a dog, followed by angry barking. Orsian moved on.

He did not know the city as well as he might have liked. He had ridden the Castle Road countless times, but Merivale's back alleys were a mystery. Piperskeep loomed to the north, so he headed in that direction, but the streets were tightly packed, and more than once he entered a narrow path only to find a dead end or that it led him in a wholly different direction.

And all the while, the ransacked city was silent as the creeping of a shadow. Orsian glanced in every window and down every alley, and saw nobody. One inn had smoke rising from its chimney, but the doors were locked, and when he knocked nothing within stirred. Another had clearly been set ablaze, and half the first floor had gone up in flames before someone had seen fit to put it out. Blackened beams protruded from the wreckages like the ribs of a carcass picked clean by scavengers.

A riot. Hessian had probably sent in the guards and

hanged the instigators, now the rest of the citizenry were hiding. But then where were the guards?

He did not have to go far to see the first body. The man had been dead a day or two, and stripped naked. The side of his head looked to have been caved in with a rock.

Orsian passed two more corpses, and as he neared the gated streets of grand houses that ran in a half-circle around Piperskeep's walls finally heard a distant clamour of voices. This was a part of the city he knew better, and he eagerly rounded the last few corners.

But as he approached the high iron gates marking the entrance, Orsian stopped in his tracks.

The belongings cast into the street dwarfed all he had seen so far combined. Overturned stone sculptures, chipped and split in two where they had fallen; a pyramid of wooden furniture twice a man's height; more ransacked travel chests than he could count. Many of the great sandstone houses had had their doors torn off, and barely a single window had been left unbroken. There were more bodies too, mercenary guards slumped against stairs and spread-eagled in pools of blood and mud. An evil smoke hung in the air. From towards the Castle Road, Orsian heard the first signs of men: an uproar of screaming and, beneath it, the low roar of blazing flames.

He pushed the gate open and stepped inside, a pit of dread in his gut at what he might find.

CHAPTER 34

Ciera stumbled out into Piperskeep's yard, and all she saw was death. Not since the Grandsons' War had a *hymerika* been slain inside the castle walls, and now everywhere she looked there were bodies with the red mark of the king's guard upon their chest.

One was slumped next to the wall, a stain of blood marring his throat like a crimson neckerchief. Not ten yards away, two more had died together, impaled on each other's swords. There were bodies on the stairs, on the battlements, sitting against the walls such that they might simply have been taking a moment's respite, if not for the dark puddles of blood pooling beneath them. Ciera's gaze lingered on each of them for as long as she could bear. She had brought them to this, and she owed them that much.

From the battlements, a crow descended and began pecking at a man's face. Ciera launched a pebble at it, drawing an admonishing squawk and sending the bird winging upwards back towards its perch. Above, more dark birds strutted like guardsmen, cawing and eyeing the corpses below.

The *Hymeriker* was not a brotherhood for life, but Andrick Barrelbreaker had never cast a man out by reason of advanced age. Those remaining were the ones Lord Gurathet had left behind; some for questionable loyalty, some because they were favourites of Lord Balyard, but mostly because they were in the twilight of their years, still masters of a blade but ready to leave war to the younger men, with unbent backs and knees that did not click. How many years' experience had been lost in this madness? How many tales of heroism and brotherhood that would never again grace the barracks' mess room? Ciera had never cared for such things before, not until so many had chosen to stand with her instead of with Balyard.

Unable to contain herself, Ciera slipped to her haunches and vomited. She stayed there a moment, lacking the will to rise, watching her tears follow the contents of her stomach.

'Lady?' asked Haisie. Even faced with death, the girl had been unwilling to leave Ciera's side, and clutched baby Andrick to her as if he were as precious as her own sibling.

'I'm fine,' gasped Ciera, fighting back a wave of nausea.

She felt a hand upon her shoulder, and there was Errian. Sweat-stained and haggard, with dark circles under his eyes as gloomy as the water of a deep well, but alive, and seemingly unhurt.

It was the first she had seen of him since she had disappeared into the walls. While the *hymerikai* fought, Ciera had been able to flee with Andrick through the hidden passages. For a time, she had become horribly lost, even discovering a wide, sloping tunnel deep below that looked like it might run for miles. When she had found a safe exit, she had hidden in an unoccupied guest chamber with the door barred, bringing with her every servant she could find. They had cowered together, all rank forgotten. Their only protection had been Ciera's dagger, which she had gripped tight in her fist as she stood behind the door trembling, listening with horror to the screams and the sharp clash of blades.

'How did you know who was on your side?' she asked Errian.

Errian pointed to a golden cloth tied to his right arm. 'We wore these.' He shook his head, taking in the tableau of corpses. 'We had them outnumbered at first, until Balyard summoned the watchmen from the gate.' He pointed across the yard to the inner gate, where a silver-haired *hymerika* lay surrounded by a dozen corpses in the red livery of Merivale's guard. 'I sent a few men to hold it in their stead, but it was still a close-run thing. We can thank Eryi that most of the mob turned on the city once the Watch withdrew.' He offered a hand, and pulled Ciera to her feet.

'And Balyard?'

'We found him an hour before dawn. His men surrendered. We've confined him to his chambers with his family, under guard.'

Ciera would have felt better with Balyard chained in the dungeon, but she supposed there were some courtesies that had to be offered. 'What do we do now?'

Errian looked at her strangely. 'You rule, of course.'

Of course. The weight of Errian's words threatened to drop Ciera to the floor again. 'Bring all the *hymerikai* still living to me in the hall,' she heard herself say. 'Even those who fought against us. If they repent and re-swear their oath to the Sangreal line, they can serve me. Free the guards as well on condition of their loyalty. Their first task is to gather the bodies for burning.'

'By your will, Majesty.'

Errian was about to turn on his heel and leave, when the gate across the yard began to creak.

A tall youth Ciera did not know stepped between the high oak doors, with skin bronzed to the shade of teak. A beard of black fuzz dusted his jaw and cheeks, and his long thick hair had been bound at the back of his neck. He sported no uniform Ciera recognised, but he wore a sword with the ease of a man who knew how to use it.

'You!' exclaimed Errian. With a shriek of steel, he wrenched his sword from the scabbard and started towards the newcomer.

If the youth feared Errian, he did not show it, standing patiently with his hands loose at his side and his blade undrawn. He flashed the shadow of a smile. 'You know me then. I feared no one would, though perhaps it would have been easier.'

As soon as he spoke, Ciera recognised him. 'Orsian?' He had been a boy then, softly spoken, who on the road to Merivale had patiently taught her the Sangreal lineage and later shown her the city's market when the rest of the world would have been content for her to be hidden away like an invalid. Had that truly been less than a year ago? The memory felt like it belonged to another age.

Errian was shouting. 'By Eryi's balls, draw your sword so I can kill you! Coward!' Afraid Errian meant to do just that, Ciera lifted her skirt and ran towards them.

She had heard tales of the brothers' enmity, but still Orsian did not reach for his blade. 'You've not changed, Errian. Do the citizens have you to thank for the state of

Merivale? Who else could have been so foolish as to order the guards away while the city collapsed into mayhem?'

'What's happened?' asked Ciera. 'How bad is it?'

Orsian's eyes flicked towards her. 'My Queen. Merivale is in pieces. There are hundreds dead.' He spoke deliberately, as if the effort of remaining calm cost him more than he showed. 'The inner ring has been ransacked; they are hanging whole families for the crime of hoarding food. Where is the king?'

'And you let them?' Errian hacked up a laugh. 'Of course you did. All you're good for, isn't it, watching better men die? Father should never have let you join the *Hymeriker*.'

For the first time, Ciera caught a flash of anger in Orsian's green eyes. 'I have dined enough on grief, Brother. If I am to blame for Father's death, then so are you.'

Errian moved faster than Ciera would have believed possible. One moment he was at her side, and the next he was snarling, looming over Orsian like a grotesque shadow, his sword flashing high and terrible. She screamed as Orsian's blade rose to meet Errian's down-cut in a shower of sparks. She had not even seen him draw it.

Errian must have been as shocked as she was. What followed ought to have been the clashing song of steel, but instead the two combatants held their blades together, testing the other's strength, as if this was their thousandth exhausted strike rather than their first.

'You got faster,' said Errian.

'Or you got slower,' Orsian countered. Neither moved.

'Stop this,' said Ciera. 'Enough men have died today.'

Orsian's eyes never left his brother. 'Him first.' Reluctantly, Errian took a step back, sheathing his blade.

More cautiously, Orsian did the same. 'Do not speak of Whitewater to me again. You were not there when he died.'

'I know. I regret it every day.'

Orsian looked around the yard. 'Is anyone going to explain what happened here? Where is Hessian?'

Taking a deep breath, Ciera told him of Hessian's departure, and her conflict with Lord Balyard. She left nothing out, and beckoned Haisie forward with Andrick so that Orsian could meet the new prince.

Orsian spared a smile for the sleeping Andrick, particularly to learn he was named for his father, but he was frowning by the time she finished. 'But where is Mother, and Naeem, and Theodric? Why did none of them stop this madness?'

Ciera sighed. It was easy to forget how much had happened while Orsian had been away. Wherever he had been away. 'Eryispek, with Hessian.' She explained quickly.

By the time she had finished, Orsian's face was drawn with worry. He ran a hand through his beard, as though a man thrice his age with the weight of the world on his shoulders. 'And Gurathet commands the *Hymeriker*? No wonder they lost. Father used to say the man had suet where his brains ought to be.'

'They lost?' demanded Errian.

'They lost. There are thousands of refugees trapped outside the walls fleeing the Imperium. Whatever is left of the *Hymeriker* will be here any day now. We have maybe a week before the Imperials arrive, if that.'

He left unsaid what Ciera knew he was thinking: that their brief, bloody coup and the rioting in the city had left them ill-prepared to meet them. She swallowed. She had hoped only to save Merivale from Balyard; she had not meant to bring the city to the brink of ruin, and now the fate of East Erland rested in her hands. Balyard and Gurathet had a great deal to answer for. 'How many?'

Orsian shrugged. 'Twenty thousand, forty thousand? Many more than we can muster. We need to open the gates – when they arrive—'

'Are you mad?' asked Errian. 'We don't have enough to feed those we have, and now you propose to let more people in?'

'What are we for if not to protect the people of Erland? I won't let them be butchered by the Imperium because of Balyard's misrule.'

'Let them in,' said Ciera. 'The more we have, the better a defence we can raise.' She looked to Errian. 'We should go into the city. I'll want a dozen *hymerikai* as a guard.'

'A hundred would not be enough if the mob takes against us.' Nevertheless, Errian went off to find them.

'Give me a dozen watchmen,' said Orsian. 'I want to get that gate open.'

It took the best part of two hours before they were ready to leave Piperskeep, once Errian had seen to all Ciera's commands. Though it grieved her to do so, she left Andrick in the arms of Haisie, guarded by six *hymerikai*, once she was satisfied that Balyard was safely under lock and key. A stableboy led her horse out, and she mounted it in the middle of Errian and eleven *hymerikai*, those with the fewest injuries and most certain loyalties.

'At the first sign of trouble, we're turning back,' said Errian. The guards of the Merivale Watch had been persuaded reluctantly to return to their posts, but if Orsian's tale was true it would take more than a few hundred men to return Merivale to order.

Ciera tried to still the butterflies in her stomach, and to take heart from her protectors' straight-backed discipline and the gleam of their mail. She had not left Piperskeep since learning she was pregnant with Andrick, and she dreaded what she might find.

Errian gave a command, and the thirteen of them rode in formation through the arch of Piperskeep's great gate, beneath the shadow of the fortress's monolithic grey-black walls.

There were more dead between the inner and outer gates, and overhead the gargoyles over the passage leered at them like demons awaiting a meal. Ciera forced herself to look at every single corpse. Some faces she knew; not by name, but one man had always given her a brief smile when she nodded him her thanks as she passed, and another was one of Balyard's men who had taken such twisted pleasure in seeing Andrick wrenched from her grasp. Her gaze lingered on his face the longest, eyes that had once been full of twinkling malice now sightless and bathed in the blood of a head wound so deep she could see his skull.

Grizzled Laphor rode next to her. His shield arm was tied up in a sling, but he had demanded the honour of riding out with her. 'Every man who ever became a *hymerika* knew the risks, Majesty,' he said. 'May Eryi take them.'

'May Eryi take them,' she whispered back. But how many of them had thought to die on the blade of a brother?

The portcullis rose, and at a walk they joined the Castle Road. A year before, Ciera had entered the city this way the day before her wedding to Hessian, and marvelled as what seemed the whole citizenry of Merivale had greeted her, but the Castle Road was deserted now, save for a few furtive scavengers watching from behind doors or the shelter of side-alleys, and strewn with debris.

At one of the gated streets, Ciera signalled for her escort to stop. There were no guards, and a hundred yards away a fire as high as the houses that surrounded it burnt bright against the twilight, as men cavorted around it like twisting shadows. Sounds of merriment reached Ciera on the wind, hoots of laughter and the gay tune of a piper. Errian pressed his hand against the gate, and it swung open.

Every house they passed showed signs of looting; doors torn off hinges, clothes strewn across the street, smashed bottles in pools of ruby wine. The only guard they saw had been bludgeoned so soundly that his brains were leaking down the steps outside a house.

The sound of hooves on the cobbles soon drew the revellers' attention. The piping ceased, and thirty-odd assorted souls turned to look at them.

'What is this?' demanded Ciera. Her voice sounded thin and reedy beneath the crackle of fire.

A woman draped in soiled silks with bird's nest hair and black circles painted beneath her eyes cackled and clapped her hands together, each finger bejewelled in obviously stolen rings. 'Just a party. Join the fun!' She laughed, and seized a jar of drink from a man swaying on the spot and thrust it towards Ciera, until a *hymerika*'s horse crossed her path and sent her scrambling backwards.

'We ran out of rope,' slurred a man, waving a slender golden sword towards the fire.

Ciera stared into the flames, and what she saw made her stomach curdle. 'Eryi's bones,' gasped one of the *hymerikai*, followed by the sound of him noisily throwing up over the side of his horse.

There had been four of them, presumably a family. The looters had tied them to each side of a post, piled it high with kindling, and set the whole thing ablaze. Four blackened corpses remained, little more than piles of ash and bone. The smallest must have been no older than ten. The only saving grace was that they were so burnt Ciera could not see their faces.

'He squealed like a stuck pig,' said the man with the sword. 'Smelt like one too.' Behind him, the rest cackled like a coven of witches.

Ciera fought down an urge to gag. 'By Eryi, why?'

'Why did they starve us?' demanded a woman from the back. 'Why did they tax us for every grubby penny we earnt? Why did their children parade around in silks while my boy sickened and died?'

'The king would never have allowed it!' added a man, this one wearing a guard's helmet and waving a broken spear.

It was not them; it was Balyard, Ciera might have said, but what did these people care? They only knew they had not enough, and those who lived on streets like this had more than they needed. *To think this all began with a petition from the guilds.* There had been so many chances to prevent this.

'Majesty?' asked Errian. In the firelight, his eyes flashed red with murder.

She could have ordered the *hymerikai* to ride them down, but the command caught in her throat. Abandoned by those who ruled them, denied bread and justice, was it any wonder these people had turned to their own warped morality?

Then she forced herself to look again at the charred bodies of the two children, and made up her mind.

'I offer you all a choice,' she began, willing her voice to carry over the fire and the murmurs of the mob. 'Give up those who burnt them, and you might walk from here with your lives. Otherwise, we will slaughter every single one of you.'

The man with the golden sword laughed. 'And why should we listen to you? Who are you anyway? Think I've seen you down the Erland Rose flashing your parts for bits of silver.' Many of his fellows laughed, but others had started to look a little uneasy.

Ciera looked to Errian. 'Kill him.'

The man opened his mouth to protest, but all that came out was a gurgle and a stream of blood as Errian drove his sword through his throat. The man's blade clattered to the cobbles, and the mob took a fearful step back. Two foolish souls made a rush for Errian, who drove them back with contemptuous ease.

A few tried to flee, but the *hymerikai* rode them down. It did not take the rest long to surrender the family's killers: the woman wearing her weight in stolen jewellery and two men, one of whom was so drunk he had slept through Ciera's arrival.

'I'm begging you, Majesty!' cried the woman, as Laphor drove her to her knees before Ciera. 'I never knew you was the queen!'

Ciera's gaze swept over the assembled mob, passing over the wailing woman. 'Is there any here who will swear by Eryi that it was these three?'

They almost tripped over one another in their desperation to swear. Ciera settled on the word of a spear-thin old man in beggarly clothes who seemed more sober than most – she half-suspected he had only been attracted by the fire's warmth – and a young woman who claimed to be the wife of one of the culprits.

'I told him it was murder, Majesty,' she kept insisting.

It was not quite a substitute for a trial, but it would serve. Ciera needed to send a message, not just to these, but to every citizen, that justice would once again rule in Merivale.

To everyone's surprise, Ciera dismounted, and her guards repositioned themselves between her and the mob. 'Your sword, Errian.'

He looked at her quizzically. 'Majesty?'

'Your sword.'

Looking no less confused, he handed it to her.

Ciera held it aloft, watching the glow of the fire ripple down its blade. She could not recall ever holding one before, but the weight of it and the cool metal of the pommel felt pleasing in her hand. 'The rest of you may go free,' she addressed the crowd. 'Provided you leave behind all you have stolen, and swear in Eryi's name that you will do no more violence. Tell all you pass what you have witnessed here, and tell them also that no more will Merivale starve.

'An army marches on this city, twenty thousand or more strong, and what they will do to you if they prevail will make today look like a summer fête's farce. Anyone willing to take up arms in the city's defence will be given bread. This in the name of my husband King Hessian Sangreal I swear.'

It was not a rousing speech that would stir in their hearts loyalty to her or to the Sangreals, but she hoped it made the point. Without a word further, Ciera drew Errian's sword across the first man's throat.

Sharp as the blade was, it was surprisingly difficult to split a man's neck, and by the time she reached the woman, the sleeve of her gown was drenched in blood. Before the woman could protest, Ciera made an end of it.

She looked at the rest. The fire crackled, and the blood pulsed slowly upon the cobbles.

'Go,' she told them.

The mob retreated into the night. Ciera watched the flames, with Errian a silent shadow at her side.

'You do not agree with what I did,' she said.

Errian reached to take his sword from her. 'It may mean they do not murder you in your bed or betray us to the Imperium, but if you think they'll fight for us when the time comes, I have an everlasting wineskin I'd like to sell you. If you'd hanged them, it would have been justice, but this was folly.'

'Enough men have died on my account already.' *I will not rule like Balyard, nor Hessian.*

'This is war. Dying is what people do.'

Ciera remounted. Further down the street, she could see more corpses: guards who had fallen defending their masters, and merchants caught by the mob as they piled the last of their wares onto a cart.

'The guards can deal with this tomorrow,' she said. 'Back to Piperskeep.'

On their return to the Castle Road, they encountered Orsian, riding with a boy and a girl asleep at the front of his saddle, alongside a pretty, short-haired woman who looked familiar and a boy who unmounted might have towered over even Errian.

'All the refugees are inside the city,' Orsian told her. 'No sign of Lord Gurathet and the *Hymeriker* though.'

Under starlight, looking down the Castle Road, Ciera could see more than half the city. In distant windows, fire blazed – of the living, rather than the dead – and atop the walls she could see the faint silhouettes of guardsmen returning to their duties. Perhaps Merivale might return to order, at least for now.

But it was the fires beyond the city that drew Ciera's eye. An uneven glow against the horizon, of flickering torches that seemed to dance in the dusk wind and gave faint illumination to the shadow that crept towards them through the dark.

It was not the Imperium. There were too few of them. It was what remained of Gurathet's *Hymeriker*; close to a thousand beaten men, whose loyalty was still to be decided. They might join her, or they might seek to overthrow her.

Whatever happened, the promise of battle travelled with them. Somewhere beyond the horizon, the Imperials were coming. Coming for Merivale.

CHAPTER 35

On bare feet, Rymond paced the walls of his prison, around his bed on the far wall, past a high shelf packed with books, past the only door, and arriving back at the roaring fire surrounded by cushioned chairs and a low table with a flagon of wine placed in the middle.

Fifty. Each circuit took Rymond slightly over a minute, meaning that his fifty rotations added to an hour of walking, which was enough that he could feel he had not been idle all day. It was approaching the time his lunch would be delivered, so he poured himself a glass of wine.

It was strange how better suited he was to being a prisoner than being a king, but that was as much due to his jailers as to himself. No luxury had been denied to him, save his shoes to prevent escape, but why would he want to run? This was the most rest he had taken in the best part of a year. He reached for a smokestick, lit it over a candle, and as he inhaled felt every care rush from his skin like sweat over a hot spring. They had given him all his belongings, including the trunk containing his casheef. Using it sparingly, sprinkled in his regular smokesticks, he could make the supply last another month.

This peace would not last forever of course. The men he had left outside the walls were loyal to him, and he had many stalwarts inside the city also. And why would the Imperials have locked him up in a far wing of Irith Castle unless they were worried about him being freed? He suspected that at that moment, Strovac, Dom, and their Imperial partners were struggling to fight back a tide of unrest within Irith. It had only been a week; Rymond was quite confident in his restoration. The Imperials had taken the city by trickery, but they could not hold it; Irith would not suffer Imperial rule, and if they stretched their force to try and occupy the rest of the country they would leave themselves vulnerable.

He caught the sound of heavy footsteps out in the corridor and heated words being exchanged. 'Get off me!' A woman's voice, followed by a fleshy slap and a man's angry roar. There was a brief struggle followed by more shouting, and as they paused outside the door, Rymond realised with a plummeting sense of dismay who was about to be shoved into the room.

The door burst open, and two members of the Wild Brigade appeared, burly and bearded, carrying Rymond's mother between then. She was uncharacteristically unkempt, with her ordinarily coiffed hair askew, and wearing a sensible shirt and jerkin over a knee-length leather skirt. There was a trail of blood running from her lip and down her chin, which she wiped away as soon as the two men threw her onto Rymond's bed. One of them had four bright red grazes running across his cheek.

'Bitch scratched me!' he snarled. 'I'll bloody show—'

He began to advance on Breta, before the other grabbed

his shoulder. 'Strovac and the girl said she wasn't to be harmed. Let's go.' Reluctantly, the bloodied man let his companion lead him from the room.

Breta stood from the bed and dusted herself down. She looked at Rymond, taking in his relaxed pose, fine clothes, glass of wine, and smokestick. 'Well, I'm glad to see one of us has been doing well. Tough fight when they took you, was it? Did you give as good as you got?'

'Mother, what are you wearing?'

'Never mind what I'm wearing!' She stalked towards him, and Rymond felt as if he were twelve years old again. 'Why are you reclining here as if this is one of your bawdy houses? Do you not understand you've been deposed?'

'What would you have me do without weapons or even shoes? It won't last. The city will rise for me.'

'The city *already* rose for you! I was the one who got them to rise!' She smacked the smokestick out of his hand into the fire. 'I'm dressed like this because I have been leading Irith's resistance, and now I find you treating this like your own personal feast day, drinking wine and smoking—' She sniffed the air. 'Is that casheef?'

Rymond shifted uncomfortably. 'So what if it is? How do you know what casheef smells like?'

His mother stared at him incredulously. 'Eryi's teeth... I knew you were a fool, and a drunk, but I always counted myself lucky you were not the hopeless sot your father was. Even he was not mad enough to touch that stuff. Where is it?'

Inadvertently, Rymond's eyes flicked towards his trunk at the foot of the bed. Breta followed his gaze, and scrambled towards it.

By the time Rymond reached her, she had thrown the

trunk open and was haphazardly tossing his clothes across the room. Rymond seized her hand, and she turned and slapped him with the other hard enough to make his eyes water. As she reached the bottom of his trunk and came uncomfortably close to his hidden stash, he seized her around the waist and threw her onto the bed.

'I am not a child any more, Mother! I am your king! For once in my life won't you just leave me alone!'

Breta rolled off, and stood, her lips twisted in a sneer. 'King of what exactly? King of this room? The city has fallen, you fool! Our last foothold in the New Quarter was overrun this morning. Why do you think I'm here? Because I missed your company? And while the town burns, you hide here with your bare feet and your casheef proclaiming to be king?' She laughed acidly. 'You are no king.'

The door opened, and they both turned towards it. Alcantra stood in the doorway, dressed as she had been when Rymond first met her, now with a long slender rapier and golden dagger hanging from her hip. She smirked. 'I hate to interrupt. I was hoping we might have a word, Majesty.'

'Only if you move my mother to a different room first.'

'She can stay. You're to come with me.'

Rymond looked towards his trunk, which his mother was eyeing.

'Worry not, Majesty. I have all the casheef you require.'

There was danger in those deep blue eyes, like a poisoned well. 'What happened to Adfric? No one has told me anything.'

'He's dead.' Alcantra spoke as she might have spoken of the weather. 'A brave man, but not the brightest.'

Rymond had known of course. He had seen Adfric fall. 'May Eryi take him.' He sighed. 'I'll come with you.'

His mother rounded the bed and seized his arm in a vulture-like grip. 'Rymond, give them nothing. No matter what deal they offer, you must not accept. Our time will come again, but you must not let them make a pawn of you.'

Rymond shook her hand away. 'If you touch my trunk—'

She gripped him again, harder. 'Your casheef is the last thing you need to be thinking about. West Erland—'

Rymond shook her away again more forcefully. 'The way I spend my leisure time is not your concern. *Do not* touch my trunk.' He turned and followed out the door after Alcantra. As it closed behind them, he felt a moment of light-headedness, and his fingers itched for some casheef to inhale, but he recovered himself and let Alcantra lead him down the corridor, two of the guards who stood at his door following in their wake.

His feet slapped against the flagstones. Rymond had rarely entered this part of the castle, and everything they passed looked both familiar and unfamiliar: the wide, slate cobbles, the fading tapestries, the walls that changed colour partway up where a different stone had been used during the castle's construction.

Alcantra led him to an arched doorway, from which the scent of lavender and billowing gusts of steam crept between the hinges. She opened the door, and within was a wooden tub, filled to the brim with scalding water.

'Amazing the things you don't know exist in your own castle,' said Rymond. 'Is that for me?'

'You are beginning to smell. With your mother captured, we are prepared to be more generous.'

Rymond looked Alcantra up and down. 'Are you planning on joining me?' He was only half-joking.

'I would be a poor jailer if I fucked my prisoners.'

'I would be a poor man if I did not ask.'

The bathroom was tiled and spacious, lit by a chandelier of candles hung from the ceiling, and the tub was so large Rymond could have lain down in it. The room was finer than his own bathroom. 'I had no idea I treated my guests so lavishly.'

'Enjoy.' Alcantra left, closing the door behind her, and Rymond quickly removed his clothes and leapt into the bath, sloshing water over the sides.

The water was hot enough to take Rymond's breath away, and it took him a little while to get comfortable. Then, with his head leant back against the tub, he closed his eyes and dozed, his want for casheef a comfortable itch behind his eyes.

I cannot escape. Might as well enjoy it. He was not Errian Andrickson, capable of stealing a sword and carving his way out. And if he tried, there were far worse places inside Irith Castle; deep dungeons, without hot baths or comforting smokesticks.

Rymond relaxed so well that he must have slept, for when he woke, the water had cooled from boiling to merely baking. He looked around. Someone had removed his dirty clothes and left folded, fresh ones taken from his bedchamber.

By a door opposite the one they had entered, Alcantra was waiting for him.

'Finally you're awake. You snore like a boar.'

'Thanks for the bath.'

'You'll thank me for more than the bath in a moment.' She pushed the door behind her, revealing a grand bedroom as large as Rymond's own, with a high four-poster bed, a golden mirror in the corner, and carefully arranged flowers on the table. Rymond's trunk was there too, at the bottom of the bed.

Rymond followed her inside. He resisted the urge to run to the trunk. The bath had turned the itch for casheef into a nasty pricking, like bladed insects were crawling under his skin. Something about the situation gnawed at him now; why would they waste a hot bath on a prisoner? 'Why are you doing this?'

'We need you to address the people of Irith,' said Alcantra. She took a seat at the table. 'And for that you must be washed.' She reached for a flagon. 'Wine?' She was already pouring.

Rymond took the chair opposite. The wine was pink, and when he took a sip tasted of foreign fruits, rich and spicy on his tongue. He could not escape his sense of unease, and had to press down his desire to ask for some casheef. 'So, you need me to make an announcement to keep the citizens in check? It will take more than a hot bath for me to be your puppet king.' Rymond shifted uncomfortably in his chair as a light sweat broke out over his skin. The desire to scratch was becoming uncontrollable. He ran a nail down his face, and his skin was baking hot.

Alcantra's unsettling gaze felt as though he was being studied by a cat, curiosity laced with disdain. 'You don't look well.' She held up a finger, a smudge of casheef on her nail. 'Would this help?'

Rymond lunged for it, and in one graceful movement, Alcantra stood and drove his face hard into the table. He cried out as his cheek smacked against the wood, and Alcantra pushed him to the floor.

'Do you know how casheef works?' she asked, circling the table as Rymond cradled his pained face. 'It secretes itself in your pores. You've been walking around with a permanent low-level dose ever since you started taking it. That bath...' She let her neck and limbs go slack, mimicking a broken puppet. 'That bath just cleaned you out.'

'What have you done to me?' Rymond gasped from the floor. Even in his robe, he was shivering. His face felt like it was on fire.

'Teaching you a lesson as to what happens if you can't cooperate. You *need* casheef. Do not bother to kid yourself otherwise. You can do as I say, or I can lock you away somewhere until the withdrawal has you tearing your skin off.' She reached inside her mouth and rubbed the speck of casheef against her gums. She pulled a face. 'It tastes foul, but it's less addictive. Now, I'm going to reach into my pocket for another dose, and you're going to be a good little king and stay where you are. Otherwise, I'll lock you in here, and when I come back, you'll be barely a puddle on the floor. Understand?'

Rymond nodded. What else could he do?

Alcantra plucked a tiny packet from her trousers and wiped a finger inside it. It emerged with a smear of black powder on it, which she moved slowly back and forth in front of Rymond's face.

His eyes followed it hungrily. He wanted it, needed it. But he believed her. His heart pounded with fear. If he lunged for it, she would lock him in there, alone. He nodded helplessly. 'I understand.'

She smiled, satisfied. 'Good. Now, I need you to have your wits, so I'm going to give you a little.'

Rymond's eyes lit up greedily. He moved to stand, and Alcantra pressed him back to the floor with the heel of her boot. Rymond could feel his sweat seeping into his robe.

Alcantra thrust a smudge of sticky powder into his hand. 'Snort it. You're no use to anyone smoking it.'

Humiliated, Rymond held the substance to his nose. The casheef stung his nostrils, and the sensation was not so strong as smoking it, but it was sweet relief even so. He gave a wordless gasp as the drug hit his bloodstream.

Alcantra allowed him to his feet, and helped him back to his chair.

'Why?' Rymond wheezed. From the beginning, he had underestimated her.

'My employer has been planning this invasion for some time. Dom's willingness to introduce you to casheef gave us an easy way to weaken West Erland. More recently, it was for secrets. You're very eloquent on casheef; you told me all about Strovac Sigac and your plan to get rid of him. He didn't take kindly to that. I had to persuade him not to kill you.' She smiled. Her eyes were as cold as evening mist. 'After that night, I had you. I was going to tell you about Drast Fulkiro's invasion the night of your party, until your mercenary girl saved me the trouble.' She laughed. Rymond had no idea who Drast Fulkiro was. 'Your mad ride to intercept them gave me the chance to take Irith. Strovac Sigac and his band of barbarians opened the smaller gates, and we flooded the city with the Eternal Legion. I can still scarcely believe how easy it was.'

'So what now?' asked Rymond. Through the soft haze of casheef his voice was dry as cold dirt.

'That depends on you, Majesty. It's either this' – Alcantra gestured around the room, and then waved the bag of casheef in Rymond's face – 'or... something considerably darker and less comfortable. I haven't explored the dungeon yet, but the smell...' She smiled.

'All the luxury and casheef you desire is yours, if you stand up in front of all your people and swear fealty to the Imperium. You can continue to call yourself King of West Erland. In truth though, you'll be *our* king. If we tell you to take a shit, you'll lay us a golden turd.'

'What do you need me for?'

'Fulkiro has insisted on marching east, and the men he has left me are not enough to hold the city. We need to quell the madness in Irith, and we need West Erland's soldiers. Quickest way is through you.'

'Once you take East Erland, you won't need me.' Rymond blinked. The casheef was already beginning to wear off.

'You'll still have your uses. One of the best ways to keep a province under control is to change as little as possible. We've learnt that, over the centuries.'

'The people of Erland won't stand for it.'

'Give it five generations or so. The troublesome ones get weeded out. You don't have to worry about that though.' She held out a casheef-tipped finger, and Rymond greedily snorted the speck of powder. 'You tell them you've allied with us, we'll do the rest.'

Rymond's mind raced, the casheef swirling through his bloodstream like leaves on a raging river. It was a tempting offer. With surrender to the Imperium, he could return to the life he'd had before the war. Let the Imperials fight East Erland, and if they won, his reign was secure. It would be a shallow form of kingship, but power was never something he had lusted after; it had been thrust upon him. Alcantra was offering him a way out.

And the alternative... Locked away in his own dungeon, going slowly mad with casheef withdrawal. He would break within the first day, begging to be released and given another chance. When judged against that, it was no choice at all.

'If not you, I will put Strovac Sigac on the throne,' warned Alcantra.

Rymond held back a laugh. That would be amusing, to let Strovac and the Imperium tear one another apart. But he would not be there to see the moment Strovac eventually betrayed Alcantra. He would be locked away in the dark, or more likely dead.

It was no true choice. And yet, Rymond knew he could not trust her.

You will only remain alive so long as you are useful to them. That coherent thought broke through the gentle casheef haze that caressed his skin like a comforting blanket. Acquiescence would only buy his temporary survival, he was sure of it.

'What of the commander?' he asked, playing for time. 'This Drast Fulkiro? Does he know you are making me this offer?'

'Fulkiro is not your concern. Your answer, now.'

Rymond's mouth felt like sawdust. Already, he was itching for more casheef; the short rush of snorting it was a pale imitation of letting its smoke linger in your lungs.

'I need time to think,' he said, desperately. His heartbeat pulsed violently against the back of his eyes. 'How do I know I can trust you?'

'You don't.' Alcantra smiled, her teeth like sharpened swords of pearly bone. 'But it's me or the dungeon. Do this for me, and you may smoke all the casheef you desire.'

It would be a betrayal, he knew. Of his land, his people, his family, his lineage. *King Rymond the Coward*, they would name him. But better that than King Rymond the Dead.

'I'll do it,' he croaked.

Alcantra's smile widened. 'I knew you would. Here.' A smokestick stinking of tangy, earthy casheef appeared from nowhere between her fingers. She lit it over a candle, and Rymond took it from her, sucking at it hungrily like it contained the divine blood of the Norhai.

They agreed Rymond would address the people of Irith the next afternoon, but by the time Alcantra told him and left, he was barely listening. In front of a blazing hot fire, Rymond huddled inside his robe, alone with his casheef.

CHAPTER 36

The fog hung over the water like a cool white shroud, adding an eerie quality to the lake's unnatural stillness. They had long left the shore behind, and the only sound was the chopping strokes of their oars upon the surface, sending rhythmic waves that churned the water in their wake.

Viratia sat in the bow, watching the backs of the two Adrari oarsmen. Bowan, one of the young *hymerikai*, was at the stern, while Naeem had taken the narrow bench between the two rowers. The watercraft were small, and it had taken three to fit their whole company. Viratia glanced to her left and right, checking that they had not lost one another in the mist. Eryispool was vast, and if the boats were separated there was a chance they might land miles apart from one another.

Despite her wish to be on their way, it had not been until the third morning and the return of the Adrari fishermen with the boats that Hessian had seen fit to bid Fisherton farewell. Once Haim the alderman had told him that they could cut days off their journey and touch the very lowest point of Eryispek by crossing the lake instead of trekking several days across rough terrain, he had been adamant that they wait and recover, despite Viratia's protests. She would have been content to leave him and the rest behind, but Naeem had been unwilling to set out without the others.

'We don't know what's out there,' Naeem had reasoned. 'All we know is that it's out to kill us, and damn near succeeded. I'll feel happier facing it with a few extra swords at my back.'

So much for my brave protector. When Viratia had tried to get some of the Fisherton Adrari to row her across they had insisted on waiting for the fishermen's return, and refused to allow her to make the journey without a guide. Instead, she had spent two painful days at the inn, watching the young *hymerikai* drink themselves insensible while Sister Aimya tried to escape Velna's attention long enough to get the handsomest of the warriors alone. In the end, for a lack of anything else to do, Viratia had distracted Sister Velna with an afternoon of pious questioning, as if she were thinking of taking vows herself. There were many widows among the Brides of Eryi, Velna had assured her. Viratia had sworn to consider the matter further when they returned to Merivale, although by then even Velna's eyes had been glazing over.

Viratia caught the eye of Aimya from the other boat, and the girl waved to her. Viratia smiled back, recalling what it was to be so young, and hungry to escape the confines of a cage others had built for you. It was clear enough Aimya had not chosen a life of devotion and quiet contemplation for herself. Some families might give a daughter to the brides for one less mouth to feed, or in the hope of earning Eryi's favour.

The other development had been the previous evening,

when a ragged band of pilgrims had arrived in Fisherton, a
day ahead of a much larger group so they claimed. Viratia
would have thought nothing of it, if not for the whisperings
among them of a small blonde girl who had healed a broken
ankle and disappeared. The pilgrims named it a miracle,
proof of Eryi's love for them and the reward that would meet
them upon Eryispek, but Viratia knew better. Had it been
Pherri's ability to heal that had led the Adrari to kidnap her
daughter, or to kill, or something else entirely?

I am coming, Pherri.

'And I thought the Pale River was vast,' grumbled
Naeem from the middle of the boat, surveying the endless
water in every direction.

'At least there's no danger of us being dragged downriv-
er,' said Bowan.

'Just drowning to worry about then,' said Viratia.

Naeem barked a laugh. 'Times like this I wish I'd learnt
to swim.' He leant back behind an oarsman to run his fingers
through the water. 'Not that it matters if you freeze to death.'

'We're only a few hundred yards from shore that way,'
said one of the oarsmen, nodding to their starboard side. 'We
don't go into the deeper water except to hunt.'

'Is this mist usual?' asked Viratia. She would have sworn
it was growing denser, its transparent tendrils thickening to
heavy clouds that left a chill moisture upon the skin.

The oarsman shook his head. 'It's been a mild summer,
Lady. Usually this would have been burnt away by the sun
by now.'

Viratia surveyed the sky. The sun overhead was shadowed behind cloud, little more than a cool grey coin. Its
passage over the high expanse of Eryispek had done little to
warm her bones, and she huddled deeper into her furs.

Across the water, Hessian looked like a bedbound child, with only the top of his head visible over his own pile of fleece.

Their boat bobbed unexpectedly as a series of powerful waves crashed against their port side, and Viratia had to grip the sides to stop herself being lifted into the air.

'Eryi's bollocks!' cried Naeem. 'So much for—'

Whatever he had been about to say was swallowed by a roar as a finned tail the size of a horse burst from the lake and soaked them in a torrent of icy water before disappearing again.

Viratia spluttered, pushing wet strands of hair back from her eyes, her vision blurred by the sudden onslaught. She had heard of the great whales of Eryispool but had never expected to see one in person. She peered into the water, and caught sight of a shadow circling their boats in the depths below. It was inky-black, and enormous, perhaps as long as the curtain wall of Piperskeep was high. She repressed a shiver. They were said to be gentle, but the vastness of the creature was harrowing. It was big enough to swallow all three boats whole.

Her companions too were soaked, but the Adrari had managed to keep hold of their oars. 'Do they usually behave like that?' asked Viratia, still scanning the water.

'No,' coughed one of them, brushing a hand across his wet face. 'They don't usually come so close to the banks. They prefer it out in the deep water.'

As he finished, a second great tail suddenly burst from their starboard side. The wave missed them, but crashed into the two boats behind. Hessian's took the brunt of it, and for a moment was flung into the air before crashing down again.

The Adrari exchanged baffled glances, worry plain on their faces.

'They're trying to sink us!' cried Viratia. 'Row!'

The first whale leapt across their path, just tens of yards away, sending water cascading across their bow and soaking Viratia to her underclothes. This seemed to shake the Adrari from their stupor, for with a cry they bent their backs to the oars and doubled their stroke, dragging them clear of a wave the brunt of which narrowly missed Velna and Aimya's craft.

Viratia seized a bucket, and set to bailing out the ankle-high water collecting in the bottom of their boat. 'There's two more!' cried Naeem from the stern, pointing ahead of them.

Viratia turned, and the sight that met her filled her heart with awe and terror. Two whales, on a course for head-first collision with them, black fins breaking the water like ebony daggers. 'They're going to ram us! Aim for the shallows!'

The Adrari did as she commanded, and the others seemed to have taken the same idea, for they veered together towards the shore, now visible only a few hundred yards away. Somehow, Hessian's boat had got ahead of them, and Viratia caught sight of the king's fear-wracked face. He was silent and shivering, evidently too shocked to take command.

Their sudden change of direction seemed only to spur the whales on. They harried them, two either side flapping their tails to send waves across their path and one at the rear, zigzagging and rolling, setting the boats bobbing and driving them into the worst of the surf. Their easy route across Eryis-pool had turned to chaos; roaring water assaulted them from all directions, and for all Viratia's work with the bucket more was coming into their boat than she could possibly hope to bail out. Her back burnt from the effort, and at Bowan's behest she allowed him to take over.

Viratia turned to the bow, just in time to see the black maw of a whale's mouth burst from the water and fall upon the stern of Hessian's boat. In a maelstrom of teeth, it crunched the craft apart like tinder. Behind her, Naeem screamed, as the giant fell back into the water, dragging their shrieking companions down with it.

She did not need to tell the Adrari to row faster. Their oars were a blur as they sought to pull them to safety, ignoring the floating wreckage they passed. Viratia did not even give thought to searching for survivors; her only aim was to reach dry land as soon as possible, Hessian be damned.

'We're nearly there!' cried Bowan, just as another heavy wave sloshed across the boat. Their stern bounced violently as a whale broke the surface just behind them, missing them by yards.

It was only when Viratia heard the clunk of an oar against the bottom that she was prepared to accept they were safe. She fell to her knees, dizzy, as next to her Bowan tossed aside the bucket and collapsed. The two Adrari dropped their oars, breathing like their hearts were about to give out. Naeem leapt over the edge into the water and began wading to shore, willing to wait no longer to reach dry ground.

When the rest of them made it ashore, they found him with his forehead pressed to the snow-dappled ground. 'Never again,' he gasped to himself repeatedly. 'Never setting foot on another boat as long as I live.'

'Nor I.' Bowan was staring glassy-eyed out towards the lake. 'I'd sooner take my chances with those wolves again.'

'We should have known,' said Viratia, wringing the water from her hair. Of course their enemy could also turn the beasts of the water against them. She surveyed the lake for any sign of their companions, but the dense fog made it impossible. 'Did anyone see Hessian?'

Naeem rolled over to stare up at the sky, where snow was beginning to fall. 'I saw his boat go under. Damn beast ripped it apart.' He slammed his fist into the ground. 'Should have stayed with him. Andrick would never forgive me.'

'If you'd been there, you would be dead too,' said Viratia. She had no love for Hessian, but he had been Andrick's brother, and they had loved each other in their strange way. There would not even be a body for burning, and the heir was just a babe in arms. Hessian should never have come. *Damn that elder bride.* She hung her head, wishing Andrick were there. He would never have let this happen, any of it. If he still lived, she would never have let Pherri out of her sight. 'What about the other boat?'

Despondently, Naeem and Bowan shook their heads. 'Damn shame,' croaked Naeem. 'That girl Aimya was as good with a spear as any man I ever trained.'

Behind them, the two Adrari were trying to get a fire going with some damp branches they had snapped from a nearby tree. They would need it. Their clothes were soaking, and there were only a few hours of daylight left. Already, a chill wind was upon them, blowing the cold of their wet skin deep into their bones. Without fire and shelter they would freeze tonight.

Suddenly, Bowan stood, pointing out towards the water. 'Look!'

Viratia looked up, and her heart leapt. A second boat, sitting low in the water, propelled by one oar and bobbing clumsily towards the shore. 'Over here!' she cried, madly waving her hands over her head. 'Over here!'

Faces she could not make out looked towards her, and the boat turned. A few of its passengers put their arms into the water to propel them, trying to aid its beleaguered oarsman. Viratia could just make it the blonde head of Sister Aimya, and Sister Velna next to her. The boat's sole *hymerika* looked to be rowing; there was no sign of the two Adrari.

Viratia waded into the shallows to drag them to shore, while Naeem and Bowan followed. Soaked as they were, a little more water hardly mattered. As they came closer, with a start she saw a soaked cloak of red fur curled up on one of the benches, bright as a beacon in the mist.

Naeem glimpsed him at the same time. 'Majesty?'

'He lives,' said Aimya. The girl was as wet as the rest of them, but her eyes shone with youthful zeal. She took Hessian under one arm as the *hymerika* did the same, and Naeem and Bowan rushed forward to haul him from the boat.

'How?' demanded Viratia. 'I saw him go under.'

A hand grasped her, and she found herself pulling Sister Velna ashore. 'It was a miracle,' the elder bride extolled. 'We passed right by him. Aimya and I just managed to get him inside the boat.'

'But how did you escape the whales?'

Aimya climbed out, resting a hand upon Viratia's shoulder to do so. 'Speared one of the bastards in the mouth when he was about to swallow us. They didn't seem so keen after that.' Her face fell. 'We lost the Adrari though. They tried to fight it off with their oars and the bastard swallowed them whole.'

'Sister Aimya saved my life,' Hessian croaked. He stood, supported by Naeem, dripping water and shivering. 'Which is more than can be said for the rest of you!' He shoved Naeem aside suddenly, fire blazing in his eyes, and Bowan shrank back from the fury of a suddenly reinvigorated Hessian. 'You!' He raised a shivering finger towards Sister Velna, his voice rising in pitch and temper. 'You treacherous harridan. You knew this journey would kill me, didn't you!' He turned his ire upon Viratia. 'And you! You want me dead as well. You blame me for Andrick, and for your idiot daughter running off! I ought to have you both executed.'

He began pacing back and forth, rubbing his shivering hands together. 'First bandits and wolves... now damned whales... Well, no more.' He pointed to the two surviving Adrari. 'You, and you. Tomorrow at first light you'll row me and my guards back to Fisherton. I am not going another step.'

Viratia stared at him. They were mere miles from Eryispek now. 'You want to go back on that lake, after what just happened? And leave us without guides?'

'Whatever's causing this madness doesn't want us up there.' Hessian lifted his eyes towards Eryispek, so close now it took over the sky. 'I doubt it will give me any trouble retreating. If you want to stay that's your choice.'

Viratia looked to Sister Velna, expecting her to demand Hessian fulfil his oath, but the elder bride was only staring towards the Mountain, her fingers clasped tightly in front of her, whispering silently to herself. Though soaked from the lake she was not even shivering. She gave no sign she had even heard Hessian. The woman's behaviour grew stranger by the day.

Hessian turned, and stomped off in the direction of their burgeoning fire, onto which an Adrari was casting planks from one of the boats.

'Can't blame him,' murmured Naeem, standing next to Viratia. 'He wasn't well even back at Piperskeep. We're lucky he's made it this far.'

Viratia sighed. 'We were unlucky he came at all.' She could have been after Pherri days ago if not for Hessian, and now he might be dooming them by going back.

'We have his barge and his guards to thank for getting us here,' said Aimya, who had left her soaking clothes by the fire and stripped boldly down to her undergarments. 'And the Adrari say we've only lost half a day. They'll give us directions to the nearest trail. We can be upon Eryispek by tomorrow noon.'

Viratia looked to the sky, counting the hours of daylight they had left. Not enough. Not without freezing to death. She sighed, suddenly overwhelmed by tiredness. 'Rest well tonight, both of you. What we have faced so far might be nothing next to what awaits us up there.'

She looked up at Eryispek, close enough now that she could make out individual snowdrifts and white-dusted trees, and high in the distance, dark specks of what might have been Adrari villages. *I'm coming, Pherri.* But if the journey so far had almost killed them, what hope did Pherri have among her captors?

CHAPTER 37

The old man was sweating, Tansa could see from her place on the long balcony above the hall. His exposed pink pate was slick with perspiration, and his grey hairs hung in limp threads around his ears.

It was very hot, Tansa had to admit. There had been days when she was last in Merivale where she had forgotten what it felt like to be warm, but in summer the city sweltered. That was good for the upcoming siege, she supposed; people ate less in the heat.

On the dais, Queen Ciera sat on a simple wooden bench atop a cushion, her babe swaddled tightly against her chest. She wore no jewellery, save a silver tiara furnished with rubies that shone like the dawn under the glow of high wooden chandeliers.

The first time Tansa had seen her, it had been Ciera on the high balcony, back in Cliffark's playhouse. *We've both come up in the world. I'm on the balcony, and she's on the stage.* It was easy to see how the girl had beguiled her brother, with her doll-like face and bouncing curls. *You could*

have had anyone you wanted. Why was it Tam who had t
die? Had she ever wept as Tansa had? Somehow she doubte
it; people like her and Tam were just toys to these people, c
less regard than a favoured horse.

'Lord Gurathet,' the queen began. 'For your failure
recognise the Imperial threat, and your defeat at Halorc
Bridge, you are relieved of your role as *balhymeri*.'

Lord Gurathet drew himself up as if preparing to spe
then something in the queen's face appeared to change l
mind. The air seemed to leak out of him. He turned to t
crowd behind him, scanning their faces for an ally who mi{
speak for him. The silence that spread through the co
could have been cut with a butter knife, as everyone wai
for the next words that would drop from the queen's lips.

Ciera raised an eyebrow. 'That will be all, Lord.'

To the surprise of Tansa and, to judge by the faces of
court, many others, Lord Gurathet released a booming la
before reaching into his pocket and wiping his face wi
handkerchief. 'Can't say fairer than that, Majesty! At my
a man should know when he's beaten. I did what I cou
get our boys back here safe. I'll stay and serve under wh
you appoint, if you'll permit me.'

'Arrangements for our defence must be made wi
delay. We may only have a few days, perhaps a week
are lucky, in which to prepare the city.' The queen's
stirred grumpily, and she passed him behind her to a nu

'Who will it be then?' asked Lord Gurathet. His ey
to Ciera's right, where Orsian and his brother Erriar
sentry. Orsian had donned the armour of a *hymerik*
and his hair had been sheared back so that it fell no
than his shoulder. He looked a little less like Ranul
day. 'Lord Orsian?'

Orsian did not move, but next to him Errian bristled. 'I am the elder,' he said, in a voice that carried across the whole hall. 'Until yesterday, you all thought Orsian dead. I should be *balhymeri*.'

Lord Gurathet chuckled. 'No disrespect, Lord, but your accomplishments are limited to being captured by the pup Rymond Prindian and nearly drinking Hessian out of house and home. Orsian proved himself last autumn at Imberwych. He even looks like the Barrelbreaker!'

'Lord Gurathet,' said Ciera sharply. 'I did not ask for your opinion on my *balhymeri*. I have given you your freedom under assurances you will attempt no further treason, but it's possible I was mistaken.'

Tansa caught murmurs of agreement from members of the assembled court, and a few whispers of consternation. Errian's fair face had turned puce, but a gruff old *hymerika* she had heard Orsian name Laphor spoke for him. 'Lord Errian proved himself only this week. If not for his leadership we'd still be chafing under Balyard's misrule.'

That set the whole court off into debate again, and a few *hymerikai* exchanged angry words and began shoving at one another.

'They fight over honours like flies over a pile of shit,' Tansa murmured.

Next to her, Cag shrugged. He almost looked handsome in his new red livery. The commander of the Merivale Watch had been crying out for new men, and to Tansa's bewilderment Cag had answered the call.

'Why are you even wearing that? You're not on duty. Eryi's balls, you're not even old enough.'

'Some of us have to find our place where we can. We can't all get tupped by the king's nephew.'

Tansa resisted the urge to hit him. 'Just move on, Cag. Do they pay you weekly? Whenever it comes, I suggest the first thing you do is find a brothel.'

Cag opened his mouth to reply, then seemed to think better of it. He turned his head to face the hall below, hurt written in the set of his mouth. Tansa immediately felt guilty, but how else was she supposed to respond to him being such an arse? He had been sulking for weeks now.

'I swear sometimes it's like you don't even miss him,' he mumbled.

She could have grabbed his collar and punched him in the face. He didn't know, nobody did. Tam had been the other half of her. To say she did not even miss him...

'Just telling you what I'm thinking,' he continued when she did not reply. 'Here we are, in the home of the man who killed him, and you're just sitting around and shagging his nephew like it never even happened.'

'Just be quiet.' There were people turning to look at them now. 'Hessian ain't even here.'

'What if he was?'

'He'd have himself a fancy new city guardsman, with the strength of an ox and the wits of a wall.' Before Cag could reply she turned on her heel and strode to the other side of the balcony, ignoring the pointed looks she got from other members of the court. She did not know who they were and did not care to.

Below, the nobles were still holding forth. Some pompous lord had finally been able to get a word in without somebody speaking over the top of him, and was evidently eager to let the world know his thoughts.

'If we must have a son of the Barrelbreaker,' he was saying, 'let it be Lord Errian. He is the elder; how would

Andrick have intended that Orsian be ahead of him? By all accounts, he groomed Errian for command since he could hold a sword.'

The man looked as though the mere act of holding a sword might send him toppling over, but Orsian was nodding respectfully. 'I agree,' he said. 'Errian should be *balhymeri*. Give me the command of the Merivale Watch, and any citizen willing to take up arms.'

Whispers broke out across the hall. Errian was looking at his brother through narrowed eyes, as if trying to comprehend whether he was being outsmarted. Ciera though was nodding. Tansa could not help thinking how delicate she looked, like a lilac petal battered by heavy rain. 'If that pleases all, then it's settled. Errian is the *balhymeri*.'

The news was welcomed by loud cheers from Errian's supporters, and two *hymerikai* strode over to thump him on the back and clasp wrists with him. Orsian though did not even move, a strange expression on his face.

Tansa wanted to scream at him. *I came here for you, to save your family!* On the journey to Merivale, when their talks that sometimes lasted half the night turned to his family, all Orsian would ever say of Errian was how he hated him, and now he was prepared to give up his first glimpse of true power for him. Why could these nobles never say what they meant? Before the tears could form, she rushed from the hall.

Lord Gurathet was striding towards him, and Orsian let himself be grasped by the shoulder and pulled into a hard wrist-clasp. The man then seized him by the back of the neck and drew him into an embrace.

'Brave of you, lad,' he said. 'To put that much trust in your brother. I've seen enough of him to know you could do better.' Somehow, even when he tried to whisper, Gurathet's voice boomed like a thunderclap. 'By Eryi, you best not let him fuck this up.'

They were bold words for a man who had just been dismissed from the same position, but Orsian smiled along, thanking him kindly and promising to work with Errian.

The truth was, Orsian wanted to command the Merivale Watch and the commons. He had watched his father for the first fourteen years of his life, and Captain D'graw for four months, and between them Orsian believed he had gained a good enough understanding of what men looked for in a leader. Errian could lead warriors, but there were few men who could lead the rest of the city well enough to make a difference when twenty thousand Imperials came hammering at their gates.

I have to make them believe we can win. If men yet unbloodied by battle realised the odds that faced them, they would break at the first chance of death. Even the city watchmen; the closest most of them had been to war was likely breaking up tavern fights and saving penniless punters from the whores they had failed to pay, at least before the city had rioted and half of them had deserted.

His brother was striding across the dais towards him, and Orsian broke off his embrace with Lord Gurathet. Errian looked as proud as though he had already fought off the Imperium single-handed, puffed up like a bear ready for winter. Hard to believe that he had been either imprisoned or drunk for the best part of a year.

Orsian clasped his brother's wrist. 'Congratulations.' When Pherri had told him of how Da'ri, her tutor, had died

Orsian had been ready to kill Errian, and they had come within a hair's breadth of blows in the yard the day before. Now though, seeing him again, somehow Errian's prickly pride and hot-headedness seemed less of an affront. He pitied him slightly; Errian was their father's heir, and how could he ever hope to live up to that legacy?

Errian pulled him close and whispered, 'What exactly is your plan, Brother? If you mean to avoid combat and hope that I die so you can be Lord of Violet Hall, it won't work. I swear, you and your watchmen will face the same dangers as the *Hymeriker*.'

'Are you mad?' Orsian wrenched away from Errian's grip. 'I'm here to defend Merivale, just as you are. You are welcome to Violet Hall. But if you raise your blade against me again as you did in the yard, I swear there will be consequences.'

Errian laughed. 'Barely two years ago you were still practising with a wooden training sword. The day I fear your wrath, I will hang up my blade for good. See to your watchmen and commoners.' He turned and left the hall, his footsteps echoing off the cold stone, followed by a retinue of *hymerikai*.

Orsian watched him go. Why even when there was so much at stake did Errian have to make it so difficult? *Because he is Errian.*

Eager for a distraction, he looked to the balcony in search of Tansa, but she was gone. *There is no place for her here.* Some lords kept mistresses, but few would dare bring them to court, and Tansa was nobody's mistress. She was as bold and clever as anyone Orsian knew. If not for her, he would have been out at sea aboard the *Jackdaw* awaiting ransom, but who in Piperskeep would understand what they had been through together?

He looked to Ciera. She was still sitting on her cushioned bench, holding the young prince. Orsian could not help but marvel at her ascent; when he had last seen her, she had barely left her chamber, yet somehow she had risen to claim the regency at the point of a sword. He supposed that birthing a prince and then having him snatched by your step-daughter's husband was a situation that would incline a person towards ruthlessness. He approached, and dipped to a knee. 'Majesty.'

'Orsian. Few men would have given up the chance to be *balhymeri* so easily. You have my gratitude.'

He inclined his head, acknowledging the compliment. 'I have a boon I must ask in return.'

Ciera raised an eyebrow. 'Go on.'

Orsian swallowed. 'I am a second son,' he began, 'with no prospect of land unless my brother should die without an heir. My father was a great lord, not by birth, but by the strength of his sword arm. In ordinary circumstances, with my father dead, I might be free to do as I please, but as a *hymerika*, the son of Andrick Barrelbreaker, and the king's nephew, it is not so simple. When the king returns, I intend to seek his permission to marry. I would be glad of your support.'

'The short-haired girl you brought from Cliffark?'

'Her name is Tansa.'

A half-smile played on her bow lips. 'She seems... fierce. And is Tansa of a noble family? She looks familiar.'

Orsian felt his cheeks reddening. 'She's a daughter of the streets of Cliffark. She has no family.'

Ciera regarded him carefully, cogs turning behind her

eyes. 'Balyard could move against me again, as might others. I want your oath.'

'My Queen, I am of the *Hymeriker*. I knelt before the king and swore an oath to the Sangreal line.'

'I have seen what such words are worth.' Her face hardened. 'I need your oath, Orsian.'

Orsian did not see any great loss to himself by giving it. He had already sworn once. He placed a hand upon his sword hilt. 'My Queen, I swear by Eryi and by the strength of my sword that I will defend the rights of you and Prince Andrick.'

She beamed. 'And I swear that I will make your case to Hessian when he returns.' She paused. 'If he returns. We've heard no word from Eryispek. We must all pray for him.'

Orsian withdrew. Ciera evidently did not feel as secure in her crown as she looked. *A boy king.* There had been boy kings before, he knew, and the kingdom always suffered for it. Even with Hessian's unpredictability, his rule was far preferable to the alternative.

In Orsian's chamber, Tansa stalked back and forth, only the fear that she would break something expensive stopping her from kicking something. Orsian had described his rooms as modest, and she supposed they were to him, but they contained wealth that if not for the theft that had led her to Merivale the first time Tansa would never have even contemplated. The two swords crossed on the wall had red gemstones forged into the hilt, the rug beneath her feet was a lush cloud of wool, and his bed was piled high with furs of beasts she did not recognise. Even the lock to the chest in the corner shone with gold etching, and she had no doubt that more wealth lurked within. Her efforts to pick the lock to see had so far proved fruitless.

Others might have got used to such riches, to crowns dripping in jewels and the guarantee of a hot meal twice a day, but not Tansa. Well, perhaps the latter. In Cliffark, it had seemed every move she and Orsian made was fraught with danger, like a courtship dance over a pit of snakes, but even that had been preferable to here. The only time she had felt content for her and Orsian to just *be* was on their journey to Merivale, even with Cag's eyes on them and the weight of dread in her stomach growing heavier with each passing mile.

This isn't home, she reflected miserably. But neither had Cliffark been home by the end. Where did she belong now?

The door latch clicked, and Orsian stepped inside. He even walked differently here, with a stoic, martial certainty.

'I looked for you after court,' he said. 'I thought we could take a walk along the high walls before I go to eat with the city's guild-masters; hopefully they won't hold it against me that Balyard ignored all their petitions. I'll be back late, but Ciera says you'd be welcome at her table.'

'Why did you give up the command to your brother?' she asked, ignoring his suggestion. 'You said we came here to save your family, but none of them are here except the one you supposedly hate, and you've just handed him everything.'

'I don't hate him. Well, I do, or I did. He can command the *Hymeriker*, but there's no one else who can lead the city watch and the guildsmen if we're going to make a fight of this.'

She scoffed. '*No one else?* What makes you think they'll

listen to you? You're just a jumped-up rich boy with a famous dad. They'll laugh in your face.'

Tansa savoured guiltily the hurt that for a moment marred his features. Other men might have struck her for that, but Orsian's pride was of a different sort. 'I've proven myself in battle, I led men over the side on the *Jackdaw*, I saved Cag in Cliffark – well, they don't know about the last two – but I've learnt how to lead. Captain D'graw may have been a horse's arse and the scum of the earth, but I saw why men followed him, and my father.'

'You think being a pirate and watching your father boss around other rich idiots waving swords makes you a leader?' For some reason Tansa found her hands were on her hips, which self-consciously made her feel like a fishwife chiding her husband for returning home late after gambling away all their money. 'What's the great inspiring speech you're going to give? *"Please fight for me so my family can keep shitting on the rest of you while we flounce about in silk because our ancestors killed your ancestors?"* Who the fuck of them will fight for you?'

'*Hymerikai* aren't rich! They join on merit. Naeem's father was a blackmaster, and Laphor grew up in a brothel!' Orsian was shouting now; finally she had made him lose his temper. 'I don't claim to be better than anyone!'

'But you do! You claim it with your walk and your sword and your fucking fancy room and that beautiful girl who thinks birthing a Sangreal gives her the right to tell everyone else what to do! I wouldn't eat at her table if they were serving roast unicorn!'

He's going to hit me now, she thought. His fists clenched, the crimson crept up his cheeks, and his nostrils flared like caverns. She wanted him to hit her, just to prove he was an arsehole like all the rest of them.

Instead, to Tansa's surprise, he turned and reached for the door. 'I'll leave you then. To think I sought Ciera's help in getting Hessian's permission to marry you.'

'Marry me?' Tansa felt the blood rush to her ears, and before she could think what she was doing, she seized a candlestick from the bedside and pitched it at his head. Orsian narrowly ducked, and it shattered against the wall into three pieces. 'Get out!' she screamed.

And he did. Cowering in a way that was almost comical, he lifted the latch and half-leapt through the door, slamming it behind him.

Alone in the enormous room she hated, Tansa felt all the fury seep out of her. She sank onto the bed and wept.

CHAPTER 38

Drast watched the rising smoke, the blazing fire reflecting in his irises.

Only a fool would build a home from straw and dung. He was teaching these Erlanders a lesson, and unlike the belligerent Cyliriens these cow-eyed peasants looked meek enough to heed it. Those they had been able to seize before they fled into the countryside had been shackled at the wrists and were awaiting their fate in the centre of the settlement.

'What was this place called again, Forren?'

'Gladfield, Senator. I believe that's the town's lord there.' He indicated a man taller than the rest standing slightly apart, glowering at Drast while all those around him kept their heads bowed.

'Bring him to me.'

Three legionnaires dragged the man from the throng. He was taller than Drast and around the same age, with shoulder-length blond hair and clad in ugly iron-and-leather armour. The soldiers forced him to his knees, and then pulled out three more: a woman, a boy on the edge of manhood, and a weeping girl of around thirteen.

'His family, Senator,' said a legionnaire. Like their lord, they looked cleaner and better-fed than the rest.

'Hessian will gut you for this, whoever you are,' said the lord, glaring up at him defiantly. 'I am a lord; you'll treat me with—'

Drast backhanded him with a gauntleted fist, sending a bloody spray from his mouth across the face of his kneeling daughter, who immediately began screaming.

A legionnaire clasped a hand over the girl's mouth, and her mother started pleading. 'Please, Lord, she's just a girl, let her—'

'I am no lord, savage,' said Drast, in Erlish. He was still learning his way around the barbarous language. With a cloth, he wiped the blood from his hand, then looked the lord dead in the eye. 'The fate of your people and your family depend on whether you can learn to cooperate. Now, tell me – what is the latest news from Merivale? Have the citizens rebelled?' Alcantra's intelligence claimed that King Hessian was gone and the city was on the verge of tearing itself apart, ripe for an assault.

The man glowered back at him, and spat out a mouthful of blood. 'Some rose, but Queen Ciera and the Barrelbreaker's sons restored order. Merivale's walls have never been breached; you'll be—'

Drast flicked a finger towards a legionnaire, who clasped a hand over the lord's mouth. *Interesting.* It seemed Merivale would not be so defenceless as the loathsome Alcantra had claimed. 'We may have more questions later. For now, just remember – things can always get worse, for you and your family.'

As the lord and his family were dragged back into line with the rest, Drast cast his eyes over the throng, and what he saw turned his blood to ice.

Beyond the crowd, Krupal was staring at him, smiling. He still wore his brown robe. He flicked a coin up and caught it.

Then Drast blinked, and Krupal was gone. An elderly Erlander stood in his place, with a bent back and nervous, watery eyes. No threat to anyone.

Drast let out a breath. *A trick of the light, that's all.* He needed more rest. He had not been sleeping well; Erland was a miserable place, and a part of him was still looking out over his shoulder for Krupal. No wonder he was seeing things. But Krupal was gone, he had to be; otherwise Drast would have been given the same treatment as Kvarm and Hrogo. He could not halt the shiver that ran up his spine.

Drast stalked away in the direction of the stone tower that had previously been the lord's residence, the only building in the settlement they had not set aflame.

'It seems Merivale may not fall as easily as the girl hoped,' said Forren once they were inside the bleakly appointed chamber that Drast had taken as his own.

'All the more impressive when we take it then,' said Drast. 'We press on.' After the fiasco in the west, it was just the opportunity he needed to restore his reputation.

Alcantra had cheated him. She might plead innocence, but he knew. Only his foresight in keeping several zebrephants with him had frightened the Erlanders enough that they withdrew before matters could get worse. His force had nevertheless been decimated, and the two wings Alcantra had told him to separate had through her trickery taken Irith in less than a day. Drast had reached the settlement with his dispirited army and found the Imperial flag already flying overhead.

Her victory, not his, and Drast had no doubt she had already informed Saffia Murino. She would be laughing in Ulvatia. Drast smashed his armoured fist into the table in front of him, splintering it and sending chips of wood flying.

Well, Alcantra had taken Irith, the Parmé-damned bitch could bloody hold it. He had left her a few thousand and told her to start suppressing the rest of the country. It was an impossible task. There was a risk, Drast supposed, that the Erlanders might counter-attack and leave him trapped between west and east, but it was a risk he was willing to take for the sake of wiping that smug smile off her face.

A more cautious man might have ensured their hold on West Erland was secure before attempting to take Merivale, but Merivale was the key to the east, and he needed a swift victory to wash the sour taste of Alcantra's humiliation from his mouth. With an outpost there, they could sweep eastward and then move west again to secure the lands they had already taken. Given their successes so far, he was feeling more confident by the day. As they crossed the Pale River, the famed *Hymeriker* had broken and ran from them, overwhelmed by the Eternal Legion. This was a land of simple peasants and dim-witted lords, no match for the Imperial war machine.

He looked around for wine and realised there was none. He pointed at a blank-looking slave in the corner. 'You. Bring wine.'

The slave rushed off as if Drast had touched his arse with a hot poker. Drast leant back in his chair and let his eyes close for a moment.

The door opened, and Drast looked up, expecting the

slave returned with his wine. To his irritation though, it was a captain of the Eternal Legion. 'Riders approaching, Senator.'

'That will be Lord Strovac. Send him up when he arrives.'

Men like Strovac Sigac were a necessary evil in war. Alcantra might think the barbarian was her creature, but she did not understand men of violence the way Drast did. He had sent Strovac pillaging with his Wild Brigade, without Imperial presence or specific orders. The best way to ensure the loyalty of such a man was to allow him his head occasionally.

However, after the slave returned with wine, the next time the door opened, it was not Strovac, but Alcantra.

'I told you to stay in Irith!' Drast exploded. 'How are we to hold—'

'I answer to the kzar, Senator, not to you.' Alcantra strode across the chamber and poured a small measure of wine for herself. 'Irith is secure, and I have sent men to take all the strongholds between there and here. Your mad rush for Merivale is stretching our supply line and leaving you without a route of retreat.'

Drast felt himself redden. 'What? You don't have the men! Irith is in rebellion! How do you mean—'

'Lord Rymond and I came to an arrangement.' Her voice cut across his like a sword stroke. 'He has secured peace in Irith and submitted to the Imperium. Once he's of no more use we'll divide West Erland between Sigac, Storaut, and Darlton.'

'What!' Drast was on his feet now. 'That agreement was not yours to make!' He had planned to take some land for himself, or to hand it out to potential supporters when he returned to Ulvatia.

'This is not a war for the advancement of Drast Fulkiro. The kzar approved my plans.' The girl was infuriatingly calm. She took a sip of wine. 'You are to leave another division of the Legion in West Erland, to secure our power there.'

'I will not. I need those men to take Merivale.' They were only days away from the city now; she could not thwart him yet again.

'All you need to take Merivale is me. My spies tell me the city is a powder-keg thanks to the regent's new taxes. One spark and the whole thing will go off. Then all we must do is open the gates.'

Drast exchanged a smile with Forren. 'Well, this is unexpected. It seems my spies know something yours do not. The people of Merivale have already risen, and been put down. The king's wife and nephews command now, and they are preparing for battle.'

'You mean to besiege them then?' Alcantra scoffed. 'That could take years.'

'There will be no siege. I mean to break their walls and storm the city.' A swift, crushing victory was what was needed; that had been their mistake in Cylirien, allowing their invasion to slow to a crawl while the natives regrouped and entrenched themselves for a prolonged conflict. Drast did not have the men for that.

'Merivale has never been taken.'

'That is because no one who tried had mangonels. How long do you think their walls will last against three of them? I will be supping my wine inside Piperskeep within a week.' The great wooden contraptions were the most important part of Drast's vast armoury, even more so than the *prifectai* or the zebrephants. 'You may be the kzar's agent, but I command this army. The kzar told me to take this country, and that is what I mean to do.'

'Fine. Do what pleases you. But if you fail, you'll answer to the kzar. Do not underestimate the Erlanders; you know the tale of Kzar Yoratho.'

'I do not require lessons on our military history.' Drast swirled his wine. 'I will be within their walls within a fortnight. Was there anything else?'

Alcantra scowled, and Drast was satisfied to see he had for once breached her icy calm. 'Nothing else, Senator. I will report this conversation to the kzar.' Abruptly, she left.

She will have more respect once I have taken Merivale, thought Drast. The city would fall, and when the dust settled, the glory would be his alone. He was not ready to give up on the kzarship just yet.

CHAPTER 39

The sky was clear. A tapestry of stars spread across the dark blue night, and together with a bold, bright full moon painted the land in silver. It was still warm from the heat of the day, but a merciful southerly wind provided a pleasant chill, despite the faint sulphuric stench of the Sorrowlands it brought with it.

Atop Merivale's western wall, Orsian watched grimly the horde that inch by inch, mile by mile crept towards them. It had begun with a dust cloud, and the beating of distant drums; it was only in the last half-hour that he had been able to see them. Foolishly, he had expected them to look like an army of Erland, in ordered lines, with bright banners and polished mail that reflected the glow of the sun to blind you. But this army bore just one banner, and he saw no mail. It shambled like a drunk, with disparate limbs that struck out on their own before being called back or overtaken as others advanced to match their pace.

Even so, before the sun had fallen, it had been a sight to stir fear in even the bravest *hymerika*'s breast.

Orsian had never seen a zebrephant before. Some accounts claimed the ancient Meridivals had hunted them to extinction in the southern wastes, but they had always seemed a fanciful thing, just another exaggeration of the poets charged with mythologising King Piper and the Sangreals' ancient brethren.

But zebrephants were real, black and white behemoths perhaps several times the height of a man. And it was not just the beasts Orsian feared, but the contraptions they pulled. Could the Imperials have dragged their mangonels across the Bleak Hills, or had they been fashioned from Erlish wood to raze Erlish walls? It did not matter, he supposed.

He turned to Pylas, Merivale's white-haired chief watchman, who like Orsian had been staring stony-faced across the plains. Chief watchman ought to have been a reward, a cushy desk job fairly earnt for forty years' exemplary service to Merivale. Instead, Pylas was staring down an Imperial host shortly after dealing with a citywide riot, and the fear was plain across his pinched face. 'Do you suppose they'll attack the Ram's Gate, or head south to the King's Gate?' Pylas sounded hopeful, as if by the Imperium heading south he and Orsian might sit out the battle all together.

'Both, if they've any sense, and maybe the Lesser Gate as well unless they give up once they realise we've fired the drawbridge.' They had the numbers. 'Unless they decide to siege us out.' If the Imperials knew how little food the city had on hand, they ought to be tempted, but a force so large as theirs would also struggle to keep themselves fed in the field.

Pylas swallowed again. 'I swear I'm no coward, Lord, but do I have your leave to piss myself?'

'I'm surprised you haven't already.' As he left, Orsian clapped him on the shoulder. 'Make sure there is sufficient watch for the night, then get some sleep if you can. They won't attack immediately after such a long march.' *I hope.*

Orsian descended a square set of steps back to ground level. The dwellings this close to the Ram's Gate were some of the very poorest in Merivale, little more than straw and mud, packed together to make squat, windowless huts that would keep the cold out in winter but sweltered and stank in summer. A young woman with a crooked lip clutching a babe looked at him furtively from her doorway, and Orsian tossed her a coin which disappeared swiftly beneath her shawl.

Orsian turned as the clatter of galloping hooves reached his ears, and Errian brought his mount to a stop with four other *hymerikai*, among them two of Naeem's sons. What Orsian would not have given to have Naeem there with them, ever ready to provide sage counsel and a wry jest. The day of Hessian's wedding when Orsian had drunk himself into a stupor with Burik and Derik felt like a lifetime ago, and Derik was dead.

'They've stopped to make camp,' Errian said by way of greeting, his blue eyes bright with battle-hunger. Orsian knew the look well; it was the same one Errian had worn when they were children and he had decided he was in the mood to pummel his younger brother. 'When they're asleep, we'll ride out and fire their siege weapons.' His eyes scanned the haphazardly arranged hovels that surrounded them. 'If they start throwing incendiaries, the whole city will go up like a bonfire.'

Orsian had heard the Imperium had uncovered secrets of fire that in Erland remained a mystery. He was only surprised Errian knew that. 'Agreed, then. Where do you want me?'

Errian did not reply immediately, but kept his gaze fixed

on Orsian, some private drama playing out beyond his eyes. 'I want you with us,' he said eventually, as if the words had been drawn from him like sap from a tree. 'We'll need an archer to take out their sentries, and I'm still yet to see anyone better than you.' He spoke the last few words in a rush, as if it had cost him his very essence and not only his pride. 'You can still shoot a bow, I assume?'

'I could shoot the legs off a spider at fifty paces.'

His bravado earnt a laugh from the assembled *hymerikai*, if not from Errian. Burik tossed a wineskin, which Orsian caught one-handed. 'Hope you shoot better than you drink,' said Burik, drawing more laughter, as Orsian took a draught of foul-smelling spirit and coughed into his fist. 'Unless you plan to defeat the Imperium by spewing on them.'

'We'll give them three hours to make camp,' said Errian once the merriment had died down. 'Once they're asleep we'll sneak out the King's Gate postern, ride south and west, and come up behind them. No torches.'

They agreed to meet later at the southern wall, and to pass the time Orsian took to wandering the ramparts, exchanging words with each man he passed. The city's watchmen were well-accustomed to sentry duty, but this was not true of the citizens of Merivale who had agreed to swell their ranks. Even in the darkness, Orsian could tell them by the way they fidgeted from foot to foot, and absently tapped and scraped the butts of their spears against the battlements.

Their discipline is less important than their willingness. In a shield wall, these new recruits would be next to useless, but even a child could be taught to throw a stone or deliver a message. Some of his charges were children, and he had even taken women and girls after Hilga, a stout-faced smith's daughter of sixteen, pointed out that she was older than him and stronger than most men.

All told, in addition to his six hundred watchmen, he had several thousand Merivalers, dwarfing Errian's command. They would need every one of them to stop the Imperium breaching their walls.

If they get numbers inside the city, we are finished. Piperskeep's great double curtain walls might stand for forever and a day, but its food would not. If they could not stop the Imperium here, they would spread across East Erland like a pestilence, until only another downtrodden province of Ulvatia remained.

Not as long as I have breath in my body, Orsian swore, gripping a parapet so tight that his knuckles turned white.

He passed Cag, conspicuous by his size, wearing a watchman's uniform that could have doubled as a tent.

'How do you like it so far?' Orsian asked him. They had barely exchanged a civil word since they had met, but they could hardly ignore each other now.

'I told him to stick with me,' said Cag's watch partner, a hoary veteran with two fingers missing on his left hand. 'If it goes to shit, at least he's big enough for me to hide behind.'

Orsian chuckled. 'No wonder you've lived so long.'

'Oldest man in the Watch,' added the man, puffing out his narrow chest. 'Name's Bertie. Was Hap before, Ol' Hap we called him, but he died just last week.'

'In the rioting?'

'Fell asleep and drowned in his soup, lucky bugger. That's how I'd like to go, Lord. You reckon it's possible to drown in a tankard of ale?'

'If you survive this, I'll have one made that you can fit your whole head in.'

'My ma always said I had the largest head of any baby born in Merivale. 'Bout time I got some use out of it.'

Orsian clapped him on the shoulder, grinning, and looked to Cag for an answer to his original question. 'Cag?'

The boy shrugged. 'Getting used to being a guard, instead of running from them. Suits me better, probably.'

Realising that was all he was likely to get out of him, Orsian nodded, and walked on.

His walk along the miles of wall eventually led him to the King's Gate to meet Errian. Below was a hive of activity, with eleven *hymerikai* throwing a few skins of wine between them. A team of grooms had led extra horses down from the barracks, and while around him other men jostled and jibed with one another, Orsian pulled himself onto the back of a roan colt with a swift look to it. He thought suddenly of Tansa, regretting not sending her a message that he was going outside the walls, but it was too late for that now.

Errian mounted alongside him, atop a midnight-black stallion that might have been the get of Valour, their father's horse. It snorted bad-temperedly as Errian pulled himself into the saddle.

'No torches,' Errian reminded them. He looked up to the battlements. 'Do you see any lookouts?'

'None, Lord.'

They made for the postern gate, heavy wood ribbed with black iron. It groaned as it opened, and they ducked through under the arch. The drawbridge had been left down for them, and they urged their horses across, every clip of a horseshoe seeming too loud in the still night.

Orsian scanned the plains, ready to reach for his blade or bow at the first cry of alarm. Nothing moved, save the sway of the grass as the soft wind whispered between its blades.

The Imperium camp was an orange glow against the sky, and as they rode south they turned to keep their eyes upon it. When it was almost directly behind them, Errian veered them right, westward, putting the camp in their eyeline once more.

Beside him, Orsian watched and listened, willing his ears to ignore the noise of his steady heartbeat. A fair fight by day was one thing, but a dozen men traipsing through the dark towards a foe more than a thousand times their number was another. Every sound they made seemed magnified a hundred-fold, and the moon and stars seemed bright as a hearth fire. Even miles from their camp, Orsian half-expected a hundred Imperium cavalry to burst from the darkness screaming for their heads.

When they were perhaps half-a-mile due south-west from the Imperium camp, Errian lifted a fist. They stopped once more and dismounted, keeping their horses near and letting them nibble at the dry grass. The cooling wind had dropped now, and the night felt close and clammy, enough to raise a sweat under Orsian's arms and on the back of his neck.

Errian pointed to a shadow against the sky. 'There, at the rear.'

Orsian squinted into the gloom. A tall machine of sharp angles and slender limbs stretched a long arm maybe twenty or thirty yards into the sky, atop a heavy wheeled frame.

'What is it?' asked Burik.

'The end of Merivale if we don't stop them,' said Errian. He pointed beyond the strange contraption. 'I think there are two more.' He glanced to Orsian and Burik. 'You two will go ahead on foot and get rid of any scouts. Go slow, and keep walking for a thousand-count. Kill anyone you see, and for

Eryi's sake don't get caught. When you get to a thousand, you should be around the edge of their camp. Deal with any look-outs, then turn back. Arrik and Drayen will be ready halfway with your horses. When you return, we ride like demons and fire the bastards before they even realise what's happened.' He grinned, and produced from his pack several unlit torches and rags drenched in oil.

Burik smirked at Orsian. 'Just like you setting our flank on fire at Imberwych.'

Orsian resisted the urge to remind him how close they had almost come to dying that day, and that one of his hands was still scarred from the burns he had suffered. Errian's plan did not fill him with confidence either; on foot, how were they meant to escape if they were seen?

'Arrik and Drayen will hear if you're seen and come for you,' added Errian, perhaps reading Orsian's stony expression. 'We can't risk the horses so close until we've dealt with any sentries.'

'We'll try and save some Imperials for the rest of you,' said Burik, with a brash grin that reminded Orsian of Naeem. 'Last man to kill one serves the drinks when we get back.'

His words set off a back-and-forth of wagers and insults, until Errian's voice cracked the night like a whip. 'If we all get back to Merivale and those mangonels are down I'll serve the bloody drinks myself. Now be quiet, all of you.'

For a moment, Errian almost reminded Orsian of their father, but looking around he was struck by how every man with them was one of Errian's fellows. Orsian might have preferred to have an older, wiser head among them, like Laphor, but it was too late now. He nodded to Errian, wishing that he had discovered this brother ten years ago, before he had come to hate him. 'Let's go then.'

Orsian and Burik handed off their horses, and crept towards the Imperium camp, Orsian keeping a steady count in his head. Every hundred-count, he turned to look the way they had come, and when he turned as the count hit five hundred was suddenly barrelled to the ground by Burik.

'There,' hissed Burik, who had pressed a hand over Orsian's mouth to stop him crying out. Orsian's gaze followed Burik's, and he cursed under his breath. There were two men coming towards them, less than a hundred yards to their left, in dark armour and navy cloaks that rendered them almost invisible. No torches either; their commander evidently knew his business.

As Burik released him, Orsian rose to a crouch and strung an arrow to his bow. He licked a finger, and held it up to test the wind.

'You sure about this?' whispered Burik. 'We could creep around behind them. That armour looks tough.'

Orsian shook his head. He pulled a second arrow and planted it in the ground in front of him, tested the bow once, and drew the string to his neck.

When the sentries were thirty yards distant, he let fly. The arrow struck the first man in his jugular, barely a half inch above his armour, and not half a second later the other whistled and sprouted from the other man's eye. The two of them fell within a heartbeat of one another.

Burik raced to close the distance, followed by Orsian, and slit the throat of the first man who was fighting to breathe and gulping like a fish. The second had died instantly. Burik appraised his corpse, wiggling the arrow around in the bloody mess that remained of his eyeball. 'Did you mean to hit the poor bastard in the eye?'

'Wind caught that one. Come on.'

Orsian had lost the count, but Burik swore he still had it. At nine hundred, they were within thirty yards of the Imperium camp, close enough to see their squat, triangular tents. Small fires burnt everywhere, as far as Orsian could see, including one at the very edge of camp with three men sitting around it.

'Can you take three with your bow?' asked Burik.

Orsian looked for the mangonels. They were still hundreds of yards away, separated by endless tents and campfires. This plan of Errian's was madness. He shook his head. 'Too risky. I'll come from their left, you from their right. If we're lucky that fire will blind them.'

Orsian was almost proven correct. He was within fifteen yards of the nearest man when a twig cracked beneath his toe. The sentry looked up, and Orsian covered the last few yards with a running leap.

He pulled his knife free in mid-air, and with a vicious backhand swept it across the man's neck. He did not wait to see him fall, already twisting away in a pirouette as he landed, reversing his grip on the knife to drive it into the next man's heart before he could rise.

Orsian wrenched the blade free in a fountain of gore. He looked for the third man, but his throat lolled open in a red smile left by Burik's dagger, as a clay pot of liquor slipped from his lifeless fingers.

As he surveyed the dead, Orsian was shocked to realise how young they were. In the darkness, silhouetted against the fire, they had looked like soldiers, but the gauntness of their faces could not disguise their youth. He had seen starving rats with more meat on them. If he was any judge, the youngest was no older than twelve. His sister Pherri might have beaten him in a fight.

'Slaves,' said Burik with disgust. With a toe he flicked over the body of Orsian's first victim. 'Not even armed. Probably drew first watch because they were the youngest.'

Orsian did not reply, fighting down the bile that threatened to surge up his throat. Their latter two victims were still sitting by the fire such that at a distance they would look alive, and Orsian manipulated the other into a seated position, propping him up with the spear the men must have shared. Then he and Burik were gone, moving fast as they dared back the way they had come.

They had made it barely a hundred yards when two horses reared up out of the darkness, and Orsian instinctively went for his sword. It was halfway out of the scabbard when he recognised Arrik, leading Orsian's horse behind him.

'Eryi's blood, when we couldn't find you I thought you were dead,' Arrik said with a laugh, only to be insistently shushed by Burik. 'Quickly now,' he added in an undertone, as Orsian and Burik swung up into the saddle.

Within a minute, the others appeared, and Errian handed them each a wooden torch with its head wrapped in an oil-soaked rag. Three times he struck a flint across his knife against Arrik's torch before they kindled a spark that set the oil ablaze. Quickly, the rest of them held theirs together, until twelve flames illuminated the night.

A dozen blades shrieked in unison as they were drawn from their scabbards. 'Ride hard for the mangonels,' said Errian, with a crack in his voice that betrayed his excitement. 'Do not stop for anything.'

With a thunder of hooves, they barrelled into the dark-

ness, and charged into the Imperial camp past the three dead
men, tents flashing past either side. A call of alarm went up
from somewhere, and soon the cries were all around them. A
frantic bell began to ring. Bewildered Imperial soldiers began
to emerge half-dressed from tents, and, as the *hymerikai*
thundered past, Burik could not resist a whooped cry of
'Erland!' The rest of them added their own war cries to his,
all secrecy forgotten.

As they hurtled by, Orsian lashed out with his sword,
breaking a man's face open in an explosion of blood and
teeth. One spearman rushed to meet their charge, going
down with a scream as Errian's horse crashed upon him in a
wave of hooves. Some simply stared, too shocked and sleepy
to so much as brandish a weapon or cry a warning to their
fellows.

It was too good to last, Orsian knew. They were halfway
to the mangonels when the horns began to blast, and the
zebrephants' trumpeting response served as a swift reminder
of the strength massed against them. A tall, armoured
commander screamed at his charges to form up, and Burik
rode him down, then threw his burning torch onto the flat
roof of a tent, setting the whole structure ablaze in a column
of fire.

Everywhere, men were shouting. Orsian swerved to
avoid a spearman whose thrust would have impaled his horse
at the neck, and galloped across a row of tents. His horse
stumbled, and Orsian barely kept his seat. He veered again,
holding tightly with his left hand to the blazing torch, making
for the mangonels.

He flashed across Errian's path, and threw his torch onto
the first contraption's flatbed. It flickered, and Orsian thought
it might not have worked, until Arrik threw his directly on

top of Orsian's, and fire began to lick along the wood and up the launching arm.

'Protect the others!' Errian cried. Gangs of spearmen were rushing between the tents and forming into walls bristling with bright metal. A group of five charged Drayen; his horse reared in terror, and he was thrown to the ground. Orsian rushed towards him, but veered away as another group of spearmen blocked his path. Two fell screaming as Orsian's blade flashed across their faces, but the rest pressed him into a retreat with their spears. Beyond them, Drayen had made it to his feet, but was sore pressed from every side. He lunged towards a spearman, and then howled as a second buried six inches of black metal in his thigh.

To Orsian's left, a *hymerika* fell buried under weight of numbers, spears rising and falling like feasting birds, and far to his right, another had set the second mangonel aflame, but now found himself trapped against it, penned in by a crescent of spearmen. Orsian tried to reach him, and again found his path blocked.

'Orsian!' Errian's cry broke through his battle fog, bringing Orsian to his senses. 'Get out!'

Orsian spun his mount in a circle. He had let himself become separated from the rest, and now spearmen were pressing in on all sides. At the corner of his eye, an arrow flashed from a bow, and Orsian threw himself against his horse's neck, the shaft flying close enough to strike his mail and deflect off at an angle. He dug his feet in, urging his horse towards a gap between two spearmen, only for them to block his path with angled thrusts that narrowly missed his head. He whirled again, spears that should have pierced the colt's flank finding only air, lashing out with his sword, dropping spearmen left and right. Another arrow skittered off his

mail, but Orsian was too battle-drunk to feel it, his only
concern to escape before the sheer mass of spears arrayed
against him became too much.

But there was no way through. *This is how my father
died, beyond the reach of his friends.* A spear grazed his
horse's rump and the animal bucked. Tansa's face flashed in
Orsian's mind. If his mount went down, he was finished.
Another spear flashed. The horse reared up, and with no
other choice Orsian pulled his feet from the stirrups ready to
leap clear.

And then Errian was there, grabbing the horse's reins and
pulling its front hooves back to earth. With a furious snarl, he
swung his flaming torch in an arc across the spearmen's faces
forcing them back, as his sword deflected a spear thrust and
opened the wielder from clavicle to temple. 'Come on, damn
you!'

Orsian did not need to be told twice. Together, he and
Errian charged the gap that had opened for them, as
spearmen fell back before the terror of the Erlanders' swords.

'East!' cried Errian. Two mangonels burnt like towering
candles, but far away from them the third still stood. Errian
launched his torch in an arc, its fiery tail curving across the
night sky like a shooting star. Orsian watched it, and realised
as it fell it was going to land short. He looked around for
another torch, but Errian's must have been their last.

And then the night exploded.

The mangonel erupted in a deafening maelstrom of fire,
shooting flaming comets of red and purple off into the sky,
and for several seconds the night was bright as day. A
wooden fragment shot past Orsian's face, narrowly missing
his ear.

Orsian whooped. There was a lull in the fighting as men

turned to stare, covering their faces against the glow before it faded. 'Did you mean to hit the incendiaries?'

Errian did not reply, but lifted the horn at his neck to his lips and blew, giving a clarion call so loud it threatened to rend the night in two. Eight *hymerikai* still stood. In the half-light of the rising dawn, they fought their way back to one another, and charged, the spearmen falling back before them like spirits before the dawn. They rode for Merivale, at a pace so furious that even the red sun seemed to retreat before their advance.

Orsian looked at his hands. His sword was still clenched in his right fist, and in his left he had somehow acquired a broken spear. His horse – he would have to think of a name for the beast now – panted beneath him, and a swift look back showed only a flesh wound where a spear had nicked its rear.

He turned to Errian. His brother was unmarked, and a determination on the edge of madness glittered in his eyes. 'Thank you, Brother,' said Orsian.

Errian looked back, scorn written across his face. 'I didn't do it for you. Do not expect to be so lucky next time.'

Orsian did not reply. He looked ahead, savouring the sight of Merivale's walls. He would live, at least for today. Tansa was waiting for him. Behind, the three mangonels blazed, filling the early morning sky with black smoke.

CHAPTER 40

Whiteness engulfed them. The storm that had been threatening to descend upon them for days had swelled to a maelstrom, reducing their vision to little more than the stooped back of the person in front of them. All else was swirling sheets of snow, and the high, frigid wind that assailed their ears like a banshee and threatened to tear the clothes from their shoulders.

Pherri clung tightly to Charones's neck, taking shelter behind his back. Several miles back the blizzard had become too thick and the slope too steep to pull the sled. Only Charones had the strength to carry her, and the hulking giant had borne her weight with pig-headed patience.

Pherri raised her head to check for the person ahead of them, and was met by a stinging shower of ice that burnt her eyes and blew the hood from her head. She grasped for it, eliciting a grunt from Charones at her shifting weight, and yanked it back over her head, dripping icy water into her face.

'Can you still see them?' she cried over the deafening

gale. If they lost their way, they might never find their companions again.

'I can still see Antares ahead of us!' called back Charones. 'He says he's not seen a storm like this in fifty years!'

'We should find shelter!' The storm howled, and Pherri had to almost bury her face in Charones's cheek to make herself heard. He had cast his hooded fur off miles ago, to give it to Maghira.

'There's a village a few miles ahead. Soon, little princess, I swear.' He punched his chest emphatically.

Pherri could have cried with relief, if not for the fear that her tears would freeze upon her face. She had never known cold like this. In places, the snow had soaked through her furs, leaving a clammy layer of frosty water upon her skin that set all her hairs on end, and a biting chill that pierced all the way to her bones. She was only glad she did not have to walk; much of the ice had dripped into her boots, and she could no longer feel her toes.

She shut her eyes, and pressed her face to Charones's back, reducing the world to the wailing of the wind and the irresistible press of the cold.

When she next raised her head, the gale had lulled, and the incline had flattened to only a slight uphill. The snow remained relentless, but now it sliced in sideways instead of swirling about them like a dancer's skirts.

Through the relative calm, Pherri saw they had kept to their companions' heels. Beyond their trudging figures were the outlines of small dark dwellings, built among stout rock formations to protect them from the worst of the wild mountain weather.

Charones turned his head, a smile painted across his round face. 'I told you, princess!'

Pherri was too tired and grateful to correct him. Once he had learnt she was a king's granddaughter, Charones had called her nothing else. She hugged his neck tightly. 'Thank you.'

He grinned and slapped his shoulder with a meaty hand. 'Adrari huts are not warm, but we shall live.'

Pherri was eager to get inside, but ahead of them the rest of their party slowed to a halt, where Maghira beckoned them in close. Many of them looked no better than Pherri felt, even some of the Adrari. Garimo's handsome face was taking on a tinge of blue, and Ruhago's beard was a tangled grey icicle. Pherri looked for Delara and Theodric, and was relieved to see them both alive, though Delara was dragging her foot slightly, and Theodric had wrapped himself so tightly in furs that only his eyes were visible.

'We should approach carefully,' said Maghira. 'If Adrari see a band of strangers emerging from a snowstorm they're likely to attack and figure out who we are after we're dead. There have been strange tales from the higher villages these last few months.'

Antares grunted. His mouth was hard, but by the way he carried himself he could have been out for a summer stroll. 'I am known in this village. I will find the alderman.' Leaning on his staff, he stomped off towards the nearest hut.

Pherri tapped at Charones's shoulder to let her down. Theodric removed his face covering and crouched to speak with her, though Pherri could see it pained him. 'I should never have brought you here,' he whispered, barely audible over the gale, his once cheery voice little more than a croak.

His gloved hands trembled, and his cracked lips were dry as dust.

It stung her, to see her mentor brought so low. He had been well a few days ago, but the storm had tired him more than most, and even Charones was not so strong that he could bear a full-grown man through a snowstorm. 'It was my decision,' she told him, covering his shivering hands with her own.

'It was not a choice you should have had to make.' A glistening tear quivered on his lower eyelid. Snow was settling on his face. 'I would barely be able to *phisika* a coin right now, but still the strength drains out of me like a sieve. Magi were not meant to go this long without proper food.'

Antares's round-shouldered silhouette appeared from one of the huts. 'There's nobody there!' he cried. 'All of them, gone.'

Maghira cursed. 'Where would they go in this?'

Pherri had to wonder the same. The storm was rising again, and the grey, distant sun was beginning to dip towards the horizon.

'I don't know,' called Antares. 'Let's talk about it inside, before we freeze to death.'

Together, they stumbled towards the hut, just as a great rush of wind howled down Eryispek and showered them with snow. Her legs still numb, Pherri was blown sideways into a snowdrift as she tried to keep up, and Charones picked her up to stop her falling behind.

He ducked inside under the doorframe, and through the hut's gloom Pherri saw Antares already trying to set fire to a bundle of sticks. After a few tries, they sparked into life, and a pale orange glow illuminated the dank interior. It was little more than a wooden frame, bolstered with what by the smell might have been a combination of clay and animal dung.

They shuffled inside, forming a circle around the walls to fit everyone inside. Even then, there was barely enough room, and the roof was so low at the edges that even sitting down the top of Charones's head brushed the ceiling.

Nobody spoke for several minutes. Most of them sat with their knees up to their chests, huddling into themselves for warmth. The wind was a constant cry, a stark reminder that no matter how uncomfortable they might be, it was better than being outside. The first to move was Garimo, taking some food from his pack and tossing it in a pan with some snow, then holding it over the fire.

'We'll stay until the storm settles,' said Maghira. 'It can't blow like this for much longer.'

'Says who, girl?' said Antares. 'I've seen storms that lasted for weeks.'

'Never this far down the Mountain,' said Ruhago, in a low voice that betrayed his exhaustion. 'Tell me I'm wrong, Antares.' His foreboding tone sent an icy chill down Pherri's spine.

Antares looked back at him sharply, as if he meant to disagree. Then after a moment, he sighed. 'I'll give you that. Maybe the folk who lived here started heading down, hoping to get out before it got worse. We should check the long hall further up; they might've gone there.'

'Are we close now?' croaked Delara. The old woman spoke without opening her eyes, leaning against the hut with her head tilted back.

Maghira shook her head. 'Days away. If we can find our village. In this weather we could walk right past it.'

'Speak for yourself,' said Antares. 'Even from here I could find my home blindfolded.'

'If this weather keeps up you may have to prove it.' Maghira leant towards the fire, stirring her brother's stew with a long spoon made from bone.

'Hush,' said Theodric. 'Listen.'

They fell silent. Pherri listened, her heart suddenly beating like a blacksmith's hammer. She strained her ears, searching for some sound other than the wind, the crackle of their small fire, and the gentle snowfall atop their shack.

'I hear nothing, wizard,' said Charones.

'No.' Theodric was a far cry now from the weakened state he had seemed outside. His eyes were bright, his voice sure and insistent. 'There's something else. Be quiet and *listen*.'

They did, and this time Pherri heard it. It came on the breeze, as soft and subtle as shadow, like a whisper of sunlight through leaves. The crunching of snow, as something approached their shack. Alarmed, Pherri looked to Theodric, who met her eye, and by the faces around her everyone else had heard it too.

'It's not close yet,' he said. 'It might be the villagers returning.'

Antares seized his axe. Though made from bone, its edge looked sharp enough to shave with. 'Or it might not be.' He came to his feet, crouching low under the roof. 'Charones, with me.' Charones awkwardly manoeuvred himself towards the door, drawing his club.

'We'll be back soon,' said Antares. His blue eyes were sharp as steel. There was not a shred of hesitation in him, only a cold readiness to do what must be done. 'If it's the villagers, we'll speak with them. If it's not...' His grizzled features fixed themselves menacingly. 'Count to two hundred. If we're not back, get out and start running.' He pushed open the door and pressed out into the storm.

Their departure left among them an unnerving hush. Pherri's mouth was dry, yet somehow also watered for Garimo's stew. Garimo and Maghira seemed to have forgotten about it; Maghira had stopped stirring.

'It will be the villagers,' said Garimo. 'Just the villagers. I don't know why you're all thinking the worst.'

'Pray for the best, prepare for the worst,' said Delara. 'Shut up and count, boy.'

They sat there in silence. Pherri was pressing her nails so hard into her palm it hurt. *Pray for the best, Delara says. Pray to who?*

One hundred seconds passed, and neither Antares nor Charones returned. Garimo started tapping out the count on his thigh, until Delara shot him a look.

One hundred and fifty. Theodric's eyes shot open. 'Pass me some of that stew,' he whispered, holding out a bowl to Maghira, who started at the sound of his voice.

The last fifty seconds passed in a deep quiet, save the slow slurp of Theodric's stew. At two hundred, they looked to one another, hoping for the slow creak of the door that would welcome their friends back.

'The wind has stopped,' said Garimo.

It had. The howl had dimmed to a murmur, and though the snow still fell, it sounded softer than before. The storm had ceased, as suddenly as if it had never been there in the first place.

'Bugger this,' spat Ruhago. He was rising already, reaching for his axe. 'I'm going out there.'

'We're all going out there.' Theodric tossed aside his bowl, and wrapped his furs about himself.

Ruhago opened the door, and they stumbled out into the snow, Pherri following behind them.

Dark had fallen. A shrouded moon illuminated the gently falling snowflakes like tiny white candles, and painted the ground in silver. The storm had ceased, and yet what met them outside was worse than any squall.

Antares's head lay on the ground before them, sheared at the neck, his once penetrating blue eyes now dull, his fierce visage frozen in terror. Some distance away his body knelt in the snow, his torso leaning back at an impossible angle. A warm trickle of urine ran down Pherri's leg. There was no sign of Charones.

The silence was broken by an anguished scream. And then the night stirred before them.

They came from the darkness, from the trees, garbed in rags and bearing bronze weapons. Some walked proud as kings, others stumbling on one foot, dragging useless, twisted limbs behind them. Each though bore the same face, gaunt and dead-eyed, some missing eyes or ears or their nose, others hale and almost handsome.

The dead men began to encircle them, and when Pherri and Theodric turned to run, more appeared behind. Their pale faces flashed as the moon appeared from behind a cloud, and Pherri saw the boy from her nightmares. Gelick White-doe, dozens of him.

'By all the bones and teeth of Eryi...' said Theodric. 'Get behind me.'

Pherri would have, but everywhere she looked the circle around them was being filled in by more dead Gelicks, endless numbers of them. Next to her, she felt Garimo and

Ruhago tensing, their bone weapons gripped tightly, and Theodric summoning every ounce of focus, will, and energy he could. Pherri readied her will, though what use *phisika* might be against such creatures she did not know.

But these dead man-creatures did not attack. They stood, watching unblinkingly as the snow continued to fall.

'What are they waiting for?' asked Delara.

He stepped from the darkness like a wraith, bathed in moonlight, holding a spear in one hand and something else in the other, with a white doeskin around his shoulders. He was near as thin as his doubles, but he was whole, and with a glow of life that suggested a heart still beat under his sinew and gaunt muscle. His servants separated, and he stepped inside their circle.

Garimo and Maghira gasped. He threw something to the ground, and Pherri did not need to look closely to know it was Charones's head.

'Gelick?' Delara was staring at the newcomer in astonishment.

'Once.' His voice barked like a discordant melody, and his eyes flashed pale as death. 'Stand aside.'

'I thought you were dead.'

'Death is sometimes only an illusion.' He smiled and gestured to his servants. 'I have died a thousand times or more, and yet here I stand.' He raised an arm, and with a crooked finger pointed to Pherri. 'The girl. Give me the girl, and I will let you live.'

Pherri was peeking out from behind Theodric, but he shifted to block her from Gelick's view, and the Adrari crowded in around her. Pherri closed her eyes, as if shutting him from her vision would protect her. She could feel the malevolence and ill-intent rolling off him in waves. She would not go with him, never.

Theodric had been silent, but now stepped forward with fire in his eyes. 'Enough of this.' He locked eyes with their foe, and Pherri felt a slight change in the air as he reached out with *inflika* towards Gelick's mind.

She could not tell what vision Theodric was trying to press upon Gelick. Perhaps that they had disappeared, or a fierce beast risen from the snow. Could *inflika* even work when the target knew what you were doing? Perhaps if he were not so weakened from their journey, Theodric might have tried *shadika* or *phisika,* but those required reserves of energy he did not have.

She had seen Theodric make men imagine the impossible, but Gelick's face was a mask of disdain. 'You think to bandy tricks with me, wizard? I learnt magic when the world was young. Try that again, and I will destroy you.'

Theodric's gaze flicked above Gelick's head, to the shadowy fir trees from which he and his dead brotherhood had emerged, and Pherri knew immediately what he was going to try. With an imperceptible brush of *phisika*, Theodric tore the nearest tree from its roots, and with a creak set it falling towards Gelick.

Gelick did not even look up, and for a moment Pherri allowed herself to think it would work, right up until the trunk came within a hand's-breadth of his head. Her companions gasped as it stopped still in mid-air, with Gelick standing calmly underneath it.

He cackled; a high, dissonant sound that set Pherri's teeth on edge. She felt Theodric straining as he poured his energy and will into forcing the tree trunk down those last few inches. Instead, slowly the tree began to rotate, end over end.

'I warned you,' said Gelick. Theodric's eyes grew wide as the spinning tree became a blur. It should not have been possible, Pherri knew; even expertly wielded *phisika* could not hold a tree spinning in mid-air. 'I gave you a chance, wizard. More of a chance than she would have done. One day, men might learn not to test their will against a god.'

Whip-fast, the tree swung towards Theodric, as if heaved by an irate giant. Pherri felt him push against it with *phisika*. The trunk slowed, but it was too late. Pherri cried out in horror as it smashed against Theodric's chest, shattering bones and crushing organs and drawing from his lips a wild scream of terror.

The tree dropped, and Theodric fell with it. He slumped to the side, his torso a bloody pulp. Pherri dodged around Delara's outstretched hands and the three horrified Adrari and raced to him, falling to her knees next to her mentor.

Somehow, he still lived. His eyes were closed, and his breath came weak and laboured, misty in the cold night air. She could see the shape of his skull under his skin, emaciated by the energy he had expended. He grasped her hand, surprisingly strong. 'I'm sorry, Pherri.' He coughed, and flecks of blood sprang upon Pherri's face, hot against her cold, tear-stained cheeks. 'Should never... have come here.' His voice was barely a murmur, as light as the snowflakes melting upon his head.

Pherri sniffed, wiping at her frigid tears with a gloved hand. 'It will be okay, Theodric. I won't let him take me.'

He grasped tightly at her, pulling her closer, and for a few seconds his tired eyes sprang open. 'Fight him, Pherri. *Fight him.*' The light left his eyes, and his head collapsed into the snow. Pherri buried her face in his neck, tears flowing like a torrent. Theodric, her mentor. Dead, hundreds of miles from home, where not even magic could save him.

'Enough of this!' Gelick cried. 'Bring me the girl.'

Blinded by tears, Pherri heard the rush of undead servants, and the hopeless cries of her companions as they fought to hold them back. Cold hands seized her, pulling her from Theodric. She beat her fists vainly against dead flesh, and Gelick's army lifted her and carried her into the trees, as a rising maelstrom of ice and snow roared through the night.

CHAPTER 41

It was raining the morning after the burning of the mangonels, but the humid air clung to Orsian's skin like velvet. He climbed the steps to the western battlements with a trail of guardsmen, after two hours' sleep huddled in a corner of an abandoned inn, too weary to return to Piperskeep.

Across the grass, the Imperium camp sprawled; a city of tents sprung up overnight, even larger than it had seemed the night before. At the far edge, the three mangonels had been extinguished, but one was reduced to a pile of black ash, and the others were twisted and charred beyond use.

It would not be enough, Orsian knew, not with the number of tents and drilling soldiers he could see. Riders had been sent out, to the Gough lands to the north and to the lords of the south moors beyond the Little River, with no response. Fear of Hessian might have roused them, but not letters sent in the name of the little prince. Given the host they faced, Orsian could hardly blame them. He could see armoured men on horseback, riding to and fro and setting their men into lines ready for an attack. The Imperium commander clearly did not mean to waste time.

Errian was there also, stony-faced and surrounded by *hymerikai*. Orsian approached, and the others parted to let him through.

'You'll command the guard at the King's Gate,' said Errian in greeting. 'I'll take half the citizens, for all the use they'll be, to bolster our number here. You can have the rest. If their attack falls only on the Ram's Gate, leave a token force and bring the rest here.'

Orsian had a higher opinion than Errian of the citizens. Many had come from the guilds, and whether mason, fletcher, weaver, tanner, or smith understood the value of discipline. Some also played in the city's viciously contested hogball matches. He would accept though that a bruised head or broken ankle were not comparable to the very real risk of having a sword run through your bowels.

Orsian expected the hammer of the Imperium to fall all along the walls, probing for weak points. Small numbers of volunteers had been spread along the eastern wall as well, ready to watch the Lesser Gate and drive back any attempt to scale the ramparts there. The bulk of their attack would fall upon the two main gates though. Assaults elsewhere would draw their resources, but there was no prospect of an entire army making it over the wall. He turned to his watchmen. 'Pylas, go. I'll meet you there.' Pylas saluted, then he and the rest hurried away.

Orsian looked back to Errian. 'Do we know how they'll clear the moat?' he asked. On the western wall, Merivale's moat was twenty yards wide, twenty feet deep, and waist-high with the city's grim, brown sewage.

'Get shit on their boots.' Errian pointed to something in

the distance. 'Or use those.' Orsian squinted through the drizzling rain, and saw slaves in brown linen carrying long wooden ladders.

'We should break the drawbridges,' said Burik. 'Once they're across the moat they'll smash the chains and have a clear ride to the gate.'

'Then they'll starve us out,' said Errian, 'and it won't take long. We *want* them to attack, remember?' He looked again to Orsian. 'You sure you can hold the King's Gate with watchmen?'

Seeing the foe they faced in the cold light of day was a sobering reminder of the odds confronting them, yet Orsian found himself nodding. 'They'll hold it.'

'They better. I'll send ten *hymerikai* to bolster them.'

Orsian walked away from their brief meeting feeling vexed. Part of him believed that he would have been able to fight his way free of the spearmen, but the larger part of him knew that Errian had likely saved his life. Why had the first words out of his brother's mouth not been a mocking reminder of this?

The meaty slap across his face when he reached the bottom of the steps shook him from his reverie. 'What—?' His assailant followed up with another, but Orsian was ready this time and caught them by the wrist. Once his eyes could focus again, Tansa appeared in front of him, red-faced and furious.

'I thought you were dead!' She slapped him again across the face with her other hand.

Her attack had drawn the attention of the men milling around the base of the wall, so Orsian pulled her away into a corner behind the stairs, and mercifully Tansa let him.

'I was too exhausted to return to Piperskeep,' he explained. He waited a moment, expecting Tansa to cut over him, but continued. 'I only got two hours' sleep. That would have been even less if I'd returned.'

Tansa sniffed. 'When he got back, Cag said you'd gone out to fight the Imperials and hadn't returned when his watch ended. When you didn't come back, I thought...'

Orsian bit back some choice words about what he would say to Cag. Could he not see how little their rivalry mattered, given what faced them? He had expected Errian to be his worst foe inside the walls, but Cag was comfortably in front so far. He took Tansa's hand and kissed it. 'I'm the king's nephew. If I die, you'll know about it.'

'Is that meant to make me feel better?' She wrenched her hand away. 'You don't know what it's like, cowering behind walls while the only two people you care about risk their lives. It's torture. I can fight, or help, or something, please.'

'I won't risk you. Everyone else I care about is gone; I won't lose you as well. You've got Pitt and Esma – they need you.'

Tansa's eyes flashed, and Orsian's hand twitched as he thought she was about to strike him again. 'I'm not their bloody mother, Orsian! You've got boys as young as twelve running around here, and you expect me to just hide with all the noble ladies and old women, while they hold their noses and giggle every time I walk past. I'm not like them. I saved you on the *Jackdaw*, I can help!'

'You can help by staying in Piperskeep! If something happened to you, I...' Orsian searched vainly for the words that would make her understand. 'I'm in charge of hundreds of men. Some of them will die, probably today. If I make the wrong decision because I'm worrying about you, I put them in jeopardy, and their families, and then everyone in Piperskeep. For the sake of Merivale and everyone in it, I need you to be safe.' Orsian had a sudden inspiration. 'There's meant to be a tunnel running from below Piperskeep all the way beyond the city walls; if the Imperials find it, they could sneak an army in under our feet. The queen might know where it is – you could take a look down there just to make sure it's clear.'

'That's the worst idea I've ever heard.' Orsian reached for her, but Tansa pushed him away and stepped back. 'But fine, I'll go, for the sake of having something to do. If you won't let me fight, you can at least take Pitt off my hands. He's been stealing from the kitchens, and if it happens again the cook swears she'll brain him with her rolling pin.'

She stalked off, and Orsian threw his hands up in frustration, ignoring the sniggering of the guards on the stairway above. Why not Pitt as well? He was already babysitting another of the strays he had picked up in Cliffark, and the boy would likely be less trouble than Cag.

A bucket lay on its side in a nearby pile of straw, and Orsian kicked it as hard as he could, putting a hole in the base and breaking it to splinters against the wall. Even with Cag and everything else, on the ride from Cliffark he and Tansa had grown if anything even closer, sharing a blanket, making love, and whispering to one another long into the night. Ever since their arrival in Piperskeep though he could do nothing right with her. When not avoiding him, she was telling him all the reasons he was a fool, and now she was angry because he had not thought to tell her he was alive! It was maddening.

After flicking the remnants of the bucket out of the way, Orsian found where he had tethered his still unnamed horse, and rode for the King's Gate.

Pylas awaited him atop the battlements, surveying a view

that was most unlike that from the Ram's Gate. The plains were almost serene, mile upon mile of rippling grass, with only the distant drumbeat of the Imperium camp to indicate that anything was out of the ordinary.

'If they do not strike here, I'll take half our force, and leave you in charge,' Orsian told him. 'Have a line of beacon fires ready along the wall for if you need me.'

The veteran guardsman paled, like a man bound for the gallows. 'I'm not sure which idea I like worse, Lord, being in charge here, or being under attack.' Pylas puffed out his cheeks and hurried off to give orders to two of his lieutenants.

Orsian let out a long breath. Tansa had scorned the idea that he could command the city's watchmen, and while Pylas was agreeable enough, he was beginning to fear she was right. *They serve Merivale, but they never thought they might have to die for it.* A truncheon was not a spear, and a watchman was not a warrior. Some had been on the job for decades without ever holding a weapon with an edge on it. He looked up and down the parapet. They looked fearsome enough, in their leather armour and red surcoats, holding eight-foot spears of dark oak tipped with steel, but if they broke, they would break hard.

Interspaced with the watchmen were his guildsmen, all those considered sound enough with a bow to make a difference. Every man of Erland was expected to train one day a week with a bow, but arrows were limited, and these were the best of them. Mostly they were fletchers, skilled with the bows they made, but also others, including Hilga, the burly smith's daughter, and the huntsman Yarl and his three sons who were as good as any *hymerika* Orsian had seen.

'Lord! Lord!' Orsian looked up to see Pylas hurrying towards him like a baker whose bread was burning. He

stopped, gasping. 'We won't need those beacon fires, Lord.'
He raised a quivering arm, pointing west along the wall.

Orsian saw them just as they rounded the far south-west
corner, still hundreds of yards away but making a clear path
towards their gate. Row upon row of men in brown tunics,
perhaps a thousand of them, with an armoured horseman for
every five-by-five square riding between their ordered lines.
At the rear, a shirtless man with a belly like a pregnant sow
rode upon a palanquin borne by eight slaves, beating a staccato rhythm on an enormous upright drum.

At any other time, the sight might have seemed comical.
Offered an eyeglass by Pylas, Orsian pointed the lens
towards one of the twenty-five-man squadrons. Ten of them
bore two long ladders, and the other fifteen squat, curved
blades with short bows across their shoulders.

'If this is the best they can offer, Pylas, you'll be back
patrolling the streets within a week.' Orsian knew though
that was a lie. This was the least of the Imperium army,
starving slave boys like those he had slain around the fire.
He trained the eyeglass upon one of the horsemen, and
took note of the long black whip in his hand. Halfway
along, it split into ten slender cords, each tipped with a
metal claw that would tear flesh from bone as easily as
pulling meat from a roasting pig. A shiver ran along the
stripes Abner had left on his back. If the mate had held
such a weapon, Orsian would be dead. As if putting on a
show, the rider lashed out with it, and Orsian winced as
five ladder-carrying slaves cried out in pain and increased
their pace.

'Just slaves,' he called, for all the men on the gate to hear.
'Archers, to the wall!'

The watchmen stepped aside, and Orsian's bowmen

stepped forward, and the air was filled with the sleek sound of arrows being pulled from quivers.

At a snail's pace, the Imperium's square formation approached the moat, the fat man's deep drum growing ever louder. Orsian could feel the rising tension, not least because he could hear Pylas's spear shaking.

The first slaves were within twenty yards of the moat now, and still Orsian remained silent, while all along the wall bowmen looked at one another quizzically.

'Lord?' asked Pylas.

Orsian did not reply. The first slaver's whip cracked again, urging his reluctant charges on, so close now that Orsian saw the blood splatter as the slaves' clothes were rent in two.

Orsian shouted a command, and along the wall, archers placed an arrow to their bow and pulled the cord tight against their jaw.

The slaves stuck the ladders in the ground, ready to be tipped forward. Others pulled the bows from their back. The slavemaster shouted something, but Orsian heard nothing over the beat of the deafening drum.

'Loose!' Orsian cried.

All at once, the tension along the wall broke, and time that had slowed to a crawl accelerated to the speed of the shafts that flew from the Erlanders' bows. The drum dropped to a distant whisper, as men cried out in elation and fear. Almost an entire squad of slaves went down, some all the way into the moat and the shallow pool of filth, and one of the ladders clattered in after them.

Fresh men were already rushing forward to replace them, as riders' whips lashed out left and right. Arrows of their own flew, most coming up short but one narrowly missing Pylas, too busy shouting in fury along with the rest of them to notice.

'Loose!' cried Orsian again. Another hail of arrows soared, and a dozen more Imperials fell or stumbled as shafts sprouted from their chest, neck, or leg. The first squad were attempting to rise as the whip beat down upon them, but the second volley sent them cowering back to the dirt.

But other slaves were still pushing forward, spreading their line of battle wider along the walls. A ladder thirty yards from the gate fell with a thud across the moat, and a bold slave began crawling across on his hands and knees, his ugly blade clenched between his teeth.

'Spread the fire!' Orsian paused to allow his bowmen to adjust. 'Loose!' A fletch appeared in the man's knee, and with a scream he plunged head-first into the moat.

'Can you keep the count going?' he asked Pylas, drawing his own bow.

The watchman looked at him blankly. 'What do I do, Lord?'

'Just say "Loose" every ten seconds or so. Not too fast.'

Orsian moved forward. The Imperials' arrows were still mostly falling short, and he had seen only one Erlander retreating, a fletcher with a shaft in his shoulder. Orsian lifted an arrow to his eye, and trained it upon the nearest horseman, targeting his face below his helmet. When Pylas cried, 'Loose,' Orsian fired with the rest of them, and was rewarded as the fletch found its mark and the man toppled from his horse soundlessly, dead before he hit the ground.

Emboldened, Orsian drew again between Pylas's count, and trained his bow upon another slavemaster, snarling and whipping his charges forward towards the moat. A sudden gasp of wind threw Orsian's aim, but that was not enough to save the man. It caught him at the joint of soft leather between his shoulder and neck, and the whip fell from the limp fingers of his suddenly useless arm.

Erlanders cheered, and then cheered louder as the slaves under the man's charge turned tail and fled.

Pylas cried, 'Loose!' and another deadly volley soared. The slaves were having to climb over the corpses of their fellows now, offering targets so easy that Orsian might have thrown an arrow and found flesh. All along the line, the masters were struggling to keep order.

'Aim for the horses!' Orsian crowed.

The next volley filled the air with the keening of horses, shafts sticking from their tough flesh, bucking and kicking as their riders fought to keep their seats. One was thrown, landing heavily on his head, and did not rise. Another was dragged away by his fleeing horse, trying desperately to release his tangled foot from the stirrup. One leapt free before his tumbling horse crushed him, but then sought to whip the slaves forward again from the ground. That was a mistake. A slave grabbed him from behind and wrenched his helmet off, and another stabbed him through the neck.

The arrows were already drawn back for another barrage, but Orsian turned and signalled for Pylas to call a halt. The damage had been done. The other slaves had seen the master go down, and decided they liked their chances against the men with whips better than against the men on the walls. The horsemen tried to rally together, striking down the first slaves to come at them before sheer numbers overwhelmed them and they were dragged from their mounts.

Twenty-five against one with a whip is still twenty-five against one. Fear would only lead men so far. The surviving slaves ran off in several directions, keen to be as far away from both Merivale and the Imperium as fast as possible. Meanwhile the eight slaves who had borne the palanquin were currently beating the fat drummer to death with their own chains.

The Erlanders cheered and stomped the ground, and Orsian allowed himself a small smile. *This was just the first tickle of the spear though.* They had sent the weakest of their forces first in the hope of easily securing the drawbridge and a route to the gate. The true thrust might even now be falling at the Ram's Gate.

Orsian headed for the stairs. 'Pylas, send for me if you need me. I'm taking the *hymerikai* below to the Ram's Gate.' He had placed the ten Errian had given him on the ground to cover the gate and to give those up top an opportunity to take confidence from their victory. The warriors would be furious with him, but giving them another chance to impale an Imperial was the swiftest way to forgiveness.

But Pylas did not seem to be listening. 'Look, Lord.'

Orsian turned, fully expecting to see a second Imperium force heading for their position. But Pylas was pointing north, into Merivale, towards three figures riding down the Castle Road, two soldiers flanking a tall figure in heavy red robes. His head was slouched forward and, as Orsian watched, the man almost fell from his horse, before seemingly coming to his senses and grabbing the cantle of his saddle.

Orsian raced down the stairs two at a time and stopped, staring, hardly believing what he was seeing. By what trick could they have bypassed the wall with no one noticing? *Of course, the tunnels.* They might have encountered Tansa down there.

King Hessian Sangreal brought his mount to a halt, and

Orsian sank to a knee before him. Open-mouthed, the rest followed, some even dropping their weapons in astonishment.

For several moments, there was silence. A silence so sharp it threatened to wound anyone who broke it. Somewhere, a crow cawed, then stilled, as if someone had quietened it with a look.

After an age, the silence ruptured. A lone cry of 'Hessian King!' burst from the walkway, and was swiftly followed by a tumult of noise. 'HESSIAN KING! HESSIAN KING!' came the cry, as men beat their fists against shields and pounded their spears upon the flagstones.

With the noise, Hessian stirred as though woken from death, and gazed about himself, with the cast of a man remembering who and where he was. Light brightened in his eyes, and he stared straight at Orsian. He raised a fist, grimacing as though it pained him, and the soldiers fell silent.

'Nephew.' The king wheezed, and let out a harsh, broken cough. 'When I heard of the invasion, we rode through many days and nights to be here. It is a balm to my heart to see you alive. It seems I have missed much in my absence.'

CHAPTER 42

Pherri woke, bundled under furs, inside a shallow cave walled with ice. Somebody had lit a fire for her, but it was little more than embers now, and even beneath so many layers she could feel the cold deep in her bones. She moved closer to the tepid ashes, shivering. The air was thin, and her breath came in icy mist like puffs of smoke.

The world outside the cave was a blur. The open sky beyond its mouth was obscured by tendrils of ice and snow, blown by a shrieking wind that seemed to sweep through the whole cavern.

She groaned and flexed her joints, aching from chill and so many miles carried by creatures without a concern for her comfort. She remembered the lumpy cold of the unGelicks' dead fingers against her flesh and shuddered. She recalled too their pitiless eyes, and the pale gaze of the Gelick who lived. There had been no shred of humanity behind his grim visage. Whoever he had once been, that man was gone.

Gone too was Theodric. Pherri slammed her eyes shut, holding back a sob. She had never truly felt in danger on their journey. Even with the men in the forest and when the Adrari had taken her, she had known he would save her. How naïve she had been. They had known there were forces on Eryispek they did not understand, and now she knew that their powers were beyond even Theodric. He had told her to fight, but what hope did she have? Their foe was almost a god, and even his servant had been too strong for Theodric.

Pherri rolled closer to the fire, hoping that its scant warmth might burn away the debilitating fear in the pit of her stomach. What did Gelick and Eryi want with her? She was untried and untrained, barely capable of feats Theodric could achieve effortlessly, yet they had taken her and killed him.

Pherri took a deep breath and held it, searching for calm and trying to think, pushing down her terror to a level below conscious thought. She was not dead, so for now they needed her alive, and that meant she had time. Time to figure out an escape. She willed herself to her feet, and stumbled towards the cavemouth.

The storm was so fierce she had to lean into the wind and press her fingers to the walls to make progress. She craned her head outside, searching for a sight of anything, holding a hand up towards the biting hail that raked painfully against her face.

She saw nothing. There was daylight somewhere, but such was the gale's ferocity she could not even see the sky. Gripping the cave's edge, she looked down instead, and with a gasp scrambled back inside.

The world ended no more than a foot past the edge, and beyond that there was only abyss, a curtain of white shadow descending into forever.

Pherri grasped at the wall, trying to control her breathing. There was no hope of escape, not unless she learnt to fly through a snowstorm.

I am near the summit. They had dragged her to the top of the endless Mountain, a place Pherri had doubted could even exist. There would be no rescue mission led by Maghira and Delara to save her. To believers, the mere existence of this place was an act of faith. The knot of fear in her stomach seemed to expand, engulfing her whole being.

Pherri watched the entrance, seeking tranquillity in the constant breath of the wind and the twisting waves of snow. Weak though she was, she still had magic, and was Eryispek not the centre of such things? The last time she had tried *spectika*, she had been blocked, but on the Mountain she doubted anything could stop her. She centred herself, feeling its benign power beneath her feet, drawing on it as a focal point for her focus and will. When she could hear nothing but her own heartbeat, she reached outward.

It was nothing like the last time she had tried it. Then, the whole world's existence had rushed her consciousness, almost overwhelming her with the scope of her awareness. If not for intervention, she could have learnt anything of Erland she wished to know. Now though, it was as if an invisible fog pressed in at her from all sides, reducing her perception to little more than a few feet outside the cave. She could sense the path of every falling snowflake, every shard of sleet that melted upon the cavemouth, but beyond that, nothing. The world below was as far removed from her as the shadow realms from which Theodric drew illusions.

Then, just as she was ready to give up, she felt something. Something that set her heart pounding.

There was a presence, of such malevolent authority that

it soaked into everything, dimming Pherri's small world to shadow with its incandescence. Upon the fresh snow, its feet echoed like the ring of a great bell, every step a knell upon Pherri's soul.

She tore herself away from *spectika*, and backed away towards the fire as something rounded the cavemouth.

A tall shadow appeared, blocking out the dull daylight that penetrated the storm. Pherri retreated, pressing her back up against the rear of the cave. The shadow ducked inside.

Its features sharpened. The top of its head brushed the roof of the cavern, and the dim light revealed a man's face, smooth and unlined, surrounded by six plaits of dark hair. He wore no furs, only simple tunic and trousers, and by the firelight, Pherri saw he cast no shadow. He was a mirage, without physical essence, like a *shadika* summoning. His eyes were real enough though, pupilless orbs of such pale blue that they were almost white. The power rolled off him in waves, so bright Pherri could barely bring herself to look at him. If not for the cave wall at her back, Pherri would have run on instinct, like a deer before a bear.

'Pherri.' His voice was like the thunder of drums, and at his feet the grey embers flickered. His mouth smiled, but the cheer never reached his pale eyes. 'Welcome.'

Pherri thought her thudding heart might leap out of her gullet. 'Who are you?' she whispered.

'You know who I am.'

And she did. For who else but a god could have held such power without a body in which to hold it? 'You're Eryi.'

His lips peeled back in an empty smile. 'Indeed.' He lowered himself to sit before the fire's cold ashes, and as he cast a hand over it the flames sprang to life. 'Join me.'

Pherri hesitated, but the warmth of the rising fire beckoned her, its glow hot upon her cold cheeks. *He could have killed me already. Whatever he wants me for, he wants me alive.* Cautiously, she approached, and sat opposite, placing the fire between them.

'I apologise for your treatment,' he continued, his voice deep and rolling. So close to him, she could see the imperfections of his disguise. His face was so smooth as to be incomplete, as though its rough edges had been sanded away. 'My servants are... limited.' He sighed. 'Yet while my influence is bound by my... intangibility, I must make do.'

'Then how did you kill Georald?'

'Magic is wasted on such as him. Limited talent, and no will to use it. He would have gone to his grave a servant. I had to hurry you along; I could not risk your mother catching you. She has proved... troublesome.' His mouth twitched. 'Not the question I thought you would ask. Most would want to know how I summoned you here, and why.'

'You didn't summon me here,' retorted Pherri, surprising herself with her boldness. 'We came here seeking answers.' *We.* It was this monster who had killed Theodric, as carelessly as he had murdered Georald. She resisted the pointless urge to grab a log from the fire and strike him with it.

'Come then.' He rose suddenly. 'I will give you your answers.' For a moment his body flickered, like a pond rippled by stones, and Pherri saw the truth under Eryi's glamour. Beneath the body was only bones, held together by an act of will. Pherri hesitated to follow him, then found her body moving of its own accord. She tried to slow, but her legs kept going as if dragged by invisible strings.

He looked back to her impassively. 'Do not waste your

energy fighting me. Come.' He passed a hand over the cave-mouth, and the storm broke, revealing clear blue sky.

Pherri stepped forward, looking outward and down, and gasped. As she had known, the slope was almost vertical, but now she could see the swirling blanket of cloud that marked where from Erland you could no longer see Eryispek. It was so far below them; she was miles above the village where the unGelicks had seized her.

'How did I get here so fast?'

He ignored her. 'Come.'

Eryi led her past the cavemouth, along a narrow ledge that widened to a winding path upward. It looked to be forged from ice, but Pherri's feet did not slip. The air grew warmer. Pherri began to feel a pleasant sunshine upon her neck, as if she were taking a summer stroll in Violet Hall's orchard.

The path carved its way through mounds of snow, ever upwards, until eventually it flattened. Eryi stopped to wait for her, at a flat, circular plaza like a frozen lake. A throne sat at the centre, high-backed and shimmering under the strange sunshine.

Eryi stepped to the throne, and sat, as from nowhere an ice staff appeared in his fist and a gleaming white crown upon his brow.

'I never liked the cold. But I have made do. You get used to it, after a few thousand years. I have found ways to serve myself. Men rarely climb so high, but animals do, and I have always had an affinity with beasts. They do not fight *inflika* the way men do.'

'This is the summit,' said Pherri, staring with wonder up at the sky, so close it threatened to fall on them. A slate of bright blue spread out above her, endlessly from one horizon to the other. As she stared, it began to spin, and with a sudden nausea Pherri had to avert her eyes and place her hands upon her knees, breathing hard at the thin air.

Eryi gave a high laugh. 'Like the cold, you get used to it.' He rapped his ice staff on the ground, and Pherri felt the vibration it sent across the plaza under her feet. Somewhere below, she heard the rumble of an avalanche.

'The centre of the world,' he said. 'The totem of the Norhai.' Pherri felt the sensation of the whole earth turning about them, as though this high point of Eryispek was the spoke of a wheel about which it spun. The dizziness overwhelmed her, and she collapsed to her hands and knees, pressing her forehead to the cold floor.

'Get up!' he snapped. 'I did not bring you here to cower like a child.'

Despite her sickness, Pherri felt her limbs obeying. This time she kept her gaze focused upon Eryi and his throne. 'Then why did you bring me here? If it is to kill me, then be done with it.' She had hoped to sound brave, but her voice wavered under his pale gaze.

'First, to show you. To show you everything, so that you will understand what it took. Witness.'

He slammed his staff to the ground again. The sky spun, until everything became a dizzying blur and Pherri had to close her eyes.

She felt the spinning cease, and opened them. She still stood on Eryispek, with Eryi sat upon his absurd throne, only now, the spiralling sky was gone, and a thousand windows of a thousand shades took its place.

'*Errian.*'

Her father's voice. Pherri whipped her head towards it,

and a vision loomed large before her. Her father, and Errian, face to face, in their father's chamber at Violet Hall.

'*You are a hymerika now, and you must obey me.*' He wore his armour, and though Errian was a hand's breadth taller than him, Andrick seemed to loom over him like a giant. '*We fight for the King and for Erland, not for glory. Jarhick will go to Thrumbalto, and you will go to Basseton.*'

This was last year, Pherri remembered. *When Gelick Whitedoe attacked Basseton.* Errian had been meant to go to Thrumb, but Prince Jarhick had gone instead.

'*Yes, Father,*' said Errian, with only a flicker of prideful reluctance. '*I will leave on the morrow.*'

Pherri blinked, and the sky of windows spun again. A new scene rose before her eyes, even more vivid than the last.

She stood inside a grand tent, bathed in a low warm light by the rising dawn. Nearby, a sleeping, naked woman lay curled over a bedsheet, illuminated by a single flickering candle. A tall figure stood at the entrance with his back to her, in a robe of fine red silk, a glass of ruby wine clutched in his hand.

He turned towards her, naked beneath his robe, a young man with blond hair cropped short, sharp cheekbones, and an aquiline nose. She had glimpsed him only at a distance before, but she knew him. Her cousin, Prince Jarhick, dead now for over a year.

This is Thrumb, she knew instinctively. *The night he was killed.*

She blinked, and the scene changed again. The woman who had been sleeping stole up lithely behind Jarhick, and drew a dagger across his neck. The prince clawed at his maimed throat, the blood seeping between his fingers. He

fell, gargling, and was still, the wound pulsing to his
heartbeat.

The images were coming faster now, spinning before
Pherri's eyes like wooden tops. There was no sight nor scent
of Eryispek now, only a wild maelstrom of a hundred new
places and events, with Pherri at their centre.

But for all the strangeness, the flurry of visions stopped
somewhere she knew. Lordsferry, the river town closest to
Violet Hall, the warm summer air alive with the cries of
merchants and the scents of their stalls, roasting meat and
carved wood and sweet spices, and somewhere, the
squawking of cockerels.

The summer fair. Before the scene could settle, Pherri
slammed her eyes shut. 'No, please!' she cried out. She did
not need to see this, not again.

'You will see it, all of it!' Eryi's voice came from everywhere, and Pherri found her eyelids opening of their own
accord under his command.

She was not where she had been that day, when Errian
had spared her the worst of it. Her old self's screams receded
into the background as Errian carried her away, leaving Da'ri
to the mob. Instead, Pherri stood over his mangled body, his
clothes torn and filthy, his once kind face a mess of blood and
bruises. Dead, where he had once been so full of life.

The old anger rose in her, from before she had distracted
herself with Theodric and magic. *That only happened
because Jarhick died*, she realised. That's what had set Errian
against the Thrumb.

A dark laugh penetrated her skull, echoing through it like
clashing steel. 'You begin to see,' said Eryi. 'All that
happened was according to my design, like the single
snowflake that begins the avalanche.'

More images flashed before her. Delara at her bedside, giving her the ghastly brew that had closed her dreams and almost flushed away her magic. Theodric, in the Piperskeep library, speaking kindly and leading her to his study. Both of them, fighting over her in front of her mother like dogs over a bone. All of Theodric's teaching, and that day on the battlements when she had floated away on her magic and the whole of Erland had spread out before her in a flash of *spectika*, until Eryi had slammed the door in her face. They had not left until months later, but that had been the day their journey began.

'Enough,' said Eryi. She felt his will and focus pressing down like a weight, trying to pull her away from the swirling visions, by now so real that Pherri was sure she could have reached out and touched the figures within. There were hundreds of them, but she saw only the ones Eryi willed her to, the rest never settling long enough to become discernible. They were slowing now, the solidity of Eryispek coming back into her vision.

No, thought Pherri. There was more, things Eryi did not wish her to see. She remembered Theodric's words. *Fight him.* Anger rose in her like a flash flood. This creature had killed Da'ri and Theodric, and now taunted her by forcing her to watch their deaths. *No!* A great effort of will burst upon the pressure that drove at her, and the images began to speed up again. She felt Eryi's sudden alarm inside her head, and before he could stop her, Pherri leapt for one of the windows.

The scene she found herself in was different to the others. Where they had been as vivid as life, this one was grey, as though coated in heavy fog.

Below her, the Pale River spread across Erland like a

white-blue ribbon. A horse fought against the current, struggling to stay afloat under the weight of its rider and the bundle it carried. There was fighting on the near bank, while on the far shore a woman squeezed the water from her hair. Somehow, the horse and its cargo made the other side, and two soldiers rushed forward to take the bundle. Pherri realised it was an unconscious woman, her limbs limp and soft as she was lifted from the horse.

This isn't right, realised Pherri, recognising Queen Ciera's inert body. *They never got her across the water.*

She blinked, and the scene shattered into spiderweb, revealing beneath it a scene every bit as lifelike as the earlier ones. Orsian, spluttering for breath as he dragged Ciera's body above water, and swam her to the bank, where she spat up half the river while Orsian looked on.

Orsian saved her, Pherri remembered, feeling a pang of loss for her missing brother. What had the grey scene been? The alternative, what might have happened had he not been there?

There was a shriek, like a sharp knife drawn against stone. 'Enough!' Eryi's will broke against her like the rush of the Pale River, and as the windows slowed to a stop Pherri fell to her knees, dizzy from the sudden return to Eryispek. She pressed her forehead to the ice, taking slow, deep breaths against the nausea.

'You see.' Eryi still sat upon his throne, triumphant. 'With the simple act of taking Gelick as my servant, I set in motion the chain of events that brought you here. His attack on Basseton sent the prince to Thrumb, and while your countrymen fight over Erland like curs over scraps, I have advanced, and that one simple act eventually led you to me. For millennia, I have waited, knowing that some day the one with the blood and power to free me would be born.

'Millennia, and yet in a sense, no time at all. My Mountain is the centre of existence; all that has been and will ever be happens here at once. I have only to look.' He shifted his staff slightly, and a vision of Pherri and him as they were now appeared in the sky, him on his throne and her collapsed to her knees.

With an effort, Pherri staggered to her feet. She did see. From Gelick Whitedoe's doomed war to this moment, in a series of unavoidable events, all at Eryi's hand. The Thrumb. The war. Da'ri's death, and the letter he never sent with his plan to go to Eryispek. Delara, Theodric, and *spectika*. It had all led here.

And yet... Some part of that design had faltered. That grey, waning world, where Queen Ciera had been taken across the river. What did a god care for the Queen of Erland?

Orsian. Orsian had saved Ciera, and in doing so had changed something, something that Eryi had intended.

'There are so many possibilities,' he continued. Around him, visions of alternatives swirled like dancing shadows: Pherri, older, laughing as she and Da'ri strode through a forest; Pherri, older still, practising with Theodric at Piperskeep; Pherri, as a woman, garbed in robes and deep in discussion with Prince Jarhick, who wore his father's crown. 'And through patience and cunning, I have created the only one that suited my purpose. With you, Pherri, I can finally escape this prison, and none shall stand against me.' He beat his staff on the ground, and the storm began to swirl once more, as through the snow the shadowy figures of his undead army closed in on her. Eryi's eyes fixed on Pherri, like bottomless pools of unnatural moonlight. 'There has never before been one whose strength was enough to be a worthy sacrifice. With your help, I shall finally be free.'

Pherri's heart was beating fit to burst, but against all her instincts she took a step towards him. 'I won't!' With her *phisika*, she bent her will against his, spinning the storm of ice fast enough to push back the deathless wraiths closing in on her. 'You're wrong!' she cried over the wailing winds. 'Orsian saved Ciera, and you couldn't stop him!'

The cold curl of Eryi's lip sent spasms of fear through her, but proved that the barb had struck home. 'A minor inconvenience. A rare misstep. Your brother is nobody, nothing. The fate of the Sangreal line is nothing next to bringing you here.' The unGelicks pressed closer, as the swirling barrage of ice tore their lifeless skin to shreds.

Pherri laughed, savouring the glorious madness of the storm. She could turn it against him. All that held his shattered bones together was his own will; they would not survive a blizzard. 'Orsian thwarted you!' she shrieked over the deafening noise. 'As will I!' She pushed more of her energy and will into the storm, accelerating and bringing it closer to them, just yards from Eryi's throne. Her nose and ears were bleeding, but she did not care.

'Enough.' Eryi's eyes met hers, and in a burst of focus penetrated her mind with *inflika*. The force of it sent Pherri's mind and body staggering. Theodric had taught her to use *inflika* to change people's perception, but Eryi's use of it was nothing so subtle. He bombarded her with images: Orsian, drowning on smoke as a burning boat sank into the water; her mother, wounded and dragging herself through the snow on her hands and knees as a group of unGelicks stalked her; Erland, reduced to ash, and at its centre a pulsing volcano. Screaming, Pherri fell to her knees as her control of the storm collapsed, her nose dripping blood onto the ice. An unGelick seized her, and once again Pherri felt the profane touch of dead flesh as she was thrown over a shoulder.

'Back to the cave with you!' came Eryi's cry as she was dragged away. 'Take some rest, Pherri. Together, we shall fulfil your destiny.'

CHAPTER 43

The *prifecta's* strike sent a shuddering vibration down Orsian's sword and up to his elbow. Before the sensation faded, he was on the defensive again, catching the steel-garbed warrior's second blade on a shield already on the verge of being torn to splinters.

It had taken five days and four nights of battle for the Imperials to send a detail of their most famed warriors against the city, and this was the first to scale the walls, ascending the long ladder in head-to-toe steel plate.

Orsian weathered another blow, stepped back and kicked a brazier into the *prifecta's* path, showering hot embers like fireflies into the darkness, but the Imperial slipped around it and readied another blow.

The *prifecta's* sidestep took him close to the battlements' sheer inner edge, and Orsian launched his ruined shield into the man's eye-slit. As the warrior tried to catch his balance, Orsian feinted with his blade then stepped in to hook the man at the back of the knee. The *prifecta* toppled, grasping at thin air.

The heavy clank of steel against the flagstones below told its own story, but Orsian looked over to see the job was done. The *prifecta* had landed on his head, and no weight of armour would protect a man from that. To make sure, a watchman wrenched the helmet off and buried a dagger in the man's eye.

Orsian looked around his section of the western wall. Two days ago, they had fired the drawbridge to the King's Gate, when both bridges had fallen under the Imperium's assault and they were no longer sure they could hold them in two places at once. There were still many miles of wall to defend, but for now the Imperium was focusing all its strength upon the Ram's Gate.

But Merivale still held. To Orsian's left, a head appeared above the parapet, and was met immediately by Hilga's boot. The legionnaire went over screaming, and the smith's daughter pushed the ladder after him. To his right, Cag hauled an axe-wielding slave soldier over his shoulder and threw him down into the moat.

Hilga reached for a discarded bow and set an arrow to it, before Orsian placed a stilling hand on her shoulder, almost taking an elbow to the face for his trouble. 'They're fleeing.' He pointed towards the dimly lit drawbridge while watchmen hurled rocks and abuse at the retreating Ulvatians.

'You never said we couldn't shoot them in the back.'

'I would encourage it, but we're low on arrows.'

He looked around. Just on this stretch of wall he could see as many as fifty dead and dying. Most were Imperials, but they could afford to lose men; Merivale could not.

'They're getting closer every time,' said Hilga as she wiped the blood from her black iron hammer. There were deep bags under her eyes, and the glow of her sweat in the light of the braziers gave her skin a yellowish tinge.

They were. There was word that Yriella Gough had left her lands with a few hundred men and was making raids upon the Imperial camp, but otherwise Merivale stood alone, and every day, the Imperials threw something else at the city. The poorly armed slaves of the first day had given way to better-fed slaves clad in leather armour bearing throwing spears and slingshots, who in turn had given way to black-robed, tonsured acolytes with incendiaries that belched burning clouds of choking red fumes. It had been they who had finally got the drawbridge down, rushing in under cover of smoke and coating the chains in some strange gel that turned the metal links to rust. Now only the gate and the walls stood between the Imperium and Merivale.

And us, Orsian reminded himself. The defence of Merivale had driven ordinary folk to extraordinary acts of heroism. He had seen Hilga bury her hammer in a man's skull even as a long cut across her forehead bled down into her eyes, and old Pylas skewer a spearman with an arrow just before he buried his weapon in Orsian's gut. Pylas was dead now though. A well-aimed arrow had taken him through the knee, and a fever had set in too fast for the healers to do anything. Smeared with poison, most likely. He had died only that morning.

Yet for all that, the hero of Merivale was Errian, fast as the wind and furious as a wildfire. His every waking moment was spent upon the walls, retreating for sleep for barely an hour at a time, and none had slain more Imperials than he. If a glut of foes somehow made the battlements without being thrown down, it always seemed to be Errian who met them, against impossible odds carving through them like a scythe through wheat.

When he was younger, Orsian had thought that one day he would be able to match Errian with a sword, but had his brother followed through on his threats in Piperskeep's yard there would have been little Orsian could do to stop him.

Orsian watched the retreating Imperials for a time, until behind him the sun began to rise over Merivale, and a great cheer went up from its defenders. He handed the defence of his section of wall to Horath, a slightly younger version of Pylas, and headed for the stairs, where he encountered Errian coming the other way. Other than necessary commands, they had scarcely spoken to each other in the past days, and by his vague eyes Errian was as tired as Orsian.

'Six more *hymerikai* dead,' grunted Errian, falling into step beside Orsian. 'They're taking us apart piece by piece.'

It was true. There was no help on its way, and every day left their numbers more depleted. They could bleed the Imperium for every step of Erlish soil, but the enemy were too many.

'The king and queen could flee,' said Orsian. 'Hessian might raise an army in the east.'

'I've already suggested it, and he won't hear of it. Yesterday he was even speaking of joining us on the wall. Said he can still wield a spear as well as any man.'

That Hessian's famed stubbornness endured was enough to give Orsian heart. The king had been so weak on his return that for a time they had worried he might die, but after two straight days of sleep Hessian had risen from his sickbed and demanded wine, as though he had never left Merivale.

They had reached the bottom of the steps when a shout

of 'Lord!' drifted down from the battlements. With a sinking feeling, Orsian turned, preparing himself for the news that a squad of *prifectai* was advancing on the bridge.

At the top though, Horath was almost breathless with excitement. 'They've raised a white banner! They want a parley!'

Errian and Orsian reclimbed the stairs. Left and right, Merivalers were jeering the banner-wielding *prifecta* who stood across the drawbridge, his steel plate bright under the rising dawn. 'Silence!' commanded Errian. 'We will hear him!' The walls quietened, and Errian called down at the man. 'You have a message?'

The man removed his helmet, revealing a bronzed face and black hair pulled back in a widow's peak. His voice was deep, and accented with the long vowels of the Imperium. 'Senator Drast Fulkiro, Commander of the Eternal Legion, requests a representative of Merivale outside your gates within the hour, to discuss your surrender. He guarantees safe conduct.'

This pronouncement was greeted with more jeering, and Errian had to call twice for silence before he could make himself heard. 'Agreed. One hour.'

The *prifecta* nodded, replaced his helmet, then showily whirled his horse on its hind legs to more jeers from the Merivale battlements. He rode away, the white banner streaming.

Errian looked to Orsian. 'Will you ride out with me, Brother?'

'Is that *your* decision, Errian?' came a croaking voice. The brothers turned, and there stood Hessian, tightly gripping a cane as he climbed the last stair. A whisper passed along the wall, and men fell to their knees as the King of

Erland ascended the ramparts. He unfolded his skeletal frame to its full height to look Errian in the eye. 'Last I checked, I still ruled in Merivale.'

'I am your *balhymeri*,' said Errian. 'I would have thought it my place to—'

'It is not your place!' Hessian barked. 'I *rule*, you *serve*. Is that understood?'

Errian lowered his eyes. 'Yes, Majesty.'

'Good.' Hessian's cane trembled in his hand and for a moment Orsian thought he might fall, but the king kept his feet. 'I will treat with this Imperial commander, and you will ride out with me.'

The sun was still low against Piperskeep's silhouette when they rode out of the Ram's Gate, arrayed in a column with Hessian and Errian at its head. Orsian rode behind them, next to Burik.

The portcullis rumbled, and they passed beneath the murder holes. Orsian could not resist looking up at them, ominous hollows in the stone that promised swift retribution to any foe who stepped beneath. If the Imperials broke the outer gate, an inauspicious greeting awaited them within the claustrophobic tunnel. Above, cauldrons of water sat, ready to be fired to boiling and poured down upon the invaders. Burning oil would have been better, but they needed every *hymerika* on the wall, and Orsian did not fully trust anyone else to handle such a task; the risk of the defenders being overcome by smoke before they could pour the substance was too great.

A larger party of Imperials waited beyond the drawbridge. Two dozen *prifectai* hung back, cloaked crown-to-heel in steel, but it was the group at the end of the draw-bridge that drew Orsian's gaze. A hawk-nosed man with a shaved head and green eyes glittering with cold calculation rode at the centre, in white armour so bright it almost hurt to look at, flanked by an older man bearing the purple banner of the Imperium, and an unsmiling blonde woman dressed as if selling wares at market rather than for battle. There were representatives from West Erland too; Orsian recognised the ancient Lord Storaut and the portly Lord Darlton the Younger, and, at the edge of their party, a sight that set his blood beating so hot that for a moment all he could hear was the thudding of his own heart.

Strovac Sigac, small-eyed and smirking, so large that he made his warhorse look like a donkey. Orsian blinked, and the scene flashed again across his eyelids. His father riding like a man possessed, Strovac's axe flashing in the low spring sun, and the warning cry that caught in Orsian's throat.

For a moment, it was as though he had forgotten how to breathe. Sigac seemed to sense Orsian's eyes on him, and for two pregnant seconds met his gaze, before leaning to his right to whisper something to Lord Storaut, who replied with a tight smile.

'Pay him no mind.' Hessian's voice snapped Orsian from his trance. He looked up to see the king staring at him. 'That goes for all of you.' He looked in turn to Errian, Burik, and the rest. 'His time will come.' The king drove his horse forward, spurring them to follow.

The white-armoured man raised a palm in greeting, displaying a silvered gauntlet threaded with gleaming gold. 'King Hessian.' He spoke the Erland tongue haltingly, but with only the barest trace of an accent. 'I am Senator Drast

Fulkiro. I come only at the urging of my advisors. They assure me that even the stubbornest of foes may be shown reason.'

'I do not see Kvarm Murino among them,' said Hessian. 'When I heard of your invasion, I was sure he would be with you.'

The senator shifted awkwardly in his saddle. 'We need not concern ourselves with Kvarm Murino. I claim all the lands of Erland, in the name of the Ulvatian Imperium. Open your gates and submit, and you and your people will be spared.'

Hessian met his gaze evenly, a faint smile playing around his lips. 'I will give you all the land you need, Senator.'

The senator's advisors exchanged confused looks. 'You will?' questioned Fulkiro.

'Oh indeed.' Hessian looked Fulkiro up and down. 'You are not a tall man. Six feet of Erlish soil should serve.'

The senator scowled, while Orsian and the other *hymerikai* could not hold back their laughter, doubly so when Fulkiro called for them to be silent. Orsian even saw slight smiles from the blonde woman and Lord Darlton. 'Keep your jests,' barked Fulkiro, a red rash seeping up his neck. 'Your pride will not serve you as slaves.'

'No jest, Senator. Do you think me ungenerous? Very well. Discard your amour and weapons. Leave Erland. Turn over your West Erland conspirators. And tell your kzar that Erland knows no ruler except King Hessian Sangreal.'

Before the senator could reply, Lord Storaut spoke. 'Hessian, even before this invasion you did not hold all of Erland. The senator's offer is a fair one. Darlton, Strovac, and I have submitted and agreed to divide West Erland between us.'

'So you are turncloaks twice then? I knew the boy

Rymond had little sense, but at least he had a spine. I would sooner treat with a den of vipers than the likes of you.' Hessian cast a scornful eye over Storaut. 'The lands you claim as yours today will be Sigac's tomorrow. There are earthworms beneath my horse who are likely to outlive you.'

Storaut merely muttered darkly in response, but Strovac chuckled. 'Storaut will live longer than you, I wager. Do you suppose we cannot see the way you cling to your reins to stop your fingers trembling?'

'Enough of this!' barked Fulkiro. 'I did not come here to listen to your provincial squabbling. If you will not submit, there is no more to say, and I am glad for it.'

Strovac ignored him. He reached into a saddlebag. 'I had expected Andrick the Bastard's widow to be here. Rymond asked me to give her this.' He flung something off-white and egg-shaped to the ground, and it rolled to a stop before Errian's horse. The empty eye sockets of a human skull stared up at them.

Orsian tried to swallow, but his throat had turned to ashes. Somehow though, he sensed Errian going for his sword. He spurred his horse forward and barely caught his brother's wrist when an inch of dark steel showed from his scabbard. 'They'll kill us,' he hissed. Errian stared at him. His face had turned to chalk, his pupils so large that his eyes looked like a pair of new moons, but Orsian felt his grip relax, and the blade slid back into its sheath.

'The skull of Andrick Barrelbreaker!' Strovac cried. 'You can see the hole I left in it if you don't believe me. Half his brains leaked out of it before the birds got to him. I'd have saved you his cock as well, but they ate that.'

The pounding of blood in Orsian's ears threatened to deafen him. A fierce, red-hot anger swelled in his heart like a bloated corpse. He would have reached for his sword there and then, certain death be damned, had his right hand not been wrapped around Errian's wrist.

The next thing Orsian knew, he was looking down at Hessian. In his private struggle with Errian he had not seen the king dismount. Hessian lifted the skull from the grass and held it to his forehead.

'You are home, Brother,' Orsian heard him whisper, and in that moment he saw Hessian as his father must have: a brother, as close to him as Errian was not to Orsian; a father-figure, without whom he would not have been able to raise two sons to manhood; the only person who knew him not only as a king, but loved him as a brother.

Even Fulkiro and his retinue seemed to have been shocked into silence. When he was finished, Hessian handed the skull to Burik, who helped him reclaim his saddle, where-upon Hessian took the skull and held it to his breast.

'Thank you, Strovac, for returning my brother's head to me.' Hessian sounded as though he might choke. 'It may be the most honourable act you have done in your miserable life. I ask only for an hour's grace before battle, so that we might burn it in the ritual fashion.'

'I had forgotten how superstitious the tribes can be so far from civilisation,' said Fulkiro. 'It's charming. Have your ritu-als. Soak it in piss; bless it with goat entrails. Regardless, we will be inside your walls by nightfall.

'You are too few, with too many miles of wall. Even as we speak, there are sappers digging below your eastern wall, and by the time it falls, our assault against this western gate will have begun. You cannot defend against both. The legion-naires are making bets as to which side will fall first.

'And once we are inside, your people can expect no

mercy. When they beg for quarter, I will tell them their king spat my offer back in my face.' He turned his horse back towards camp, and the rest followed.

Strovac Sigac was slower to retreat. He rode within yards of Orsian and Errian, goading them to strike. 'When your father looks down from above the clouds tonight, you'll be dead, or at least you'll wish you were. I've told Fulkiro that when he's divvying up the slaves, I just want you two and your mother.'

'Run along to your new master, Strovac.' Hessian's voice dripped with contempt. 'The greatest regret of my reign is that I allowed a sword to be put in your hand when I should have ordered it be put through your belly.'

Fury flashed in Strovac's eyes. 'Your brother was a dog, and died like one.' He wheeled his horse and galloped away.

'Back to the city,' said Hessian. His breath was coming low; even just riding out had tired him. He looked to Errian. 'Is it true? Can they bring down our wall?'

Errian hesitated. 'It would take years to dig through! They can't possibly have.'

Orsian was less sure. The defenders had hardly bothered to patrol the eastern wall once they had fired the drawbridge to the rarely used Lesser Gate. The Imperium's only assaults on it had been the odd foray by poorly armed slaves. But what if this had been their plan all along? 'We should go,' said Orsian. 'See if we can find a tunnel.'

Hessian nodded. 'Yes. Take who you need.'

They rode back to the city, and the gate creaked closed behind them. 'To the battlements!' cried Errian, to the beleaguered troops, some of whom were leaning against the stairs or taking a quick nap in the shadow of the walls. 'If I find any cunt asleep I'll throw him into the moat!'

Orsian leapt down to assist Hessian. The king was still clutching the skull like it was worth its weight in gold. Orsian did not even want to look at it.

Hessian's cheeks glistened with tears. 'You're home, Brother,' he whispered, pressing his forehead against it again. 'I'm sorry, for everything.' He sniffed, and cast his bloodshot eyes upon Orsian and Errian. 'We'll burn him quickly, now. Someone fetch me kindling and a torch.'

It was not the funeral his father deserved, Orsian reflected, as Hessian held a burning brand to the straw pyre they had hastily built in the dirt. But when Hessian reached out and gripped Orsian's hand, he felt the tears about to come. He wiped his eyes and willed them away. *He would not want my tears. He would want me to save Erland.*

The fire burnt out, leaving behind a skull even more sinister than before, charred black and red and with deep dark sockets that seemed to stare at Orsian in reproach. He turned away.

Heedless of the dirt, Hessian had collapsed weeping to his knees, bloodlessly pale. Errian whispered something to a *hymerika*, and two of them led him to his horse, and sent it in the direction of Piperskeep.

'At least he held it together until we got back,' said Errian, but Orsian could see the shadows of tears lurking beneath his eyes as well. 'Go to the eastern wall. Eryi's balls, if they've dug underneath us...'

'If it's there, we'll collapse it,' swore Orsian, though he was oblivious as to how. There was so much the Imperials had that they did not; next to steel plate armour, chemicals that could burn through metal links, and the ability to dig deep enough to collapse a city wall, what good was the *Hymeriker*? 'Or smoke them out or something.'

Errian could spare no *hymerikai*, so Orsian took six others with him: Hilga the smith girl, Cag, and four city watchmen. As they were riding away, he noticed Pitt calling to him, and dragged the boy up into the saddle. Since Tansa had insisted that Pitt be taken off her hands, Orsian had taken him on as something in between a groom, a servant, and a messenger boy.

'Tansa's still angry with you,' the boy told him. 'The queen invited her to eat last night, but Tansa sent Esma back to say no.'

Orsian winced. Since the attack had begun, he had returned to Piperskeep only once. He and Tansa had lain together, both before and after he had slipped into an exhausted sleep for the few hours before dawn, but it had done little to quell Tansa's obvious misery.

This is not her place. When it was over, if they lived, it would be for Tansa to choose her path. One of the reasons Orsian had kept Cag close was to keep him safe. Not that he needed it now; every kill seemed to only increase Cag's confidence with sword and spear. What he lacked in skill he more than made up for in strength and reach.

There was a skeleton force of watchmen patrolling the eastern wall, just two men for every quarter-mile. As they brought their mounts to a stop, a spearman hailed them from atop the ramparts. 'Was beginning to think you'd forgotten about us!' he called down. 'We've not been idle, Lord. Had some try and climb down into the moat and up across the other day, but a few arrows sent them packing.'

Orsian dismounted, handed the horse's reins to Pitt, and raced up the stairs. It was odd that the Imperium had not turned more of a force against the almost deserted Lesser Gate, but he had been too tired and occupied by assaults on the Ram's Gate to think of it. A grim, sinking sensation settled in his gut.

'Have you seen anyone digging?' he demanded. 'Any strange noises?'

The spearman frowned. 'Digging?' He scratched his head. 'Nothing of the sort. One of the lads the other night thought he heard voices, but we shined a light down and didn't see anything. Also saw a boy running off this morning back towards their camp. We shot an arrow after him.'

Orsian gritted his teeth. He was about to reply when a cry came from Cag. 'There!'

He looked up, and far to the south saw the slow march of Imperial legionnaires, unmistakable with their long shields glinting purple and the sunlight reflecting off their polished helms.

'They're going under the walls!' Orsian declared. He did not need to see it to know Drast Fulkiro had spoken true; he could feel the truth in his bones. He looked to the spearman. 'Send word to my brother: we need reinforcements here, urgently, as many as he can spare. We're going out there. We'll collapse the tunnel.' If they could find it.

One of the watchmen he had brought with him paled. 'Lord, there's thousands of them coming up, we can't—'

'What will it matter if that wall comes down?' said Hilga. 'If Lord Orsian says we're going out there, we're going out there.'

Shamed by the girl, Cag and two watchmen followed Orsian and Hilga out of the gate, as the other two hauled the portcullis up.

'Stay there!' Orsian commanded. 'We may need to close that quickly.' Already, he could see the Legion perhaps only a mile away. They marched slowly to maintain formation –

on the summer breeze he could almost hear the shuffle of their feet and the cry of their leader keeping time – but he judged they were twenty minutes away at most, which meant the sappers might be right under the walls.

He rushed to the edge and peered down into the moat. It was some yards apart from the walls here, and the water was shallower than at the southern and western sides. *We should have it flush with the wall and filled entirely with water,* thought Orsian as he looked down. A dream for another time. This close, the putrid stench of stagnant water and excrement made his eyes water. 'Look for anything. Any sign of digging or earth being disturbed or anyone being around.'

'There's something there!' came a voice, and Orsian looked down to see Pitt had sneaked out of the gate to join them. Orsian did not even bother to command him to get back inside.

Orsian squinted. 'I can't see anything.'

'It's a spade,' declared Pitt, pointing more insistently.

Once Orsian had trained his eyes to see past the layer of scum over the brown water, he could see Pitt was right. The shadow of a spade lay underneath.

'Do you really think they're digging under the walls?' asked Hilga. 'That's still yards of earth to dig through before you'd reach the foundations.'

'Maybe their tunnel's already collapsed,' added Cag.

'No, they're down there,' said Orsian. 'You saw what those acolytes did to the drawbridge chains; who's to say they've not got something that can melt earth and stone as well?' He cursed inwardly; they ought to have seen it sooner. *He* ought to have seen it sooner. If they broke through here, they could fall upon Merivale's defensive positions on the south and western wall from behind. It would be a slaughter.

'We're going down there. Please tell me someone has some rope.'

It quickly became clear that none of them had rope, so one of the watchmen was despatched to find some. Orsian paced the bank, periodically shifting his gaze from the gate to the advancing Legion to the earth beneath his feet, imagining he could hear the scrape of sharpened iron against stone as the Imperial sappers chipped away at the foundations.

It's not over yet, he swore to himself. Even if the wall fell and collapsed into the moat, the Imperials would still need to scale down the far-side bank, which would require ropes, patience, and time, unless they jumped in full armour and risked breaking their legs. Time enough to bring a force from the other side of the city. It might only be a mob wielding cleavers and eating knives, but it would be something.

I should tell Tansa to get out of the city. But if he insisted Tansa leave, she would likely do just the opposite. And there was no way she would leave without Cag.

Cag was standing nearby, looking near as anxious as Orsian felt. The large youth seemed to sense Orsian's gaze, and shot a glare back at him. 'You should tell Tansa to get out of the city,' said Cag. 'She won't leave unless you tell her.'

It was fitting that they should both have been thinking of Tansa. 'If all is lost,' Orsian said, 'you have to get her out. There's an underground passage out of the keep, Tansa's seen it.'

'I found it!' A shrill voice called up from the bottom of the moat. Disbelievingly, Orsian turned, and looked down to see Pitt, shin-deep in filth and waving up to them. 'There's a hole that way!' He pointed northward. 'I listened, but I couldn't hear anything. It's dark.'

Orsian resisted the urge to vigorously berate Pitt for

wandering off. How had he even got down there? 'That's great, Pitt!' he called back, hoping their conversation was not audible down the Imperium's mine. 'Just *wait there!*'

By the time the watchman had returned with a length of rope to secure to the outer gates, the distance between them and the legionnaires had halved. Orsian descended swiftly, his feet sinking into the soft dirt of the moat's edge. The others followed, and they ran north, sloshing through the brown water.

Within a few hundred yards, they found the opening, a dark fissure in the earth several feet across, widening into a tunnel that snaked below the walls. Straining his ears, Orsian swore from within he heard the tinny sound of pickaxes against the city's foundations.

'What do we do?' whispered Cag.

Orsian's eyes surveyed the ceiling, then the walls, searching for the supports he was sure would be required to prop up such a construction. He could barely fathom the bravery of such men, to descend into this strange foreign earth armed only with spades and axes, ever aware that their work might bury them.

Unfortunately, he would have to follow them.

A few paces in, Orsian's left hand touched upon a wooden support down the earthen edge. He traced his hand upwards, and along the cross-beam connected to the support on the opposite side. Through the gloom, he could see a few feet further in.

Orsian signalled to the others, and moved forward. He was not sure whether it would be enough to bring down the supports closest to the entrance; they had to go deeper. Other than Hilga dogging his steps, Orsian could sense his companions' understandable reluctance to follow. He turned his head towards them, just as an arrow whistled past his neck.

Had he not turned, it would have caught Orsian directly in the throat. A second arrow whizzed past, missing him by a foot. Not prepared to wait for a third attempt, Orsian charged forward, hacking blindly into the darkness.

In the narrow tunnel, he could barely miss. A third arrow skittered off his mailed shoulder, and then Orsian was upon them. There were two of them, holding the foreign crossbows so derided by Erlanders, who trained from their youth with a bow. They required less skill, but were slower; to draw one a man had to place his foot in a stirrup and pull back. Orsian fell upon them just as one was lifting his weapon while the other cocked his foot to the stirrup. A single slash cut a crimson scarf across the first's neck, and the second across the face, sending them both spinning to the earth.

'Back!' cried Orsian to those behind him. There was no prospect of going deeper now. Further down the tunnel, he could see a flickering light, silhouetting the clumsy shadows of his foe as they raced up the shaft to meet him. Orsian threw his weight against a wooden pillar to his left, and it cracked slightly. The beam above him sagged, and spots of dirt began pouring down into his face. He ran, nearly tripping as he threw himself against the next pillar, bringing down another shower of earth. A great, ominous rumble followed behind him, and he leapt clear of the shaft just as it began to collapse, dirt coming all at once in a torrent, drowning out the screaming of trapped men within.

The supports further down the passage where they were still digging might hold, but there was little Orsian could do about that now. He could only hope the others had been crushed in the earthfall, or that they would be too focused on getting out to fully undermine Merivale's walls. He rose to his feet, dusting himself down. 'Anyone hurt?'

A groan rose from the moat wall. With a sense of dread, Orsian turned, and found Hilga bending over Cag, an arrow embedded below his chest. The bolt had punched through Cag's light armour like parchment.

Orsian rushed over. Cag's clothes were already drenched in sweat, and his face had a sickly, clammy pallor to it. 'Did it go all the way through?' Orsian asked. If it had, they could treat it – remove the head and the fletching and draw it out the other side.

Hilga shook her head.

'Was meant for you,' said Cag, grimacing, his breath coming low and laboured. 'Just my luck.'

Orsian knelt and pressed two fingers to Cag's torso where skin met shaft, drawing a pained cry. 'That has to come out, quickly.' He left unsaid how many of their soldiers had sickened from Imperial poisons even after an arrow had been removed, their veins and arteries slowly turning black. 'Hold him down, I'll have to push it through.'

'I've checked!' said Hilga. 'It's up against the bone. He needs a healer.'

'I'm fine,' said Cag, though the fear in his eyes was plain as day. 'Just might need some help walking.' With a deep groan, he hauled himself to his feet, and stumbled sideways; Hilga barely got herself underneath his arm before he fell, and Cag hissed and grimaced as his weight came down on her shoulder.

A cry came from above. 'They're nearly here!'

Orsian looked up, and saw Pitt standing at the edge of the moat, silhouetted against the clear sky. 'Pitt, damn you!

How did you get up there?' Facing Tansa would be bad enough now; if Pitt hurt himself as well she would kill him.

'Climbed out,' he said with a shrug. He pointed into the distance. 'They're nearly here. You need to get out.'

Orsian tried to still his rushing blood, coursing with his narrow escape from being buried alive. They had been down here long enough that the Imperials could be almost on top of them by now. 'Back to the rope,' he said. 'Cag first, I'll go last.'

'We should leave him!' said a watchman. 'There's no hope for the rest of us if we take him with us!'

Orsian turned on him, resisting the urge to seize his neck and strangle the life from him. 'Even with an arrow in him, he's still more bloody use than you are. Maybe it would be you, if you weren't such a coward. Would you want us to leave you behind?'

'N-no, Lord.'

'Then help us get him to the rope. Maybe if you're quick about it I won't make you go last.'

Between them, Orsian and Hilga managed to shuffle Cag along the moat. His legs were fine, but every step brought a grunt of pain as bone and body shifted against the arrowhead. Heat was rolling off him like a furnace.

By the time they reached the rope, Orsian could hear the beating of deep drums echoing off the city walls. If he was any judge, they had only a few minutes to get to the gate, assuming they had not closed it against the approaching Legion. 'You two, go,' he said to the watchmen, who did not even bother to wait for him to finish speaking before they rushed to the rope and began climbing. 'Wait at the top!' he called after them.

'You next,' he said to Hilga.

'Balls to that. How are you planning to get him up by yourself?'

'I'll tie him on. You and the others pull him up then throw it back down for me. Don't wait.' From his position against the earthen side, Cag mumbled something incoherent. The short walk through the moat had sapped the last of his strength; he did not even seem to mind that he was sitting in several inches of filthy water.

'Not a chance.' She jutted her jaw out as if she meant to fight him. 'The city can't stand without you. *You* go up and I'll tie him on down here. Get the others and haul us up together.'

'But—'

'Go!' Hilga shoved him towards it. 'Be a lord, damn you!'

As the two watchmen reached the top and disappeared over the ledge, Orsian leapt onto the rope and began hauling himself up, digging his feet hard into the earthen side and pulling himself up hand over hand.

Orsian heaved himself over the edge. He came up to his knees, and was relieved to see the two watchmen had not abandoned them.

His relief was short-lived. He turned back towards the moat, and the sight that met him took his breath away.

At a distance, it had not been possible to appreciate the sheer scale of the foe marching towards them. Thousands upon thousands of soldiers, shaking the earth with each synchronised step of their perfect formation, each alike with their purple-golden shields, plumed helms, and spears twice a man's height.

The Lesser Gate will never stand against so many. Orsian could only hope that Errian had heeded his message and sent more soldiers.

'We're pulling them up!' he told the watchmen, who like him were gazing at their arriving foe, their eyes wide with fear. It was even harder work then Orsian would have imagined, straining against the rope and trying to avoid tumbling forward as they dragged the weight of two people up. Hilga would be doing her best to help, but Cag was little more than dead weight now. At one point, the rope slipped through a watchman's grip, almost sending them all stumbling towards the moat, and Cag cried out as if he had been speared.

He was whimpering like a babe as they finally hauled him and Hilga over the edge, but holding a hand to where the arrow shaft penetrated his flesh he managed to get to his feet. His face had turned as grey as rancid meat, and though he could meet Orsian's eye, his eyes were red-rimmed and inflamed, with a yellowish tinge to them.

'Tell Tansa,' he whispered. 'Tell her—'

'Tell her yourself,' said Orsian, tucking himself under Cag's arm as Hilga did the same the other side. The Imperials were so close now that their drum seemed to be beating inside Orsian's ears. The two watchmen were already running towards the gates, and the three of them shambled together after them.

They were only yards from the threshold when Orsian heard the thrum of a bowstring and the first crossbow bolt punched into one side of the wooden double gate. 'Come on!' he cried. He looked back, as the first of the legionnaires began crossing a long plank of wood they had tipped over the moat and the wall's few defenders began launching arrows. One took a shaft in the neck and fell, just as another crossbow bolt whirred past Orsian's head.

'Close the gate!' he cried. Another bowstring thrummed. 'Close it!' As they passed under the wall into the gatehouse,

Orsian felt himself being dragged sideways. His feet went from under him, and he landed in a heap with Hilga and Cag.

He groaned. 'Everyone alive?' It had been closer than he would have liked, but their collapsing of the tunnel might have gained the city a few more hours at least.

Cag whimpered, but from Hilga there came no reply. With an awful feeling, Orsian crawled to where she lay face down on the cobbles.

She had not worn mail. Only a few layers of thickened leather had been there to protect her from sword and shield and shaft. In the last few days, Orsian had seen the well and poorly armoured alike struck down and killed. The strongest armour in the world could not save you from a well-placed thrust from a skilled foe, nor from a moment of bad luck. In battle, sometimes one moment was all you needed, for good or ill.

The crossbow bolt had not needed to be well-placed. It had caught her in the back, and plunged through layers of leather, skin, and muscle to penetrate the heart. It jutted from her body like a flag of victory, as thick red-brown blood began to pool beneath her.

This was not the first time Orsian had been touched by death. Andrick Barrelbreaker had lived for battle, to better serve his brother the king and his country. To die by violence had been the only fitting end for such a man. Hilga though. Hilga had been sixteen. She had fought not because she was trained to, nor for glory, nor for the rule of a king who would never even know her name. She had fought for survival, of herself, her family, and her city. In better times, she would have grown up to inherit her father's smithy, and to birth heavy-jawed, golden-haired sons and daughters, to laugh with her and run about under her feet. To die as a young woman by a crossbow bolt to the back from a foreign soldier was no fitting end for brave Hilga. Orsian hung his head, and though there was no time, allowed himself a moment to weep. To Hilga, it was the least he owed.

This was where they found him, kneeling and weeping over her corpse, while outside the deafening Imperial drums beat on, over the whistle of arrows and the screams of the men they struck.

'They're at the gates, Lord!' declared a watchman. 'What should we do?'

'Fight them,' said Orsian hoarsely. He looked to Cag, grey-faced and soaked in sweat, his breath little more than a rattle, the arrow still jutting from his torso. Somehow, though he looked worse than poor, dead Hilga, the giant boy had got to his knees. 'Get him to a healer,' added Orsian.

His voice seemed to stir Cag. 'I can go myself,' he said, somehow mustering some resistance from his feverish state. With a noise that was half groan and half snarl, he pushed himself up, and stumbled onto the supportive shoulder of a city watchman.

'There's too many!' insisted the watchman. 'They're over the moat.'

'Then throw them back.' Orsian came to his feet. 'Where are the reinforcements?'

The watchman pointed towards two *hymerikai* waiting beyond the walls. 'There, Lord.'

'Two? He sent two?' Orsian could have laughed. What was Errian doing? He stalked towards the two *hymerikai*. 'Are you all he sent? Where's the rest of you?'

'Lord Errian sent us to fetch you,' said one of them. 'You're needed at the Ram's Gate.'

A loose helmet was rolling on the ground nearby, and Orsian kicked it furiously towards the wall. 'Get to the battlements then! I'm going to beat some sense into my brother. The city will fall if he doesn't send men here!'

He found Pitt, relieved he had made it back inside. Orsian tried to persuade him to go and help Cag, but the boy refused to be separated from him.

As Orsian vaulted onto his horse, he heard banging and shouting against the outer gate. 'Close that inner gate!' he called to the guards. 'Get that water in the gatehouse boiling, and if they break through pour it on their heads. Just hold until I come back!' He pulled Pitt up in front of him, and galloped away, praying that there would still be a Lesser Gate to defend by the time he returned.

The city was still full to bursting, most having nowhere else to go. As Orsian rode past, distressed citizens reached out to him, begging for any hopeful news he could offer them. When the fifth such person stopped him, Orsian finally relented, pulling to a stop in a burst of sparks as horseshoes skidded against the cobbles in front of a large bald man wearing an apron, next to a skinny wife with bird's nest hair and a gaggle of half-clothed children under their feet.

'Gather all the folk you can and go to Piperskeep! Tell them Orsian Andrickson sent you!' Before the man could reply, Orsian rode on.

He galloped on through Merivale's narrow streets, past crooked hovels, deserted inns, and knots of pale, terrified people. Twice more, he stopped to urge people to gather all they could and flee behind the walls of Piperskeep. He could only hope his name was enough to earn them entry; most had already pulled back from the walls, but that would only delay matters if the gates fell. Orsian suddenly remembered

Errian's scheme to destroy the mangonels, without which the city would surely already have fallen.

As he neared the Ram's Gate, over the clatter of hooves he heard the unmistakable sounds of battle: a hubbub of confused shouting, the sharp clash of steel, and the blast of a horn so deafeningly loud it must have been twice the length of a man's arm.

And then, a sound that twisted Orsian's blood with horror.

The horn sounded again, and hundreds of voices cried out in terror. 'Retreat!' he thought he heard someone shout, followed by a great rumble as if the very sky was collapsing in on itself, more shouting, and a thunderous explosion.

They've gone under the western wall as well. Dreading what he might find, Orsian drove his horse on around the last two corners.

For a foolish moment, he saw the wall still stood, and felt a second of relief, until he saw the state of what had once been the Ram's Gate.

At a distance, it had been impossible to judge the true size of the zebrephants. This one might have been close to twenty feet high, were it not currently dying noisily amidst the ruins of the gatehouse, trumpeting mournfully beneath several tonnes of rubble. It had been armoured in thick mail, but that had done nothing to protect its eyes from the arrows the Erlanders had peppered it with as it made its doomed charge towards the gate, now protruding like hedgehog spines around its blind, dead eyes.

It had not been enough. Barely audible beneath the zebrephant's death throes were the groans of the Erlanders who had been there when the gate fell. Some were lying with their legs crushed by fallen masonry, while to judge by the screams there were many more who were trapped beneath the rubble.

Errian, thought Orsian immediately. His brother would have put himself right where the danger was thickest, atop the gatehouse. He dismounted. 'Pitt, ride for Piperskeep! Tell them to get everyone inside! Go!' They could not hold the city now; already he could see Imperial legionnaires picking their way through the rubble to engage the stunned Erlanders. Before the boy could object, Orsian slapped the horse's rump back towards the way they had come, then threw himself into the fray.

Someone had mercifully put the poor zebrephant out of its misery, and as a few bold legionnaires bearing their vast rectangular shields trod gingerly across its back into Merivale, Orsian let off a few quick arrows. Two at least struck their targets, and sent their victims toppling from the zebrephant's back as the barbs found the opening of their helmets, but the rest could not penetrate the Imperials' armour, and they came on.

A tall, helmeted *hymerika* was bellowing orders. 'Shield wall! Shield wall!' Orsian's heart leapt as he recognised Errian, unharmed, rushing towards the breach. '*Hymeriker,* form up! Back the rest of you, get back!' He grabbed a stunned citizen standing with his ugly sword hanging uselessly at his side and thrust him out of the way. 'Get back, damn you!'

'Errian!' Orsian ran after him, casting aside his bow and drawing his sword and shield. 'Errian!'

His brother gave no sign he heard him. As more legionnaires came through the ruined gatehouse, dozens of *hymerikai* were already forming up on Errian's mark, locking their shields and crowing for the Imperials to come and meet their death.

'Errian!' Orsian shoved his way between his brother and the man at his right and locked his shield in with the rest. 'Errian, we need to retreat!'

Errian looked at him in surprise. 'The *Hymeriker* do not retreat! We can hold them here!' Their ranks were swelling, and the Imperials were holding back, waiting for the reinforcements appearing behind them. A few arrows flew overhead, and a legionnaire fell screaming with a shaft through his eye.

'The Lesser Gate can't hold them!' Orsian shouted. 'We need to get everyone back to Piperskeep!'

'Eryi's bloody cock, Orsian, I said we can hold them!' Errian looked at him with madness in his eyes. 'We will make them bleed for every inch of Erlish soil. Flee and hide behind the walls if you want, but I swear when this is over I'll come and drag you out of there and hang you! I am your *balhymeri*!'

He thinks he's Father. But Andrick Barrelbreaker would have seen the situation for what it was. They might hold here for a time, but when the Lesser Gate fell the Imperials would pour into the city and they would be trapped, cut off from Piperskeep.

Orsian was ready to protest again, until he looked up and saw it was too late. The Imperials had spread out to the width between what remained of the western wall and the hovels and houses on the *Hymeriker*'s right, and with steady, purposeful steps were advancing upon them with their own shield wall raised.

CHAPTER 44

Through a world of white, they trod upward, stumbling over steeply packed snow and hidden tree roots. Flakes were falling gently, and the wind rushing through the pines scattered powder across their hoods and shoulders. The mists seemed to seep from the trees, and yet reveal them with every step forward, each fresh trunk proof that they were moving and not trapped inside a bubble of fog.

Viratia forced the tree branch she had taken as a staff to the ground, and pressed on, the mantra that kept her going spinning in her head with every stride. *Just one more step. One more step and I'll rest.* The exhaustion was in her bones, in her frozen feet, in the lungs that rattled with each breath of bitter air. Behind her, she could hear Sister Velna whispering words of prayer, as she had been ceaselessly for days, ever since they had escaped Eryispool and Hessian had left them. Ahead, Naeem's breath came low and steady, as dogged and untiring as a veteran *hymerika* ought to be.

Viratia looked past Naeem, to where Aimya led the way, levering herself through the snow with her spear. Sister

Velna brought up the rear, and Viratia was sure to look back occasionally to make sure they were not separated.

'By Eryi,' gasped Naeem in between breaths. 'Always thought I'd die among *hymerikai*, not surrounded by women.'

'We'll stop soon,' promised Viratia, as much to herself as to Naeem.

'Eryi lends strength to our feet!' cried Velna, though she sounded just as exhausted as the rest of them. 'He is beckoning us on towards his glory! I am coming, Lord! Pray with me, Sister Aimya! All of you, pray with me!'

Velna's piety quieted everyone. They returned to their trudging, in silence.

At first, they had followed the track pointed out to them by the departing Adrari, but, when there was no sign of anyone travelling ahead of them, had gone deeper into the pine forest in search of any marks of passage. They had found enough to pick up a trail; burnt-out fires with the bones of small game left nearby, branches stripped for kindling, the odd footprint that had not yet been claimed by snow. Viratia had been glad of Aimya's youthful eyes; she sensed the young bride was now near as invested in this quest as Naeem and herself.

In her more optimistic moments, Viratia assured herself that Pherri had been there, that she could sense her daughter. But who could say for sure they were following Pherri and Theodric, that they were following anyone?

Viratia tried to quieten the voice that asked how a girl as small as Pherri would have survived this climb, and the plunging temperatures that came with the fall of night and did not rise again until the pale sun came to pass over them. Whether her daughter was alive or dead, Viratia would find her.

She heaved herself onward. They all did. As the slope continued to steepen, Naeem took up a second, staff-like branch and began using both hands to push himself forward. 'Used to know a woman who did a trick with two bits of wood. I liked hers better though.'

Only Aimya laughed at the jest. That Velna did not reprimand her fellow bride served to prove how tired she was.

Viratia was about ready to call them to a halt when Aimya gave a cry and stopped. 'I see something! It might be a village!'

Viratia had felt close to sleeping on her feet, but that roused her. The ground seemed to be levelling, and she looked up, squinting through the heavy mist for what Aimya had seen.

'I can't see a thing, girl,' said Naeem. 'But I'll trust those young eyes of yours. March!'

The prospect of salvation spurred them on, and they attacked the snow with renewed vigour. Within a few steps, what Aimya had seen emerged from the mist like a mirage: a few scattered huts, set among a snow-dusted formation of dark rocks.

'Eryi has answered our prayers!' cried Velna, raising her hands to the sky. 'Eryi sees all! I am coming, Master!'

She sounded half-crazed. Viratia turned again to check on the woman. Velna looked back at her, but there was no understanding in her glassy expression. Viratia had begun to wonder if the cold had driven the elder bride to madness, but she had been strange even before the temperature plummeted.

As they approached, Viratia's foot caught on a snow-hidden rock, and would have fallen if not for her staff. Now outside the cover of the trees, the wind seemed to blow even colder, and the Mountain loomed above them like an endless shadow. She hurried on with the rest of them.

Up the slope from the huts stood a wooden hall, with long log walls and a flat roof. Aimya reached it first, and with Naeem's help threw open the double doors.

Viratia had hoped to be welcomed by a warm, well-lit space full of Adrari eager to pull weary travellers before a roaring fire, perhaps with Pherri whole and hale among them, but as she stepped over the threshold the sight within was bleak. In cold semi-darkness, four hooded figures huddled around a single smoking fire, below an empty dais and surrounded by vacant benches.

The door closed behind them, shutting out the snow, but the hall seemed no warmer for it. Viratia could still see her breath forming white in the air.

Naeem raised a hand in greeting to the four figures. 'Well met, friends. We've travelled here all the way from Merivale, and we'd be most grateful to share your fire.'

His words brought all four figures to their feet, as if woken from a trance, and the one nearest lowered her hood to reveal a pale, pretty girl with rosy cheeks and a thick braid falling over her shoulder. 'By—' The girl seemed momentarily lost for words, but her eyes softened in relief. 'You came. The goddess said you would. You're Pherri's mother.'

In a moment Viratia was striding across the hall, tiredness forgotten. 'Do you have her? Where is she?'

'She's gone,' said an older man with a tangled, greying beard. 'Days ago.'

Viratia's heart seemed to skip a beat, and then sink. She was about to ask where her daughter had gone, and who had taken her, but then the squat figure across the fire looked up, and Viratia's blood twisted with loathing.

'*You.*'

Delara stepped forward, shadows playing about her wizened face. 'I warned you. Both of you. Magic is a curse.'

Viratia grimaced. 'Naeem, give me your sword.'

'Now, hold on!' said the Adrari girl, stepping between them. 'Delara fought—'

'Vile servant of darkness!' Someone shoved Viratia aside, sending her sprawling to the floor. Moving impossibly fast, Velna swung her staff towards the Adrari girl's head.

'Maghira!' Another of the Adrari, a young man, pushed the Adrari girl aside, and lunged forward to place himself between her and Velna with his arms raised. The staff struck his elbow, and he screamed as if it had been a hammer blow. He collapsed with a wail, his lower arm hanging limply at an unnatural angle.

Velna stalked towards the girl, who was crawling frantically backwards towards Viratia. The look on Velna's face as she advanced was like nothing human. Her eyes were glassy, a blue so pale they were almost white. She pulled back her lips in a rictus grin, and her mouth was as deep and black as endless night. '*You have no power here, Goddess.*' Velna's mouth moved, but the rough, pitiless voice that came out did not belong to her. '*You will not—*'

With a snarl, the older Adrari man swung his bone axe from behind. It met Velna's flesh at the shoulder, and her whole arm thudded to the floor, splattering blood across the hall. Sister Velna turned towards her assailant, her face twisted in fury, no sign that she had even felt the blow. Wide-eyed, the Adrari pulled back for another swing.

Velna raised a palm, and the Adrari was thrown across

the room. The far wall broke apart in an explosion of splinters, and the man disappeared into the snow.

Viratia shook herself to her senses. What was happening? 'Naeem—'

But the grizzled *hymerika* was already moving forward, his sword drawn. The thing wearing Velna's skin turned its pale eyes on him and raised its staff. Naeem tensed on the balls of his feet, holding his sword in both fists.

A bubble of fear rose in Viratia's throat. Blood was still pouring from Velna's armless shoulder, but the elder bride gave no sign of slowing. Whatever Velna was now, Naeem could not hope to fight it. Naeem stepped forward, too fast for Viratia to cry out a warning.

From the side, Sister Aimya dashed forward and impaled Velna with her spear. It went up through the ribs, into her heart, and out her back.

Velna opened her mouth in a silent scream and, for a moment, her eyes returned to normal, and Viratia saw only a confused priestess. Aimya yanked the shaft free, and Velna's one-armed corpse sagged to the ground.

Aimya let her spear fall. 'I've dreamt about that.' She looked down at the corpse and grimaced. Velna's face looked almost peaceful. 'Sorry, Sister.'

'Eryi's shitting testicles, what the fuck was that?' swore Naeem. His face shone white as a sheet in the firelight. 'Damn near pissed myself.'

The girl Maghira was getting to her feet, but did not answer him. Instead, she ran to the young man, who was still whimpering on the floor over his dislocated elbow. She looked up at Delara, eyes blazing. 'Some use you were! What sort of magus are you?' Delara cackled. 'I'm no magus. And I'm certainly not going to fight a god for your sake. You saw what happened the last time someone tried that.'

'That thing was a *god*?' said Aimya. 'You mean there *are* actually gods?'

Maghira had managed to crack the youth's elbow back into place. 'Just two. That *thing* that just possessed your friend was Eryi.' She looked at Viratia. 'And it's him who has your daughter.'

Viratia looked the girl in the eye, searching for the lie, but her face betrayed nothing except certainty.

Naeem sheathed his sword. 'Explains the wolves and the whales then. I'd be mad not to believe you after seeing Sister Velna shove a man through a wall without touching him.' They all looked to the hole, where the cold was now rushing in.

'It was her faith,' said Aimya. The girl was kneeling by her elder bride, clutching her hand. She seemed almost surprised to be there. 'He possessed her. All she's done since we left Fisherton is pray. Don't think I even saw her eat. Was starting to think she'd gone mad.' Aimya reached out to close the lids of Velna's staring eyes. 'I suppose she did. Least I know for sure Eryi's real now. Makes sense he'd be a total bastard.'

Viratia stepped forward and placed a hand on Aimya's shoulder. 'You saved us.' She looked at Maghira. 'I'll give you about thirty seconds to explain what's going on here, and why *she*' – Viratia pointed an accusing finger towards Delara – 'is with you.'

Maghira met Viratia's eye, opened her mouth to speak, but seemed to falter under the older woman's penetrating gaze. 'It's hard to know where to start,' she said weakly.

'Think I might know.' They all looked towards the voice,

and the older Adrari limped through the hole, clutching his side and with blood trickling from his scalp. 'We can start at the beginning. But afterwards you can all help me find my axe.'

'Ruhago!' Maghira cried out, and ran to him. Her brother followed, gingerly clutching his elbow.

'I'm fine,' said Ruhago, wincing as he allowed Maghira to embrace him before roughly shaking her brother's uninjured hand. 'Or alive at least. Think a rib might be broken.'

The seven of them gathered around the fire, with Aimya seeing to Ruhago's badly bruised torso while he sat on a stool preparing to speak. Viratia made sure to keep as far as possible from Delara. Their eyes met over the fire, and the Lutum woman stared back at her. Dark questions swirled in Viratia's head. Had she killed Theodric and handed Pherri over to whatever dark thing had possessed Velna? She could not bring herself to think of the presence she had felt as Eryi. But if Delara had played any part in it, Viratia would kill her.

Once Ruhago's injuries were bound, he was ready to begin. The fire danced and smoked amidst the gusts of wind that whistled through the hole Ruhago had left, and the shadows of the hall seemed to close in around them, until it was only their band of seven and the fire.

'There are two powers on this Mountain,' said Ruhago. He winced as he shifted on his seat. 'Gods, if you like. Vulgatypha is the last of the Norhai, after she killed the rest. Many thousands of years ago, she sought to take dominion over our realm as well. Eryi was the magus who sacrificed himself to stop her, imprisoning her within the heart of the Mountain and him at its summit. The Adrari have always sought to balance the two, to keep them both bound, but now Eryi's too powerful, and centuries being caged have not made him kind. He's breaking free, and if he does, Vulgatypha will too.' His deep-set eyes shone orange in the firelight. 'We were to bring your daughter to Vulgatypha. We thought it might restore the balance between them, giving her what she wanted, but Eryi's army of dead men got to us first. They took your daughter.' Ruhago reached for a skin of something, took a long drink, then passed it clockwise to the youth still cradling his elbow.

For a moment, no one spoke. The fire crackled and the wind shrieked through the opening. Viratia had a hundred questions, but hardly knew where to begin with them. Part of her wanted to leave again immediately in search of Pherri.

'That's it?' said Naeem. 'Sounds like you're telling me both Erland's gods are murderous bastards who need to be kept under lock and key.'

Ruhago shifted again on his stool. 'Aye, that's about it,' he said. Garimo passed the skin to Delara, who declined and handed it to Aimya. 'Maghira said we had to wait for you, and now here you are.'

'Vulgatypha says she can save Pherri,' said Maghira. 'But you have to come with us. She says we're to bring you to her.'

Viratia realised she was clenching her hands so tightly she was pressing her fingernails into her palms. *Vulgatypha.* The name sounded ominous in Viratia's head, as if even to think of her might draw the goddess's attention. She thought for a moment to offer a prayer, but to whom? Her stomach rumbled, and she realised she was overcome with hunger. 'Do you have any food?' she asked.

Maghira frowned. 'Did you understand what Ruhago just told you? Your daughter—'

'But you're not proposing to take me to my daughter,' said Viratia. 'And you kidnapped her, so why should I trust you?' Her voice rose. 'And if you want me to come with you to this Vulgatypha, you'll give us all some forsaken fucking food.'

Maghira looked at her, a desire to bite back at Viratia dancing in her wide, expressive eyes. Then it faded. 'There's some salted venison. Garimo, help me please.' The siblings disappeared into the back of the hall.

Viratia looked across the fire to Delara. 'You knew, didn't you? You knew there were two powers on Eryispek. That's why you left.'

Delara looked at her. 'I'd suspected for decades. I felt the powers that burnt deep beneath the rock and high above. It wasn't till Gelick Whitedoe started this madness that I knew though. She whispered to me.'

Viratia's heart was thudding behind her eyes. 'What did she say?'

'I barely knew at the time. It was so faint that I didn't even notice it, but it became a compulsion. It was only when I failed and felt her rage that I realised. Vulgatypha sent me to stop Pherri learning magic.'

As the words left Delara's lips, anguish lanced through Viratia's skull. Delara had been right. Viratia had to clasp her hands together to stop herself tearing at her own face. She felt a firm hand on her shoulder, and Naeem placed the skin of ale in her hand.

'Not your fault,' he told her, his voice heavy with regret. 'None of us knew. I was never one for the gods really, but my dad was. Feels like my head's been turned upside down.'

Aimya spat into the fire. 'That's for these gods. Always knew I was right not to believe in any of the cunts.'

Viratia drank some ale, wishing it was something stronger. This was impossible. What interest could two gods have in her daughter, fighting over her like crows over a carcass? She wiped her mouth. 'And Theodric... was he Eryi's man?'

'You can ask him yourself,' said Ruhago.

He led them to a chamber divided from the main hall by a thin curtain, and as Ruhago pushed it aside, Viratia felt a deep sense of foreboding. There were a few candles lit within, revealing a simple room with a low table and thin sleeping cot.

It took Viratia a moment to realise the man on the cot was alive. Beneath a thin blanket, his body was so gaunt that she swore she could hear the rattle of bones with each shallow breath. One arm was strapped to his chest by a sling, and as Viratia approached, she realised that his torso had been caved in on one side.

'Maghira says there's nothing we can do for him,' said Ruhago. 'He refuses to die though. Thought he'd go today, but he's clung on again.'

Theodric's eyelids shot open, revealing a pair of orbs so bloodshot they were more red than white. 'Lady Viratia...' His voice was as thin as spiderweb. 'I'm sorry... Tried to save her...'

Part of Viratia wanted to scream at him, to rage at him for bringing Pherri here, for ever teaching her daughter magic in the first place. It was pointless now though. Theodric would die, perhaps today. 'Have you given him something for the pain?' she asked Ruhago.

'We don't have anything like that.'

'Good.' Viratia looked to her companions. 'Aimya. Return to Merivale. Tell them of what's happened here, what you've heard. If Eryi uses Pherri to break his bonds... They will need all their strength for what's coming.' She paused. Hessian would never believe it. 'Go to Queen Ciera; you must tell what we face, and persuade her.'

'And where will you go?' asked Aimya.

Viratia looked down at her hands. They were dry and chapped, and when she moved her fingers the joints ached like they had been stuck with iron pins. She had come too far to balk now. Pherri needed her, even more than Viratia had imagined. These vengeful gods would not have her daughter.

'Naeem and I are going to see Vulgatypha. She might be Pherri's last hope.'

CHAPTER 45

'Through the tunnel...' the boy whispered again. 'Through the tunnel...' His cracked lips never seemed to moisten, no matter how much water they dribbled into his mouth, and his hair was sodden with fetid sweat.

It was all Cag had been saying for three days. He lay in Orsian's bed, eyes closed, covered in every fur they could find, with two dozen candles burning beside him on the twin bedstands.

On a chair next to him, Tansa clutched his hand between hers. It was burning, like grasping freshly forged iron. She took what solace she could from that; it meant he was still alive.

'Through the tunnel...' he whispered again.

Lorna, the young apothecarist, bent over him, laying a hand against his cheek. There were hundreds of wounded within Piperskeep, but only Cag had been granted the honour of Orsian Andrickson's own bed, and that made him special enough for Lorna's private attendance twice a day.

Tansa had sent the rest of them away; the stern, pious

Brides of Eryi with their judgemental eyes and their endless praying, and the ancient Eryian priests who insisted that Cag's humours were unbalanced and he needed to be bled. Most of the true healers had been nearby when the Ram's Gate had fallen, and few had managed to escape unharmed.

Lorna made an indecipherable noise, pushed back her single blonde plait, and pressed two fingers to each side of Cag's neck. His breath was slow and steady, but as putrid as Merivale's moat.

'I don't understand why he's not getting better,' bemoaned Tansa, clutching Cag's wrist more tightly. 'You took the arrow out three days ago.'

'The Imperials' poisons are beyond my learning,' said Lorna, now rubbing a soothing balm into Cag's temples, lips, and behind his ears. 'I have seen tens of men fall to them these past days. It is likely only his size that has kept him alive this long.' She sat back on the edge of the bed. 'I can do no more. He is in the hands of the Norhai now.'

Tansa felt her bottom lip beginning to quiver. 'There must be something else we can do.'

'Keep the candles burning, and the blankets piled high. And pray that he sweats the toxins out.'

The apothecarist left, and Tansa hung her head between her legs, taking deep breaths to hold back the tears. When she felt ready, she looked over to where Esma was playing with two dolls on the carpet. Tansa had promised the girl that she and Cag would be fine by themselves, but still Esma would not leave her side.

'Esma.'

The girl looked up.

'I have to leave for a bit. Could you come and sit with Cag?'

The girl nodded. 'Maybe Poppy and Buttercup can help wake him up.'

When Tansa stepped out, Esma was sitting beside Cag, walking the two dolls across the furs. Cag murmured something, and Tansa did not need to be next to him to know what it had been.

'Through the tunnel...'

Tansa did not require Cag's fevered advice to know that it was time to go, but she would not leave without him. She knew the tunnel he spoke of; she had seen Hessian's secret way, a cramped stone passage below the earth stretching into the boundless darkness. And yet Cag held her here. For as long as he drew breath, Tansa would not leave.

She would never forget the moment she had helped Hessian from the tunnel below Piperskeep. When she had seen him last, he had stood tall and proud, laughing on his balcony as her brother suffocated and died, but up close he was only a beggarly old man, with cadaverous circles beneath his eyes and an ill sheen to his grey skin. Pitiful as he was, she might have killed him there, if not for the guards at his side, but when she had seen his delight at hearing Orsian was alive she could not help but be glad with him, almost as if there were a kinship between them.

Tansa had often imagined, during those long, sleepless nights after Tam's death, what she would do to the man responsible; the weapons she would use, and the words of vengeance she would whisper in his ear as the life left his eyes. She had never though expected to help him. Yet when it had mattered, she had chosen Orsian over Tam, the living over the dead, and the guilt of that was like a noose cutting into her neck.

We're all dead anyway, she reflected as she stalked the

halls searching for someone who might be able to give her more blankets and candles for Cag. The Imperium's drums had thundered outside their walls for so long they had become just one of the noises of the keep one learnt to ignore, but they were still there, an unrelenting reminder that Merivale had fallen, and with it, all hope.

The Imperium held the city now. Their purple banners hung over every watchtower and high building, like brightly feathered birds ready to peck the slow-decaying carcass of Piperskeep to the bone. It was said the final battle would be fought between the fortress's inner and outer gates; not even the most optimistic *hymerika* seemed to believe they would hold the Imperials outside the curtain wall.

Tansa continued her search, wondering where one would keep blankets and candles in such a vast castle, but when she descended to the floor below, the sight that met her brought her to a stop. Dozens of women and children lined the corridor, bundled in rags, with fearful eyes and nostrils dripping snot. Several children were crying. A harried servant was walking among them, ladling small portions of thin stew into trenchers.

'Please can you spare some more,' pleaded a woman clutching a bundled babe. 'My granddaughter, she has a—'

'That's all there is!' insisted the servant, already hurrying on to the next person. 'There'll be more this evening!'

'But the babe, she—' The woman's appeals descended into a flood of sobbing, as more pitiful figures shuffled forward towards the servant's cauldron of stew.

Tansa watched, feeling disgusted with herself. *Blankets and candles should be the least of my worries.*

It was disturbing, how quickly it was possible to become accustomed to being companion to a lord, sleeping in his feather bed, having your food brought by servants, and your injured friend receiving the personal attention of any healer you desired, while every other wounded man was crowded into the great hall, divided and treated based on how likely they were to die.

If not for Orsian's name, I would be in this corridor and Cag would be dead downstairs.

But there was nothing she could do for them. Not even the stores of Piperskeep could feed so many mouths, already diminished by the famine of the winter just passed. Tansa slowly backed her way up the stairs. Cag's life would not rise or fall by the measure of a blanket or candle. She would not ask anything of a servant again, not while so many went cold and hungry just a stone's throw from her room.

As she reached the top step, a familiar voice called to her from along the corridor. 'Tansa!'

It was Orsian, of course, pale and dark-eyed, but still brimming with hope and vigour. He stank like the deepest depths of Pauper's Hole now; he had not washed or removed his armour in days, sleeping in shifts with the rest of the men when they were not manning the curtain wall.

The saviours of Merivale, she had heard the men calling him and Errian, though Merivale was lost. Orsian had saved the eastern wall, slowing the Imperium advance, and Errian had commanded a desperate rearguard from the Ram's Gate that had given time for people to reach the shelter of Piperskeep.

She smiled weakly as he approached, the most she could summon. When she looked at Orsian the *hymerika* lord, it was hard to believe she had ever known a boy called Ranulf. She had long ceased to be angry about that, about any of it, since Cag had fallen. Even after many sleepless days with his life resting on the edge of one knife or one lucky arrow, Orsian the *hymerika* still suited him better than Ranulf ever had.

There is no place for me here, she thought as she returned his kiss.

'Where's Pitt?' she asked, suddenly realising the boy who had become Orsian's shadow was not there.

'Sleeping,' Orsian assured her. 'He's refused to take rest for three days; I had to hold him wrapped in a blanket until he dozed off.'

Tansa felt an inch of tension ease out of her. She knew what it was to lose a brother; she did not want Esma to experience the same.

'I just looked in on Cag,' he continued. 'He looks... calm.'

It felt like years ago they had found ways to joke together even as Cag's life depended on their plotting. A siege left little room for laughter. 'How is it on the wall?' she asked.

'I gave the command to Errian an hour ago.' The brothers fought in eight-hour shifts, never together. 'We're holding best we can, but the outer gate won't last forever. That's not what the king wants to hear though.' Orsian coughed. 'Lord Gurathet died last night. One of their legionnaires fell from a ladder and pulled him off the parapet.'

It was strange, the way these noble folk spoke, as if Lord Gurathet had been the only one slain and not one of dozens. Orsian might have commanded common men and been loved by them, but he was still a lord.

They were interrupted by an impatient call from the far end of the corridor. 'Orsian! Orsian!'

Hessian strode towards them, tall and terrible, murder in his eyes. Instinctively, Tansa moved behind Orsian. He was ghost-gaunt, and his cane shook in his palsied hand, yet he was almost unrecognisable from the grateful old man she had found below the castle. There was a presence to him that made Tansa feel as though she were standing in the eye of a storm.

'Orsian! You should have been in my solar a half-hour ago, so I must fetch you like a bloody servant, and I then find you cavorting in the corridor with this... this...' His eyes found Tansa's, and she froze under his gaze.

He sneered at her, and faster than Tansa would have believed he was capable of, Hessian flung out a hand to whip Orsian about the ear. 'We're in the middle of a siege, you fool! My solar, now! I need your report.'

Orsian the lord merely nodded. There was blood on his ear where Hessian's ring had caught him. 'At once, Majesty.' He clasped his hands behind him, and without a look back at Tansa followed Hessian down the corridor, and disappeared up a flight of stairs.

For several moments, Tansa stood in shock, scarcely able to breathe. *He did not even recognise me.* Of course not. She was nobody, as Tam had been, worthy of no more than a sneer or a length of rope. That was the man who had slain her brother, who she had helped from the tunnels, and now only stood there as he berated Orsian. In the presence of her brother's killer, she had done nothing, twice. Tansa walked the few yards back to Cag's sickroom, shame coursing through her like icy water.

Esma was asleep, curled up in the crook of Cag's huge torso, the two dolls clutched between her fists. All that broke the room's stillness was the soft crackle of candles and Cag's laboured breathing.

Tansa retook her chair. 'We should never have come here,' she whispered.

'*Through the tunnel...*' came his weak reply. The yellow sheen of his skin was like curdled milk.

'You wouldn't have stood there. You'd have killed him.'

'*Through the tunnel...*'

'Please, say something else. Anything else.'

But Cag did not speak again.

The dying had been long, but the death when it came was as short and swift as a gust of wind slamming shut a door. Cag's chest expanded under the furs, and for a moment his eyes opened, and he took in a breath so deep Tansa thought it might never end. Then it did, and Cag of Cliffark lay still.

Tansa blinked away tears, but managed to get the words out. 'May Eryi take him from this earth and above the clouds.' Cag had always slept soundly. Tam had said it was like trying to wake the dead.

She sniffed, and touched a cold hand to Esma's cheek. The girl rubbed at her eyes with her fist and murmured something.

'He's gone, my sweet,' Tansa whispered. She picked her up and laid her sleeping frame on a second, smaller mattress under the window, away from Cag's corpse.

She might have sent for servants and asked for his body to be prepared for burning, but that could wait. Tansa gathered up the heavy pile of blankets into her arms, leaving Cag cold in his watchman uniform. Tam had seemed smaller in death, but Cag's corpse seemed larger if anything, like some ancient, excavated giant.

Carrying the vast pile of furs, Tansa descended again to the corridor of Merivale refugees. They were unmoved from earlier, with so many children still wailing that Tansa wondered she did not hear Cag rising from death at the sound of it.

They stared at her with glassy eyes. 'I brought furs,' Tansa declared, trying not to feel foolish. 'I thought—'

'Can we eat them?' demanded a young woman with a child at each tit. 'Come back when you've food, whoever the shit you are.'

Under the woman's ire, Tansa's old street instinct took over. 'Well don't bloody well take them then.' She dropped the furs indignantly to the flagstones. 'I just thought—'

She was interrupted by a deep tolling of bells. Some children were shocked to silence, while others only redoubled their screaming or began anew. Somewhere, dogs were barking, and Tansa swore she heard the rattle of armour and weapons as warriors roused from their slumber.

A girl barely older than Tansa who had sneaked forward to claim a fur had gone white as a sheet. 'One of them warriors told me that when the bells ring, it means they're through the outer gate.' The blanket trembled in her hand. 'They'll make slaves of us all.'

'Hush, child,' said an old woman. 'Bells could mean anything.'

The corridor descended into bad-tempered arguments over whether bells meant their deliverance or their doom.

The rattle of weapons and the tread of heavy boots gave them their answer. Tansa threw herself against the wall as a troop of *hymerikai* descended the stairs. She looked for Orsian, but these warriors were even younger than he was, with smooth cheeks, their armour bright as the day it had been forged, and their wide eyes glistening white with fear.

Tansa stared after them. *They're all dead*, she realised, watching the spears shake in their hands as they passed.

Within an hour, or a day, each of them would be dead as Tam and Cag, brought down before they had even had a chance to live.

And as she watched them depart towards their doom, she knew, whether Piperskeep fell or prevailed, that there was one task she must do before she fled. Not only for vengeance, but for justice; justice for Tam and Cag and the rest, all those who died in the name of a nobility that promised safety while delivering only misery.

Without a word to the women, she returned upstairs. She claimed her knife from her cloak that hung on the back of the door, and began a twisting walk through the grey halls of Piperskeep.

In corridors and staircases she passed endless soldiers running towards the yard that led to the outer gate. They paid her no mind, and when Tansa thought she saw Orsian among them she threw herself into an alcove until they passed. Her knowledge of the keep was limited, but she moved instinctively, searching for the stairs that might lead to a high tower.

A servant girl rushed past, and Tansa grabbed her arm, causing her to gasp and drop the bundle of wood she carried. 'I'll give you these if you exchange your dress for mine,' said Tansa, eyeing the dyed red wool of a Sangreal servant and producing from a pocket a pair of gold coins with Hessian's head on them.

The girl hesitated, even as her fingers moved towards the coins. 'I'll get in trouble.'

'What do you care? The whole keep's about to be swarming with Imperials. Do you *want* to be a slave? Take the coins and run.'

The girl glanced each way down the corridor. A long

trumpet blast sounded, so close it was hard to tell if it came from within the keep or without. 'Quickly then.'

They swapped clothes in the shadow of an alcove, Tansa making sure to turn out her pockets and retrieve her knife before thrusting the bundle of clothes into the girl's arms.

'I'll need your wood as well,' she told the girl.

'It's yours.' The girl looked around furtively, then set out at a run around a corner.

'The Norhai grant you good luck,' Tansa whispered after her. She walked briskly away, the close sound of men marching to the gate drowned out by the blood pounding in her ears.

Twice she had to throw herself around a corner as a servant hurried past carrying something or lighting candles. If she was mistaken for a true servant and put to work the disguise would be wasted.

It took her longer than she would have hoped, but she navigated her way to the bottom of a set of spiral stairs. Tansa gazed upward at a row of bright wall sconces that lent little warmth to the forbidding steps before her. With a deep breath, she pulled her bundle of firewood close, and placed her foot on the first stair.

Don't think, she told herself. *If I think, my courage will fail me.*

Atop the stairs were two more young *hymerikai*, both pale, blond, and so slender Tansa fancied she could have drowned them in a bath like a pair of rats. 'I've brought firewood,' she said, lowering her eyes in her best imitation of a downtrodden Piperskeep servant.

The first *hymerika*'s eyes narrowed. 'They don't need firewood.'

'The king requested it.'

The boy jutted out his jaw. 'I don't remember any command going down about firewood.'

'Just let her in, Hal,' said the second one. 'What if he shouts at us again?'

Hal assessed her critically up and down. He scowled. 'Well, get on with it then.'

The second guard opened the door a crack, and Tansa slipped inside. The door clicked closed behind her.

She took in Hessian's solar: a vast room filled with high bookshelves, soft furnishings, a table in the shape of Erland, and a fire next to a pile of wood and kindling as high as Tansa's navel. It was fortunate for her the two guards were so unobservant.

It was also empty. Tansa frowned, until she noticed the doors to the balcony were open a crack, and heard the faint murmur of conversation. She felt a moment of dread. *If Orsian is out there...* If Orsian was out there she would lay down her bundle and leave, then find some way to explain later why she had exchanged her own clothes for a servant's dress.

Tansa strained her ears. There were two voices, and far below them the clamour of clashing steel, and the desperate cries of the warring and wounded. She caught the terse bark of Hessian, and the high tones of a woman, with the clipped vowels of a lady. Or a queen.

Tansa's heart was like a hammer against an anvil, but she lowered the wood to the floor, and turned to slide the black iron door bolt quietly across.

Drawing her knife from the bodice of her dress, she crept across the soft red carpet towards the balcony.

As she approached the door, something stirred in the corner of her eye, and Tansa froze. Time stopped, but after a moment, when no one called for her to halt, she turned towards the source.

She had not seen it before, when the lower half of the bookshelf had been hidden by the table. It looked like little more than a tight bundle of rags. Then the bundle gurgled, and raised a tiny pink fist in the air.

The prince.

For the briefest moment, Tansa could not resist the evil thought that entered her head. *I could end the whole male Sangreal line today.* And who knew how much future evil that might undo? How many future Tams and Cags might live to raise families of their own, instead of dying for a man in a tower who did not even know their name?

The shame of thinking it flooded through her like the poison that had flown through Cag's veins. She looked down at her knife. *I am no murderer. No shedding of blood will bring them back to me.*

'What are you doing?'

Tansa turned, and recoiled as Hessian's long frame loomed over her. With a snarl, he grasped for her knife, his yellow fingernails tearing at her hand as his other hand curled around her throat.

She clung to the knife, barely noticing the skin of her wrist being torn to ribbons while his grip pressed down on her windpipe. She tried to jab the blade into his stomach, but his grasp held her tight. Her other hand punched uselessly at the wrist about her neck. He was stronger than her, stronger than he had any right to be. She could feel her windpipe collapsing. Tiny stars flashed in her eyes.

Desperately, Tansa aimed a kick at his groin. Hessian twisted to avoid it, but it caught him even so, and he released his grip long enough for Tansa to suck down a breath before it tightened again.

Hessian grunted and pushed her hard against the wall. Tansa's head bounced off it painfully. She tried again to drive the knife into him, but his grasp on her wrist was firm; she could feel the blade being turned back against her abdomen. The edges of her vision were darkening, but she released her futile attempts to free her neck, and with both hands tried to retake control of the knife.

Hessian was so close she could taste the wine on his breath. He snarled, and pressed his whole weight upon her as the blade shook in their three hands. Tansa's vision shrunk to pinpricks.

He's killing me. There were tears on her cheeks, and she felt her bladder relax and warm urine soak into her underclothes. Her weakening fingers holding the knife seemed like they belonged to somebody else. *I'm coming, Tam.*

Then the baby began to wail.

Hessian's bloodshot eyes looked away from Tansa as the prince's ear-splitting shrieks filled the room, and with the last of her strength, she drove the knife into his gut.

Something hot gushed over Tansa's shaking hands, and Hessian's eyes widened like carriage wheels. The fingers at her throat slackened, and she sank to her knees, taking great, wheezing breaths. She pressed her hands against the stone, never so glad to feel the cold of Piperskeep against her skin.

With a great effort, she pushed herself up, feeling almost a stranger in her own body. She needed the knife. She whirled on the spot searching for it, awful bile rising in her throat.

But the blade was still buried in Hessian's stomach. Blood was spreading like a wine stain across his robes, pooling beneath him like a lake. He was not dead, though. His shrewd eyes bored into her like arrows to a bullseye.

'End it,' he hissed. 'End it, whoever you are.' He coughed, and a spurt of blood burst from his mouth.

Tansa looked down at him. 'It's a better death than you gave my brother.' It hurt to speak, and her voice came out hard and raspy.

The king laughed, and it turned into a cough as more crimson spurted up. 'Who was he? Some boy? They usually are.' He tried to laugh again, and before he could drown on the blood in his mouth, Tansa made an end of it. She pulled the knife from his stomach and drew it across his throat. The skin split like suet, and with a torrent of gore and a deathly sigh, King Hessian Sangreal breathed his last.

Feeling suddenly sick, Tansa rose, and looked down at the king's corpse. His eyes were like two pink marbles, glassy and lifeless. It ought to have been harder, to kill a king. In the end, they were all just blood, skin, and sinew.

Something creaked behind her, and Tansa whirled on the spot. She was in no state to fight again. If they meant to kill her, they were welcome to. Hessian was dead.

Ciera Istlewick stood in the balcony doorway, so serene and beautiful it was as if she had appeared from another world, where knives and revenge and murder did not even exist.

Tansa held the blade out before her. 'Don't come any closer.'

The queen kept her hands clasped in front of her like a priest. 'I remember you now. You're Tam's sister.'

Tansa blinked back tears. 'I was. Your husband killed him.'

'I know.'

Tansa hardly knew what to say to that. She thrust the knife towards Ciera. 'He'd still be alive if not for you.'

'He died for me, yes. But his choices were his own. Might I see to my son?'

In the confusion, Tansa had managed to forget about the child. He was still screaming, fit to bring the whole tower crashing down around them. 'Aren't you going to call the guards?'

Calm as water, Ciera indicated towards a volume on the bookshelf. 'Pull on that book and a door will open. Take the stairs down as far as they will go, then take the left-hand fork and follow the right wall. It will lead you to the tunnel that runs under the city. You've seen it, I believe.'

Tansa watched her warily. 'Why are you helping me?'

'For Tam. I'm sorry.'

Tansa backed away towards the bookshelf. She pulled out the volume the queen had pointed to, and to her amazement the entire wall rotated, revealing a dark, cobwebbed passageway with a set of stairs spiralling downwards.

Ciera had seized her son, and stepped past Hessian's lifeless body to the table, laying the child down to be cleaned and changed. 'Take a torch from the wall. You'll need it.'

Tansa did as she said. The Norhai were smiling on her, she supposed. As she ducked through the open bookshelf, she turned. 'You could come with me? The keep might have fallen by dusk.'

Ciera smiled, in a way that Tansa could not figure out the meaning of. 'I rule in Merivale now. As long as this keep stands, I will be here. I will say goodbye to Orsian for you.'

Orsian. Tansa felt a pang of regret. She turned, and made for the stairs.

CHAPTER 46

For days, Eryi left Pherri alone in her cave. The snowstorm swirled constantly, leaving her imprisoned in a constant semi-gloom, hidden from both the sun and night, illuminated only by the ever-burning fire. Pherri measured the passage of time by the meals his undead servants brought her, and though the thought of food touched by their flesh turned her stomach, she ate it all: hunks of fire-cooked venison, with root vegetables, washed down with weak beer. Whatever Eryi's plan for her, he clearly did not intend for her to starve.

Draped in furs, Pherri shivered next to the fire, remembering the horror of his *inflika* inside her head, and how foolish she had been to think of fighting him. Even Theodric had succumbed, and that had been when Eryi worked through Gelick Whitedoe.

For the umpteenth time, she stood and walked to the cavemouth, pulling her furs tight around herself. She stared outward, and, as ever, all she saw was snow. Above and below it danced, driven by the howling wind, obscuring the air itself.

She put her toes to the edge, and steadied herself against the wall when the wind's hard breath threatened to pull her from her feet.

'It is time,' came a voice from behind her.

She whirled round, almost slipping on the ice. Eryi sat at the fire, still garbed in tunic and trousers as if not even the cold could touch him. *It is a glamour*, she reminded herself. Beneath the illusion he was only bones.

'Time for what?' *Time for him to sacrifice me.* Fear rose in Pherri's heart. 'Why now?'

'Today, death casts its long shadow over Erland. Where there is death, men cry for their gods. Do you know how many men will swear oaths to me this day? They will throw themselves upon their foes' swords, all the while praying they could live. And where there is sacrifice, there is change, and the gaps between realities move, inch by inch. Your sacrifice will be the greatest of all.'

Pherri's bottom lip begin to quiver, but she willed it to be still, holding back her childish tears. 'I don't want to die,' she whispered. The cave seemed colder now, though the fire burnt bright as starlight.

Eryi laughed, a high tremor that shook the ground beneath their feet. 'Nobody said anything about dying. I paid for my servants with death, but you have seen the limits of them. Little more than dumb beasts; no eyes to see nor minds to sense.

'With your life, I will pay for my life, and with your body, my body.'

Pherri blinked back her tears, remembering suddenly Theodric's first lesson with her on the power of *shadika*. '*It is too much for a human mind to bear… summoning a human mind as well as a human form is beyond our limits.*'

'You're going to use *shadika*,' she gasped. 'You think you can bring your body from another world. That's what you did with Gelick: you killed his companions, and used *shadika* to replace them with dead copies of him from other realms.'

He nodded, smiling. 'You are a remarkably clever child. *Shadika* to bring a shadow is one thing, but *shadika* to bring a form... To bring a living, breathing creature... The focus is there, but for a magus to bear such energy... impossible. That's why the Lutums had to die. With their corpses, I drew other Gelicks from other worlds. Worlds where he was already dead.

'I did not know it would work... I only suspected. I controlled Gelick, why not other Gelicks? Dumb creatures, but capable of following simple instructions. Suitable for my purpose.

'Now with your sacrifice, I will have a body of my own again. My full powers shall be restored.'

'But you can't! You just said yourself that to bring life is impossible. Theodric told me that to bring a human mind from another world would destroy it.'

'All the better. I have no wish to share my body with another, even another of myself. I have planned this for centuries, but I faced a problem: in almost every future I saw, the magic did not work. Either the body I sought failed, or taking possession of it left me powerless. Even when riding other people, I have some measure of my strength, but restoring my own body and holding my magic looked impossible.

'Until I found you. With you, I shall have my body, and power that would make the Norhai tremble. I have seen it. Magic demands sacrifice, a part of ourselves every time we cast, and with yours, you will herald my descent from this forsaken prison.' His eyes had taken on a wild gleam, as if he was no longer seeing her. 'Too long have I fed on the prayers of men without the means to use my power. Now I shall be a god worthy of the name. All will bow before my coming; Erland, and then the world.' His pale eyes flashed, and outside the wind howled louder than ever, like a chorus of banshees.

Pherri stared at him, backing away slowly. 'You're mad. If you leave this place, Vulgatypha will free herself.'

'Not even she will stand before me.' He smiled, like a brief flash of sun behind a black storm. 'I feared her once, but no more. She will bow with the rest of them, or she will die.'

Pherri remembered Ruhago's words. '*A war that almost split the sky in two, raining meteorites and lightning as men cowered and prayed for the gods' mercy.*' If Eryi went to war with Vulgatypha, the same would happen. She could not allow it. 'I won't do it. I'll never help you.'

'Did I sound as if I was offering you a choice?' Eryi flicked a finger, and the strong limbs of the real Gelick Whitedoe grabbed her from behind, drawing from Pherri a high scream. She struggled, but his grip was as unyielding as iron. This was madness. With a burst of *phisika*, she tried to throw him off, but Eryi's will held her like a fly trapped in a web.

'Take her to the summit.' In a flicker of magic, Eryi was gone, and Gelick dragged her from the cave.

Stumbling, she let herself be led up the slick, icy trail, thinking furiously for some escape. *Eryi needs me alive*, she thought. That would be true sacrifice: to kill herself rather than be used in his twisted reincarnation ritual. She threw herself against Gelick, but his grip held firm.

'You still live,' she said, looking up at him. 'We could escape together.'

But Gelick Whitedoe gave no reply. Eryi's grasp upon his mind had left him as senseless as his dead brethren.

Atop, Eryi waited, seated upon his throne of ice. Overhead, the stars were already beginning to shine under the rose-tinted twilight, sending scattered points of twinkling light across the summit.

'There is a battle, in Merivale,' he said flatly, as the unGelicks swarmed and led her forward. 'Your brothers are there.'

'Orsian?' The question was out of her mouth before she could stop herself.

'He lives, for now.' A vision flashed in the sky: Orsian, a little older and taller than she had known him, beset from all sides, his sword flashing like a burning brand as he dodged death by inches, sweat pouring from his brow. 'We can make this easy, Pherri. If you cooperate, your brother will survive. If not...' He gestured, and a blade cut inside Orsian's guard, grazing his cheek just below his eye.

The threat was clear. Pherri nodded, her throat suddenly dry as sand. Her refusal would not defeat him.

'Good.' A silver dagger materialised in his fist. 'Hold out your hand.'

Pherri did as she was bid, and with a flash of the blade a small incision appeared on her palm, pulsing tiny beads of blood. Eryi then raised his other hand, and ran his own palm down the blade. The cut hissed, and the amber-red liquid that spilled from it was viscous, more like bone marrow than blood. He enveloped Pherri's hand in his. His touch was at once both cold and warm, and sent a numbness all the way up Pherri's arm.

'Blood magic,' he said, with faint distaste. 'It was old when I was young, but powerful, given the right source. We are bound, Pherri.' She could feel the liquids mingling, his strange ichor somehow finding its way into her cut and entering her bloodstream. Disgusted, she tried to pull away, but his grip was firm.

'Watch,' he said softly. The blade was gone, and in his hand rested his high staff once more. He twirled it in his fingers and slammed it on the ground.

Once again, the world before Pherri swam with visions, running past one another in a swirling vortex. It was dizzying, faster even than last time, but Pherri could not tear her eyes away. What she saw too was different, not scenes and events, but all of Erland, its centuries rolling back before her eyes. One by one, the four bridges over the Pale River came down, while the course of its flow changed, and settlements fell and rose with the coming and passing of different tribes. She watched the constructions of Piperskeep and Merivale in reverse, their walls and towers falling until all that was left was a forested hillside.

The passage of time slowed, and she felt Eryi exerting his will upon it, searching for something. Pherri had been transfixed by the rolling back of the years, but remembered suddenly that she had to stop him: regardless of Orsian's fate, Eryi could not succeed. Tentatively, she tried to break their connection, to drag herself back from the fascination of the past to the cold mountaintop of the present.

'No.' Eryi did not speak, but his voice echoed inside her head, and Pherri felt the weight of his will pressing down on her, holding her in his visions of long-gone days. She pulled harder, resisting him, and for a moment thought she felt him struggle to bring his will to bear before time began cycling again.

'*I warned you.*'

Pherri screamed as she felt Eryi rip her consciousness in two, holding one half with him in the past as the other was wrenched back to the present. The sensation was terrifying, like having an eyeball torn from your skull and turned back upon your face. Eryi continued to roll back the years, while in the present, his gaze turned upon Merivale, and Pherri could not resist his will that she watch.

She saw through the eyes of an enemy soldier, with a strange, curved sword and armour bright as the sun. Inside the shattered outer gate of Piperskeep, between the high walls of the passage that led to the castle, two shield walls formed to face one another, screaming wordlessly. At the centre of the East Erland line, Pherri recognised Orsian through the open face of his helmet. Errian was next to him, taller than Orsian, his hair golden and a blade once more in his hand.

'*I could make one kill the other. Alas, we do not have time for such poetry.*' Like a vice, Eryi's will pressed upon the strange enemy soldier, and though it offended every instinct for self-preservation he held, he threw his sword, sending it spinning straight for Orsian's eye.

Before it even left his hand, Pherri knew the throw was true, and that the wound would be mortal. Somewhere, someone screamed with anguish. Herself. She took one last look into her brother's eyes, and as he blinked beneath his helmet, so did Pherri.

The next thing Pherri knew, the sword was spinning towards her, and with the whip-fast reflexes of a trained soldier she lashed out with her own blade to send it clattering to the ground.

She glanced down at the hand that held the sword, and saw the mail-armoured sleeve of the king's *Hymeriker*. Her arm rippled with taut muscle as she turned her hand, honed by hours of training and combat, physical strength she had never even imagined.

The sensation of being watched made her look up, and across the ground, she saw the man who had thrown the sword staring back at her through eyes pale and pitiless – Eryi's eyes.

Pherri watched through Orsian as the enemy force advanced upon the Erlanders, with bright shields and high purple hair sprouting from their helmets. Their numbers dwarfed the *Hymeriker*, and beyond the shattered gate, thousands more pressed forward, enough to cut through the Erlanders like threshers through wheat.

But the *Hymeriker* were not trained to fear. They were trained to fight. A war cry burst from their lips as one, and the Erlanders forged forward to meet the Imperium.

The world shook as the two lines of shields crashed together in a cacophony of wood and iron, and soon the air was filled with the high melody of sword and spear, together with the desperate, clamouring shrieks of men. Pherri screamed with the Erlanders as they fought for every inch of Erlish soil, and for a moment forgot that she was a girl of twelve, hundreds of miles away.

The clang of steel against Orsian's helmet brought her back to herself, and as her brother's assailant pulled back for another strike, Pherri acted on instinct. She lunged with a sword, and the man fell back with his face gushing blood.

But it had not been Orsian's blade. Through her brother's eyes, Pherri looked up in astonishment at its wielder, Errian, before a second foe pushed forward with his shield and forced Orsian back on the defensive.

'*What are you doing?*' demanded Eryi. Pherri felt the alarm in his voice as it pounded against her skull.

What had Theodric told her about *phisika*? It could not achieve what was physically impossible. But this was not impossible; outnumbered though they were, this was only swords and spears and men's flesh. The power of Eryispek hummed through Pherri's body like a tidal wave.

'Saving my brothers.'

Pherri withdrew from Orsian, pausing for only the merest moment as she felt her name on his lips. 'Pherri?' She opened herself outwards, letting the clamour of combat fill her consciousness, and then she set to work.

Through *spectika* and *phisika*, she became the battle. Every swing of a sword, every thrust of an Imperial spear, and every arrow that threatened to fall upon a *hymerika*. She felt them all before they happened and all at once, as if within the walls of Piperskeep time ceased to exist, and there was only the constant churn of the shield wall, from now stretching into eternity. And every time a *hymerika* would have fallen beneath the frenzy of Imperial steel, Pherri was there, guiding their arm, or the arm of the man next to them, or even an arrow in flight as an errant gust of wind caught it and sent it hurtling towards the enemy who dared to try and strike an Erlander.

A battle is a thousand small moments, whether determined by strength, or skill, or simply chance. And the Erlanders won every single one. They poured over the Imperials like a sea of steel, like a great thousand-legged spider driven by a single awareness, and soon the Imperials were running, turning for the gate as if the fires of the heavens had been unleashed upon them. Sensing victory, the *Hymeriker* rushed forward, and Pherri howled with them, feeling every single strained voice as if it were her own.

And then, once the *Hymeriker*'s victory seemed all but certain, exhaustion threatened to overwhelm her. Suddenly, Pherri was aware of the frailty of her own body, of the overwhelming energy she was having to expend to guide every sword strike.

'Be safe, Orsian,' she whispered, though she had no idea if he heard her. She could only pray to whatever power there was left to believe in that they would both survive to meet again.

Her fight was on the Mountain. She tore herself away.

The force of her consciousness remerging with her own body blew Pherri's breath from her, and in a moment Eryi was on her, his will dragging her back through time. The windows to other worlds had become a second layer upon her vision, Eryispek's summit flickering back and forth between icy cold and a smoking crater of magma as the years rushed back before her eyes.

'*It's almost time.*' His voice was a whisper, but she could feel the desperate longing beneath his words. The visions were slowing now, like he was searching for something close. '*Your brothers' battle for Erland is irrelevant.*'

Pherri's mind raced, still reeling from having her mind split, the unnerving sensation of being inside her brother's body and then seemingly nowhere and everywhere all at once, and abruptly having the two halves shoved back together again. '*Fight him,*' Theodric had told her. She had shown she could do that by saving Orsian and turning the battle, now she only had to thwart him here. But Eryi's hunger merely strengthened his intent; trying to fight against his dragging of her back through time was like swimming against a riptide.

Abruptly, the whirl of visions ceased, and Pherri stumbled as the world solidified. They were back on Eryispek, but a second image flickered in her eye: Eryi, trekking up a mountain of ash and flame, towards a great crater belching magma and spewing dust into the sky.

'*A world where I failed,*' said Eryi, with wry amusement. '*Left to her own devices, Vulgatypha would have brought our world to an end, as she did in this one. I will save my body from this fool's failure.*'

Pherri felt the impossible sensation of being thrust from her own reality into the other, as Eryi's *shadika* sought to bargain her for the copy of himself. *I'll die*, she realised. *If my mind isn't burnt out by the trauma, my body will burn with that world.* Desperately, she threw everything she had into resisting Eryi, every drop of focus and will and strength to fix herself in her own reality.

She might as well have fought against the wind. Eryi's power was as irresistible as the tide, and Pherri found herself being pulled towards this other Erland. She could feel the heat of the volcano upon her face, and the burning dust filling her nostrils. She closed her eyes, trying to disregard the sensation as she fought hopelessly to stay in her own reality.

To her shock, a second vision appeared: Eryispek became a verdant hillside, with grass as high as her waist and a rainbow motley of bright meadow flowers. A high yellow sun bathed her in warmth, and a gentle breeze filled her ears with the sounds of chirping crickets and the rustle of wildlife through the grassland.

She was out of options. Eryi might force her out of her

own world, but he would not choose her destination. Pherri fixed this other reality in her mind, and when with a final burst of energy Eryi sought to send her from her own world, she did not resist.

For a moment, Pherri was not sure it had worked, and then she collapsed, and felt soft grass beneath her hands. Behind her, the roar of Eryispek's winds faded to a whisper, replaced with the high, anguished scream of Eryi. She heard him raging, clawing for this other world, and beneath it all, felt his terror. Easily, worlds away from Eryi's power, she did what she could not do before, and severed his hold upon her mind. His screams fell silent.

My mind is still here, she thought, dazedly, gripping the warm earth as if to stop herself from falling off. *Unless the mad do not know they are mad?*

With that thought, exhaustion struck her like an avalanche. This fertile new world faded to black, and Pherri slipped into oblivion.

CHAPTER 47

Helana tossed and turned under her thin, scratchy sheet. She had never been the soundest of sleepers, but when she did, the dreams were waiting. She had never dreamt of Jarhick after first taking casheef, but now he was in all of them. Sometimes he was whole and hale, but more often he was dead or dying. The worst was when she had the power to save him, but the faceless assassins slipped through her defences like mist, and with their shadowy blades slit his throat, before Helana woke covered in a layer of glistening sweat.

Frustratedly, she bundled up the blanket and threw it into the corner, then rose to stand barefoot at the window, looking over the forest.

'They're both mad,' she told herself for the dozenth time. 'Raving.'

She'ab had told her more, after the revelation that they were seeking her cousin Pherri, of bound gods and magic and Eryispek wrapped together in a tale that made less sense the more you considered it. The potency of casheef liquor was well-known; she had begun to wonder if extended use of its leaf had perhaps driven She'ab to insanity.

Helana could barely recall the last time she had seen Pherri. It had been two, perhaps even three years ago, and she had been a furtive, bookish child with no more interest in Helana than Helana had in her. The idea that fearful girl was the key to some cosmic masterplan was ridiculous.

But then why did She'ab and Ba'an know who she was?

A knock at Helana's door nearly made her jump out of her skin. Scowling, she wrapped a blanket over her night-dress, and gripping a blunt eating knife stepped to her door.

It was She'ab, as expected. He looked as tired as Helana felt, with circles under his eyes and his grey plaits frayed and unkempt. He looked down at the knife Helana was gripping. 'I hope that is not meant for me.'

Helana stepped back to grant him entry. 'One cannot be too careful.'

'Indeed. Our last messenger to Barthrumb has not returned, just like the others. We can only conclude that Hu'ra means to make war.'

Helana had not considered Hu'ra capable of a great deal, but the night she had spoken with Ba'an and She'ab, the chieftain's first son had escaped Thrumbalto to join the rebels in Barthrumb as their leader. It was said that more Thrumb were gathering there every day. 'I don't even understand how he's doing it.'

She'ab had taken a seat on her bed. He sighed wearily, showing his age in a way he never had before. 'There are some who have long been dissatisfied with the concentration of power in Thrumbalto. It was also they who suffered the worst from your brother's invasion, and they resented Ba'an for making common cause with Rymond, an Erlander, for they do not care for the distinction between East and West and Sangreal and Prindian. Now Erlanders are pouring across the border, fleeing the Imperium, and the rebels have found a new matter to be upset about. That Ba'an is also hosting the sister of the man they call the Butcher of Barthrumb is the bird that broke the branch. Still, I never thought Hu'ra had the stomach to challenge his father.'

'Hu'ra would be a terrible ruler.'

'Undoubtedly, but his followers see these as desperate times, and in desperate times all people want is change. They seldom look for the consequences.'

Helana stepped to a corner table to pour them each a measure of honey liquor. 'You do have a way of making everything seem worse.'

'Indeed. But I did not come here to speak to you of Hu'ra.' He accepted the cup Helana handed to him.

'No, you came to speak to me of casheef, and Jarhick, and my cousin Pherri, and how the very fact that we are having this conversation is proof that our world is crooked, as if an axle is loose and it's hurtling towards certain destruction.' She took an irritated sip of the sweet liquor. 'Just explain it to me again, briefly.'

The air in the room felt cold. A sharp gust of wind screeched through the chamber, setting the candle flames dancing. Helana stepped to the open window and closed the shutter.

This was the third time Helana had made She'ab tell her everything again. His full tale sounded like a fever dream. 'A thousand years ago or more, the god you call Er'yi was a man, of the people who split into the Thrumb and the Adrari. We had magic, but our lives were blighted by Vulgatypha, the last of the Norhai. To thwart her, every

Thrumb kept a part of their name to themselves, so that she could not use it to control them. When they sought to imprison her inside the Mountain, they almost succeeded, but it spewed scorching magma and poisonous smoke for days upon days, and threatened to destroy the land they had fought so hard for. Er'yi was the magus who saved them. He gave himself to seal her, binding himself to the Mountain for eternity.

'His sacrifice cost the Thrumb everything. Our magic was dissipated in lending our strength to Er'yi, and within a century we were forced west by the men who swept in from the sea, our numbers decimated. The Adrari were those who remained, taking refuge on the Mountain.

'I believe Er'yi is trying to free himself, and has found a way to influence the world and shape events to his will. Your brother may have died for it. Through casheef, I have seen your cousin Pherri visiting Thrumbalto, but she is not here. She is of huge significance, and if she is significant to us, she is significant to Er'yi. Pherri might be the only one who can restore the binding upon him.'

'And if he's a Thrumb why would you want that?'

'Because he is the only thing keeping Vulgatypha trapped.' She'ab was sitting like a condemned man, his head bowed and his elbows resting upon his locked knees. 'If Er'yi frees himself, the mountain goddess will soon follow. And after a thousand years, how much of that man do you think remains? Eryi the god will be very different to Er'yi the man, perhaps as cruel and vicious as Vulgatypha herself. A shadow will fall over the whole world, a shadow heavy as the heavens and as certain as the dusk that follows day.'

As she listened, Helana watched him carefully. A few times, his voice creaked and almost cracked, and his shoulders were taut as a bowstring. *He believes it entirely.* 'How do you know this? Just from the casheef?'

'In part. Casheef, what I can piece together of our history, the prophecies and the portents and reading the stars. When you saw your brother alive, I was sure. The chieftain was more cautious. He brought you here at my urging, but it took time for me to convince him we needed to bring you into our confidence. It has cost him a lot, allowing you to stay here.'

'So what now?'

'You must take casheef again. With the right direction, you might be able to save Pherri before Er'yi gets to her. I must speak with her.'

She had known what the answer would be. 'And what if I only see Jarhick again?'

'We can—'

She'ab's reply caught in his throat, as the sound of scuffling against the outside walkway floated in through the shuttered window. Helana swiftly seized her knife and flung it open. If Hu'ra had sent assassins, she would meet them blade in hand.

But it was Na'mu's face that met her, and at the sight of Helana's blade Ti'en had to grab him to prevent him toppling backwards.

She'ab was at the window in an instant, and seized Na'mu by the neck. 'What did you hear? What did you hear, gods damn it?'

'Everything,' said Ti'en defiantly. 'We knew something was going on between you two. We followed you.'

'And you never thought that perhaps it was something you did not need to know?' She'ab's face was tight with fury.

'It was something we very much needed to know! You've

been lying to us, to all of us! Years you've spent, since we were children, telling us to worship the forest gods and obey the ancestors, and it was all a lie!'

She'ab was shushing her frantically with his spare hand, and when he tried to cover her mouth Ti'en danced out of the way. 'Just come inside,' he hissed, 'before someone hears you. Gods, you are a wilful, impossible creature.' He let go of Na'mu and Helana went to the door to let them in.

'You're going to help, aren't you?' asked Na'mu of Helana once they were both inside.

Ti'en snorted. 'I don't believe it. I've seen what people get like when they drink casheef liquor. It's all just seeing nonsense.'

'Why would she see her dead brother?' retorted Na'mu.

'Not even the grave could keep that bastard buried.'

She'ab shot her a look. 'That was Helana's brother, Ti'en.'

Ti'en spat on the floor. 'He butchered hundreds of us, and you preach restraint? I'll speak of him as I please.'

It was the first time Helana could recall Ti'en expressing an opinion of Jarhick. They had somehow always avoided the topic. 'It's fine. I know my brother's invasion was wrong.'

'Wrong? It was more than wrong. It was—'

'Ti'en, that will do!' She'ab's eyes blazed. 'I will not let you derail this discussion with what happened last year. Jarhick Sangreal is dead, he and many others. What we have to discuss is greater than all of that.'

Ti'en's sat down, with no small measure of reluctance.

She'ab remained standing. 'You may stay, if Helana allows it. Another word from either of you though and I will throw you from this tree.' He looked back to Helana and continued their conversation as though Ti'en and Na'mu had never appeared. 'With control, you can master what you see with the casheef. The seeing of other worlds is the natural result, but you must resist it. If you focus upon the person you seek in this world, you might be able to communicate with them.' He produced from his shorts another tiny black-orange casheef leaf.

He held it out to her, and Helana took it gingerly. She sniffed it, and gagged at its bitterness, her body recalling how ill the last one had made her feel. 'What will I say to her?'

'Sometimes it is only when we learn the answer that we know the question that should have been on the tip of our tongue all along.'

Helana could only laugh at that. 'As cryptic and unhelpful as ever.'

'Will you do it?'

Helana hesitated. The leaf felt strangely heavy between her fingers. She was not sure she even understood what was being asked of her. 'Why me?'

'You know Pherri, and you have a blood connection with her. Try and focus upon your memory of her.'

There was little chance of that. Pherri had been an irrelevance to her, rarely seen and too young to be of any interest.

Orsian loved her though. He always said how clever she was. Helana had dismissed it at the time, the boastings of a too proud brother. What if Orsian's image of Pherri would help her though? She had not thought of him in months, that foolish boy who had believed he loved her.

She looked down at the leaf. 'Eryi's balls,' she muttered. The worst that could happen was that she would see Jarhick again, and that would not be so bad. She looked once at She'ab, raised the leaf to him in mock salute, and placed it on her tongue.

It was sourer than the one she had taken before, and for a moment Helana thought she might heave the whole thing back up, but she lifted a fist to her mouth, slammed her eyes shut, and somehow kept it on her tongue as it dissolved.

It tasted so awful that she almost forgot she was meant to be focusing on Pherri. She tried to fill her mind with a memory of Orsian, of him saying something about his sister. But the face that kept swimming before her mind's eye was Jarhick, tall and blond and smiling, with some jest ready on the edge of his lips. *No, not him.* She fought against her own longing.

Slowly, and then quickly, the casheef began to take effect. Her memory of Jarhick faded to nothing, and visions of Thrumbalto swam before her: She'ab dangling his feet over the edge of a walkway as people went back and forth like ants below; Ti'en walking between the trees hand-in-hand with Errian.

Then she saw her: a slip of a girl, dressed in the Thrumb style but with her straw-coloured hair unplaited and floating free on the wind, sat laughing with an elderly Thrumb man at the base of the Irmintree.

'Pherri!' Helana cried. She saw her cousin for a moment as Orsian must have seen her, bright and animated and fascinated by everything.

And then Helana's vision exploded into a thousand shards.

Countless Pherris swam before her eyes, as spectral and indistinct as wisps of faraway fog. Pherri, alone in a room of Piperskeep, flipping a coin over and over; Pherri, on a walkway staring over the Ancestors' Forest with She'ab's hand on her thin shoulder; Pherri, struggling through heavy banks of snow as hailstones the size of children's fists showered her.

'*Open your eyes, find her.*' She'ab's voice sounded like it was passing through bubbling water. Helana's eyelids felt as heavy as the elk's corpse, but with an effort she lifted them.

And just like that, she felt her awareness return to Erland, to her version of Erland, not just her tiny tree hut, but all of it at once, every river and blade of grass so close she could touch them.

'*Find her,*' came She'ab's insistent voice.

Armed with her memory of Pherri under the tree, Helana reached out for her.

But Pherri was not there.

'She's gone,' Helana heard herself say. Her mouth felt like it was full of wool.

'*Find her!*'

I am trying. Blindly, Helana reached out with her consciousness. The effect was horribly disorientating, and she felt burning bile rising in her throat that she had to swallow forcefully back down. She shaped Pherri in her mind, and from her visions she knew her: a girl as bold as Orsian and brighter still, with a child's endless curiosity and a will as hard as a warrior's.

Her image of Pherri flickered. It was weak, but she was there, and Helana reached for her.

As fast as blinking, Eryispek loomed before her like a ghostly white shadow, vast as the sky and clouded by a maelstrom of mist and snow, spinning endlessly atop its peak and threatening to cover the whole world with its shadow.

But Eryispek has no summit, she thought, nonsensically. Madly, she forced herself into the white horror, searching for

Pherri so desperately that she felt herself calling her name even as nausea threatened to overwhelm her.

'*Pherri! Pherri! Pherri!*' Somebody was shaking her. Warm blood was flowing from Helana's nostril and trickling onto her lips, its metallic taste a momentary distraction from the vomit at the back of her throat.

The flat summit of Eryispek swelled into view, coated with ice and flashing with the light of a thousand different worlds. And at the centre of it, her cousin Pherri, locked in a battle of wills with something that had once been a man, something that took form only through ash and pure malevolence.

And then with a flash, Pherri was gone, and Helana dived straight after her into the void.

It felt like her body was trying to turn itself inside out. A thousand worlds away, a girl named Helana screamed and fell to the floor, writhing horribly as an old man whose name she could not remember shook her and shouted over and over that she had to wake up. There were other things too, flashing arcs of flame and distant cries and the crackling of burning wood.

Helana felt her whole psyche trembling on the cusp of something, like a wavering rock upon the edge of a volcanic crater.

'*You can't pass between worlds like that!*' she imagined a voice saying, somewhere, in a time and place where words had a meaning. '*Your mind won't survive it!*'

Something in the voice's desperation shook Helana to her senses. She was following Pherri unhesitatingly into the void, and it would destroy her. She tried to draw herself back, but the pull of the other world was unrelenting. Her consciousness was trickling away, flying like a hundred birds from a tree as the leaves fell like a torrent of rain.

Desperately, out of options, Helana threw herself into the abyss, even knowing that it might be the last decision she ever took.

Instead, she felt herself land on her feet, in a room filled with heavy rugs and a roaring fire, with her mother's picture staring down at her, in a body that was hers and yet was not her own.

This is my room. A melodious laugh escaped her lips. She rushed to the looking glass on her dresser, hoping that she was right.

Helana's own face stared back at her. Cheeks a little fuller and eyes a little softer, with hair styled shorter than she would ever have agreed to, but unmistakably her own reflection. She had passed through the void and landed safely inside another version of herself.

'Am I trapped here?' she wondered aloud. But even as she said it, the cacophony in her ears proved it was not so; the shouting and the slamming of flesh into walls and the hot smell of burning in her nose.

She had run out of time. She'ab's casheef had already lasted far longer than it ought to. But Pherri – her world's Pherri – had passed through to this world as well, and she had to find her.

Helana ran to her table, seized a quill, and she scrawled upon a torn sheet of goatskin:

Find Pherri. Not your Pherri. On Eryispek. Help her.

The world was collapsing. Her view of the parchment was overlayed with visions of her hut in Thrumbalto, with shadows moving against the wall like spilt spots of ink.

She was out of time. The chamber dissolved around her,

and Helana's body seeped through the floor, back to Thrumbalto.

She woke with a gasp, sweating profusely, so warm it felt like her skin was on fire, her throat dry and aching. 'Water,' she moaned, expecting She'ab to appear with a cool cloth and a reviving drink. 'Water.' She lurched to her feet, and fell over herself, colliding painfully with the wooden floor.

Someone laughed. 'Looks like she's awake.'

Helana tried to blink the bewilderment from her eyes. By the chill air and the soft, distant glow at the window, it was almost dawn.

I've been away all night, she realised, through the fog of pain that emanated from where her head had struck the floor. 'Water, She'ab,' she croaked. Why had she fallen on the floor? She made to rise again, but her legs tangled in something and she crashed back against the floorboards.

The laughter came again, as cutting as cold steel. 'She doesn't know where she is. He did say she might lose her mind.'

She was tangled in something, that was all. Confusedly, her eyes still adjusting, Helana fumbled for her feet, and found them tightly bound with rope.

'We thought we'd leave your hands,' came the laughing voice again. 'Funnier that way.'

Helana manoeuvred herself into a seated position against the wall, and wiped furiously at her eyes. Slowly, the room came into focus. She'ab was gone. Na'mu too. She was surrounded by four Thrumb, watching her from chairs arranged in an arc. Hu'ra sat in the middle of them, next to Ti'en, both smiling like cats who had cornered a mouse.

'Surprised?' asked Ti'en, her pretty, pale face animated with glee.

'I—' Helana's mouth felt as if it had been stuffed with straw. 'I don't understand,' she said, her words coming in a rush. 'Where is She'ab?'

Hu'ra chuckled. 'The shaman has been charged with treason.'

Helana looked at him blankly, uncomprehending. Her mind was moving at little more than a slow trudge.

'Don't you understand?' demanded Ti'en, her face stretched in a rictus sneer. Helana had never seen her friend like this before; she was fierce, but never cruel. 'We've taken Thrumbalto! My brother crushed our treacherous father in the span of a single night! You're our prisoner now.'

Helana blinked, the exhaustion of passing between worlds threatening to overwhelm her. The sweat was rolling off her in streams. 'Why?'

'*Why?*' sneered Ti'en? 'After all this time, she still has to ask *why*! I'll tell you why—'

Hu'ra laid a placating hand on her knee, unusually calm. 'We do not need to explain ourselves to her, Sister. We can—'

'No, I want her to hear this. It's the least I deserve after all those months of spying, pretending to be her friend.'

Helana was suddenly overcome by a wave of exhaustion. Her eyes slipped shut, and then Ti'en drove a foot into her stomach. Helana was too tired to cry out, but in her depleted state it hurt as if she had been kicked by a horse. She cowered on the floor. 'Please—'

'Do you know how your brother died?' Ti'en demanded.

Through watering eyes, Helana looked up at her, and could not help being shocked by the naked hatred in her eyes. 'At peace talks. Someone poisoned—'

'Erland lies.' Ti'en sneered down at her. 'I did it. When my father sent envoys to the Erlanders, I sneaked along with them. That night, I went to your brother's tent. How could such a gallant prince resist? When he'd finished with me, I slit his throat.' Her crazed smile broadened. 'Father never even knew. But he was so pleased to see you and I becoming *such good friends!*' She sang the three words like a nursery rhyme and laughed. 'I knew there was more to you than they were telling me. Lucky for us that this happened to be the same night my brother came.'

Helana squirmed to the window and pulled herself up to look down upon Thrumbalto. There were fires everywhere, and people screaming, and the shapes of men, some standing with spears and some on their knees. She saw nothing of She'ab, or Na'mu.

Ti'en came towards her. 'We knew Father and She'ab were up to something with you, we just didn't—'

Helana leapt for her. Her feet may have been bound, but she bundled the girl to the ground, raining down punches, until Hu'ra and another Thrumb dragged her off, thrashing and spitting.

'You... you...' Helana could not even form the words for how much she hated Ti'en in that moment. She was breathing like a bellows, exhausted, with black spots flashing in her vision.

Ti'en spat out a bloody glob of saliva. 'Rage all you want, we've won. And you're going to tell us everything.'

Held upright and with her arms bound by two men, Helana was defenceless. Ti'en's furious punch connected with Helana's jaw. She felt a brief, hot burst of pain, before the black of unconsciousness rose up to meet her.

CHAPTER 48

The ceiling was moving. It shifted like the sea, all tides and currents and eddies. It pulsed in time with his slow heartbeat. It was austere grey, and it was not; a storm of colours like flowing stained glass lit by the warmth of a thousand suns.

In his bed, beneath a mountain of piled furs, Rymond lay, trapped somewhere between slumber and consciousness. There was a gone-out smokestick rolled between his fingers, but when had he last drawn on it? It could have been half a minute ago, or half a year. A small heap of ash had formed on his pillow. Groaning, Rymond rolled towards the warm glow of the bedside candle. He stretched towards it, and as the flame licked against the smokestick, sucked the smooth fumes into his chest. He blinked as he inhaled, held it in his lungs, and then blew it out with a sigh.

His awareness sharpened, and the ceiling's illusion faded, though it did not disappear entirely. The fire on the far wall was burning, but could not dispel the scent of old sweat that permeated the room. Rymond ran his hand through an overgrown blond beard to a mane of oily, knotted hair, and felt an instant of confusion. Rymond Prindian did not allow his appearance to become so dishevelled. So who was this man? Rymond Prindian's hair shone like gold, and he dressed in the best silks and velvets, and even if he might occasionally spill wine on his fine clothes, he did not languish all day in filthy bedding. Rymond Prindian was a lord, or perhaps a king. It was all terribly hard to recall, but logically, he could not be Rymond Prindian. That did not mean he knew who he was, but perhaps this was the natural state of things.

Satisfied, he drew the smokestick to his mouth again, only to suck at empty fingers. It must have fallen. He tried to look for it, but the candle had burnt down to an unlit stub, and just bone-grey embers remained of the distant fire. The only illumination was a cold moonlight through a gap in the curtains and a yellow glow under the door. How was he going to find more casheef trapped in the dark like a stinking mushroom? Cursing, Rymond tried to throw the covers off him, but they were too heavy. Instead, he rolled and found the edge of the bed, but somehow he had got tangled up in the sheets. He fell to the stone floor, letting out a gasp as his tailbone collided with a flagstone.

Too hard. It's all too bloody hard. He lay his head back against the foot of the nightstand and tried to sleep. There would be more casheef in the morning. Dawn would rise soon.

It was not sleep exactly, but he did dream. Rymond saw a great fire on Eryispek, armies clashing against the gates of Merivale, and somewhere Helana stood atop an impossibly tall tree, screaming into the wind. The visions flashed past his mind's eye like shards of broken glass, splintered and senseless, and all the while Rymond tossed and turned in his jumble of sheets.

A commotion outside the door disturbed his rest. Rymond's eyes snapped open. It was still night; who could be cavorting in his halls at this time? He called for them to be quiet, but the din continued, a man's deep voice and the violent clashing of steel on steel. Suddenly scared, Rymond grasped for the edge of the nightstand to pull himself up, and yelped as the whole thing fell on top of him. The noises grew louder, and then suddenly quietened.

The door burst open in an eruption of light, and Rymond had to cover his eyes to stop himself being blinded.

'Eryi's balls!' cried the first man through the door. 'It smells like—'

'Be quiet!' hissed a familiar female voice. 'Never you mind what it smells like – quickly now.'

Rymond protested weakly as a forest of hands grasped for him and heaved him to his feet. Clothes were stripped from his body, and something itchy and heavy was pulled down over his head and neck.

'He's half-dead,' said one man. 'And he stinks! Do you expect us to carry him all the way?'

'You'll carry him as far as he needs. He's your king.' Rymond could still not quite place the woman's voice. He opened his mouth to tell her that she was wrong, that he was king of nothing and nowhere, that he wanted only to be left alone, and the woman shoved a lit smokestick into his mouth. 'Maybe something other than that foul casheef will wake him up a bit.'

Rymond inhaled hungrily. This tasted different, and did not leave his limbs and eyelids leaden. With shaking fingers he pulled it from his mouth, and exhaled a billowing cloud of earthy smoke, then immediately placed it back between his lips for another drag. His eyes swam into focus, and he realised he was surrounded by four men, and two women.

'Mother,' he whispered. 'I—'

'We don't have time for this,' said the second woman. She too sounded familiar. 'Get him up.'

A man threw Rymond up onto his shoulder, and suddenly they were heading for the door. Rymond caught a glimpse of soiled bedclothes surrounded by discarded smoke-sticks, before the door closed behind them and they were in a corridor filled with rows of bright sconces that hurt his eyes.

They passed men in golden armour topped with purple plumes, sprawled on the floor or slumped against the walls in swelling pools of blood, then in a moment they were gone, round a corner, hurtling through corridors that were as familiar as they were strange.

They passed more bodies, but before Rymond could form the words to ask what had happened, they burst outside, into a dark and deserted courtyard. Rymond felt a moment of familiarity as somebody jammed his foot into a stirrup and pushed him up onto a horse. He barely grabbed the reins and steadied himself in time to stop himself falling down the other side. Someone shoved an open skin of wine into his hand, which he drank with abandon, letting the warm ruby liquid trickle down into his beard. A pie appeared in his other hand, and he bit into it. The inside was so hot that it burnt his mouth, but he devoured it hungrily, feeling more alive with every bite. He took another long swallow of wine.

The night seemed to sharpen around him. Someone had wrapped him in a cloak, but the air was icy upon his skin, and suddenly he was shivering uncontrollably. The high sides of the courtyard seemed to press in around him, over his head, walling him in brick by brick. He wanted to run. He wanted to return to his chamber. He wanted casheef. He wanted never to touch another speck of it for as long as he lived.

'Rymond. Rymond.' His mother was at his side, looking up at him. 'Rymond, can you hear me?'

'Yes, Mother.' The sounds felt unfamiliar on his tongue. He took another glug of wine and had to push a fist to his mouth to stop himself throwing it back up. 'I can hear you.'

'These men will take you to safety.' Her voice was piercing in his ear, and somehow a thousand miles away. 'This one' – she indicated a man on horseback the other side of him – 'says he knows you.'

Blearily, Rymond turned towards the man, a thin-faced youth on a piebald mare. 'Brant!' His own voice shocked him awake. 'The scout—' He saw a mad, moonlight ride down a slope towards an enemy encampment with Brant at his side. That memory belonged to Rymond Prindian, his true self, not whoever he had been pretending to be, trapped in the dark and sated endlessly with casheef.

Brant grinned. 'Good to see you again, Majesty.'

'Someone had to save your useless hide.' Rymond turned the other way to see Gruenla, her eyes hard and her jaw jutting fiercely under her helmet.

'Gruenla! By Eryi, I'm—'

'Sorry?' Gruenla laughed and spat on the ground. 'That's what I think of your sorry. You thought I was a spy! I'd have left you in there to rot, but your mother's paying us to get you out of here. Can you ride?'

'I think—' Rymond's head ached. He bit hungrily into the pie again. 'I think so. Give me a moment.'

'You don't have a moment,' his mother hissed. 'You need to go, before we are discovered.'

Rymond blinked down at her. She looked older than he remembered, and thinner. 'Are you not coming?'

'I can do more for our cause from within Irith. If I return to my chamber without being seen, they will have no idea of my involvement. What matters now is that you *get out of here*. You cannot free West Erland while you are doped up on casheef. You must be a king, now more than ever. Not just a king, but a *leader*. If you cannot free us from the Imperium, who will?'

Something in her words seemed to sober Rymond more than the smokestick, the pie, and the wine combined. He could still feel the casheef in his bloodstream, like tiny claws gripping at his veins and arteries. His body lusted for more, for the sweet, careless release of black oblivion, but Rymond found the strength to push that feeling down. 'How long was I gone?' he asked.

'Weeks,' said his mother. 'Brant and Gruenla will tell you all, but first you need to go. Raise the people of Erland, raise all of those you can. Now go.'

She slapped his horse on the rump, and it bucked so hard Rymond had to grip his reins and press his knees into the beast's flanks to avoid being tossed. He recalled the sensation; King Rymond Prindian knew his way around a horse. There was an open gate ahead of him, manned only by two more dead Imperials. He drove his mount forward, and plunged into the night, away from Irith, towards freedom.

CHAPTER 49

'I've never seen anything like it,' said Errian, approaching Ciera, who had just taken her seat on the dais. His face was bright with triumph. It was two days after the Imperials had been thrown back from the gates of Piperskeep, and the *Hymeriker* had congregated in the hall where barrels of ale had been rolled out. 'Erland will sing of our victory for centuries. Thirty or more Imperials dead for every Erlander who fell. Not since King Darien—'

'Victory?' questioned Ciera. 'The Imperials are still at the city gates, are they not?' She was surrounded by attendants, with her son, the new king, cradled in her lap.

Errian was unperturbed. 'They lack the strength to mount another assault. If they had not retreated beyond the walls we would have taken Merivale back within days. Some of their slaves are refusing to fight.'

Ciera would have liked to commend Errian and the rest for their bravery, but while the Imperials were still encamped outside the city walls she could not find the words. They could be as proud as they pleased, but she would not count this a victory until the Imperials were driven from East Erland and Andrick's crown was secured.

'How did he die?' The challenge came from a *hymerika* at the back of the hall, a tankard tight in his fist. 'What was the use in winning if the king's dead? And you let it happen; who are you to tell us what's victory and what's not?'

A few shocked heads turned towards the man, but there were murmurs of agreement. 'She killed the king!' shouted another, and suddenly the room was in uproar, with angry claims and counterclaims thrown back and forth between those who had supported Ciera, those whose loyalties were still to Balyard, and those who formed the majority, who had taken no side but still considered themselves Hessian's men.

Ciera tried to control her unease. Beneath Errian's pride, she had not detected the room's undercurrent of discontent. There were too few men in this hall whose first loyalty was to her. If enough *hymerikai* turned against her...

For a few moments, Ciera thought events might tip from words into violence, until Errian climbed atop the dais. 'Enough!' Some mutterings continued, but the hall fell silent enough for him to make himself heard. 'I will not have *hymerika* fighting *hymerika* while the Imperium still sits outside our walls! Let the queen speak.'

'It was as you have already heard,' said Ciera, letting her voice sweep across the floor before any further accusations could be raised. 'It was the girl Tansa. I came in from the balcony, and my husband was dead at her feet. She forced her way out using my son as a hostage.' That was a lie, but a necessary one.

'And no one else saw this?' cried a *hymerika*. 'Pretty bloody—'

'Silence!' Errian's hand went to his sword. 'Next man

who speaks without my permission can answer with their life.'

Ciera watched the sea of faces. Some looked sympathetic, but there were more eyeing her darkly. Some seemed almost on the verge of drawing steel, and there were many others whose expressions were unreadable. Whether they were hiding their true feelings or simply reserving judgement, Ciera could not tell, but she could see enough to say that the matter was not settled.

Perhaps true power rests with those who wield the swords. She had imagined Hessian's death would leave her rule undisputed, but instead it appeared to hang upon the whims of the *hymerikai*.

It might have been easier, she knew, if she could have found the strength to weep for him. She wore black, as was expected of her, but she knew she did not look the image of a grieving wife, sitting in Hessian's place ruling in the name of his heir, with dry eyes and a tale that made her look, if not guilty, at least foolish. It had been a mistake to come to the hall.

Andrick began to wail, and Ciera took this as an opportune moment to bring her brief appearance to a close. 'We will end matters there,' she said, coming to her feet, as hostile mutterings began to rise and pitiless eyes followed her. 'Tomorrow, we will burn King Hessian's body. May Eryi take him.' She rushed from the dais.

Before she could depart the hall, Errian stepped across her path. He looked down at her stonily. Ciera owed him her freedom and her queenship, but in that moment, she wished Orsian were *balhymeri*. He might have understood why she could find no tears for Hessian. 'I would advise you, Majesty, to consider your position.' He kept his voice low, below what might be heard by the *hymerikai*. 'The men are angry. I have said enough that they will not act rashly, but you see how it looks. Hessian is dead, and you have stepped over his corpse to claim the crown. Give up your rule, before you are removed.'

Ciera could have slapped him. 'Is that a threat?'

'It is a warning. If you stand down now, I may be able to protect you. If you don't... The *Hymeriker* will not stand by and allow me to shield the king's killers. I will do what I must.'

'Then try it, if you dare. Need I remind you that the enemy is outside these walls, not within.'

Before Errian could reply, Ciera walked from the hall, eager to be free of the pointed stares and whispers that cut like knives. She had sought to rule herself, and now she would have to live with that, and all the risks that went with it.

'You should double the guard on Balyard,' said Laphor as he strode alongside her, the rest of her guard following behind. 'There's no telling what some of his lot might do if they get the idea in their head.'

'Do it. Men whose loyalty you can vouch for.' She dropped her voice. 'And double the swords around me. And bring me Orsian. This evening.' She needed one of the brothers on her side at least; it could make all the difference with the *Hymeriker* if Orsian spoke for her.

Whatever happens, I will not run. She had fought too hard to give up now. Piperskeep was hers.

Ciera ate alone with Andrick and her attendants in his nursery, starting fearfully at every creaking door and every set of footsteps in the corridor. Laphor was not with her, and though she trusted the rest of her guards, they lacked the older man's steady, grandfatherly bearing.

She was feeding Andrick when there was a double knock at the door. 'Who is it?' she called, her voice quavering slightly.

'Orsian.'

In all her worrying, Ciera had somehow forgotten she had sought for Orsian to come and see her. 'Come in.' She handed Andrick to Lanetha and rose.

Orsian appeared with a tankard of ale in hand. He did not look drunk though, just sad. His eyes were soft, as if he did not register where his feet were taking him. Slowly, as if in a dream, he closed the chamber door.

Orsian moved towards the table like a ghost, his legs as heavy and cumbersome as two anvils. It was an exhaustion beyond the ache of his flesh and muscles; every movement was an effort of will, as if the link between his body and mind had been severed. He sat down opposite Ciera, across a small table of bread and cheese. It was at least one item of good fortune that it did not appear they would starve under an Imperial siege.

He almost smiled. That was one thing they had achieved, as futile as it all felt. Even when so much had been lost, he perhaps could cling to that.

Orsian looked up, suddenly aware that Ciera had asked him a question, and was regarding him expectantly. It was hard to imagine that this girl, hardly older than himself, was now in command. Did he answer to her? Had Erland ever been ruled by a woman in the name of a king still at the breast? Pherri would have known, but wherever Pherri had gone, Orsian could not follow. He wondered if he would ever see his sister again, or if her hand guiding his sword had been farewell, the last he ever knew of her.

He had told no one of what he had felt, Pherri shifting the tide of battle for Piperskeep when all seemed lost. They would have thought him mad. Better to let them believe that they had overcome such overwhelming odds by their own strength. As unlikely as it was, they all seemed happy to believe it.

'I'm sorry, Majesty. What did you say?'

Ciera was looking at him with pity in her eyes. 'I asked if you loved her.'

The question hit Orsian like the fist of a *prifecta*. Was it right to love someone who had killed his king? What had Hessian been to him? A distant madman, who could scorn a man one moment and claim kinship with him the next. So Orsian had thought, until he had seen Hessian clutching Andrick's skull like a lost child. That had been true grief, and for a few heartbeats, Orsian had seen the brother his father had loved, not the king he feared.

And just as Orsian had felt he was beginning to understand Hessian, to understand the horror of the alternative, Tansa had killed him. What had Tansa been to him? Had he loved her? He had never loved Helana, as much as he convinced himself he had in his childish fancy. Tansa, though...

He fumbled for the truth. 'Yes. She was the first person to show me I could be something other than what everyone else expected me to be, that I had a choice. She never wanted me to return to Merivale. I couldn't work out her reluctance.' He gave an acid laugh. Who knew how many families had been torn apart by the stern justice of Hessian and Erland? He had never drawn the connection to Tansa's brother.

Ciera reached out and placed a hand atop his. 'We are the choices we make, Orsian. You came back because you believed in something bigger than yourself. Erland is not just Hessian.'

Orsian looked across the table at her. 'Did you love Hessian?'

It was a foolish question, he knew. Hessian was no one's idea of a devoted husband. Ciera shook her head slowly. 'I... I came to respect him. He married me for duty. Sometimes I think all he did, he did for Erland, and then I remember what he did to me, and my heart fills with such rage I can barely breathe.' She was gripping the armrest of her chair as if to steady herself. 'I want things to be different. Erland must not die with Hessian. But you must have heard the whispers – if you do not speak for me, I fear what Errian and Balyard will do. My son needs you. Erland needs you. I need your help.'

Orsian hesitated. She was giving him a choice, where Hessian would have only demanded obedience. What held him back was whether he still believed in Erland. Believed in anything. He had seen his father die, his king die, and countless others, like Cag, Pylas, and dear, brave Hilga. They had believed in Erland, and died for it. His sister, mother, and cousin were all missing. What did it truly matter who ruled in Erland?

'I didn't do it for Erland,' said Orsian. 'Or for you. I came back to protect my family, but they're gone, and Hessian died for it. No matter how much I fight, everyone dies or disappears. Tansa was wrong about me, I can't be anything else – I am what my father made me, a warrior. But I've killed for duty, and I've killed for coin, and I've killed for survival, and you couldn't fill a thimble with all the fucking difference it's made. Reckon I'm done with caring.'

He thought he saw a teardrop glistening on Ciera's eyelash, but then she blinked, and it was gone. In the place of the girl sat a queen, as implacable as the sea. 'You swore me an oath.'

Orsian shrugged his heavy shoulders. 'What's an oath really? It's just words. Kill me as a traitor if it pleases you. I don't care any more.' He rose, and strode from the room, without any clue where he was going.

As night fell, Ciera found herself back on the balcony of Hessian's solar, staring out over the lights of Merivale. Since the Imperials had retreated beyond the city walls, the braver among the citizenry were returning to try and recover what remained of their lives and livelihoods. At the Ram's Gate, the mountainous corpse of the zebrephant had been cleared away limb by limb, and under torchlight Merivale's stonemasons worked to rebuild the wall.

Inside Andrick slept, oblivious to the danger he might be in. Only days before, Ciera would have given anything to have so many walls between her child and the threat of the Imperium, but that had changed with Hessian's death. Balyard had always been her enemy, but how many others inside these walls had now turned against her?

It would have been easier, she reflected, if Hessian had died on his journey, rather than been assassinated within the very tower on which she now relied for her protection. Ciera supposed she ought to have been fearful of Hessian's vengeful ghost, that she should hear its reproachful wails with every gust of wind that flew past the tower, but Hessian had already done to her all the damage she would allow. Andrick, and the chance to rule, were her recompense for that.

Already, Ciera was making plans for further reforms, and how she might get Merivale back on its feet once the Imperials were defeated. They would have to borrow coin, perhaps from her father, at generous interest rates that would not cripple them with repayments. Taxes could be foregone to encourage the recovery; Piperskeep would replenish its coffers through loans and trade.

Beyond the walls though, she saw the fires of the Imperium, diminished but far from beaten. The war would now be fought by a man she could no longer trust. Rebuilding Merivale might be a dream for years from now.

Ciera heard an insistent knocking at the solar door, and rushed back inside, still bundled in the furs she wore against the balcony's cold. With a sinking feeling, she opened it, and Laphor stood before her, with Burik and Arrik.

His face was grave, and his breathing ragged, as if he had just run the entire length of the stairs. 'They are coming, Majesty. Errian has freed Balyard. They mean to charge you with the murder of King Hessian.'

Ciera closed her eyes, and for just a moment allowed despair to overwhelm her. She let out a breath, hardening herself for what was to come. She had not known, but she had suspected, and she was ready. Their route was planned; she had located the other end of Hessian's tunnel and there were horses and provisions waiting there. Once she was out, her loyalists would make for the stables and follow her east by different routes, drawing off any pursuers.

When Ciera spoke, her voice was calm and steady, even as her heart fluttered in her chest. 'Very well. I am ready.' She stood back to allow Laphor entry. 'The rest of you know the plan?'

Before Arrik and Burik could answer, heavy boots sounded on the stairs. Together, they drew their blades and turned.

'We can hold them, Majesty,' said Arrik. 'But not for long.'

'Long enough,' said Burik, with steel in his voice. 'If we can hold them at the stairs their numbers will count for nothing.'

'Eryi lend strength to your arms, my brothers,' Hurriedly, Laphor stepped inside and bolted the door, which did little to silence the cacophony of men marching up the spiral stairs. He grabbed Ciera by the arm. 'You open the way; I'll get the prince.'

Ciera ran to the shelf and pulled the book to reveal the cobwebbed passage behind the wall. There were confused shouts beyond the door, and then the screech of steel being drawn.

Laphor thrust the swaddled Andrick into Ciera's arms. 'Once we're out, don't stop for anything.'

Laphor held the torch, and Ciera led him down the rickety spiral stairs, following her own footprints in the dust. Not wanting to leave anything to chance, she had mapped out her route earlier that evening; she wanted none of the anxious stumbling of her previous passages through Piperskeep's walls. At one point, she swore a rat the size of a small dog ran over her foot, but Ciera was too intent on her purpose to cry out.

At the very bottom of the stairs, Ciera took the left passageway that would lead them to the tunnel. The walls here were so damp they had grown a heavy green moss, and there was a criss-cross of footprints in the thick layer of dust on the floor from recent use.

They reached where the passage turned and widened into the exit tunnel. Ciera stepped past the threshold, and came nose to nose with Lord Balyard.

His lip curled in triumph. Ciera shrieked, and tried to turn back, but Balyard was too quick for her. His hand seized her wrist as Balyard's tame *hymerikai*, Tarwen and Ormo, appeared from the shadows to grab her, and together they dragged her through into the tunnel. Ciera stumbled, only just keeping her balance and stopping herself from dropping Andrick.

'Well, well.' Balyard stepped towards her, sneering, his voice echoing in the cavernous space. Ciera cringed backwards, holding Andrick out of his reach. The two *hymerikai* were holding torches, casting towering shadows upon the curved walls. 'I told Errian you were too devious to be caught in that tower. I've learnt now not to underestimate you, so I'm glad my hunch proved correct. You should have known these passages would not stay secret forever. Ciera Istlewick, I hereby arrest you—'

Balyard's pronouncement was drowned out by a blood-curdling war cry as Laphor leapt into the tunnel. His blade flashed to take Ormo in the back of the head, spattering blood across the opposite wall. He rushed to place himself in front of Ciera and turned, ready to take the next man, but Tarwen was too quick. 'Run!' cried Laphor. Sparks flew as their blades crashed together. He pushed forward aggressively, keen to make a swift end of it, but Tarwen held him off easily, as two more of Balyard's *hymerikai* detached themselves from the darkness.

'Stop!' Ciera cried. Laphor could not fight three of them. They paid her no heed. In her arms, Andrick stirred and began to cry.

Balyard's eyes were intent on the fight, and so he did not notice the pounding rush of footsteps behind him. Ciera's eyes were drawn past him, just in time to see Orsian grab Balyard from the rear and jam a dagger up under his throat.

Balyard gave a panicked cry. 'Stop! Stand down!' His *hymerikai* turned in alarm, giving Laphor a chance to retreat. He was panting heavily, blood dripping down his wrist from a wound at the shoulder.

'Both of you, run.' Orsian moved quickly, manoeuvring along the width of the tunnel to place Balyard between him and three *hymerikai* with Ciera and Laphor at his back, giving them a clear path to escape.

'You're making a mistake, boy,' croaked Balyard, as the three warriors fanned out.

'Take another step and I'll kill him.' Orsian's words made them hesitate, their eyes scanning in confusion from Balyard to Ciera.

Andrick was bawling now, his echoing cries magnified by the low ceiling. The three warriors continued forward, their blades drawn, and as Ciera turned to run she saw Orsian shove Balyard towards Tarwen and draw his sword in a wide flourishing arc that forced them back. Laphor ran alongside her, as behind them Orsian's blade met his three attackers in a slew of shrieking steel.

Balyard was screaming. 'Kill them! Kill them! Get the king!'

As they ran, Ciera took one last look back towards Orsian. He was impossibly fast, his sword little more than a silver blur throwing firelight, but the three *hymerikai* were pressing him hard.

'Come on!' Laphor cried.

Ciera turned away from Orsian, and ran.

CHAPTER 50

Inside his command tent, Drast Fulkiro stalked from wall to wall, only his need for wine preventing him smashing his cup to pieces against the table. His family's red-black-yellow colours had once put him in mind of a deadly serpent, but the walls now seemed to be mocking him with their bright vulgarity.

'Tell me again,' he commanded the hulking *prifecta*. 'Tell me again, while I decide how I'm going to kill you.'

The armoured slave did not even blink, frustrating Drast even further. The *prifectai* might have been the most effective warriors within ten thousand miles, but any inclination to guile or defiance had been beaten and bred out of them. Drast could have ordered every single one hanged and the *prifectai* would have faced the gallows willingly.

'We might retake the city, Senator,' the nameless *prifecta* said again through his helmet, 'but we could never hold it. The Piperskeep counter-attack has slain too many, and now the residents are pouring back into the city; they hide in abandoned buildings, attack with weapons discarded by our dead, then disappear before the Legion reaches them. Every day, more slaves desert. The Legion and the *prifectai* are too few to hold such an area.'

Drast resisted the desire to strike the man, knowing the *prifecta* would simply accept the blow like a lump of rock. When they had withdrawn from Merivale, Drast had thought it a temporary embarrassment, not a finality.

And after victory had been within his grasp. He could not even begin to understand how the Erlanders had turned the tide. The gate to Piperskeep had been smashed, the Eternal Legion had been through in overwhelming numbers, and then when the castle's last defenders ought to have been overrun, they had somehow rallied. Their shield wall had become impervious, as unyielding as if they had been imbued with the very stone and mortar of Piperskeep, and every swing of their swords seemed to find Imperial flesh. Drast had seen in Cylirien how desperate men found new reserves of strength, but never anything like the Erlanders had done. Defeat for the Imperium should have been impossible.

Drast downed his wine, and flung the cup across the room to shatter against his trunk. He seized another from the table and filled it to the brim. 'We'll starve them out then.'

'We lack the strength to maintain a siege, thanks to your folly,' said Alcantra from her place at the table. Drast could not help but recognise the smugness in her pronouncement. 'And how long do you think before the rest of East Erland rallies? The raids by their Lady Gough are becoming more frequent. If we face an enemy outside these walls and those within attack—'

'We can go through the forest to the north,' suggested Forren, who was leaning against a tent-pole with a brooding look on his face. 'That takes us right up to the castle without having to hold the city. From—'

'Go look at it and see if you fancy marching an army through there,' said Alcantra scornfully. 'They could pick us off one by one from the walls.'

Drast had the sudden urge to fling the fresh cup of wine in Alcantra's face. '*Prifecta*, you are dismissed.' He turned and looked to the slave quivering by the tent flap, one of those too stupid to have deserted yet. 'You. Find me my Erlish lords: Sigac, Storaut, and Darlton.'

He would leave it to the natives to think of something, and if they failed, he would hang them as a lesson. If one of them had a plan that succeeded, Drast would make him King of all Erland. Drast was sick of the sight of Erland, with its rains and weak sun and its ugly people. His place was Ulvatia, and though all might appear lost now, if he could snatch victory he could still return a conqueror.

This is because of the Urmé-damned mangonels, he thought, seething. All the trouble of bringing them across the Bleak Hills only to see them burnt, and nobody had thought to bring anyone who knew how to make more. He had set slaves to felling trees and carving them into beams and planks, but not a single fool in the army had the wit to know how to construct one. He might have asked Alcantra to seek assistance from Saffia through her mirror, but that would have been the most brutal humiliation of all, to ask that thieving witch for help.

'We should retreat across the river,' said Alcantra, as if Drast had simply been waiting in silence for her counsel. 'With the loyalty of those lords we can hold West Erland, then send for reinforcements from Ulvatia.'

'Never,' spat Drast. 'You think we'll hold their loyalty if

they think we've lost? Strovac Sigac would murder us in our beds.'

Strovac Sigac. Another culprit for their defeat. The brute had assured Drast the commanders within Piperskeep were little more than children. Drast turned away from Alcantra and began pacing the tent from wall to wall.

'What is taking them so long?' Drast demanded of Forren after his dozenth crossing of the tent. He had drunk another cup of wine by then, which was doing little to quell his temper.

Forren pushed himself away from the pillar he was leaning on. 'I'll go and find them. That slave is a simpleton.'

As Forren departed, Drast surveyed the tent. On the far wall, two of his own bodyguards stood to attention, dressed in a silver mimicry of the Eternal Legion's golden armour, with Fulkiro colours on the plume rather than Imperial purple. Alcantra was still sitting at the table, thoughtfully rotating a smokestick between her fingers, a disdainful expression on her face. Even though she was pointedly not looking at Drast, he knew it was meant for him.

He looked again to the guards on the rear wall. There was no one else within the tent other than the four of them. *I could have her killed,* he mused. He could blame Alcantra; say to Forren and the rest that it had been self-defence. His guards would never tell. Would anyone mind, other than Saffia? She would be too busy running the Imperium to be troubled by the distant death of a minor servant.

Drast's murderous imaginings were interrupted by the arrival of Strovac, who insolently threw aside the tent flap and strolled into the tent as if it were the common room of an inn rather than the centre of the Imperial command.

'Took you long enough!' roared Drast, switching from

Ulvatian to Erlish. 'When I ask for you, I mean *immediately*. Where are the others?'

Strovac smirked. 'They're dead. Them, and this one.' He threw something round and heavy onto the table. It bounced twice, and rolled to the floor, landing with a thud in front of Drast. He looked down, and recoiled in revulsion as Forren's cool grey eyes stared up guilelessly from his decapitated head.

'By the moons!' Drast drew his sword. 'What are you doing?' His two bodyguards had already roused themselves, and behind their shields were advancing towards Strovac, their spears thrust out towards him. 'Guards!' Drast called out for the other two standing beyond the tent flap, before realising they were likely also dead.

Alcantra stood, and sought to place herself behind the two bodyguards, but Strovac's long strides had already brought him to the table, and with an arm he grabbed her by the hair and pulled her back, sending the chair tumbling.

Drast felt an inappropriate frisson of pleasure at the panic on Alcantra's face as she struggled uselessly against Strovac's grip. 'I'll let you live,' he whispered, looking over her with a grim, yellow-teethed grimace. 'You'll be well-treated, so long as you make yourself useful.' He threw her to the corner of the tent like a broken toy.

'Kill him!' screamed Drast at the two bodyguards, but they seemed reluctant to advance, just standing there and mindlessly jabbing their spears still several feet from where Strovac stood. The Erlander had not even drawn his sword. 'What do you want, Strovac?'

Strovac's grin was as dark as an empty skull. 'From you? Nothing. I'd have killed you already, but my friend here insisted you would want to see him first. He's made quite an impression on me.'

Drast could only look at Strovac in confusion, until the tent flap was thrown back again.

The man who stepped inside could not have been more different from Strovac Sigac. He was old and slightly portly, with a fearsomely twisted grey beard. He wore no sword or armour, just a simple brown robe. Nevertheless, the fear that until now Drast had been keeping under control began to course through his bloodstream like liquid fire.

Every mote of Drast's conviction crumbled, as if someone had taken a hammer to his heart.

Krupal, very much alive, radiating his invisible mastery. He looked at Drast, and though Drast had expected to see hatred, he saw only indifference specked with remote amusement, like a bird of prey sighting a worm.

'Kill him!' Drast cried. Why weren't his bodyguards moving? 'Throw your spears, you idiots!' He looked at Strovac pleadingly. 'You don't know what he is, I'm telling you—'

Krupal was smiling now. 'He knows. Lord Strovac here is considerably more forward-thinking than you.'

'There's a war coming, Drast,' said Strovac. 'It's nothing personal. I only want to be on the winning side.'

Drast suddenly remembered he was still holding his sword, trembling uncontrollably in his fist. Krupal was there right in front of him, and Drast swung at him clumsily.

As the blade passed through him, the shadow that was not disappeared in a puff of smoke. The true Krupal had not moved, and still stood there, smiling eerily at Drast.

'Be glad that I'm merciful.' The magus gave a bloodless sneer. 'As much as it would please me to banish you to another realm, I must withhold my strength.' He flicked a finger imperceptibly, and the Fulkiro bodyguards jerked like marionettes. They turned slowly towards Drast, their spears raised.

By the time Drast realised what was happening, it was too late. The spears flashed through the air. He felt one burst through his breastbone, and in the merest moment before the second pierced his heart, he saw Krupal smiling.

'I never thanked you for waking me, Senator,' came Krupal's voice as Drast lay dying, from a hundred miles away. 'I will remember you as the herald of a new dawn. The magi shall rise again.'

EPILOGUE

Beneath a mountain of ice, the fire without fuel still burnt. There was no wind deep within Eryispek, but still it flickered as if it were alive, casting weaving grey shadows on the frozen walls. It was hot enough now that they could have taken off their clothes and danced naked around it in some primitive ritual as ancient tribes might once have done, before they learnt that gods were real and endowed with a pitiless hunger that could not be appeased by dancing and prayers alone.

As the narrow passage came to an end, Maghira led the way into the chamber, following the fire's glow. She grieved her dead companions, but still, it seemed for the best that Antares was not here to see this; Maghira revealing the Adrari's secret to two flatlanders would have set him to beating them all with his staff. Viratia and the noseless man Naeem came behind her, with Ruhago and Garimo at the rear. The Lutum woman, Delara, had disappeared on the way, and nobody seemed troubled enough to look for her.

Behind Maghira, Naeem stepped through after her,

nearly losing his footing on the slick ice and steadying himself against the sheer wall. He stared at the dancing fire, casting off his hood and letting its warmth roll against his brutish face. 'Why does none of this melt? And where's the wood for that fire?'

'The fire without fuel,' said Ruhago. He moved stiffly with his wound. 'Like the Norhai, it emanates from nothing, and so cannot be quenched.'

Naeem sucked in a breath, and looked to his mistress. Maghira was not sure of the exact nature of their relationship, but Naeem seemed devoted to her. 'You sure about this, Lady?'

'If she believes she can save Pherri, I will speak with her.'

Maghira had come to admire the lady's fortitude. When Adrari spoke of the noblewomen of the flatlands, it was to mock their soft, safe lives, eating and stitching and birthing behind stout walls, far from the sharp winds of Eryispek that threatened to scour the flesh from your bones. Viratia though had pursued her daughter up the frozen wastes, with little more to guide her than her own sense and determination. She spoke of Vulgatypha as if she were some lesser noble, to be cajoled and threatened into granting Viratia her desires. Their names even sounded slightly alike.

They approached the fire, casting off their gloves and furs like they were entering a warm, welcoming inn. 'What happens now?' asked Viratia as they sat before the flames.

'We wait,' said Maghira.

Maghira could not claim to understand the mind of a divinity. Was it possible to understand something that gave you a sense of fear so deep that it almost became part of you? Vulgatypha's anger when they had lost Pherri had been so painful that Maghira feared her skull would split in two, and even now the great weight of the goddess's awareness upon her made her feel as though upon a precipice, where the slightest breath of wind could send her plummeting into madness.

What an innocent she had been, the last time she was here, blithely wandering into the cave believing she wanted to know what lurked within, what the great secret of the Adrari was. Maghira would happily have forgotten it all: Tremares's burnt and twisted body; the horror of Charones and Antares's murder; the army of corpses that spoke with the voice of a god; the way the very fabric of truth and possibility seemed to sunder under Eryi's will; the helplessness she had felt as Pherri, that sweet, brave child, had been dragged away. Maghira would have wed anyone her father asked, only to forget it all.

And yet here she was, answering Vulgatypha's summons, returning with the second prize of Pherri's mother. The desire to serve Vulgatypha was a terrifying compulsion she could not escape, and if she made one more wrong move, the goddess would destroy her. She could only hope that Viratia would sate Vulgatypha's hunger.

They did not have to wait long. The flames crackled purple, and for a moment the stars of the night sky flashed on the ceiling. '*Viratia, the mother. Come to me.*' The chamber rumbled, and Garimo recoiled in fright from the fire.

Maghira steadied herself. It was a relief to hear Vulgatypha's voice aloud, rather than resounding inside her own head. Nevertheless, when she stood, she found her legs were trembling.

Viratia rose, looking as composed as if she were readying herself for a dinner invitation. Naeem made to stand also. 'Should I come with you?'

No sooner had the words left his mouth than the fire flashed again. '*I have no use for you. She is to come alone.*'

Naeem paled. 'Right. Got you.' He sat back down, and Maghira detected more than a hint of relief. 'Reckon I'll do as she says,' he said to Viratia apologetically.

Viratia reached down to squeeze him on the shoulder. 'You have done all I asked of you. Thank you for seeing me here safely.'

There were tears on his cheeks. 'I'll see you back safely an' all,' Naeem replied, sounding as though he was almost choking. 'You and Pherri.'

Without another word, Viratia found the passage, and wormed her way into the darkness, up the twisting tunnel towards Vulgatypha's chamber.

Maghira watched her leave, as the rest of their party assembled themselves around the fire, all seemingly too tired to speak. She could not help wondering what Vulgatypha wanted with Viratia. The goddess had never mentioned Pherri's mother. What could they be discussing, and why could Maghira not know about it? She had done Vulgatypha's bidding for months; if anyone deserved to be within her confidence, it was her.

With a glance to ensure she was not watched, Maghira followed after Viratia.

The path twisted into the chamber above, illuminated by a starlit night sky that stretched above them like an endless, indigo banner. It had been almost peaceful when Maghira had come before, but now forks of yellow lightning at intervals shattered the heavens, their thunder echoing against the ice walls.

Maghira crouched at the entrance, tucking herself into

the shadows to listen. The Erland lady had her back to Maghira, a black silhouette against the erupting sky.

'Did you summon me here to frighten me with tricks?' Viratia demanded. 'I did not need to journey to the heart of Eryispek to see the sky.'

The sky crackled. *'Use not that name here. The Betrayer has no claim to this Mountain.'*

'But he has claimed my daughter. I want to know why.'

'Your daughter has the power to make or break the world. He sought her as a sacrifice, because she has the strength to restore to him his true form and release him from his prison. Alas, she is beyond my sight. She may have thwarted him. She may be dead.'

'I came here because I was told you could find her. Where is Pherri?'

Maghira watched in awe. The sheer power and force of will behind Vulgatypha's words made her want to run, or to curl up in a ball, and yet Viratia bore it all.

'If she lives, she has passed beyond our world and into another.' The sky crackled with repeated bursts of lightning, and Maghira felt an unnerving malevolence in them, as if the sky were cackling. *'I can show you how to bring her back, if you'll help me. Give yourself to me, and save your daughter's life.'*

Maghira thought she saw a crack of doubt appear in Viratia's mask of scorn. 'You have servants. What do you want of me?'

'They are weak vessels. Men have never been suited to my purposes, and the girl is a fragile, feeble thing, for all her pride and beauty. You though... The widow to a warrior of peerless renown, who when his sword slipped from his grasp took up his burden and made your enemies quail before you. You, who

have crossed through all the Betrayer's trials to meet me here, though you have no magic of your own, through sheer force of will. And the mother to the girl who can break the world. You would have been a worthy Norha.

'*To escape this prison, I require a vessel, a body with the strength to hold me. I see that in you. Surrender yourself to me, and together we will have the power to bring your daughter back.*'

Maghira realised her mouth was hanging open. This could not be allowed to happen. They had done this to bind the two powers on the Mountain, to thwart Eryi and thus keep them within their frozen cages, not to give Vulgatypha the means to escape.

Silently, ominously, Viratia nodded. Strands of her long golden hair twisted before an invisible wind. Her face was rapt with wonder. 'Very well. What must I do?'

'No, you can't!' Maghira leapt from the shadows.

Maghira felt the goddess's sight fall upon her, and the weight of it froze her in place. She tried to cry out, but found her tongue fixed to the roof of her mouth. Vulgatypha's aura flickered with pleasure. Maghira could feel it growing, expanding to fill the chamber, as the night sky sizzled and flashed. '*You have done well, girl. One more task, and you shall be free of me.*' Like a moon sweeping across the sky, Vulgatypha's focus returned to Viratia. '*There can be no victory without sacrifice. Kill the girl, and free me.*'

Vulgatypha's final words stirred something in Maghira. Her legs were suddenly free, and her mouth could move again. She opened it to scream, and it caught in her throat as Viratia turned, and carved a knife across Maghira's wind-pipe, spraying blood in a fountain of crimson.

The last thing Maghira saw was Viratia's gore-covered

face, and two eyes in which sorrow and savage certainty mingled in an impossible, illogical tableau. 'I'm sorry,' Maghira heard her whisper, as Viratia lowered her almost tenderly to the floor.

Above them, the night sky looked down upon the chamber deep inside the Mountain. A hundred bolts of lightning flashed together, and then were gone.

A LETTER FROM R.S. MOULE

Dear Reader,

Thank you sincerely for reading *The Hunger of Empires*. And, assuming you read this after reading *The Fury of Kings*, thank you for sticking with the Erland Saga.

If you enjoyed *The Hunger of Empires*, I would be profoundly grateful if you could leave a rating or review with whichever retailer you purchased it from. It makes a huge difference, firstly to know that someone enjoyed it, and secondly to encourage interest in the series.

If you have any thoughts you would like to share with me, I would love to hear from you. Please get in touch through any of the links to social media below. These are also a good way to stay notified of my new releases.

If you would like stay informed about the next book in the Erland Saga, just sign up at the following link. Your email address will never be shared, and you can unsubscribe at any time.

www.secondskybooks.com/rs-moule

Book 3, as yet untitled, will be the final volume of the Erland Saga, and at time of writing is a work in (rapid) progress. I shall endeavour not to keep you waiting too long; I hope you are as anxious as I am to discover what happens to Pherri, Orsian, and all the rest.

Thank you so much for your support.

Roger Moule, June 2023

 twitter.com/RS_Moule

ACKNOWLEDGEMENTS

It does not feel all that long ago I was writing my acknowledgements for *The Fury of Kings*. Thank you again to everyone I mentioned then. My gratitude, also, to the following.

The whole team at Bookouture/Second Sky. My editor Jack Renninson spotted all the problems I was hoping he wouldn't notice and made me fix them. Publicity guru Noelle Holten. Richard King, Mandy Kullar, Alba Proko, Melanie Price, Myrto Kalavrezou, Melissa Tran, anyone I've missed. Thank you for publishing my books.

Colin Mace for his incredible work on the audio versions of *Fury* and *The Hunger of Empires*. I hope one day to be brave enough to listen to more than five minutes of my own prose.

All the reviewers and book bloggers who made positive noises about *Fury*. I fear there are too many of you to mention by name, but I am so grateful to you all just for reading it – that you also took the time to write about it is extraordinary. I hope you enjoyed this one as well.

My sister-in-law, Nina, for spotting the mistakes nobody else did.

Finally, my wife, Eloise. One day, perhaps I will not spend whole evenings chained to my keyboard, appearing only to brew more mint tea or pour more whisky, but I am afraid it is not this day. Thank you for your patience.

Printed in Great Britain
by Amazon